MURDERS AT THE
MONTGOMERY HALL HOTEL

A PRUNELLA PEARCE MYSTERY

BOOK TWO

GINA KIRKHAM

www.bloodhoundbooks.com

Print ISBN: 978-1-5040-8183-2

ALSO BY GINA KIRKHAM

For my beautiful daughter, Emma

'I love you to the moon and back and all the stars...'

PROLOGUE

31 OCTOBER 1977

*H*e bit down hard on his bottom lip; a slight metallic tang touched his tongue. He had drawn blood. Quite ironic really under the circumstances. He swished the black cloak behind him and adjusted the horns that adorned his dark curls. The band that held them aloft dug into the skin behind his ears, but he knew he should ignore the discomfort. All the great actors he had read about had suffered for their art and no matter his age, he should be no exception.

His brother, older by mere minutes, ran around the room, the white sheet draped over him billowing and flapping as he jumped excitedly from sofa to chair, howling and wailing. The cut-out eyes offered him very little vision and contributed to his clumsiness, but he didn't seem to care; he was caught up in the moment. The temptation to prod him with his devil's trident was quite overwhelming for Daniel, but he knew the soft plastic would have next to no impact on David's fair skin, which was such a bitter disappointment for him.

Halloween was celebrated as keenly as Christmas at Montgomery Hall. Daniel's fingers traced the ornate panels of the Somerset Room as he swooped around the four walls, his cloak billowing around him. Montgomery Hall was his family home, a place that harboured imaginary ghosts that would sit comfortably beside fake cobwebs, bats and pumpkins.

Daniel plonked himself down at the window seat and looked out at the swaying trees devoid of their finery. They scared him a little. He imagined their black, gnarly fingers silhouetted against the drab sky reaching out to pluck him from his safe place, to steal him away. He giggled, wondering what his parents would think if all that was left of the eight-year-old him were the ridiculous horns from the top of his head and a cheap plastic cape left crumpled in a heap on the floor of the Somerset Room. He watched as David launched himself from the arm of the fireside chair and sailed through the air, his chubby hands reaching out from under the sheet to clutch the heavy velvet curtain draped next to him.

'Wahooo! I'm a ghost...' he howled.

His brother landed awkwardly, a jumble of boy, polyester, cotton and plush baroque red. The ornate gold metal of the rigid holdback hook gave slightly, allowing one roped loop to slip. David's excited hollering was quickly exchanged for another, more chilling, sound.

A thick, guttural choking, naturally designed to draw attention to a rapidly evolving nightmare, filled the room.

Daniel, his breath caught in excitement, stood mesmerised, preferring to be a simple onlooker. A member of the audience rather than the star.

He watched fascinated as David flailed and fought the fabric, his muffled grunts filling the room as the twisted bronze cord of the curtain tie-back, stark against the white sheet, caught and tightened around his neck. He watched the small imprint of David's mouth under the cotton suck in and out like a waning heartbeat. He watched his legs kick and his Thunderbird slippers squeak against the woodblock floor, desperately trying to find purchase. He watched his brother's futile fight for life as the metal curtain rings scraped backwards and forwards against the heavy brass pole with each turbulent quake of David's body.

Swish. Swish.

He watched and waited – until there was silence.

Daniel tilted his head in a moment of feigned sympathy for his brother, then flung back his cape, jutted out his chin and took a bow to his audience of lit pumpkins and black paper bats. An excited fire now burned within him.

And just like a season, he had awakened...

In the blink of an eye, autumn had become his most favourite season of all.

'Strange children should smile at each other and say, "let's play".'

F. Scott Fitzgerald (*Tender Is The Night*)

MOVES LIKE JAGGER...

PRESENT DAY

*P*runella Pearce turned the Victorian 'open' sign to face out onto Winterbottom High Street, happy to announce to those that cared to venture into her little village library the welcome she felt they deserved. She reverently wiped the dust jacket of Ann Cleeves' new addition. All her books in the converted shop that served the close-knit community deserved her respect, but she did have just that little extra admiration for Vera and her detective skills. She was a woman after her own heart, intrigued by murder, mystery and a bit of mayhem thrown in for good measure.

Winterbottom had certainly seen its fair share of those in its time. Pru's recent foray into several grisly murders; committed by one of their own no less, had given her the inspiration to set up a part-time detective agency, together with her best friend, Bree Richards. They were both currently enjoying the remnants of their youth before hurtling towards mid-life, she having recently said 'hello' to her forties, whilst Bree was still clinging on for dear life to her thirties at the grand age of thirty-nine years, four months and sixteen days. They had agreed that it was now or never to turn their hands to something a bit different, something that would bring a smidgeon of excitement to their lives. It hadn't quite got off the ground yet, but they had gone as far as throwing around a few business names, which, by Pru's calculation, would be – she checked her watch – finalised over several gin and tonics in the Dog and Gun later that evening.

'Cup of tea, Albert?' she said as she swept past the elderly gentleman who was engrossed in the latest edition of the *Winterbottom News*, gently patting him on the shoulder as she made her way to the kettle and teabags in the corner of the shop. Her little coffee-break corner was squeezed in between the shelves that held the colourful spines of books from P to T and U to Z.

'Ooh that would be lovely, thank you, Pru.' Albert neatly folded the newspaper and placed it on the worn mahogany desk in front of him, the soft light from the reading lamp casting a glow that made his smile even more endearing. 'Mrs Tytherington was all of a twitter this morning; I had to sneak out before I could partake of my cup of Earl Grey!' He added a small harrumph to the end of his sentence to show his disappointment.

Pru smiled to herself. Ethel Tytherington, stalwart member of the Winterbottom Women's Institute, of which Pru was their current president, was renowned for her excitable nature and occasional sharp tongue. Very few members took offence to her gossip because more often than not it was touched with observational wit, risqué humour and very gentle sarcasm. The timing of her legendary one-liners was a joy to behold.

'Oh dear, what on earth has got poor Ethel into a pickle this time?' She carefully poured the boiling water onto the teabags and watched them bob up and down in the pot before giving them a vigorous stir with a teaspoon.

'Holidays!'

Albert's one-word response left Pru feeling unsure if she should coax more from him or leave the matter to rest. She placed the delicate cup and saucer in front of him and tucked a digestive biscuit on the edge as a peace offering. 'Holidays?' she quizzically repeated.

'Yup, holidays – or lack of 'em!' Albert took a sip of his tea. 'Now, Pru my dear, you tell me, what would a couple in their seventies want with a ruddy Swinging Weekend in Bath, I ask you?' He rummaged around in the pocket of his tweed jacket and pulled out a folded sheet of paper. Pressing it on the desk he ironed out the creases. 'See–' His bony finger prodded the writing. '–I never swung in the 1960s, and I'm sure as hell not starting to fling myself around now to Mick Jagger, am I?' He bit into his biscuit, and then suddenly decided to push out his lips in an effort to replicate young Mick's famous pout. The chunk of digestive momentarily wavered between his lips before losing its hold. It flicked upwards, executed a double flip, and landed with a gentle thud on the desk in front of him. He quickly swept it up with a jerk of his hand and rammed it back into his mouth. 'If Ethel thinks we can energetically wiggle our arthritic hips without putting them out of joint and ending up in Winterbottom Cottage hospital, she's got another think coming!' He harrumphed again to prove his point.

Pru took the sheet of paper from him and quickly scanned the flyer. Her eyes widened as she scrunched her lips tightly together, trying not to giggle. 'Oh, Albert! It's not a dancing weekend, it's a–' She tried desperately to think of the most appropriate way to explain it. '–it actually says *Swingers' Weekend*.' She waited for his response.

'I know. That's what I said, my dear; the daft old mare wants me to swing my hips and gyrate all weekend, when I'd much rather be on my allotment tending to me shallots.'

'Mmm... yes, I'm sure everyone will be swinging their hips and gyrating, Albert, but it won't be to music.' Pru laughed as she folded the paper and gave it back to him. 'Leave it with me. I'll speak to Ethel if you'd like me to.' Albert nodded in appreciation and went back to sipping his tea and reading his chosen book, the routine he always followed on his days at the library – paper, tea and biscuits, then book.

Pru turned her back to him and blew upwards, sending her fringe into a frenzy. How on earth she was going to explain to Ethel that her chosen weekend was more bedroom than ballroom antics with a bit of a 'Ladies Excuse Me' thrown in was anyone's guess.

THE MONTGOMERY HALL HOTEL

*T*arragon Montgomery, the reluctant owner of the Montgomery Hall Hotel, tapped the nib of his pen on the register in front of him. He used the nail on his little finger to pick at a remnant of lunch wedged between his front teeth, ran his tongue over the offending porcelain pegs and then offered a very loud '*tsssk*' to the empty reception hall.

'Smithers...' he barked. The ensuing echo drifted up the carved oak staircase and bounced from the full height of the stained-glass window on the first-floor landing, before throwing the name back into the vaulted Great Hall. Tarragon waited for the little crystal droplets on the chandelier to quiver with the arrival of Smithers from the servants' quarters. Smithers didn't disappoint. His plump little body encased in a black tailed jacket set off by a tapestry waistcoat hurried through the heavy door. He crossed the bronzed marble floor tiles and stood, with great poise, in front of the reception desk.

'You called, sir?'

'Of course I did, Smithers. Who else is in residence in this bloody mausoleum?' Tarragon dramatically waved his arms around him, and then immediately felt guilty for taking out his low mood on his always pleasant and willing member of staff. Smithers had been with the family since before he was born and had often acted as *in loco parentis* to Tarragon and his twin cousins, Daniel and David Beaumaris, when they had all lived under the same roof. He gave a slight nod of his head, as if that would offer a small acknowledgement of his rudeness. 'Can you ask Cook to prepare a lightly scrambled egg on toast for Mrs Montgomery, please? Her appetite hasn't been quite up to scratch today.' He pointed up to the ceiling, indicating the top floor suite occupied by his elderly grandmother and the matriarch of the family, Cecily Montgomery.

Smithers gave a formal bow. 'Of course, sir, right away, sir.' He turned swiftly on his heels and waddled quickly back towards the hotel kitchens, his highly polished shoes squeaking against the tiles as he went.

Tarragon couldn't help but liken him to a penguin. He watched him disappear before picking up the telephone.

Stephanie Montgomery traced her finger down the side of her gin balloon, clearing a little road through the chilled droplets before taking a large gulp. She relished the coldness of the ice and the mellow smoothness of fennel and lavender before she spoke. 'Look, darling, there's no point in harping on if you're not going to make changes, take chances. This place is dying on its feet, people want excitement, they want something different.' She kicked her shoes off, stretched out her legs and wriggled her toes. 'I mean, we can't even offer them a spa, sauna or swimming pool; we've dropped off the radar for weekends away, let alone a mid-week market for business travellers.' She sighed loudly as though she were chastising a naughty child.

Tarragon feigned interest in his wife's pep talk. He wasn't really in the mood. Christmas was barely three months away, and the only booking they had taken to date was the regular festive reservation for Captain Harlow and his wife. Nice people, but their bar bill would hardly cover a week's pay for the chamber maid, let alone eat into the debt Montgomery Hall was accruing with dodgy plumbing, rattling windows and draughty corridors. 'It's at times like this I wish I'd been born further down the line, then I wouldn't have inherited this dilapidated hellhole.' He poured himself a large scotch from the antique glass-fronted drinks cabinet. 'We could be anywhere now: Barbados, the Seychelles, even Bali, but no... David strings himself up from a curtain and Daniel goes down like the bloody Titanic and drowns...' his voice tapered off.

Stephanie set her lips into a thin line and scowled. She certainly would like to be anywhere else now, other than stuck here with Tarragon the Tedious and his 102-year-old grand-mother, who was currently disintegrating before their very eyes. She suppressed a snort of laughter; she could swear the woman was dropping perished body parts all around the thickly carpeted corridors of Montgomery Hall as she defied the Grim Reaper. She had certainly chosen the wrong branch of the Montgomery family to marry in to. Hell, she would have closed her eyes and thought of England had she secured Tarragon's decrepit, but very wealthy, great uncle Bartholomew. A few months with him and her *pièce de résistance* in the bedroom would have seen him off with either a heart attack or slow suffocation from her eye-popping 38Ds, encased in a rather delicious Bravissimo bra whilst hollering *'Make Me Smart, Bart'* at the top of her voice. If Tarragon wasn't in the room with her, she would have laughed out loud at that thought. Bartholomew hadn't acquired the Montgomery fortune, but he had been successful in his own right and, more importantly, hadn't been tied to the crumbling Mont-gomery Hall. Instead, she had settled on Tarragon, and now she had to wake up to him every single morning for the rest of her life... or his.

Stephanie padded over to the drinks cabinet and held out her glass for Tarragon to replenish it. She watched him sparingly measuring the gin into her glass. 'I mean really, darling, what would be wrong in pumping the old dear just a little? She *must* know where Hugo squirrelled away his fortune; she was his wife, for God's sake!' She tipped her glass towards him, not so much in cheer but more in frustration at his apathy. 'It could save this place or, better still, save us!' She fell silent, wondering what she would do with the missing Montgomery millions and her wet-as-a-fish husband.

Tarragon shook his head in frustration. 'It's a myth; he lost most of it in the 1970s on that commercial build; you already know that, so just leave it be.'

Stephanie pouted to show him her displeasure. 'I'm not talking about the official line; what the tax man was privy to. Come on, Tarragon; you know he was a clever man. That money has got to be somewhere, and it should be ours!'

All around her on the wood panelled walls of the Montague Room, ghastly portraits of Tarragon's family glared disapprovingly at her and her impertinent suggestion, making her squirm uncomfortably in her Fendi frillies. They portrayed stories of tragedy, greed and incompetence, but the saddest of all was the painting of twin boys with dark curls sitting side by side in the very room they now occupied. The engraved gold plate underneath held their names:

Daniel and David Beaumaris
31 October 1976

'Penny for them.' Tarragon slipped his arm around her waist. She shuddered at his touch, but it went unnoticed by him. 'Both of them gone before their time; did you know David was only eight years old when he had his accident?'

Stephanie nodded. Of course, she knew. She was well versed on each and every untimely death in the Beaumaris and Montgomery clans. The death of Tarragon's aunt and uncle in a boating accident in Marbella had shaken the very foundations of the family; their collective grief added to by the loss of their son Daniel Beaumaris, the remaining twin, in the same incident. Less than three years later on Halloween, a fatal car crash had claimed the lives of Tarragon's own parents.

Their untimely deaths had thrown the inheritance ladder into total disarray, and after the passing of his grandfather, Hugo Montgomery, Tarragon had become the reluctant heir to the Montgomery estate, which included this dilapidated pseudo castle of horrors stuck in the middle of a man-made island, along with a nice wedge of trust money he had somehow managed to fritter away on his wife's excesses.

Tarragon had cursed the day Hugo had unfortunately missed ten out of the fifteen available steps down to the wine cellar, instantly breaking his neck. He was sad for all of two minutes, until the realisation hit him that the bottle of 1959 Dom Pérignon clutched in Hugo's left hand had been lucky enough to survive the impact.

'They thought he was somehow implicated, you know...' Tarragon turned his attention back to the portrait of the young twins.

'Who was?' Stephanie felt obliged to ask, just to keep him sweet, but in truth she really wasn't interested.

'Daniel, in the death of David. He was a very strange boy. Even his mother was afraid of him. He wasn't much better as an adult, to be honest; we all gave him a wide berth. There was a cold cruelty to his eyes; we didn't rush to mourn him.'

Stephanie scrunched up her nose and sneered in distaste before slugging back her G&T. She carefully examined each portrait in turn. All dead. Departed, swimming with the fishes, the big adios – whatever you like to call it – and she had the utter misfortune to be left with the last two remaining family members who were shaping up to be pretty adept as coffin dodgers.

What a ruddy pity Tarragon the Tedious couldn't fall victim to an untimely death too. Now that *would be something to make her future a little more bearable.*

THE CURIOUS CURATOR & CO

'Two pink G&T's and a packet of pickled onion crisps, please, Jason.' Pru tapped her nails on the bar, being careful to avoid the recent spill of lager and the tackiness of a chunk of cranberry sauce left by the previous occupant of her bar stool. Bree was happily ensconced in their usual snug under the window, deep in conversation with Andy Barnes, Pru's Delectable Detective boyfriend with the amazing buns of steel. Pru sighed wistfully. She'd give anything to be able to give them a nice little squeeze right this minute, but in the interests of public decency that would have to wait until they got home.

'Pru, Pru...' Andy shouted over the general hum of conversation and the throb of music coming from the jukebox on the far side of the Dog and Gun. She turned, tilted her head and gave him a teasing smile. 'Yes, my dearest one?' She waited, trying to lip-read and make sense of his frantic arm gestures. She gave him a thumbs up to reassure him she had understood. 'Jase, can you add a packet of pork scratchings?' She tapped her debit card onto the reader and watched Jason load up the tray, finally flinging a packet of scratchings into the middle. She edged her way through the crowd back to her seat, being careful not to spill any of their sacred gin. 'Here you go!' She plonked the tray onto the small round table and gave Andy's hair an affectionate ruffle.

'What are these, my Loony Librarian?' He held the packet of pork scratchings aloft between his thumb and forefinger.

'Duh, let me see, oh Fabulous Detective... in my expert opinion, I'd say they're a packet of frazzled pig rind dipped in excessive salt and guaranteed to raise your blood pressure. Why, what do you think they are?' She grinned.

'Erm... how about a pint of Watkins like I asked for?'

'A *what?*' Pru shuffled herself along the booth seat.

'Watkins, beer, ale – you know, the stuff men like to drink in pubs.' He gave Bree a wink before turning his attention back to Pru.

She screwed up her nose. 'Jeez, don't ever let me play charades partnered up with you, Andy Barnes, you're bloody hopeless.' Pru took the first sip of her drink and acknowledged Bree, who was still shaking with laughter. 'He did say a packet of pork scratchings, didn't he?'

Bree shook her head. 'Nope, definitely a pint of Watkins...'

'Well, whatever–' Pru waved her hand to indicate she wasn't in the least bit perturbed by the fact that Andy would have to forgo his pint unless he went to the bar himself. '–we've got work to do if we are going to get this detective agency off the ground.'

Andy covered his ears with his hands. 'I don't think I should be privy to this; you know crime stuff should be left to the experts, that is, the police, i.e., me!' He hastily stood up, rattled the change in his pocket, and counted out how many pound coins he'd 'stolen' from his Mr Grumpy savings pot.

'It would be low-level stuff, Andy, nothing major or dangerous, maybe extramarital affairs and wayward husbands – or wives...' Pru quickly added. 'Finding lost relatives, stuff like that. Bree and I were very good during your Winterbottom WI murders; we helped, didn't we?'

Andy shook his head. 'Oh yeah, right. Remind me: which one

of you nearly got throttled in the doors of The Old Swan Hotel with a chiffon scarf, and which one of you almost got electrocuted at the hands of Phyllis Watson?'

An uncomfortable silence settled over their table as they both considered his pointed question and their mutual close shaves with death.

'I know, how about using a bit of your name and a bit of mine for our business venture?' said Bree, breaking the stalemate.

'Ooh, I like the sound of that.' Pru brightened immediately. 'We could be the *PruBe's Detective Agency*, a little bit of Pru and a little bit of Bree.' She grinned.

Andy popped his eyes at them. 'Seriously! And you honestly don't think that sounds like a mass of unmentionable body hair? Good grief, girls, I'd be worried as to what type of clients you'd attract with that name!' If he had been fortunate enough to have had a pint of Watkins in his hand, he could have spluttered it mid-mouthful. Instead, he had to settle for a very loud guffaw, whilst accidentally releasing a splatter of pork scratchings down his shirt. 'Look, if you're hell bent on this venture – but definitely don't give up your day jobs – how about the one you first thought of: *The Curious Curator & Co?*'

Pru and Bree sat quietly, pondering his suggestion. The only sound was their collective crunching of the shared packet of unwanted scratchings. It definitely had an air of Dickensian mood about it, something Pru loved, and it did conjure up a more professional image. They gave each other a smug side glance and grinned.

And from that moment, the *Curious Curator & Co Detective Agency* was born, amid pink gin and tonic, pork scratchings, and a quirky but loyal friendship.

THE WINTERBOTTOM LADIES

I'm telling you, Ada Millington at the Dog and Gun is definitely bisexual, I heard it from Florrie Patterson at the Twisted Currant Café. Our Ada's been painting both sides of the fence for donkey's years.' Ethel Tytherington delved into her handbag, pulled out a white embroidered handkerchief, and dramatically dabbed at her nose. 'I always knew there was something quite naughty about that woman. I've seen the way she eyes me up from behind the bar when I've been sipping my sweet sherry!' She pursed her lips and dipped her head towards the other WI ladies who were currently hanging on to her every word. Ethel loved a captive audience.

'Oh, Ethel, for goodness' sake!' Clarissa Montgomery intervened. 'First, don't flatter yourself, and secondly Florrie told me the same story, Ada can speak two languages – she's *bilingual*, you silly woman!' She took a bite from the slab of fruit cake and wiped the crumbs from her chin before continuing. 'She was a nanny for a wealthy family when she was younger, and used to travel all over with them. I've heard her speak French fluently.'

'Pah, bilingual, bisexual it's all the same!' Ethel tartly snapped back.

Clarissa grinned. 'Well, one speaks with tongues and the other...'

'Ladies, ladies, that's enough!' Pru jumped in quickly. She was desperate to laugh, but she could see the tone of this conversation rapidly dropping through the floorboards of the Winterbottom St Michael's Parish Hall, home to the Winterbottom Women's Institute meetings.

'Ooh look, here's Hilda.' Millie Thomas waved wildly to let her friend know where they were sitting. They all budged along one seat to make space for her. Hilda Jones took her time crossing the vast hall. Millie couldn't help but feel a touch of sorrow for her; they had all noticed that her forgetfulness was getting worse. Dementia was such a cruel disease, stealing a little bit more of a person each day, but Hilda took it all in her stride. She eventually reached them, took off her coat and placed it over the back of the chair, sat down, smiled at her friends, and just as quickly stood up.

'Well, it's been lovely seeing you all, but it's time for me to go. I'll see you soon at Florrie's café no doubt.' She picked up her coat, jiggled her arms into the sleeves, and turned to leave.

'Hilda love, you've only just arrived...' Millie, a look of concern on her face, gently took her arm and sat her down.

'I know!' Hilda winked and gave a huge grin, making the ladies laugh out loud.

'You little minx!' Clarissa offered her a slice of cake. 'I can never tell when you're being serious or having us on.'

'Right, whilst you're all enjoying your tea and cake, ladies, Bree will hand out leaflets giving lots of different choices for our days out and, I think–' Pru checked the accounting book in front of her. '–maybe an odd weekend or two away if our budget can stretch to it.' A gentle murmur of approval ran through the gathered women. 'So, if you'd all like to have a ponder on where you would enjoy going to and pop any ideas into Bree's suggestion box. Similarly, if you spot any hotel mini-break deals you think might interest the ladies, let her know.'

Clarissa was the first to give her opinion. Her hand shot up into the air like a schoolgirl, desperate to offer the answer to the teacher. 'Yes, Clarissa?' Pru gave her undivided attention, even though some members had already broken away into little groups chattering ten to the dozen.

'How about a murder mystery weekend? That would be so much fun,' Clarissa offered.

Pru let out a long sigh and caught Bree's eye. Murder mystery! Jeez, hadn't they experienced enough of that with the Winter-bottom murders? They'd lost six members in that awful event. No matter how much time had passed, it still sent collective shivers down their spines.

'Lemon drizzle cake, anyone?' Brenda Mortinsen's cheery voice suddenly interrupted the proceedings as her chubby, shiny face loomed out of the kitchen, cake-stand held aloft with great pride. Pru couldn't understand why Brenda baked that particular cake for every WI meeting; she wasn't sure if it was a tribute, or if she just didn't seem to grasp the significance of it. Poor Mabel Allinson, who had been the first to die, had been found face down in that delicious delicacy and, quite understandably since that day, nobody had touched so much as a crumb of lemon drizzle cake.

Ethel suddenly became very animated again. Perched on the end of her seat, she waved her arms as though conducting an invisible orchestra. 'I like the sound of that, don't you, ladies? Oh, what fun we could have: guessing who did it, but without the risk of being garrotted, stabbed or poisoned.' She was beside herself with unbridled excitement.

'I went to one once at a restaurant in town; they had actors playing the part of waiters and bar staff. Even the chef was one.' Millie gaily trilled.

'Did you guess right? Did you find the murderer?' Clarissa

was deeply invested in her own brilliant idea and was starting to feel a shiver of self-importance in the hope the Winterbottom ladies might consider her suggestion.

Millie paused to think. 'Mmm… well, the food wasn't up to much and we all got it wrong on our table, but that was more to do with our over-indulgence in the Merlot, Malbec and Baileys.' She faked a hiccup and winked. 'By the time the third bottle had gone down a treat, we were that tipsy we didn't give a bugger who'd dunnit!' She let out a hearty laugh.

Pru sat quietly at the president's table, cup of tea in hand. Millie's mention of wine had made her hanker for a glass of Merlot herself, but listening to the ladies chatter and giggle, throwing ideas around for the coming year, gave her a warm feeling. To know that Winterbottom village, for all its little foibles and odd characters, still held a great community spirit, which regularly revealed itself at their twice monthly meetings, was a joy.

'Penny for them.' Bree sat herself down on the second chair at the table. She took a large bite from the huge slice of chocolate cake that was balanced on her plate. 'Mmmmfph, been finking… mmmm, mmmfph nom nom… Shhhaterday…'

Pru grimaced, wrinkling her nose. 'For goodness' sake, Bree, don't speak with your mouth full, I can't understand a word you're saying!' Bree swallowed and wiped her mouth with a tissue. 'Funny you should mention that; my last boyfriend said the same thing…' She laughed loudly as she squished her index finger into what was left of the cake.

Pru's cup rattled back onto the saucer. 'Eeewww, too much information, matey. You'll give Ethel a run for–'

'Time, ladies, please!' Eric Potter, the village postman and volunteer caretaker for the parish hall, made his presence known. He stood centre stage, flat cap at a jaunty angle as he checked his watch. 'I need to be locking up in the next ten minutes; Mrs Potter has a nice hotpot waiting for me at home.' He grinned.

'I bet she does–' Ethel Tytherington quickly retorted. '–we've all heard the saucy rumours!'

Amid laughter, much clattering of crockery, and the scraping of chairs on the oak flooring, they cleared away any trace of their occupancy of the venue and the last August meeting of the Winterbottom Ladies Institute came to an upbeat and cheerful close.

A SHARP EXIT

*S*mithers let out a slight groan as his knee gave way on the first stair to the main gallery of Montgomery Hall. He stopped momentarily to get his breath back before placing the tray down on the walnut console table. He stretched out his back and then gave his left knee a vigorous rub. Man and boy he had run these stairs several times a day, often jumping two at a time in his youth; now his joints popped like a sheet of bubble wrap, and he moaned more out of pain than youthful pleasure. That thought made him smile. Ah, his dear Emily. She still led him a merry dance, even at their age, although it was no longer a quick-step but more of a shuffle.

'Come on, Smithers old boy, get your act together...' he gently chided himself as he picked up the tray and took to the stairs once again. With a final great effort, he at last reached Miss Cecily's floor.

'Oh, William, why don't you use the dumb waiter from the kitchens instead of dragging yourself up all these stairs?' Ellie tucked the duster into the waistband of her apron and took the tray from him. 'Or you could have asked me. I always clean Miss

Cecily's suite on Tuesday mornings; I could have brought it up for you.' She gave him a warm smile that lifted his heart.

Smithers was very fond of Ellie Shacklady; she was such a sweet young woman and still, in his opinion, very innocent. Sometimes far too innocent. Many times lately he had found himself respectfully reprimanding Master Bentley, the Montgomery's twenty-three-year-old delinquent son, for his colourful language in her presence. No matter how hard he tried, he just could not bring himself to like that boy one little bit. In his opinion Ellie had been a breath of fresh air in Montgomery Hall, and it had never looked cleaner since she had arrived and taken up the post. He would go to any measures necessary to ensure she was happy here, and if that meant slightly overstepping the mark in his role, then he would do so. His recent upgrade from butler to head of staff, an acknowledgement for all his years of loyal service, had been very welcome, but in his heart he would always be 'The Butler' – just as old Ernest Montgomery, Hugo's father, would call him.

'Ellie, can I ask you something before I advise Mr Montgomery of a situation that has arisen?' Smithers tipped his head and waited for her response.

'Of course. Anything I can do to help, just ask.' She gave him another warm smile.

'Well–' he hesitated, trying to pick the right words; the last thing he wanted to do was to cause offence or leave Ellie feeling he was pointing the finger at her. '–there have been certain, shall we say, objects of note that have been mislaid lately around the Hall. I do so need your assistance, Ellie; you know the placing of virtually everything here. Have you noticed anything untoward?'

Ellie pinched her lips together in thought and frowned. 'Like what?'

'Oh, small ornaments missing, trinkets, that sort of thing.' Smithers adjusted his waistcoat as a diversion from his awkwardness. 'See, just here on the dresser outside Miss Cecily's suite, her Ladro figurine, "The Dancer" – it's gone!'

Ellie looked at the space left by the ornament that had always been her favourite. The dancer's red ballet shoes and the delicate pink rose held in her hand reminded her of her own childish ambitions. 'Oh my goodness, I hadn't noticed. Has it been moved somewhere else, maybe?' She looked at him hopefully.

Smithers sighed. 'No, my dear, I've searched everywhere. I even asked Mrs Montgomery if she had moved it. We have no guests at the moment, so I fear we may have someone on staff who is a little light-fingered.' Smithers felt sad to have to think, let alone say out loud, that he was losing trust in a member of his household.

Ellie placed the tray on the dresser and, all protocol pushed aside, wrapped her arms around him and gave him a hug. 'Don't worry, I'll keep my eyes peeled for anything suspicious...' She grinned and pointed two fingers towards her eyes and then down the corridor to indicate she was going to be all-seeing.

'Thank you, my dear, it is very much appreciated.' Smithers picked up the tray and made his way to Miss Cecily's suite.

Cecily Montgomery sat in the plush green tapestry chair in front of the fireplace. The carved cherubs underneath the mantelpiece kept a watchful eye on her. She clasped her gnarled fingers together and jutted out her chin. 'I don't know how many times I have to tell you, Stephanie, there is no money, hidden or other-wise!' she barked in annoyance.

Stephanie controlled her breathing as best she could and bit down on her bottom lip in an attempt to stop herself from losing her temper. There was no point in annoying the old biddy any more than she had done already. Sunlight from the floor-to-ceiling window caught the myriad of diamonds in Cecily's ornate ring, shooting a flash of painful light directly into Stephanie's eyes. 'Look, Cecily, we are in dire straits here. The hotel is dying on its feet; there is nothing, and I mean nothing, coming in.' She waited for the old lady to acknowledge her, but Cecily sat stoic and silent. She tried again. 'By the end of the year, unless things change or there is some sort of cash injection, we won't be able to pay the staff; we will have to let them go.' She hoped that would be the thin end of the wedge for a woman who had spent the best part of her life being waited upon hand and foot.

Cecily finally spoke. 'There is still you, isn't there? You're not bloody incapable of bringing a tray up here, are you? For goodness' sake, woman, stop bleating like a sheep!'

That was the final straw for Stephanie. She could feel her décolletage and throat flushing red. 'How dare you, you... you horrible old crone–'

'Good afternoon, Miss Cecily, your lunch is ready to be served.' Smithers ensured his entrance into the room was loud enough to halt whatever proceedings were taking place. Cecily gave him a curt nod of her head and smiled, a smile that belied the anger she was currently feeling towards her silicone-pumped granddaughter-in-law.

'Now, now, Stephanie darling, don't be a bitch to me or I'll have to be a bitch back.' Cecily genteelly placed the napkin across her lap and tilted her head, gifting Stephanie a superior smile. 'And believe me, my dear, I can do it so much better than you can!'

Smithers placed the tray in front of her, giving Cecily a conspiratorial wink. He adored the feistiness of this woman whom he had faithfully served for almost sixty years.

Stephanie flounced across the Persian carpet, her heels clattering when she reached the polished wood floor. Grabbing the door handle she turned to give Cecily one last piece of her mind, but she didn't get the chance to even open her mouth before the wily old creature beat her to it.

'Oh, and Stephanie–' Cecily serenely smiled. '–don't let the door smack you on the arse on your way out!'

PERKS OF THE JOB

The early morning sun forced its way through where the curtains met and cast a shaft of light across the bedroom before settling on Andy's face. Pru loved lying in bed just watching him sleep. She poked her fingers into the dust motes to make them dance and swirl, stuck out her tongue, stretched it to see if she could reach her chin, and when that failed she grabbed the tip of it and pulled in effort to bridge the gap.

'Yeeeow...' All that did was make her eyes water.

Andy sat up like a coiled spring bouncing to full height, his sleepy eyes scanning the room. 'What's up, what happened?'

Pru huffed loudly, 'It's not long enough...'

'What isn't?'

'This!'

'Your tongue?'

'Yep...'

'For what?'

Before he could say another word, Pru threw herself across the bed and straddled him. 'For this...' She laughed, sticking her tongue into his ear.

'Bluuuurgh, you can be so disgusting at times, Prunella Pearce,' he berated her as he kissed the tip of her nose.

Pru fell back onto her pillow and stared at the ceiling. 'So, what's on the agenda today, my Delectable Defective?'

Andy swung his legs over the side of the bed, dropping his feet onto the woven rug. His hair sprang randomly in several directions. He clacked his tongue against the roof of his mouth. 'Yuk, it feels like Binks has slept in here... in fact where *is* that dratted cat?' He bent down to check under the bed. Experience had taught him that if Binks was in the bedroom his ankles were at risk. 'Not much, leisurely morning before lates.' He checked his watch. 'Three o'clock start today, but with a shedload of paperwork and court files to catch up on, I just might go in a little earlier. What are you up to?'

Pru watched him saunter out of the bedroom to the bathroom. She could never tire of that view of him, in fact it was the first thing she had noticed when they had met: his rather delicious derrière. 'I'm seeing Bree later for lunch... after I've put a wash on.' She picked up his discarded socks between her thumb and forefinger and flung them towards the laundry basket. They missed. 'We've got a few ideas for a road trip and a weekend away for the WI crew, so we'll be looking at some options.'

'Over a few glasses of wine, no doubt!' Andy teased as he tightened the bath towel around him.

'Now what on earth makes you think that!? Honestly, Andy, the way you...' Her mobile phone ringing interrupted her. She pointed to the bed and indicated for him to sit down so she could finish her chastisement of him once she had taken her phone call. It wasn't a number she recognised. She swiped on the green icon. 'Pru Pearce...'

Andy watched her, listening to the one-sided conversation.

'Yes, that's right The Curious Curator and Co...' Pru added a few um's, ah's and head-nodding as she listened. 'Of course, I'm sure that's something we can look into, and discreetly too.

Discretion is our speciality. If you send all the details to my email address, I'll get back to you as soon as we can put something together for you.' After a few more formalities were finalised, Pru ended the call.

'Oh my goodness, we've got our first job!' She excitedly punched the air. 'I can't believe it; I've only just put the advert in the *Winterbottom News* and Bree threw a few flyers around.' She paused to catch her breath. 'That was Tarragon Montgomery, the guy that's absolutely loaded. He owns the huge upmarket Montgomery Hall Hotel in Little Childer Thornton.'

Andy wanted to share her excitement, but he still wasn't one hundred per cent behind the idea. It worried him. He understood that Pru's part-time job of three days a week in the village library had left her wanting, but going from librarian to amateur detective was one awfully big leap. 'What's the job?'

'Theft! They think someone on the staff is half-inching valuable artefacts and ornaments, so they want it dealt with on the QT without police involvement. They definitely don't want negative publicity. A dishonest employee could cause major problems for future bookings. Gosh, wait until I tell Bree; she'll be over the moon.'

Andy watched her bounce around the bedroom, hopping on one leg as she tried to get the other into her jeans, wishing with all his heart she could have chosen something a little less risky. But knowing Pru as he did, that was the last thing she would ever do.

Florrie Patterson, the proprietor of The Twisted Currant Café turned the open sign on the door and adjusted the red chequered curtains either side of it. She smoothed down her apron, repositioned the bow at the back, and mentally ticked off the tables to chairs ratio. As she nudged against Table 3, she repositioned the flower vase so it was more central. 'Perfect!' she said aloud in a sing-song voice. She gave one more scan of her beloved café and nodded. 'Absolutely perfect.'

She had already taken delivery of her daily order for various cream cakes and fancies from the bakers in town, but she prided herself on baking her own scones, and today was no exception. Cooling on the rack were a dozen cherry scones for her regular village ladies who graced her with their presence several times a week. The little bell above the door tinkled loudly, heralding her first customer.

'Morning, Florrie.' Clarissa Montgomery dropped her handbag down onto their usual table, wriggled her arms out of her coat, and hung it on the coat stand in the corner next to the aspidistra that was still housed in Florrie's dead mother's chamber pot. She shuddered as she wondered what delights had been deposited in it prior to it being appropriated as a plant holder. 'Ethel's on her way, I just spotted her coming out of the butchers, so can you make it two teas and one of your delicious scones, please, Florrie.'

Whilst Florrie busied herself preparing the orders, her little tea shop began to fill with the gentle hum of the Winterbottom ladies' chatter as Millie Thomas, Hilda Jones, Avaline Prendergast and Brenda Mortinsen joined Clarissa and Ethel. Florrie loved mornings like this; it was the foundation of a good village community.

'Ooh, are you doing bacon baps this morning, Florrie?' Hilda excitedly enquired. 'Put me down for one if you are.' She sat down next to Millie, and absent-mindedly adjusted the floral placemat in front of her.

'Right, ladies.' Clarissa placed a pink plastic wallet onto the table. 'I've got a fantastic idea to put forward for our WI weekend away!' The gathered ladies could see she was beside herself with excitement. They would be all ears, but not before they had tucked into their scones and baps and wet their lips with a nice cup of Tetley. Clarissa, however, was not known for her patience. 'It's a psychic murder mystery weekend!' she quickly imparted, then sat back in triumph waiting for her listeners' excited response. The seconds ticked by as five blank faces stared back at her. Not to be deterred, she pushed photocopied itineraries towards them. 'It's in a very posh place: the Montgomery Hall Hotel, and well within our budget as they're doing a special offer for coach trips and, wait for it–' She gave a dramatic pause. '–it's on Halloween! Come on, girls; it'll be so much fun, don't you think?'

'Here we go, Hilda.' Florrie placed the requested bacon bap in front of her, a knife teetering on the edge of the plate alongside a napkin.

Hilda stared at it. 'What's this?'

'A bacon bap, like you asked for.' Bemused, Florrie looked to Clarissa for confirmation.

'Did I?' Hilda lifted the top half of the bread and stared at the mound of bacon. 'It doesn't look like a scone, Florrie. Where do I put the jam?'

Clarissa quickly intervened to save any embarrassment. It was clear that Hilda was not having a good day. 'It's okay, dear, Florrie will get you a scone and I'm sure someone will have your bacon butty–' She hesitated and looked around the table. '–won't you, Avaline?'

Hilda looked thoughtful. 'That's very kind of you, thank you.' She smiled gratefully and sat back in her chair to await her scone.

'Dearie me, you can't ask her to eat that. Avaline's a virgin!' Ethel spluttered, horrified at the idea of the bacon bap being passed to the one person that couldn't eat it.

The collective look of confusion proved that deciphering Ethel was on a par with being a wartime code breaker at Bletchley Park. The silence was broken only by Avaline's very unladylike snorts. 'I certainly hope not after five kids, Ethel, that would be a bloody miracle – I think the word you're looking for is "vegan"!'

As their laughter filled the cosy café, the members of the Winterbottom Ladies Institute drank tea together and counted their blessings of friendship and loyalty. They ensured Hilda had her much-anticipated scone and took a show of hands on the psychic murder mystery weekend.

Ethel carefully studied the itinerary. 'Montgomery Hall?' She looked pensive. 'That's your name, isn't it, Clarissa? Is this one of your relatives; are you keeping it in the family?'

Clarissa gave a hearty laugh. 'Chance would be a fine thing. No, I'm from the Pelham branch of the Montgomerys – the near destitute ones. These toffs have absolutely nothing to do with me, thank goodness.' She cleared her throat loudly before taking a bite of her scone. 'But it was the name that caught my eye and drew it to my attention.'

She wondered if the owners of the Montgomery Hall Hotel might think the same thing upon her arrival and give her a room upgrade, maybe even a four-poster bed and a minibar.

Mmm... that was certainly something to hope for.

DANIEL

NOVEMBER 1977

*J*osephine Beaumaris waited on the grand steps of Montgomery Hall; her head bowed, the immense stone lions either side guarding her as they had done throughout her own childhood. She looked over at her husband, but with eyes as cold as steel he stared ahead, not offering her any comfort. He could not have been more distant if he had tried, and she was sure he had endeavoured with much effort as it was. The team of horses pulling the small ornate funeral coach stood regal, the black feather plumes adorning their heads trembled in the chill November wind. Dark clouds rumbled across the sky, adding to the already sombre occasion as the first drops of rain began to fall.

Josephine looked to the heavens, but it was a futile gesture; her faith had long since deserted her. A bead of water fell on her cheek and merged with the tears she had already shed. She watched as her parents, Hugo and Cecily Montgomery, her brother John and his wife Clarice, along with their young son, Tarragon; paid their respects to the small casket which held a simple spray of white roses that looked lost against the glossy black veneer. All around her, grief was evident, even the servants had broken away from their duties to line the route her son's cortege would take to the family vault. They wept openly to display their sorrow at the loss of a child.

Daniel Beaumaris scuffed his black shoe against the pebbles and chewed the inside of his cheek. He didn't want to look at the coffin, not because it would upset him, but because there was quite simply no point. He felt no grief, or sorrow or guilt, for his brother's death. He felt nothing, so to look at it would be a waste of his time and energy.

The undertaker flicked the reign and gave a word of encouragement. The horses shook their heads in response, their hooves crunching on the gravel set the carriage wheels in motion; a slow pace began managed by the officiant in front. Josephine joined her husband and her remaining son, Daniel. She placed a tender arm around his shoulders as they took their place directly behind the carriage.

'It will soon be over, sweetheart.' She gave him a comforting squeeze. 'Don't be too sad, darling.'

Daniel looked up at his mother, his large brown eyes stared into hers. 'I'm not sad, Mummy...' he said. 'David is better off dead anyway, because then I've got you all to myself.'

Josephine looked upon her son in horror, a chill spreading down her spine. His eyes bore into her, not to touch her soul but to tear it apart. 'What do you mean?' she gasped.

Daniel looked off into the distance and smiled. 'I could have saved him, Mummy, but I chose not to.' He paused and tipped his head inquisitively. 'What's for tea?'

'No one is born evil ... They become that way through choice and circumstance.'
Victoria Aveyard (*Glass Sword*)

UNDER THE COVERS

*P*ru shoved the first load into the washing machine, slammed the door shut, and set the dial. It swished into life just as she found one sock, a pair of Andy's boxers, and her sports bra on the floor behind her. Mr Binks, her blacker-than-night cat, hooded his eyes in disgust, a second sock, not matching the first, hung from his tail. 'Damn, every time!' she muttered to herself as she deftly plucked the cat's unwanted accessory from him and kicked the other items into the corner. Never a wash day went by without her finding some random piece of clothing dropped in a trail from bedroom to kitchen; she really should use a carry basket. She glanced at the wall clock. Just enough time for a quick change of clothes before Bree would arrive.

Her optimism about timing hadn't quite hit the mark; she was barely halfway up the stairs when the doorbell rang. She turned and skipped two steps down and energetically jumped the last three in one leap before skidding to the front door on the Scandi weave rug. 'Taadaa…' She flung open the door and took a bow, leaving a very bemused Bree to edge past her. 'Welcome to the house of missing socks and holey underpants!'

Bree rummaged in the green slouch bag she was carrying and pulled out a bottle of Shiraz and a pink plastic folder, placing them both on the kitchen worktop. 'Please don't tell me you've had Andy's tighty whities blessed by Reverend Baggott!' She helped herself to two glasses from the cupboard over the sink.

Pru danced past her, sweeping a grey sock under her nose. 'Sniff that, if the Reverend B has incanted a few choice words, then I don't think it's olibanum incense he's used for it!'

Bree scrunched her nose and followed up with a vigorous rub of it with her index finger. 'Come on, then, what's the news you couldn't wait to tell me? You said it was super exciting in your voicemail.' She carefully poured the wine ensuring the levels were equal.

Pru had never once managed to pour wine, gin or any other liquid known to man or woman, in equal amounts; someone always got more... or less, as the case may be. She admired Bree for that talent. She took a deep breath and held it for a second before excitedly imparting her news. 'We've got a job, a real, honest-to-goodness detective job at a place called the Montgomery Hall Hotel!' She sat back and took a slug of wine in triumph, waiting for Bree's reaction.

'That place in Little Childer Thornton?' Bree hastily grabbed the folder, popping it open.

'Yep, that's the one. They think a member of staff is being a little light-fingered, but want it dealt with discreetly so as not to upset the guests.'

Bree shoved a leaflet across the breakfast bar towards Pru. 'That's so spooky. Look where the WI tribe have suggested we go for a weekend away. Montgomery Hall is hosting a psychic murder mystery weekend.' She patiently waited for Pru to digest the contents. 'All within our price bracket, too.'

Pru intently examined the glossy pamphlet which promised two nights and three days of fine dining, luxurious rooms with Egyptian cotton bedding and full entertainment in the guise of

Psychic Selma and the cast of the Dingleberry Amateur Dramatics Society. 'Perfect,' she whispered to herself. 'Simply perfect!'

As the clock ticked away the hour and the bottle was drained of its contents, they sat giggling and planning, not only their first case for The Curious Curator & Co, but also on how to combine it with a fun weekend in the company of their WI ladies as a fortuitously timed cover story.

Tarragon was beside himself with anger. He slammed his hands down onto the marble counter in the en suite and tipped his head back, eyes closed, trying to moderate his breathing. Once he felt he had gained some control, he resumed a more erect stance, one that was befitting of a Montgomery male. The stark mirror lights that Stephanie favoured for her daily cosmetic regime picked out the florid hues of his complexion; he watched fascinated as they dappled, flushed and faded the calmer he became.

How ruddy dare she! Without a by your leave, no questions asked or permission given. This was not how a Montgomery wife should behave.

He ran his hand through his hair, pushing the odd strand that had had the audacity to break away from the rest of the heavily gelled pack, back into place. He straightened his tie. Cecily hated an untidy and ungentlemanly appearance, and considering what he was about to impart to her and the resulting volcanic eruption he was anticipating, he didn't want to give her anything more to add to the emotional fallout.

'Tarragon, darling...' Stephanie's voice grated on him like fingernails on a blackboard.

He didn't answer.

'We need to talk about this; it's for the best,' Stephanie simpered. She handed him a tumbler with a good whisky mix. 'The bookings are already up, there's a full contingent from a local Women's Institute group already down for the weekend, and the entertainment posse have taken up the rest of the rooms. It will be the first time we've had a full hotel in bloody years.'

He still didn't answer, preferring to let the burn of the whisky in his throat sear away any words he might have for her that were threatening to escape.

Stephanie wasn't giving up. She absent-mindedly refolded the fluffy hand towels as she rattled on about how good her idea had been, how it was all arranged and couldn't be changed without incurring a financial penalty. She regaled him with her work so far: glossy handout leaflets, an advertising spread in the *HOTELS Magazine*, and she'd even slipped a tempting piece in the aptly named *Witch* magazine, calling for all supernatural lovers to indulge themselves at the Montgomery Hall Hotel on All Hallows Eve.

For a second time in as many minutes, Tarragon could feel his blood pressure rising to epic proportions. '"Indulge themselves..." you make it sound like a ruddy orgy! Christ knows what Cecily will make of this.'

It was now Stephanie's turn to explode. She deliberately swept her hand across the bottles of perfume, face creams and soaps, making them clatter and drop like ninepins into the sink. 'I don't give a rat's ass what Cecily thinks. If there's any justice in this world she will have, I hope, kicked the bucket by then. She's shaping up to be Little Childer Thornton's version of the *Walking Dead*!'

There, she'd said it!

A chilled silence followed her little outburst. She desperately tried to backtrack. 'I didn't mean I wanted her dead, just that she's a little overdue her dinner date with the Grim Reaper...'

Shit. That sounded even worse.

'Oh for God's sake, Tarragon, it's a psychic murder mystery weekend. It's not the end of the world as the Montgomerys know it.' She gave him a weak smile.

Tarragon slugged back the whisky and rolled the glass in his hands. 'It's the psychic bit that's the problem... you have no idea what you have started. Cecily will be furious...'

As if on cue, a loud bang resonated from the Somerset Room next door. A room that had been closed off for almost forty-five years until Stephanie had taken it upon herself to send Ellie in to open the drapes and windows, clear the air and make it presentable.

'... no idea at all.' Tarragon sighed.

Stephanie haughtily fixed her eyes on him. 'Maybe not, but that–' She pointed towards the Somerset Room. '–with its gruesome history, is what will bring the punters in.'

PSYCHIC SELMA

$\mathcal{E}$stelle Evans had always hated Monday mornings. Why? She had absolutely no idea. Not once in her excess of fifty years on this mortal coil had she ever stuck to a routine or had a job that would give a touch of those much bleated about Monday morning blues.

She just simply hated them.

She rubbed her eyes and yawned. Another day, another dollar – or whatever cash she could prise from a desperado's fingers. She had become very adept at various disguises over the years, flitting from one money-making scheme to almost bordering on criminal activity the next. Her latest foray into gathering a little bit of wealth to get by on was as Psychic Selma, a woman with the gift of precognition, and she was doing pretty damned well out of it too. She'd had a few close calls and accusations of being a fraud, but as far as she was concerned, she could *see* a wealthy target a mile off, so she wasn't really lying.

She padded into the spare bedroom which doubled as her costume and make-up studio. All around her were cascades of fabrics and colours hanging from the rails: dresses, suits, shirts, blouses; you name it, she had it. She was fortunate to be of androgynous appearance which enabled her to switch between female and male characters. It was such a talent to have, and ensured any trail to her would soon unravel; people only saw what they wanted to see. Polystyrene heads gave host to a multitude of wigs: long, short, curly and straight. A wall mirror displayed a horizontal rectangle of bulb lights, whilst underneath the dressing table held the tools of her trade. Stage make-up, greasepaints, liquid latex, on-skin silicone, false eyelashes and a fair plethora of contact lenses, which could give Estelle any eye colour she wished. She pulled two outfits from the rail and hung them on the door. She would decide later which colour she would be today.

Tying the belt of her robe tightly around her waist, she made her way downstairs, pausing to flip up the blinds on the window.

'Let there be light...' She laughed as the early morning sun shone across the landing, almost blinding the ginger cat that was stretched out on top of the wash basket. 'Morning, Chester, come on boy, outside for your ablutions.' He slinked after her on his belly, almost sliding down the last two stairs like a melted orange Smartie.

'Tea or coffee, that is the question: Whether 'tis nobler in the mind to suffer Tetley or Maxwell House...' She chuckled heartily at her own joke. She reached for the coffee canister and spooned two decent helpings into her mug whilst simultaneously backheeling the kitchen door closed. Chester curled himself up in front of the radiator and went back to sleep. She always marvelled at how he could sleep all night, go for a wee, return to his home comforts and then sleep all day. She checked her watch and opened her diary.

'Nice little booking for Halloween, Chester.' She held the mug with both hands, feeling the warmth seeping into her fingers. 'Very timely indeed, I must say. Now should I wear emerald green or a nice hussy red today?'

The cat raised one haughty eyebrow, a definite sign of indifference to any colour she would eventually choose. 'Mmm... like that, is it?' She gave him a ruffle between his ears. 'Right, quick shower and then it's supermarket day.'

She grabbed a warm towel from the airer and slung it over her shoulder, pausing long enough in the kitchen to rinse out her mug and set it on the draining board before making her way into the little ground floor bathroom of the two-bed cottage. Humming gently to herself she turned on the shower...

It would always amaze him that people could be so careless with their home security; it wasn't just personal possessions that could potentially be at risk, as dear Estelle was about to discover...

He stretched the black leather glove further onto his wrist and wriggled his fingers, relishing the slight squeak the material gave off, before pressing down on the black lever latch. The door popped open easily to reveal a small but neat kitchen, two ladder-back chairs and a round table. Stretched out underneath the radiator was a large ginger cat that paid no heed to him.

'Gypsies, Tramps and Thieves' Estelle warbled, her lilted song echoing from the tiles to bounce back and be broken by the swish of the shower curtain being pulled around her.

He waited silently, biding his time; the blue cord wrapped around one hand. He would make it as quick as he could. Even though he would relish more time, there was no point in dragging it out; it would only cause him problems, problems he didn't need.

A swift death is a blessing for the unwilling, and he couldn't think of anyone that would be more unwilling than Estelle herself.

He smiled.

This was one event that she definitely wouldn't see coming.

Estelle continued with her song as the hot water spray pricked and stung her skin. She saw her daily showers as a ritual cleansing of her soul: it washed away the previous day's indiscretions. For at least an hour afterwards, she would feel quite angelic – before she would concede and take up the mantle of scam artist once again. It wasn't always for the money; she actually quite enjoyed doing it. Being Estelle hadn't brought her much pleasure in her life, so all the characters she regularly created truly were a joy to her.

She could be anything and anybody she wanted to be – and she frequently was!

'Psychic Selma you absolute beauty...' she trilled. 'Red hair and enigmatic smile... an absolute fusion of rainbow colours!' Her vocal self-admiration was suddenly cut short by the rattle of the shower curtain being yanked along the chrome rail. 'What the fu–'

Estelle flailed her arms as she was yanked backwards over the rim of the bath. She grabbed the only thing she could, the plastic shower curtain, to no avail. She landed heavily on her tufted mat. If the circumstances had been different, she would have viewed that as a euphemism and giggled loudly; but sadly, this was neither the time nor the place. Her shriek of terror was quickly silenced by a tightening around her neck. A pulsating throb in her ears as her eyes bulged and her cheeks swelled with the pressure, muffled her grunts.

Estelle was acutely aware of her unshaven legs riding high in the air before hanging over the edge of the bath. In the seconds that followed, the realisation hit her that there would be no more tomorrows, no more adventures and no more personas...

She was going to quite simply snuff it here and now, and be known to all and sundry as 'Estelle Evans with the hairy legs'.

She seriously wished she had spent more time on what was below her waist rather than what was above it. Two minutes with a Bic razor would have made all the difference to the elegance of an untimely death and less hassle for the undertaker.

Her fingers plucked vainly at what she now knew was a pretty good grade of polypropylene rope pulled tightly around her neck. In fact, it was probably the very same rope she had recently purchased to shore up her classic cream Vespa scooter underneath a nice piece of tarpaulin in the back garden.

A versatile blue rope that can withstand large weights and lots of pressure... the advertising blurb had promised her, and it was currently living up to that promise.

As her legs stopped spasming against the bathtub and the blackness began to take her, Estelle couldn't help but wonder if she'd gone for a cheaper version of rope – would her outcome have been any different?

The beat in her ears became slow, like a heart monitor trace.

One, thump...

Two, whump...

Three, beeeeeeep...

And just like that, Estelle Evans was gone.

He stood back to admire his handiwork. The shower curtain adhered to the wetness of Estelle's skin, clinging to her like a cheap bodycon dress, whilst her bulbous bloodshot eyes stared at the ceiling.

Bravo, sir, bravo...

With the imaginary roar of his audience ringing in his ears, he took a bow and swiftly left the stage. Time was of the essence for a quick change in preparation for his next scene in this particular piece of work, the part he loved best...

The Becoming...

THE DINGLEBERRIES

'*P*laces, everyone, quickly please...' Llewelyn Black, director of The Dingleberry Amateur Dramatics Society, limply clapped his hands together to ensure he had the rapt attention of his cast members. He swept his hand through his thick silvering hair and rearranged the sleeve on his navy Burberry rollneck sweater. It was more an action to ensure that those assembled would be treated to a glimpse of his new TAG Heuer watch than for his own personal comfort.

Marilyn Peacock, his second in command and producer, made no attempt to disguise her admiration, not just for the watch but for Llewelyn himself. She rolled her tongue across her upper lip and momentarily dipped her eyes, before sneaking a quick glance to see if he had noticed her sensual signal.

'Okay, listen up, ladies and gentlemen. The murder mystery evening at Montgomery Hall is less than a week away...' Llewelyn held his arm in the air and waved the cast list.

Mmm... clearly he hadn't.

Marilyn tried again, this time with a little more pout and a tad more sass.

Llewelyn continued in blissful ignorance. 'You have your role sheets, and hopefully you have been practising hard to become your allotted character. Remember, you will have to *be* them, totally *live* them, over the three days we are there.'

Marilyn sighed loudly at his indifference to her and reluctantly studied her sheet.

THE CAST

The Waitress ... Julie Shute
The Waiter ... Ralf Barnard
The Spinster ... Marilyn Peacock
The Doctor ... Phil Timkins
The hard of hearing elderly Dowager ... Eleanor Rimple
The handsome Bachelor / The Murderer ... Dirk Diamond
The Niece ... Francesca Moore
The Busybody / The Victim ... Clara Toomey
The Inspector ... Llewelyn Black
Wardrobe / Costumes ... Caryn Davies / Clara Toomey

Eleanor being cast as the deaf old biddy was perfect, because in reality she was exactly that, a deaf old biddy, and the choice of Phil Timkins for the doctor was spot on; he was, after all, their local GP. But to give her the role of spinster was quite simply an insult.

She sat down heavily on a nearby chair, almost on the brink of tears. *Spinster indeed!* She rummaged around in her handbag, pulled out a clean handkerchief, and tore open a new packet of Polo mints. She gave her eyes a discreet dab and popped a mint into her mouth. *Spinster, pah!*

'Everyone happy with their characters?' Llewelyn paused briefly, hoping against hope that everyone was, as he really wasn't in the mood for a clashing of egos or histrionics from his crew.

One hand shot up. He resisted rolling his eyes. 'Yes, Marilyn?'

'You've got me down as the spinster…'

'Yes, that's right. Because this is a little different, I've tried to cast everyone in a role that is as close to their own personality, or circumstance, to make the transition easy over the three days.' He gave her a sympathetic smile.

'I don't understand...' She tilted her head and waited.

The little warning voice that often invaded Llewelyn's thoughts suddenly began to scream at him; *Don't go there, quit now whilst you're ahead, son...* but it was too late.

'But you *are* a spinster, Marilyn; that's why you are perfect for the role.'

Marilyn began to turn several shades of pink, her lips pursed tightly together lest what she really wanted to say should spill out. Granted, he was right, but that didn't make her feel any better about her life and her marital status. She wasn't single from the want of trying. Suddenly the tense atmosphere was mercifully interrupted by Francesca and her unfortunate lisp.

'Oooh look, *Thikick Thelma* is appearing with u*th*, how cool is that?'

'Who?' Marilyn quizzically asked.

'*Thikick Thelma*! My friend saw her at the Winterbridge *th*ummer fayre, cry*th*tal ball*th*, predictions and *th*pooky readings, yer know, communing with the dead.' Francesca was beside herself with excitement. 'Tha*tth* really going to add to the atmo*th*phere.'

Their excited chatter about Psychic Selma's extraordinary gift continued over tea and biscuits, followed by an intense discussion about their individual roles, character development and the storyline, which was actually pretty fluid in places. At these type of murder mystery weekends they would often take their lead from the other guests and go where the action took them.

'So, we're all happy with the script and what each cast member is doing?' Llewelyn once again waited. He gave them less than ten seconds to respond before he continued. 'Speak to Marilyn before you go, she's got the room allocations and coach pickup point. Right, as ever, thank you for your presence, and see you all on Tuesday.'

As the Dingleberries emptied out of the Winter Gardens Theatre, a sinister shadow moved fleetingly across the car park before disappearing into the nearby woods.

TURNING TURTLE

*A*ndy propelled his chair across the newly laid carpet tiles in the incident room at Winterbridge nick. They were a nice shade of dark grey, picked solely for their ability to hide tea and coffee dribbles, squashed-in biscuits, cake / butties, and any other disgusting deposits the CID team managed to bring in on the soles of their shoes from various crime scenes. They had been a long time coming, waiting for the police authority budget to afford them had taken a lifetime, but everyone now welcomed their fresh smell and smart appearance.

'I actually quite miss our one rumpled carpet tile, to be honest,' Detective Constable Lucy Harris quipped to no one in particular. 'That solitary one that peeled itself up in 1994. I still find myself jumping over the spot to avoid tripping up on it.' She laughed as she banged a staple into the file in front of her. That particular tile had become a bit of a legend over the twenty-five plus years since it had made itself known, acting as a random booby trap to anyone who unwittingly entered the room and didn't look down. 'By the way, how's Pru? I haven't seen her for ages with being out of the force as the family liaison officer for the Pendlebury case.'

Andy grinned. 'Please don't tell me the Terrible Trinity haven't had a boozy get-together recently. The Dog and Gun profits will be at an all-time low!'

Lucy gave him a middle finger. Although he was her sergeant, he was also the boyfriend of her best mate, so as long as the rest of the office didn't see the familiar and near-the-knuckle comedy exchanges between them, she could often get away with murder. 'I bumped into Bree briefly in Dylan's Dispensary, but we didn't have long to chat as I had an interview booked.' She savagely punched a hole into the thick cardboard of a green Q-Connect document folder. 'Ouch!' She quickly pressed her finger into her mouth and sucked. 'Oops, blood!'

Andy quickly propelled his chair over to her desk to assist, and in the process rucked up one of the new carpet tiles. 'Oh dear, is that your middle finger out of action, Luce?' he laughed.

Lucy pointed to the floor. 'You're not that lucky, Sarge, although I think you'll be out of action when the DI sees that.'

The forlorn grey carpet tile sat with its cavernous wave of a mouth stuck in the air, and as coincidence would have it, it was in exactly the same spot as their much-loved tile from 1994 had been.

Andy grimaced. He hadn't felt the *Wrath of Holmes* for months. Detective Inspector Murdoch Holmes was head of the Winterbridge Investigations Team, and possessed a quick, dry wit coupled with a terrible temper when things didn't go according to his rule book. Andy made a feeble attempt to settle the tile by jumping up and down on it and stamping his feet rhythmically. It made little impact.

'*Riverdance* – I got it in one!' Lucy laughed.

'Speak of the devil...' Andy quickly returned to his desk as the incident room door was flung open heralding the arrival of the DI.

'Morning, troops.' Murdoch Holmes strode purposely to the front of the room, dropped several files onto his desk, and with knuckles firmly placed onto the tattered blotter in front of him, he jutted his chin, leant forward, and surveyed his team.

'Right, straight from the Command Team meeting this morning, we have an out-of-force request for two detectives to assist with the Nether Walloping double murder.' His eyes searched the room. 'It's a DS and DC they're needing, so, Andy, nice little jaunt for you, and take Lucy with you; she could do with the experience.'

As much as Andy enjoyed being farmed out to other forces, this couldn't have come at a more inopportune time for him. His plans for popping the question to Pru would now have to be put on hold. He'd spent weeks arranging the right moment; he'd even roped Bree in by asking her to discreetly palm one of Pru's dress rings to give him an idea of size. The stunning solitaire diamond on a white gold band was being held by the jewellers pending his last-minute arrangements. They would now have to keep it a bit longer. He pulled their card from his wallet and keyed in the numbers. Disappointment dug deep, but as always the job came first.

Pru pulled down on the top of her suitcase and grabbed the zip, yanking it until her fingers were sore trying to make the edges meet. 'Damn, damn and damn again!' she cursed as it popped open, throwing out a Shetland wool jumper, fleecy pyjamas, and one slipper.

Andy ambled into the bedroom, a towel tied tantalisingly around his waist, allowing her to admire his tanned and toned upper torso as he rubbed at his hair with a smaller hand towel. He gave her one of his delicious grins, the one that made her toes tingle and her tummy flip. She still wondered after all this time why she deserved to be this happy.

'You're not going until next week; you'll have packed and repacked by then! Take something out. That should do it.' He sat down on the bed next to his own small suitcase which he had earlier packed for his imminent trip. 'Look at mine, anticipated two weeks away and it's all in there. You're going for a long weekend, and you've got the whole bloody wardrobe in yours!'

'I can't take anything out; I need absolutely everything that's in there – everything!' Pru stood, hands on hips and sighed with frustration.

Andy rummaged around in the depths of her case and pulled out a bottle of Shiraz, a bumper packet of variety crisps, four packets of Haribos and a bottle of Alnwick Gin. 'Really!' He waited for her reaction.

'Yes, really. I'll be working long hours on the investigation, so nibbles always come in handy when I'm hungry.'

'And the wine and gin?'

'I get thirsty too!' Pru pouted.

He grabbed her by the waist and pulled her down onto him, his lips gently brushing hers as he swept her underneath him, her chestnut curls spreading out across the bed. 'How thirsty, my Loony Librarian?'

'Ooh, about this much.' She held her thumb and index finger millimetres apart and giggled. 'I'm going to miss you so much.'

Andy kissed the tip of her nose. 'I'll miss you too, but more to the point I'll also be worrying myself sick. Just promise me you won't do anything stupid at that place. If it looks as though it's getting out of hand, you phone the police and let them deal with it – regardless of what Mr Terrapin Montgomery wants.' He was quite emphatic.

'It's Tarragon…'

Andy checked his watch. 'Mmm… we've got an hour or two before I'm *ta-ra and gone*; maybe we could, you know…' He laughed.

Pru groaned loudly as he nuzzled into her neck. 'Not funny, my Delectable Detective, not funny at a… ohhhhh!'

Suitcases temporarily forgotten, Andy and Pru set about making up for their two weeks of enforced separation.

ALL ABOARD

'For goodness' sake, Ethel...' Clarissa huffed. '... don't stop there, my nose almost wedged itself between your very ample buttocks!' She used both hands on each well-rounded cheek to push Ethel up the coach steps.

'Ladies, ladies, let's settle down. Find your seats and get comfortable, Frank has already taken care of your luggage.' Pru winced as she checked everyone's name on the list. She was sure she had already started to sound like Kitty Hardcastle, the WI's former president. She seriously hoped not; as well meaning as Kitty had been, she was much like fingernails on a chalkboard. Irritating as hell and guaranteed to make you wince. 'Millie, can you make sure Hilda is okay?'

The excited chatter from the ladies of the Winterbottom WI filled the coach. The prospect of a long weekend away with like-minded friends had been the hot topic of conversation for weeks, and just as quickly as they had taken the unanimous vote to stay at the Montgomery Hall Hotel, the date had finally arrived.

The dilapidated coach of Rubber Springs & Gaskets Tours was to be their mode of transport. Lumpy, bumpy and having had its best days during the late 1980s, Pru was amazed that it was still roadworthy. Frank Atkins, the owner, had always been their go-to for trips away from Winterbottom. He was happy to oblige with his services and a decent discount, just so long as Kitty Hardcastle was on the list. Frank and Kitty's liaisons were legendary amongst the Winterbottom ladies, making it all the more difficult to believe that the pair were still under the mistaken notion that their clandestine meetings were secret.

'Budge along a bit, girlfriend.' Chelsea Blandish, all peroxide and leopard print, inched her curvy posterior into the seat next to her best bosom buddy, Cassidy Parks. 'Bosom buddy' was an apt moniker for them, having both indulged in cosmetic enhancement at the Brassiere or Bust clinic in Winterbridge.

'I can't pull me tray up now...' Cassidy wailed.

Chelsea hiccupped loudly. 'Aren't you the lucky one; I can't get mine down!'

Pru shook her head in despair. The biggest mistake she had made was having the pickup point outside the Dog and Gun. It was obvious that Chelsea and Cassidy, the youngest members of the WI, had made use of Juicy Jason's services whilst propped up at the bar. Twice she had been inside to try and drag them out. 'What on earth's the problem now, girls?' She edged her way along the aisle to their seats to assist, pausing to take in the sight before her. 'Oh!' was all she could utter.

Cassidy's over inflated 38 double Ds were firmly splayed out on top of the pulled down seat tray whilst Chelsea's recently added-to boobs now ballooned to an incredible 36G, were firmly wedged underneath the tray on her side. Pru's mind raced, desperately trying to think of a lateral solution to their problem without her having to go hands-on. The thought of just one finger touching the over inflated silicone filled her with horror.

'How on earth have you managed *that*?' Pru asked incredulously. 'Honestly, ladies, even a five-year-old couldn't get themselves into that much of a fix! You'll just have to help each other out, or share the one tray that's already down.' She quickly turned on her heel, eager to put as much space between herself and the four over inflated barrage balloons. A fleeting vision of Chelsea's tube of sour cream Pringles wedged neatly between Cassidy's cleavage made her shudder.

'Have they got any singers at this place?' Hilda Jones plonked her tapestry holdall on her knee and almost disappeared into its depths. She pulled out a white paper bag, unfurled the top, and offered it to Florrie Patterson. Florrie dipped her fingers in and pulled out a pineapple chunk covered in sugar, examined it, and swiftly popped it into her mouth.

Ethel shook her head. 'Not as far as I'm aware; it's just a Murder Mystery with a psychic thrown in for good measure.'

Hilda looked crestfallen. 'Oh, that's a shame. I love a little sing-along. Did you know I went to see Engelbear Humperdicker in my youth. Now that's a man that could croon!' She blushed at the memory. '"Help Me Make it Through the Night" really does it for me.'

Clarissa couldn't resist. 'I find a packet of TENA ladies helps me, Hilda – I can pull an all-nighter with one of them in place–' She chortled. '–and I don't need the loo until at least 7.30am! Oh, and by the way it's Engelbert Humperdinck.'

Hilda shook her sweetie bag and offered it out again. 'Who is?'

'Who you went to see, you know; "Help Me Make It Through the Night"?' repeated Clarissa.

Hilda tutted loudly. 'Well, if you insist, but only if we're sharing the same room…'

Llewelyn Black checked his watch and nodded a personal appreciation for its perfect timekeeping, which was more than he could say for some of his Dingleberrys. There was always one. He watched Clara Toomey jauntily stride along the road, her suitcase bouncing and kicking behind her as she hauled it over the beautifully tended flower bed outside Chapperton Bliss railway station. He gave a furtive glance at Stan Suggett the station master, who looked fit to burst as Clara continued in her quest to reach the coach whilst dragging several pansies and a cyclamen with her, caught in the wheels of her case.

'Come on, Clara, put a little more gusto into it.' Llewelyn tapped his watch to prove his keenness for her to quicken up her pace.

Clara reached the doors of the coach and stopped to catch her breath, offering her suitcase to the driver, happy for him to deal with it as he saw fit. 'My apologies, I was just going over the script with a nice cup of tea, and time seemed to have run away with itself.' She hauled herself up the steps.

Marilyn, keen to keep as close to the object of her desire as possible, had chosen one of the front seats on the coach, directly in line with Llewelyn. 'Clara, you're the "victim", you don't have any words, you just have to lie down and be dead,' she huffed in annoyance.

Clara quickly spat back. 'That's rich coming from the "Spinster"; did you need words or are you just acting from experience?' She didn't trouble herself to wait for a reply, preferring to edge along the aisle to the next available window seat, wafting the scent of lavender and chamomile as she went.

'*Thum* people...' Francesca Moore lifted one eyebrow and sighed. Holding a small compact mirror, she applied a liberal slick of red lipstick and smacked her lips together to even out the coverage. She clicked it shut and looked up. Several thumbs from her fellow cast members greeted her. 'It's me li*th*p...' she testily responded.

'Ah, you mean *some people*? Well, I suppose we can't all be perfect!' Marilyn sniped.

Francesca grinned. 'Oh yeah, and I am! Have you ever tried *thaying*, "*Thally thells thee thells on the thee thore*"?'

That was all that was needed to break the ice. As the laughter of the Dingleberry Amateur Dramatic Society made way for excited chatter, all temperamental and artistic friction was soon forgotten.

'Right, all accounted for, all sitting comfortably. Next stop Montgomery Hall Hotel!' Llewelyn bounced down into his seat as the coach set off, exactly on time as he had meticulously planned. He was looking forward to this weekend away, not least because he had ensured the ravishing Julie Shute, his new extra-marital interest, would have the room next to his.

YOU RANG...

$\mathcal{C}$ ecily Montgomery pushed the tray away from her. Her usual of scrambled egg and toast had not seemed the least bit appetising today; in fact, halfway through she thought she would choke. Ever since Tarragon had imparted the news that her beloved Montgomery Hall was to be host to charlatans and actors, she had been beside herself with fury. If Hugo were still alive he would be turning in his grave. That thought almost made her laugh; it was a perfect example of an oxymoron, something that idiotic grandson of hers would never understand. Montgomery Hall played host to an extensive library, and she couldn't recall one moment in his wasteful life when he had deigned to entertain anything within it.

She reached out to grab the bell pull to call Smithers. She had stayed him on his suggestion of a cup of tea, but the more she thought of Stephanie's betrayal to the Montgomery name, the more she had a craving for a very large brandy.

To goose with the time of day... she waved her hand dismissively to no one in particular as she was, as always, on her own. 'Harlot, whore,' she mumbled to herself, 'floozy, hussy, slut...' She paused to catch her breath. 'Tramp!' If she could have conjured up more suitable descriptions for Stephanie, she would have done so. Cecily had tried to put a stop to their plans by threatening to withdraw any further financial support if they went ahead with their ridiculous weekend. The last thing she wanted was a load of commoners tramping through her beloved home, but they had continued with their plans, despite her protests and threats.

She yanked the bell pull a second time, and then carefully pushed herself up from the chair. Once on her feet, she ensured her cane, tipped by the silver head of the Montgomery Eagle, was firmly in her hand as she began her journey across the Persian rug towards the telephone. It was time for her to take a stand; she had the means, and all that was needed now was a discreet call to the family solicitors, Froxton, Bell and Blunder. Picking up the telephone, her index finger tremored slightly as she found the first number. The whir of the dial, followed by the muffled *dink* of the bell as it returned to its starting point, was the only sound that broke the silence in her room.

Cecily was so engrossed in the next stage of her plan to oust the snivelling Stephanie from the Montgomery clan that she didn't chance to hear the door to her suite open and quietly close. She didn't hear the slight squeak of a shoe on the polished wood flooring, or the controlled but laboured breath of her visitor. If she had, she might have had the good fortune to have reached her up and coming hundred and third birthday.

Before she could squeal – actually, no, a true Montgomery would never squeal; before she could loudly shout her need for assistance, Cecily was propelled forward by an unseen hand. She tottered and fell heavily against the bookcase. Her head slammed into the intricately carved door with such force, her neck cracked and bent at an unnatural angle. The black Bakelite telephone followed her, landing with a heavy thud onto the rug as her cane rattled across the floorboards.

She lay slumped against the rich oak of the bookcase. The hand that only moments ago had caressed the lush tapestry of the

Montgomery bell sash, fell limp across her chest. Her now unseeing eyes reflected the silhouette of her assailant, held in a macabre bubble of light.

As the longevity that Cecily had enjoyed for over one hundred and two years ended, the intruder calmly watched and waited. Finally, satisfied that she would never again draw breath, they left the Montgomery Suite as they had arrived.

Silently.

Tarragon stood motionless in the middle of his grandmother's much treasured Persian rug with an equally stunned Stephanie by his side. He wanted to cry, but his eyes were refusing to co-operate. Instead, the ability to swallow was fast eluding him, which in turn meant he had little vocal control to elicit more than one word.

'How?' He sniffed.

Smithers sighed. 'From the angle of her head, I'd say it's her neck, she must have landed awkwardly when she fell.' He couldn't bear to look at her milky, vacant eyes any longer, so he quickly utilised Cecily's soft angora throw as a respectful, albeit temporary shroud for her. 'She was so frail; it wouldn't have taken much.'

Tarragon nodded. 'I suppose we need to contact someone. Police? Ambulance?' He turned to Stephanie for guidance.

Stephanie tutted loudly. 'I think she's a bit too far gone for a bloody ambulance, Tarragon, don't you?' She made her way over to Cecily's drinks trolley and poured herself a brandy. She checked the side of the glass, tutted again and added more for good measure. 'It's not like she's just a "little bit dead", is it?'

Smithers respectfully bowed his head. 'I'll make the necessary telephone calls, Mr Montgomery…'

Stephanie became apoplectic. She flushed pink and spat out

her first mouthful of brandy. 'No, no... no... absolutely not! Don't you dare call anyone. We need to think what's best to do next' she hissed through clenched teeth, her eyes sparking in fury.

Tarragon looked at her in horror. 'What? For God's sake, we can't just leave her here!'

An unnatural silence followed. Smithers, Tarragon and Stephanie looked at each other and then allowed their eyes to rest upon the body of Cecily Montgomery.

'Tarragon Jasper Montgomery,' Stephanie squealed, 'if you think after all I've been through, all the planning, all the money already spent, that this old hag's sudden and inconsiderate demise is going to ruin everything I've worked for to make this weekend a success, then you've got another think coming!' She took a large slug of the brandy.

Tarragon stared at her, his mouth opening and closing like a goldfish. 'But... but...'

'But nothing!' Stephanie continued. 'I have a coachload of old dears from the Winterbottom Women's Institute due to arrive any minute; the Dingleberry actors have already ensconced themselves in their rooms and have started acting out their roles. If this becomes knowledge, it'll ruin everything, the weekend, the hotel and us.' She sat down heavily in Cecily's chair. 'We've got to think this through.'

Smithers knew better than to offer his thoughts on the matter. He was, after all, just a servant in their eyes. Tarragon winced; he had quite suddenly become very afraid of Stephanie, her narrowing eyes, her cruel mouth and her bizarre ideas. They stood waiting as she mulled over her next move.

'I'll grab a sheet from Cecily's bedroom. Tarragon, make sure the dumb waiter is empty, Smithers, you ensure all the staff are kept away from it and from the cellar.' She jumped up, almost tipping the elegant side table over. It tottered slightly before settling back into its usual place. She clapped her hands together, much like a teacher would to ensure attention and action from her pupils. 'Come on, jump to it; no time to waste.'

Ten minutes later, against his better judgement, Tarragon found himself winching his poor late grandmother down into the depths of Montgomery Hall via their butler's dumb waiter. The very dumb waiter that Cecily had upgraded and then refused to part with during the Hall's great renovations in 1991, as she had sworn it would come in useful one day. Well now it had, and it struck him as being quite ironic that it should host her almost final journey.

Smithers, also against his better judgement, found himself waiting in the cellar, the walk-in freezer door open ready to accept his recently deceased employer. It struck him too as being quite ironic that it would host her temporary resting place next to several legs of lamb, half a cow and two hundred pork chops. Particularly as Cecily had been a lifelong vegetarian.

'*C'est la vie*, Cecily Margaret Montgomery – what will be, will be,' he whispered to himself as he propped her up against two boxes of frozen chicken fillets. 'And may God have mercy on my soul as well as hers!' he quickly added in a moment of fearful contrition.

THE BECOMING

$\mathcal{T}$he theatrical style mirror lights blazed in sequence, lighting up the room, casting shadows over the rails of colourful costumes. His fingers pinched and caressed the various fabrics, a sleeve, the hem of a skirt, and then the soothing softness of a faux-fur coat.

He flicked out his right hand elegantly and began his walk, the walk he needed to perfect if he was going to pull this off. He struggled, the bulky foam of the body suit hindering any chance of natural movement. He shimmied, and lazily stretching his stride he slinked and turned a pirouette on a ten-pence piece. Exasperated at his lack of progress, he ripped the blonde wig from his head and flung it across the room.

'No, no, no,' he raged at his reflection, 'it's all wrong!'

He tried again.

A slightly quirky gait that rolled his hips felt good. He swayed his head with each step, adding more and more little touches to his character. A flick of the head, a squint of the eye, a show of jazz hands. All very theatrical, just as he liked it.

He picked up the discarded wig and placed it reverently on the polystyrene head on the dressing table and sat down in front of the mirror, the tools of the trade laid out before him. The nylon skull cap held down his naturally dark curly locks, providing him with a blank canvas on which to paint.

He began. An outline here, a sweep of eye liner there, the thick foundation covering every imperfection. He twisted the gold case of the vibrant red lipstick and began to apply it to the cupid's bow of his lips.

'Perfect!'

He had already chosen his costume in colours that soothed his soul. He stepped into the dress and allowed it to seductively slide over his body.

'One, two, three, four...' He counted the buttons as the fabric moulded to the new shape his body now possessed. 'And now for the finale.' His fingers caressed the gentle waves of the wig as he plucked it from the vacant faced polystyrene head. Teasing it into place he applied glue under the mesh, pressing it firmly onto his forehead before rising to stand in front of the full-length mirror.

'All right, Mr DeMille, I'm ready for my close up...' She puckered her lips and blew an imaginary kiss from the palm of her hand.

This would be the performance of a lifetime, an Oscar-winning performance. Like a butterfly shedding stages of its life, she had reached her Becoming.

THE ARRIVAL

'Welcome to the Montgomery Hall Hotel…' Stephanie simpered whilst standing in the middle of the huge reception hall. The central staircase behind her elegantly curved both left and right, where the steps reached the floor-to-ceiling stained-glass window. In that moment she had felt a sudden surge of power, fuelled not only by the secret knowledge that she was now the mistress of the Montgomery household, but by the rays of coloured light that burst behind her, feeding the charge of excitement through her.

Stephanie graciously moved towards the gathered Winterbottom Women's Institute ladies, who not less than five minutes ago had been hastily deposited on the grand steps to the hotel by Frank. Their suitcases had just as quickly followed, chucked out from the cavernous depths of his coach. Pru had winced, hoping that her secret stash of wine and gin had survived the Olympic shot-put style of delivery that Frank had subjected her own case to. The first heavy drops of rain had encouraged him to quickly empty his coach of not only people but also baggage.

Pru held out the booking acknowledgement to Stephanie. 'Thank you, we are all very much looking forward to spending time here, aren't we girls?' The participating twenty-eight Winterbottom ladies nodded their heads in unison, apart from Chelsea who had suddenly become distracted by one of the Dingleberry's finest members sauntering down the staircase towards them.

'Ooh, smack me on the bottom and call me Betty... he's a bit of all right, ain't he?' Chelsea leeringly addressed Cassidy, but then just as quickly wished she hadn't. It was never a good time to have competition in the available male stakes, and if this weekend was to pass to her liking, she wanted to ensure she had first dibs on anything that was remotely alive and still warm.

Dirk Diamond, in his role as the bachelor, ran his hand through his dark curly hair. He utilised his gorgeous green eyes, coupled with his whiter than white teeth, to elicit a twinkle and a smile that even Cary Grant would have been jealous of. As soon as he had left his room in character, he was in the moment and the game was on.

Cassidy squealed. 'Oh my gawd, bet *you* wouldn't climb over him to get to Beefy Bruce would yer, Chels?'

'Cassidy!' Bree was mortified. 'For goodness' sake, have a bit of decorum.' She gave Stephanie an apologetic look before turning her attention to the rest of the WI ladies, who were currently wandering around the reception hall like a flock of lost sheep. 'Right, ladies, let's sort out your room keys–' She checked her own fob. '–and shall we meet in the bar, say 6pm for pre-dinner drinks?'

Watching the ladies scatter across the veined tiles, some braving the staircase, the others opting for the elevator, Pru started to laugh. 'Jeez, I think we're going to have our work cut out for us, don't you?'

Bree nodded. 'Yep, but in all honesty, what trouble can they get up to here, particularly if you take into account their average age?' She twisted her mouth sideways in thought. 'Ah, I take that back, I've just had a flashback to the Old Swan Hotel, Ethel's missing dentures and their zest for life and laughter!'

Pru giggled. 'Right, come on, girlfriend, we've got some unpacking to do.' She linked arms with Bree and steered her towards the central staircase. 'I've got three pairs of lacy thongs to unwrap that are holding a choice of Shiraz or gin to soften the prospect of a whole evening with Chelsea and Cassidy, the culture twins.' She groaned. 'Second thoughts, don't bother with choice, we'll drink both!'

'Bloody hell, Clarissa, I know we're best friends, but honestly – a double bed!' Ethel was beside herself. 'What happened to a twin room, that's what I want to know?'

Clarissa carried on unpacking, carefully hanging her navy-blue cocktail dress on the brass rail inside the huge, intricately carved mahogany wardrobe. She swept her hand down the material, admiring her £1.50 bargain from the local charity shop. 'Don't worry, dear, you'll be safe with me.'

Ethel huffed. 'Well, you've never been married, have you. For all I know, you might be of lesbionical leanings.' She spread out her full-length winceyette nightie across the bed and placed a pair of fluffy pink bed socks next to it.

Clarissa couldn't help herself. 'Ethel, a vision of you in that ensemble would have me jumping out of the window and not on you! I'm surprised you haven't packed a matching chastity belt.' No sooner had those words left her lips, when Ethel dragged a humongous pair of frilly nylon bloomers out of her suitcase and held them up to the light.

'I rest my case…' Clarissa quipped. She picked up one of the leaflets that had been conveniently left next to the tea and coffee tray and began to read the full itinerary for the weekend.

Ethel, finished with her unpacking, sat down beside her. 'So, does it all start tonight, you know, the murder mystery stuff?'

Clarissa dropped her half-moon spectacles to the end of her nose. 'Well, it would appear so. I'm just wondering if we will know who the actors are. Do they make themselves known, or do we have to guess?'

'Mmm… well I'm pretty good at stuff like that, you know, picking out wrong 'un's. I have a talent for it.' Ethel preened herself. 'I was likened to a modern-day Miss Marple once, remember, at that book club we used to go to.'

'No, you weren't. They said you "were missing a marble". Honestly, Ethel, you do make me smile.' Clarissa chuckled at Ethel's misinterpretation. She checked her watch. 'We'd better get a move on. I don't want to be last at the bar and be left without a seat; I don't think my sacroiliac joints would last long.' She held both hands on the base of her back and rubbed, as if to prove a point.

'Ooh, Clarissa, you're such a dark horse!' Ethel was beside herself with mischievous glee. 'I once tried a cigarette in my teens and coughed up part of me left lung in the process, but I would never have had you down for smoking those spliffy things!' A naughty twinkle shone from her eyes. 'You haven't brought some with you, have you?'

Clarissa quietly shut the bathroom door behind her. She loved the bones of Ethel, but sometimes… well, just sometimes, it could all get a little bit too much.

THE STORM

A sudden squall whipped through the dense trees surrounding the Montgomery Hall Hotel. It rushed across the lawns, catching patio tables and chairs unawares. They wobbled and danced momentarily like drunken guests at a party, before being flung upended into the flower beds.

Smithers stood by the window in Cecily's suite, quietly watching the display below him. The ominously dark clouds rolled in, pushing the rain noisily against the glass, making him feel that Montgomery Hall was under attack.

A punishment maybe.

He tenderly folded the angora throw and placed it on the now vacant chair. He had said nothing to Mrs Smithers, explaining away his melancholic mood as simply being exhausted from running around after Master Bentley, rather than admitting his active participation in concealing a death and preventing a proper and decent burial.

'I looked it up, Mrs Montgomery.' He spoke to her as if she were there with him in this very room, rather than being propped up in the freezer, keeping company with half of Little Childer Thornton's stock of beef cattle and a couple of ethically sourced tuna fish. 'It was in one of your books–' He adjusted the small side table, so the feet sat properly in the age-worn indents of the carpet. '–and, do you know, I could get life imprisonment or an unlimited fine.'

He sat wearily down on the window seat. How on earth life in prison could be put side by side with an unlimited fine for such a serious offence was beyond his comprehension. It was like saying hide a dead body and you'll get a ticket for fly-tipping.

A loud flash of hailstones forcefully hit the window behind him, making him start. He looked out, trying to judge if the storm would blow over, or if it was as the weather news had predicted, here to stay. His attention was drawn to a black hackney cab below which had just disgorged a flash of vibrant colours from its rear door.

A flurry of red hair and an emerald velvet cloak were buffeted by the wind as a late arrival dragged her suitcases across the stones towards the entrance doors to the Montgomery Hall Hotel.

As Smithers made his way down to Reception to meet the new guest, he didn't yet know that he had just watched the dramatic arrival of Psychic Selma herself, resplendent in peacock finery and other worldly auras, ready to dazzle and entertain.

'Oh my goodness, that's a bit of a howling hoolie, isn't it?' Selma almost physically blew into Montgomery Hall, her legs pushing forwards faster than the rest of her body. Her cloak billowed around her as she brought with her a flurry of leaves that skipped and swirled across the marble tiles before coming to rest beside the reception desk once their method of propulsion was blocked by the closing of the doors behind her. Not to be defeated, the wind continued to do battle outside against the aged wood, making the hinges groan.

She dropped both cases and shook her hands, as though the short journey from taxi to desk, gripped to a handle, had made them devoid of feeling. The stack of gold, bronze and copper bracelets jangled on her wrist. She pressed the index fingers of each hand to her temple and began to hum. 'Now let me see...'

Stephanie stood bemused behind the desk, her expensive Montblanc fountain pen poised for action, hovered over the guest book.

'Yes, yes, I see it all now, my spirit guide is here! There's a woman, an elderly woman on the other side, and she's telling me her name begins with...' Selma made a great show of communing with someone standing beside her, someone Stephanie couldn't see and if truth be told, she didn't want to hear either.

In the time that Selma had opened her mouth, Stephanie had turned several shades of puce. A wave of panic overtook her before she found her own voice and interrupted her guest. 'Good evening. Selma, is it? We've been waiting for you. Just sign here. Here's your key; dinner is served between 7pm and 9.30pm. Smithers will take care of your luggage.' And with that she chucked the key fob across to her, clicked her fingers high in the air to alert Smithers to his task, and promptly turned on her heels and disappeared into the reception office.

The key teetered on the edge of the oak desk before dropping to the floor. Selma stood amused, a wry smile touching her blood-red lips. She loved being the one responsible for such a reaction. She touched the burnished bronze clasp on her cloak and pulled it central to her neck before bending down to pick up the key. As she did so, her beautiful copper red curls momentarily juddered before slipping to one side.

She quickly pushed the wig back onto her head and pulled up the hood of her cloak, using the weight of the fabric to hold it in place, cursing the wind and damp that had weakened its hold. She made a mental note to use more glue next time. She had a plan, one that had taken months in the making – and now was certainly not the time to reveal her true identity.

Smithers beckoned to Boris the bellboy to assist with Selma's suitcases. He didn't care to wonder why she would have two large valises for such a short stay. That type of thought, after being married to Mrs Smithers for more years than he could remember and having the joy of a daughter, had taught him women never travelled light. He watched Selma march after Boris, matching his length of stride with her own, her green cloak wafting behind her, causing the fronds on several areca palm plants to quiver in her wake. He took his place behind the reception desk and returned to watching the comings and goings of the Montgomery Hall Hotel.

Bustling and alive once more.

It felt good to see the old building soak up the presence, spirit and character of each guest as they passed through. He could almost feel the stonework, the oak and the soft furnishings inhaling as they absorbed it all.

'My dear, it is a simple case of hives – an allergic reaction, that is all,' Phil Timkins, dramatically playing his role as the Doctor, loudly addressed Francesca Moore, who was doing a grand job of fluttering her heavily made-up eyes as the Niece as they passed across the Grand Hall.

'But she's *th*wollen – *all over!*' Francesca emphasised the last two words as though they would elicit a more attentive response from the Doctor.

Smithers stood watching them, finding himself becoming increasingly more entertained, wondering where 'all over' actually was. He now knew each of the Dingleberries and the roles they were playing, but he still had absolutely no idea of their script, so he was quite happy just to follow the exciting enactment as it played out. He had become quite adept over the years at people watching, as all good butlers should be. In his transition to head of staff once Montgomery Hall became a hotel, that talent had become an absolute godsend to him.

'Doctor, Doctor... I'm not a well woman!' Clara Toomey as the Busybody / Victim swooned; pressing the back of her hand against her forehead, she gave Phil a side-eyed glance. This was her moment. She had already checked there were plenty of other genuine guests milling around the great hall and bar area to enjoy her performance; some were knocking back G&Ts, others were happy just to enjoy late afternoon Earl Grey tea. She had practised this swoon to perfection; the timing had to be just right for Phil to catch her. 'I think I'm fading...' she whispered as she dramatically fell backwards.

Phil, unfortunately, had become otherwise distracted by the sight of Chelsea and Cassidy gliding down the central staircase, all lips and enormous frontage. He stood startled, his mouth open and his tongue almost touching his chin, glad to have made the decision to specialise in orthopaedics rather than breast augmentation. Poor Clara, unable to stop the momentum of her swan dive, hit the marble tiles with a resounding *whump* and a clatter, as the force of the impact propelled her top set of dentures out of her mouth. They skittered across the shiny floor, ending with a spectacular pirouette before smacking into the skirting board and coming to a halt.

A collective gasp filled the high vaulted ceilings of Montgomery Hall Hotel, quickly followed by an eerie silence as the scene froze around them.

'Oh shit...' The dulcet tones of Cassidy Parks broke the impasse, causing Chelsea to collapse with a fit of the giggles as she watched Smithers gingerly pick up the offending porcelain pegs in his crisp, white handkerchief. 'What an absolute bloody bummer; you won't be getting yer teef into much tonight, now, will yer, girl!' she saucily added before staggering into the bar.

THE DISTRACTION

*P*ru padded over to the bedroom window. She scrunched her toes into the thick carpet and tentatively touched the ornate Victorian radiator with her fingers to test its heat output. She could hear the water still running in the bathroom and checked her watch. Bree could always make a 'quick' shower last longer than your average bath.

She pulled back the heavy brocade curtain and looked out into the gloom. She could just about make out the edge of the woods and the top of the trees against the dusk sky. There had been a respite in the torrential rain, but the wind was still blowing savagely. The TV weatherman had said to expect localised flooding and wind gusts of up to sixty to seventy miles per hour inland. At the moment it was a yellow warning, and she really hoped that the very rarely implemented red one wouldn't materialise. She checked her phone for a signal; it was so weak it barely made the little pointy triangle bit at the bottom of the cone. The promised text or call from Andy had failed to materialise; the ones she had sent him remained on her screen unsent with a red warning exclamation mark.

'Gosh, I needed that!' Bree sauntered out of the bathroom,

dragging steam in her wake. Fluffing her hair with the thick white towel, she tipped her head forward and shook the curls. When her head flicked back, each tight auburn ringlet fell perfectly into place. Pru wished her unruly mop would do the same, instead she had to spend forever blow drying and teasing it into shape.

Pru glanced at her watch again. 'About time, I thought you'd drowned in there. My tummy's grumbling, and a bottle of Merlot is definitely calling me!' She checked her reflection in the mirror and quickly ran her tongue across her top teeth to remove a sliver of Petulant Pink lipstick. 'Can't wait to see what this murder mystery has in store for us; the ladies are going to love it.'

Bree shoved one leg into her pants and executed a pretty deft hop, skip and a flop onto the bed so she could accommodate the other leg without doing herself an injury. 'We'll have to keep an eye on Chelsea and Cassidy, though. I think murder mystery and Psychic Selma are the last things on their minds.' She clipped her belt into place, pulling the clasp to the front. 'They'll be bed-hopping before you know it.' She reached for her bra.

'Oh blimey, I hope not.' The last thing Pru needed was two rampant sex addicts cavorting around Montgomery Hall, and she being the one to keep them in check. 'Those silicone bra straps are crap, Bree. What on earth possessed you to buy a flopper stopper with them on?'

Bree pulled on each strap and let them slap back into place. 'They're invisible; they don't show if you're wearing something that's slightly off the shoulder – like this.' She held up a gypsy style top.

'Mmm... I'm not convinced. I wore one once and started off with my norks at a level any twenty-year-old would have been proud of, but once the straps warmed up they stretched and my poor boobies ended up splayed out over my desk, completely obscuring the space bar on my keyboard!' She laughed, which then set off a coughing fit. 'They'd drooped so much they even chaffed my knees when I took a stroll to the coffee machine.'

It was Bree's turn to giggle. 'Well, judging by the minuscule size of mine, I won't have that to worry about. Anything from Andy?'

'No, my texts aren't sending, no signal on the phone to ring him, and I tried the hotel phone too, but he must be having the same problem his end as even a landline isn't connecting. I wouldn't be surprised if this storm has brought down the cables.' Pru scrunched up her nose and shrugged her shoulders. 'He's a big boy, I'm sure he'll be fine, and he's got Lucy to look after him. Come on, time to go down, we've got a lot of drinking to catch–'

A sudden commotion outside their room interrupted her. Footsteps pacing up and down, accompanied by mutterings and audible gasps that filled the corridor. Bree was first to the door, yanking it open, quickly followed by Pru behind her.

'The spirits are active tonight, I can feel their presence...' The unnaturally tall woman with bright red hair, a host of bangles on each arm and attired in a myriad of colours paced up and down the corridor, pausing momentarily to lean over the oak banister to look down into the reception hall below. She waved her arms in a dreamy, swaying motion, the metal bangles jangling and the wooden ones clattering as she then proceeded to dance up and down the patterned carpet. 'Yes, yes, yes...' she breathlessly chanted whilst slapping a nearby dresser with her hands as other guests stood incredulous outside their rooms.

Pru looked at Bree, Bree returned the glance. 'Ooh, it's a game of charades. I've got it – it's *When Harry Met Sally*, isn't it?' Bree punched the air in triumph.

Pru was not convinced. 'If I didn't know better, I'd say we've just met Psychic Selma, our entertainment for the evening. Come on, let's leave her to it, I'm sure she'll find someone on the other side to show her where the bar is – there'll be plenty of spirits there for her to indulge in, like gin, brandy, vodka…' Grinning, she counted them off on her fingers.

She closed the door to their room and pushed Bree forwards so that she would be the first one to edge through the gap that Selma had left between herself and the staircase. She would have loved to have stated, hand on heart, that she didn't believe in all the guff about spirits and an afterlife, but there was always an unnatural shiver that ran down her spine at the prospect of saying it out loud and being damned – or haunted – for all eternity.

A MURDER IS ANNOUNCED

*T*he Winterbottom Women's Institute posse made their way from the bar to the dining room, the majority mostly sober, having tempted themselves only with tea or soft drinks, the rest slightly tipsy on wine, prosecco, and several fine schooners of sherry. Ethel and Clarissa led from the front.

'I've checked the seating plan, we're all together, girls.' Clarissa wore the mantle of being in charge with pride. Admittedly it was a rather worn and shabby mantle, one that had been passed around between them as nobody really relished having the responsibility for Chelsea and Cassidy after they had consumed a couple of bottles of Lambrini in their room before dinner. Cassidy had already excelled herself by tottering on her six inch stilettos into the giant palm plant in the reception hall, landing face first and bottoms up on the marble tiles, gifting the poor young bellboy an eyeful of something he probably hadn't experienced before. But Pru's timely arrival in the bar had relieved them of that mantle so they could happily settle back to enjoy their respective aperitifs, leaving Chelsea to untangle Cassidy's thong from a large feathery frond.

Clarissa continued to play 'mother' to her friends. 'Ethel,

you're next to me. Millie, can you take Hilda; make sure she's not too close to the speakers – it's her left ear, dear, the left one with the hearing aid – it whistles. Avaline, can you take charge of Brenda. Make sure she's not too close to the cakes.'

'Good evening, ladies and gentlemen...' Llewelyn Black stood regal on the small stage that had been set up in front of the floor-to-ceiling burgundy velvet curtains in the Belvedere Dining Room. He made a show of tapping the microphone. There was momentary feedback, which assisted in bringing everyone to attention. 'If you'd like to take your seats, I will introduce myself.' He gave a respectful pause to allow those that hadn't yet found their allocated table places to organise themselves. Once happy that all attention was on him, he continued.

'Good evening, once again. My name is Llewelyn Black. I am the founder and director of the Dingleberry Amateur Dramatics Society, and for this weekend of murder mystery, I will be taking on the role of the Inspector from the Chapperton Bliss Constabulary.' He paused, waiting for an acknowledgement of appreciation from his audience, but the response he got from one of the Winterbottom ladies' tables wasn't quite what he had anticipated as a flutter of consternation met his ears.

'Oh my goodness, I'm going to be arrested, I confess it's me...' Hilda suddenly wailed before tipping out her handbag onto the white linen tablecloth. An array of items bearing the crest and logo of Montgomery Hall clattered onto the table. Her hearing aid squealed loudly. 'It was just a few soaps – oh, and these.' She held up three Tetley teabags and a sachet of hot chocolate that had come from her room, along with four silver teaspoons. 'I've never stolen anything before in my life...' she keened.

Millie swiftly took hold of Hilda's hand and began to pat it gently to soothe and reassure her. 'There there, Hilda, it's all right. He's just an actor; he's not a real policeman, and you haven't stolen anything. They're included in the price of our stay.'

She wasn't sure about the teaspoons, but she'd worry about that later.

Llewelyn bristled with indignation. *Just an actor, how very dare she!* He would have loved to have expressed his pique verbally, but resisted the temptation. He coughed loudly, forcing another screech of feedback from the microphone to fill the large room. 'As I was saying, there will be several other members of the Dingleberries mixing amongst you throughout the weekend, playing their roles to perfection.' He held up a limp hand and waved it in a foppish manner around the room. 'You will, of course, be unaware of who they are, but doesn't that add to the excitement?'

Several lilac-rinsed heads on Table 3 nodded in agreement. Pru, her attention drawn to poor Hilda's predicament, was more concerned with her welfare than what Llewelyn had to say. She watched as Millie carefully placed the scattered items back into Hilda's handbag.

'Oh blimey, we'll have to have a discreet look in Hilda's bags before we leave, Bree. God knows what she'll end up nicking to take home with her if we don't.'

Bree took a large swig of her gin and tonic. 'Talking of which, what did Tarragon Montgomery say when you spoke to him? Had he got any ideas on who is half-inching the family heirlooms from here?'

Pru popped her eyes. 'Sshh, shout it out, why don't you!?'

Bree looked uncomfortable, and to help ease the flush of embarrassment she had just experienced she took another large gulp of her gin, pulled her mouth down, and hunched up her shoulders in contrition. 'Sorry.'

Pru playfully punched her arm. 'It's okay, but just remember, there's only you, me and Mr Montgomery in on this. We're going to set something up, see if we can entice them out of the woodwork.'

Bree looked thoughtful and then laughed. 'Yep, bringing

something out of the woodwork has just given me flashbacks to my ex-hubby – he was a bit of a worm too!'

'I can't and I won't. My last will and testament remains as it is. You will inherit the Alexandrite ring...' Clara Toomey, having recovered from her scripted bout of hives, loudly declared to her Niece. She shimmered a dazzlingly large, but totally fake, ring on her finger. 'If it was good enough for the czars of Russia, it should be good enough for you; it's worth an absolute fortune!' Clara slammed her hand down on the table, bouncing a fork onto the floor. Julie Shute as the Waitress tucked a strand of blonde hair behind her ear and quickly made her way over; she dipped down at the knee and retrieved it. Polishing it vigorously on a napkin, she then placed it back on the table.

This action wasn't lost on Pru, who straight away tagged her as one of the actors. No waitress worth their salt would return a dropped piece of cutlery to a dinner guest and the flirtatious smile she had given to Llewelyn when she had brushed past him to retrieve the fork was another giveaway. She watched the guy in the tuxedo on the next table, his dark hair slicked back, his eyes darting backwards and forwards between her and the Waiter, as though waiting for a cue. She also noticed that he had taken an intense interest in Chelsea.

Dirk Diamond relished his role of the Handsome Bachelor / the Murderer, even more so now he had caught the eye of a delightful little blonde sitting amongst a host of old ladies on Table 4. He gave Chelsea one of his disarming smiles and winked at her. He thought that she had winked back, but due to the size of her false eyelashes, he couldn't be sure. Dirk had already pegged her for a chat-up line later on, but for now he had to concentrate on the Busybody / Victim and the Niece, the latter played by the delicious, but out of his league, Francesca Moore.

The 'set-up' was to be played out this evening, the murder would take place during the pre-dinner drinks tomorrow night and the reveal would be on Sunday before the guests checked out. This would allow the audience the whole evening to scribble in their little notebooks, sleep on it overnight, and hopefully solve the crime.

As the Winterbottom ladies tucked into a very fine three-course dinner, they were happily entertained by the comings and goings of the Dingleberries as their story of greed, lust and eventual murder was played out before them.

I DIDN'T SEE THAT COMING...

*S*elma had taken to her room for a large whisky after her impromptu performance on the second-floor corridor. She had hoped the commotion she'd caused would bring as many guests as possible out of their rooms, including the Montgomerys themselves, Tarragon and Stephanie. She needed to know exactly where everyone was housed.

Selma knew that made them sound like rabbits being bunched together in a hutch, but after seeing some of the comings and goings between the rooms, clearly for a bit of rampant afternoon delight, then rabbits probably wasn't too far off the mark.

Flinging the ginger wig onto the dressing table, she resisted the temptation to take a cleansing wipe to the gunk she had plastered on her face. It had taken the best part of an hour to put on, and she didn't relish wasting another minute of her evening reapplying it before going down to start her performance proper. She poured herself another drink, but this time watered it down with a dry ginger tonic. Jumping onto the bed, she propped up the pillows and sat in quiet contemplation, the storm outside still unrelenting, battering the window with hailstones. Whilst she was there, she would remain in character, the only respite from being Selma would be in that room. She picked up one of the sheets of paper from the bundle on her bed and took another slug of the whisky. She really didn't need to study it, but it was comforting to know it was there and it did help to visualise her route for the recce she would embark on later when everyone had retired for the night.

Knock, knock...

Her heart thudded as another series of knocks sounded on the door to her room. She leapt from the bed. 'Just a minute, let me throw something on, I'm not decent.'

Shit! That vocal was a bit on the baritone side – almost forgot who I was supposed to be.

She coughed, trying to find the right pitch for Psychic Selma, before plonking the wig back on her head and padding over to the door. She opened it just enough to see who it was.

'Stephanie! What a nice surprise,' Selma simpered, even though in truth, it was far from a pleasure. She could have kicked herself for sounding so ridiculously subservient. She needed to get rid of the snobby bitch as fast as she could. Then a second thought hit her. Maybe Estelle's body had been discovered and the Montgomerys were now aware she was a fraud!? A small rivulet of sweat began to trickle down her back.

Heavens to Betsy, that was all she needed.

Stephanie didn't wait to be invited into the room. She elegantly squeezed through the gap, pausing only to marvel at the bushy eyebrows Selma was cultivating. It was on the tip of her tongue to offer a bit of advice, a sort of woman-to-woman chat, but the more she marvelled at the sprouting hairs, the more she was beginning to doubt the pedigree of her guest in Room 27. But then again, in this day and age it wasn't hers to wonder.

'I just wanted to touch base with you before our little band of actors take their final bow for the evening. Dinner is almost over; I think they're on the dessert now.' Stephanie stood with an air of superiority in the middle of the room as she checked her watch.

'The guests will retire to the Somerset Room – it's all set up for you, so I just wondered if you require any little extras; anything to add to the atmosphere, or things you need to know about the history of Montgomery Hall?' She tipped her head waiting for a reply.

Selma was stumped. She had hoped to be able to carry this one off on her own without any outside, or, heaven forbid, any inside interference. There were many things she already knew about Montgomery Hall and its layout, the Somerset Room being one of them, and she was more than familiar with the original plans and additions that had been completed in the 1990s.

No sooner had she remembered the plans when her eyes widened and her stomach plunged to the depths – almost down to as far as the bowels of Montgomery Hall itself. Her eyes just as quickly narrowed and then darted sideways to look at the bed. Spread out were those very plans, the copies she had obtained from the National Archives.

Bollocks!

Selma quickly turned away and made a grab for her velvet cloak that was draped over the back of a chair. She enthusiastically swirled the vibrant material around before dropping it haphazardly across the bed and, fortunately for her, across the scattered sheets of paper. Stephanie appeared to be none the wiser.

'Just subdued lighting, I can do the rest,' Selma testily responded.

'Well, if you're sure…'

'I am.'

Take the bloody hint, woman.

Selma bit her tongue and ensured that remark remained only a thought. She would have blown everything if it had popped out of her mouth and offended the snooty cow. She would have been given her marching orders by the Montgomerys before her work had even begun.

It was Stephanie's turn to narrow her eyes. There was something very strange about this woman standing before her, and not just because she claimed to speak to the dead. She was pretty sure it was all a very elaborate act designed to entertain and amuse, with the potential to make money from unsuspecting, and often desperately sad, people, but it wasn't her place to judge. All she cared about at this moment in time was her guests and their financial contribution to the upkeep of Montgomery Hall.

'Selma, have we ever met before?' Stephanie chewed her bottom lip. She had no idea why she had asked that; maybe it was the strange feeling of familiarity that had begun to niggle her. 'I just feel as though our paths have crossed at some point.'

'I shouldn't think so, my dear – not unless you make a habit of slumming it in back streets or at second-rate fairgrounds and seaside promenades.' Selma smiled at her.

It was not a particularly nice smile; it didn't shine.

And there was that little niggle again.

The smile didn't reach her eyes.

It was a will-o'-the-wisp feeling, one that drifted just out of reach...

And then it came to her. Stephanie's heart skipped a beat.

It was the eyes – but where on earth had she seen them before?

BENTLEY

*B*entley Montgomery stood in front of the full-length mirror in his private suite at Montgomery Hall. Wearing just a brightly patterned and very tight man-thong, he flexed his barely perceptible biceps. Posing first one way and then the other, he desperately tried to elicit some form of a six-pack by breathing in and pushing down on his stomach muscles. When that failed, he executed a nifty bit of rhythmic buttock-clenching in time to Gloria Gaynor's 'I Will Survive' that was blasting out from the speakers on his wall.

'Body of a God...' he grunted, as the exertion and lack of oxygen made his lips turn blue. He moved closer to the mirror and checked out his chest, stroking between finger and thumb the solitary hair that adorned his smooth skin. Bentley coveted that one slightly curly hair, having spent the best part of five years waiting for more to join it. He had slapped on hair restorer and used his mother's moisturising cream to no avail. He couldn't understand why the latter had failed to offer him even a small amount of peach fuzz, because it sure as hell had helped the old boot to cultivate a fair smattering of upper lip bristles over the years. He had watched her pluck, shave and wax more times than he cared to remember, usually in what she thought was the privacy of her bathroom, so his dad wouldn't cotton on to the fact he was married to something akin to a werewolf.

The theme tune to *Rocky* suddenly burst forth from his mobile phone. He quickly cut Gloria off in her prime, just as she was about to extol the benefits of not crumbling or lying on the floor to die. The pulsing beat from his phone sent him ducking, weaving and punching the air from mirror to bedside cabinet. He picked it up and checked the caller ID.

His heart sank.

Bentley's index finger hovered over the red circle on the screen; every fibre of his body screamed for him not to answer. He exhaled loudly and touched the green circle instead; he knew his life wouldn't be worth living if he didn't.

'Hello...'

Dead air.

He tried again. 'Hello...'

'Bentley, mate, have you got what you owe me?' The voice was calm but firm. The Ganja Man was always measured in his request for payment, but he had a chilling talent for coating it with a hint of threat.

Bentley wanted to shout down the phone that he was no mate of his, but the words stuck in his throat. All he could do was meekly shake his head as he waited for a very strained 'No' to eventually leave his lips.

A further silence followed. It was just long enough for Bentley to feel that his arse was on the verge of dropping out of his posing pouch. That struck him as rather funny because, as everyone knew, thongs didn't possess enough material to provide a bum covering to actually drop out of. As quickly as the funny side of the situation crossed his mind, it left him; with just his heart hammering in his chest as evidence that he hadn't yet succumbed to a fear-induced heart attack.

'You've got until midnight on Sunday, kiddo. I'm sure a smart boy like you needs both legs. I don't want to be running around in circles for my money, and with one leg, neither do you. Capiche?' The threat was thicker with this sentence.

Bentley wanted to laugh. *Capiche!* The unfortunate situation he currently found himself in wasn't like something out of *The Godfather*, and Little Childer Thorton as a setting for a bit of kneecapping was hardly ruddy New York.

'You know where; just make sure you're there...' the Ganja Man snarled.

The line went dead.

Bentley slumped down onto his bed and ran his hand through his sweat-soaked hair. He'd been close on a few occasions when he'd struggled to come up with the dosh, but either good old Cecily had come up trumps for her great-grandson by coughing up from her vast fortune, or he'd found a little trinket or two lying around Montgomery Hall that fetched just enough to get him out of the shit. The first option was no longer available to him, so it would have to be another little trinket.

He checked his single chest hair again, fearful that the pounding his heart had just indulged in might have shaken its roots and caused it to drop off. To his relief, it was still there. He stroked it softly with his finger whilst he considered his next course of action.

There was only one thing for it. He would have to master-mind another night-time recce around Montgomery Hall once everyone had checked into dreamland. He already had his eye on a particularly nice piece. Cecily had refused him outright for the first time ever when he had slinked into her room earlier, asking for more money. Her lips had set firmly, her eyes had been steel when she had, in no uncertain terms, told him to get out. He had never felt such fury – and dare he admit it a touch of fear, as he stomped back to his own suite, muttering under his breath that she deserved everything she got. There was not one member of the clan who had an ounce of affection for her, they only feared her and what financial penalties she could impose on them.

Who would've thought toking on a doobie a few times a week could cause him such a headache? He grabbed the green metal tin from his bedside cabinet. The lid was embellished with a leaf that wouldn't take the brains of Britain to identify, and which gave a clue as to what it contained. He sighed heavily as he rolled the Rizla paper.

It was probably more like one a day at least – but what the hell else was there to do in a mausoleum like Montgomery Hall except get higher than his mother's legendary mini-skirts?

THE SOMERSET ROOM

'*O*ooh that flighty young thing on Table 2 has more cheek than Chelsea Blandish shows when she bends over wearing one of her thongs!' Ethel pursed her lips and dabbed at the corners of her mouth with her napkin as she singled out Francesca Moore from the Dingleberries. A ripple of laughter travelled down the Winterbottom ladies' main table.

'I think she's definitely one of the actors, don't you, Millie?' Clarissa was busy making notes in a small book she had only ten minutes earlier plundered the depths of her handbag to find. 'The one that's the Waitress… and the other one, the guy that's had his tongue hanging out all night ogling Chelsea; I bet he's an actor too.' Clarissa licked the end of her pencil and scribbled studiously.

Hilda, desperate to participate in the investigation, finished off the last of her sherry before standing up to make her announcement. 'I know who did it…' she breathlessly declared. 'It was him!' She pointed a bony arthritic finger accusingly at poor Smithers who was standing by the door with a white ceramic serving boat in his hand. Startled, he bowed respectfully and beat a hasty retreat from the dining room lest an escaped geriatric from the *Golden Girls* could accost him.

Apoplectic that her murderer was making good his escape, Hilda began squealing at the top of her voice. 'After him! He's getting away; he did it...' whilst slopping the remnants of her cherry sorbet over the tablecloth.

'Hilda dear, sit down – nobody has died yet. That doesn't happen until tomorrow evening; everyone is still here and very much alive.' Clarissa once again soothed her friend by placing an arm around her shoulder, ushering her back to her seat.

'I heard her say it – her over there...' She pointed to Julie who was playing the Waitress. 'She just said he'd murdered Gracie.'

'The gravy, he murdered the gravy, it was full of lumps, dear. Are you sure your ear trumpet is working properly, Hilda?' Clarissa scrunched her eyes and grimaced as Hilda's hearing aid took the opportunity to let out a loud screech of feedback, which proved there was something amiss with it.

Pru folded her napkin and nudged Bree to finish her drink. Bree side-eyed her and grinned; she had a pretty good idea of what was required of her. For some, the murder mystery weekend so far had been great entertainment, and Pru had been delighted to see the ladies laughing and cosying up to each other with their respective notebooks and ideas on where the storyline was going. She stood up and draped her jacket over her shoulders.

'Right, girls, time for Psychic Selma, I believe.' She could feel the sudden change of mood in the ladies; their notebooks and pens were quickly consigned back to various handbags and their chatter became very animated. 'They have opened the Somerset Room for this event, which is an honour in itself as it has been closed for forty years.' Pru tentatively threw in that snippet, hoping she had remembered it exactly as Stephanie had told her earlier on in the evening.

'Over forty-five years to be precise.' Stephanie, elegantly

dressed in a white chiffon box-shift dress with her hair swept into a side chignon, glided to the microphone, pausing momentarily to impart that correction to Pru before coughing to test it was on. 'Ladies and gentlemen...' she smiled knowingly, '... the Somerset Room was closed due to an unfortunate family tragedy that took place on 31 October 1977. Our family grief was so raw, no one has been able to enter the room since that fateful evening.' She paused again for dramatic effect.

Tarragon was standing watch by the main doors. His heart was heavy, not just with sadness, but with a feeling of dread too. He still couldn't comprehend what his wife had become. The anger he felt towards her was starting to eat away at him. She was using his family tragedy to set a scene for a charlatan of a clairvoyant to ply her trade. This was, in his mind, the most hurtful and disgraceful thing she could have done to him, second only to coercing him into concealing the death and body of dear old Cecily.

Stephanie continued. 'All Hallows Eve – a night synonymous with ghosts, ghouls and demons, with witches and the walking dead. The night an eight-year-old boy was tragically taken, strangled by the very same corded rope tie-back that still holds the original drapes of the Somerset Room.'

Tarragon could listen to no more. He turned away from her and left as quietly as he had arrived.

Ethel, Clarissa and Millie stood squished together, almost holding each other's hands with their mouths wide open as they listened to Stephanie and her tale. Poor Hilda's hearing aid had given up the ghost, so she was now sitting in comfortable silence, juggling glasses and sweeping the sherry dregs from the table, offering a rather loud burp after the last tot had passed her lips. The rest of the Winterbottom crew were just content to sit and listen.

'So–' Stephanie geared herself up for the final teaser. '–the Somerset Room has been a source of ghostly bumps in the night, of fleeting shadows and soft voices. Tomorrow night is Halloween and the spirits will be getting stronger. Tonight, Psychic Selma will be attempting to contact those that walk amongst us unseen at Montgomery Hall, those that have no earthly form, in preparation for the All Hallows Eve gathering.' She dipped her head and swept her eyes across each individual table in the Belvedere Dining Room. 'Ladies and gentlemen, are you ready to meet the spirits of Montgomery Hall?'

An eerie silence fell across the room as eyes widened and heads nodded in excitement. Stephanie's face resembled the cat that had got the cream. 'In that case, may I–'

A loud clattering from the back of the room broke Stephanie's monologue, making every head turn towards the source. Several seconds passed before a head appeared over one of the dining chairs on the table next to the Winterbottom ladies.

'Oopsy, it's only me...' Chelsea hiccupped loudly. 'Did somebody say stronger spirits?' She unsuccessfully attempted to haul herself up from the floor, but only succeeded in inelegantly splaying her legs out whilst losing her one remaining shoe. 'If it's vodka, count me in!'

'I think you've had quite enough, Chelsea, come on...' Embarrassed, Bree looked at the ceiling in exasperation and formed a wry smile on her lips to show the rest of the room that she was doing her best to contain the wayward member of their group. She hooked her hands underneath Chelsea's arms and pulled her up from the floor. '... honestly, can't you behave yourself for five bloody minutes?'

Chelsea grinned, giving a coy look to Bree, her glazed eyes desperately trying to focus. 'I *have* behaved myself, I'm a *very* good girl...' She bent down and peeked under the tablecloth that was draped over Table 5. '... aren't I, Mr Diamond?' She giggled loudly, much to the embarrassment of Dirk Diamond who was sitting underneath the table, knees up to his chin like a garden gnome, desperately trying to look as though he wasn't there.

He made a great show of pretending to look for something. 'I've dropped my napkin,' he announced in actor fashion, as though projecting his voice would excuse his current predicament.

Pru bent down to look at him. 'It's under your chin, Mr Diamond, tucked into your shirt.' It was taking everything she had not to laugh out loud as she took in Dirk's tousled locks, the smear of Mac Ruby Woo red lipstick across his face, and the left shoe of Chelsea's much coveted Jimmy Choos held in his hand and dripping Prosecco all over his trousers.

Jeez, it's true what they say – you can certainly take the girl out of the trailer park but not the trailer park out of the girl!

I HEAR DEAD PEOPLE...

*S*elma adjusted her cloak and arranged the silk scarf around her neck. The soft material hid a multitude of sins, not least the very obvious protuberance on her throat. She had wondered if she could pass it off as a festering goitre, but decided to go for the Gloria Swanson effect instead. It was so much more mystical.

She folded the architectural plans and pushed them into a folder before hiding it under the mattress on her bed. She had memorised all she needed for her imminent night-time wanderings around Montgomery Hall. Checking her make-up for the last time, she swept out of her room, closing the door behind her. She pushed against the wood to ensure the lock had engaged. Satisfied it had, she made her way along the galleried landing to the Somerset Room. She had privately rehearsed the little show she was going to put on whilst having a luxurious bubble bath. The acoustics in there had been wonderful, so she had practised several different voices that would engage and, she hoped, chill her audience, along with an assortment of facial expressions that included rapid eye flickering, a rather impressive trance-like stare without blinking, and lots of tics with a bit of teeth-baring.

A little chuckle escaped from her throat as she turned the corner, her cloak billowing out behind her. If her plans for the future didn't come to fruition, and she had no reason to believe they wouldn't, she could just see herself taking on this persona for real. What a laugh that would be, and a bit of a money earner too. It was amazing how gullible desperate people could be. Totally engrossed in her own thoughts, she was suddenly jolted out of her reverie.

'Yeow, feck me...'

Selma stopped dead in her tracks, tipped her head and listened. A muffled bang came from the oak wall panel next to her. She placed her ear against it, straining to hear. She moved forward, placing her ear against another panel. Silence. She repeated the process on two more panels, knocking gently to elicit another response. Still nothing.

'Selma! What on earth are you doing?'

She almost jumped out of her skin, her arms shot into the air making her array of bangles jangle and clank together loudly. If a little lady wee in fright had been possible, she would have released one. Her heart thumped loudly against her chest. She was in two minds, whether to make a rapid sprint back to her room or stay frozen to the spot like a myotonic goat when she saw Stephanie striding along the corridor. 'Dear God, woman, you nearly gave me a bloody heart attack! Did you hear that?' This time Selma didn't have to think about the pitch of her voice; it had shot up several octaves on its own accord.

Stephanie shook her head. 'Hear what?'

Selma tipped her head and listened intently again. When nothing was forthcoming, she eventually answered her. 'That voice, it was coming from the...' She suddenly realised her mouth was just about to run away with itself, and in doing so would reveal that she knew more about Montgomery Hall than Stephanie did. She was supposed to be psychic so it was obvious that she would claim to hear voices, and standing there with her knees knocking together didn't give a very good impression. She quickly recovered herself. 'I think the spirits are very active tonight... in this area here, they're flooding my aura.' She dramatically waved her hands around as though she was conjuring up something from another realm, making her cheap bangles and bracelets rattle and jangle again.

Stephanie sniffed the air between them, detecting a faint whiff of whisky. She gave a superior smirk. 'Mmm... yes, but I don't think we'd agree on the type of spirits affecting your aura, would we?' She gave Selma a disapproving glare. 'Right, we're just bringing everyone to the Somerset Room now, so I just wanted to make sure you are ready for your entrance... You *are* ready, aren't you?'

Selma composed herself. 'Lead on, Stephanie, lead on...'

In truth, Selma didn't need anyone to show her the way, this was a route she had walked many, many times before.

Now it was her turn to give a superior smirk.

Pru and Bree led a jaunty, and somewhat tipsy, pack of WI ladies into the Somerset Room. Ethel and Clarissa, with Millie and Hilda in tow, ensured they had the best seats in the house, right at the front, by engaging in a spurt of energy to bag a velour chair each. A huge floor-to-ceiling stone mullioned lunette with a sumptuous red window seat stood out, bold and impressive. The matching red velvet curtains were swept upwards at the sides, held by bronze rope cords that were looped over ornate metal hooks in the shape of feathers. All around them works of art adorned the walls. The vast marble fireplace, edged by pillars with lion heads, rose up from the floor. Candles burning on the mantelpiece illuminated two marble wall statues either side of a gilt-framed portrait of Hugo Frederick Montgomery.

Pru could only look on in awe. His pose gave no doubt that he was a formidable man, but there was a coldness to his eyes; they resembled ice, pale with a dark inner. She shivered.

'I do hope Betty comes through, don't you?' Ethel suddenly became a little misty-eyed. Betty had been her best friend until her untimely death at the hands of Phyllis Watson, the notorious Winterbottom mass-murderer. Poor Betty had been victim number five out of six in that dreadful episode. She had sadly met her maker sitting in the Dungeon of Doom ghost train carriage with a screwed-up packet of half-eaten Martha's Marvellous mint imperials on her lap. Ethel dabbed at the corner of her eye with her handkerchief.

Clarissa thought about that prospect for a moment. She was actually more concerned that Phyllis herself might decide to sneak through the spectral veil to finish off her murderous streak. 'Oh blimey, can you imagine if Phyl–'

Clarissa's tummy-churning observation was noisily cut off as the first bars of 'Hall of the Mountain King' blared out. It built in crescendo, pouring from the speakers in the four corners of the room, as everyone present sat in reverence. The faster the tempo became, the longer Clarissa held her breath. She glanced at Ethel who, judging by the colour of her face, was pretty much doing the same.

The cymbals crashed, once, twice, three times, and then the dramatic drum roll which preceded the final crash filled the room as a flash of purple light dazzled their eyes. And suddenly she was there.

Psychic Selma was amongst them, resplendent in emerald, gold and bronze.

Ethel gasped, the hairs standing upright on her arms. It had taken away what little breath she had left. Behind Selma was a round table draped with a dark green cloth, edged with golden tassels. A large glass ball hosting a purple mist sat on top, finely balanced between smoking incense sticks and an array of detailed Tarot cards. Ethel couldn't remember seeing the table when they had first entered the room, nor when they had taken their seats. It seemed to have magically appeared at the same time that Psychic Selma had.

'Ladies and gentlemen!' Selma dramatically surveyed the room. She made it look as though she was connecting spiritually with them, but in truth she was looking for the more eager and gullible. 'The spirits are strong...' she announced as she swished her cloak and did a couple of hand passes across the misty orbuculum, at the same time muttering incantations under her breath.

Little did the gathered audience know that all she was reciting was the last online shop she'd done at Tesco. It was amazing how one could make five pounds of spuds sound spooky when you uttered it with a slight accent. When she got to the last item on the list, a prawn ring, she gave an added flourish to her carefully orchestrated hand movements and then dropped to her knees, head bowed.

She let the seconds pass to elevate the expectation and heighten the anticipation. Eventually she lifted her head, and bringing her hand up, one finger pointing towards her audience, she singled out Hilda. 'You, yes you...' Selma gave the impression she was listening to someone invisible to everyone else. Head tilted she mumbled. 'Mmm... I know, yes... I have that, I understand...' She stood up and floated closer to Hilda. 'I have a message for you, a message from the other side.'

Hilda, minus the hearing aid she had just popped into her handbag to muffle the screeching feedback, was now completely deaf and totally oblivious to what was going on. She grinned inanely at Selma and nodded, only because she felt that was what she was supposed to do.

Selma continued to build a fake aura around her. She knew it was all about staging it right, making the audience believe what they were seeing and hearing. 'He's telling me his name is Bert and that he loved you very much...' She waited for a response. She had overheard Hilda talking about her recently deceased Bert whilst she had been enjoying a cup of coffee and a cake in the tearoom that afternoon.

Hilda continued to grin inanely.

Selma carried on regardless. 'He's showing me his hair, he's sweeping his hands through his hair, it's a very dapper grey...' Selma knew she was on safe ground with that one. With Hilda having one foot in the grave, her Bert must have been old enough to have cultivated a few silver hairs before he'd popped his clogs.

Millie thought it was about time she helped Hilda out. 'She said Bert's showing off his hair, it's grey,' she shouted loudly, exaggerating the words with her mouth and hoping that Hilda could at least lip-read a little.

Hilda smiled. 'He was ginger...' she innocently offered.

Selma dramatically turned, and with arms waving she skipped back to the table. She ran her hands over the glass ball again to give herself a little more time to think. 'Aha, he's telling me he was a burnished copper in his youth, but in his twilight years he turned grey. He looks very distinguished in his suit; he's standing right beside you now.'

There, that should shut the old bat up...

'He was ginger with a cream tip to his tail, and he liked tuna!' Hilda was not going to be silenced.

A ripple of laughter ran through the audience, which in turn threw Selma into a flurry of off-the-cuff activity in an attempt to cover her gaffe. 'Moving on, I have someone here called David...' She danced around the room tapping a tambourine. 'He's young, he's showing me – oh wait, yes, yes.' Selma spun around, cloak flapping in the sudden rush of air she had generated as she fleet-footed over to the mullioned window. She caressed the drapes and then her fingers settled on the rope tie-back whilst she murmured to herself. '*A tub of margarine; six eggs; half a pack of bacon; a tin of spaghetti hoops...*'

And then, as if a jolt of electricity had run through her, she stiffened, pointed a rigid finger at Stephanie and moaned loudly before dramatically slumping to the floor in a dead faint.

THE SECRET OF MONTGOMERY HALL

The level of commotion in the Somerset Room was such that any spirit or ghost residing in Montgomery Hall would have taken the opportunity to make a very quick exodus in search of a more tranquil location.

'It can't be, it can't, no, no...' Stephanie, as white as the dress she was wearing held the back of her hand to her mouth, her bright red lips stretched to a very large 'O' shape. The hand action did very little to muffle the next sound from that particular orifice. Her scream reached the decorative plaster mouldings of the ceiling before bouncing back across the audience who, stunned by the sudden *now you see me, now you don't* performance from Selma as she disappeared behind her spooky table, sat with their mouths agape after emitting a very audible and collective gasp.

Pru and Bree were first on their feet to tend to Selma, who was lying in a most undignified heap on the floor. Pru checked her pulse whilst Bree, happy that it was just a faint, began to roll Selma into the recovery position. It wasn't easy.

'Bloody hell, our Selma's a bit of a big lass, isn't she?' puffed Pru as she shoved and pushed the dead weight over.

Bree grinned. 'Not 'arf! You can say that again; she's as sturdy as a jersey cow on steroids.' She'd also had chance to notice something else that was a little strange about Selma whilst she was splayed out on the floor. Her floaty skirt had become hooked under Pru's left shoe as they turned her, and Bree had spotted a pretty fetching pair of boxer shorts cladding her posterior.

'Psst...'

Pru looked at her friend quizzically. 'What?'

Bree frantically pointed to Selma's nether regions as she made a show of smoothing down the skirt whilst exaggeratingly mouthing the word: '*Skiddies!*'

Pru made a discreet peep under the floral material and, sure enough, Selma was wearing a pair of paisley patterned silk boxers in a nice teal colour. They were bunched up over her thick 80 denier tights. Pru pulled each side of her mouth downwards and squeezed her shoulders up towards her ears in a 'beats me' fashion.

Selma quickly opened one eye. It swivelled around in its socket as she took in the lie of the land. A good old-fashioned fainting act had been the only thing she could think of to get her out of the shitty mess she'd made with Hilda and her ruddy ginger pussy – and, as an added bonus, it had scared the pants off Stephanie. Talking of which...

'Oh, my dears, what on earth happened?' Selma simpered as she pushed herself up from the floor. 'And look, my best shorts have become a little rumpled.' She made a great show of read-justing them, before straightening her skirt. 'I know they seem a little unusual, but they do keep out the chill without being too restrictive. Anyway, who said only men can wear them?' She tittered to herself and tilted her head at Pru waiting for a reaction.

Pru was quick to respond. 'Aww, Selma, don't worry; I've worn my boyfriend's thermal leggings before now... here's to unisex clothing, hey?'

Bree smirked. She loved that Pru always went that little bit extra to make people feel better, but she seriously doubted that Pru would have clad her own bum in Andy's thermals. She'd seen them hanging on the airer, and they'd definitely seen better days. They were only ever dragged out of his kitbag if he'd had to pull an all-nighter sitting on a chilly Obs post during an investigation.

'Ladies and gentlemen, may I firstly apologise for my little outburst – it did take me by surprise.' Stephanie, now accompanied by Tarragon, addressed her guests. She still looked flustered, but her voice was surprisingly calm. 'Smithers will furnish you all with a drink, courtesy of Montgomery Hall, if you would like to make your way to the bar.'

Like schoolchildren being herded from morning assembly to class, the Winterbottom WI entourage and the cast of the Dingleberries formed an orderly line and filed out of the Somerset Room, chattering ten to the dozen about their psychic experience. Most were confused, some were still laughing, some were slightly chilled, others were even more sceptical than they had been, but they agreed, all in all, that although it had not been what they expected, it had been an entertaining half hour; they just wished it had lasted longer.

Ethel and Clarissa, in the absence of Pru and Bree who were still tending to Selma, ushered the remaining Winterbottom ladies from their seats. Chelsea and Cassidy were nowhere to be seen; the first mention of a free drink had sent them tottering on their high heels through the main doors and down the staircase ahead of everyone else. Millie and the rest of the girls had opted for the elevator in blocks of four people, or whatever combined weight it would take.

Taking in Brenda Mortinsen's cuddly physique, a by-product of her delicious cake-making, Clarissa tentatively took hold of her elbow and ushered her to one side. 'Brenda, I'm afraid you'll have to go down on your own, my dear.'

'I can breathe in, will that help?' Brenda, wide-eyed in innocence offered.

'Er… not really, dear…' Clarissa pointed to Brenda's ample bosoms that were hoisted up by a 48 double-G Playtex bra. 'Shove those in the wrong direction and you'll be hitting the buttons to send us all down to the basement and back up again – several times! Best if you travel solo.'

Following the ladies along the corridor after ensuring Selma was happy to be left, Pru and Bree had already discussed which gratis nightcap they would be indulging in.

'Well, that didn't go to plan, did it?' Bree slung her bag over her shoulder and pointed to the staircase. 'Take the stairs, it'll be quicker and hopefully there won't be too much of a queue at the bar.'

Pru nodded. 'Did you see Stephanie's reaction? A bit OTT, if you ask me. After all she'd already told everyone about the relative that had died, so it should have been no surprise that Selma used it in her little show.'

As they disappeared down the staircase, behind them the Somerset Room emptied and the chatter died away, leaving Selma alone, just as she had planned. Rising to her feet she made her way over to the fireplace. Checking behind her to ensure the coast was clear, she carefully touched the head of the lion on the left-hand side. Feeling behind its head, she found the point she was looking for and inserted her index finger. A low rumble came from the oak panel next to her as it rolled back, revealing aged brick walls held together by crumbling mortar. She tentatively peered inside. To the right of the opening a stone staircase meandered into the depths behind the fireplace. *Just as she had remembered.*

The purple and green theatrical lighting still strobed the room as a haunting sing-song voice flowed from Selma's lips.

'There were two in the bed and the little one said – roll over, roll over…'

With torchlight picking out the steps, Selma disappeared into the darkness as the panel closed behind her.

THE STING

*A*s predicted, the storm that had hit Little Childer Thorton that afternoon continued to rage outside Montgomery Hall with a fierceness Pru had never seen before. She found herself drawn to the window of her room again, as though she had to see for herself what damage was being caused with her own eyes, rather than rely on the groaning, cracking and howling noises that were gripping the building and her imagination.

She peeped through the curtains and very quickly wished she hadn't. She could just make out on the edge of the tended gardens at least four trees that had been felled by the force of the winds. Their gnarled, bare branches caught in the arc of the outside security lights, glistened with rain. Her eyes adjusted slightly as she looked to the east of the estate, the small bridge their coach had crossed on arrival barely visible over the swell of the turbulent river. She wondered how much longer the banks would hold if it continued to rain at this rate. Another victim of Mother Nature.

'Have you tried Andy again?' Bree swung her legs over the bed and pushed her feet into her fluffy slippers. 'I still can't get a signal at all.'

Pru checked her phone again. 'No, but there's a text from him; it must have come through when my phone had picked up a few bars.' She read it out loud.

Hi beautiful,

hope this gets to you okay, I'm taking a chance that at some point it'll go through. Wifi here is off; phone signals are atrocious; it's like being in the dark ages.

I'm good, hope you're enjoying your weekend. Remember, don't do anything I wouldn't do.

Stay safe and speak soon.

love you. A x

PS weather is crap.

PPS Is your weather crap too?

Pru checked her own text to him, but it still carried the warning exclamation mark with the words *Not Delivered* in red. 'How come his text came through but mine hasn't sent? Surely if there's a signal for Andy's to come through mine should have gone too?'

Bree handed her a glass of red wine. 'No. I think you've got to send it again; it doesn't do it automatically. Mind you, I'm about as good at telecommunications as old Selma is at speaking to the dead!' She took a large gulp from her glass and savoured the flavour. 'Nice wine, girlfriend...' She tipped the drink at Pru in admiration. 'What a palaver that was, although I think Simpering Stephanie really fell for it.'

'Didn't she just! Blimey, that scream would have woken the dead. There's something a bit odd about Selma, though, isn't there?' Pru stretched her legs out on the bed and wriggled her toes. The shoes she had been wearing for the evening had murdered her feet. 'I wonder what tomorrow night will hold for us, apart from a very obvious, unexpected death. Have you figured out who you think it is that's going to bite the dust?'

'Mmm... difficult, that one; they've just really played it out a bit tonight, just to give us a flavour of it, but I'd put my money on the Waiter being the murderer and the Spinster... what was her name?' Bree checked the handout that they'd been given. 'Ah, yep, Marilyn Peacock; she'll be the one to curl up her toes: no family, no ties.'

It was Pru's turn to check her handout. 'Nope, I'm not having that; there's no motive for her. I'm going for either the Niece or the Hard of Hearing Aunt. I think that ridiculously expensive ring has something to do with it; they placed such emphasis on it.' She paused in thought. 'Although the Busybody could give us a run for our money!'

A gentle tapping on their door soon stopped their conversation.

'That'll be Tarragon–' Pru got up from her bed. '–he said he'd call so that we can set up the sting.' She liked how that sounded. It gave her a little quiver of excitement in the middle of her stomach.

Barely twenty-minutes had passed since Tarragon's arrival at Pru and Bree's room, but in that time, they had set their plan in motion. Tarragon had unwrapped a Lladro figurine called 'Fishing with Gramps'. It was both beautiful and comical, with a little dog expectantly hanging over the edge of the boat. Pru could actually feel the bond between the little boy and his grand-dad, such was the quality of the piece.

Tarragon carefully placed it on the antique French walnut console table that was just a short distance from Pru and Bree's room. It looked strangely out of place, the delicacy of the gloss porcelain against the heavy 1880s elaborately carved flowers, leaves and swirls of the table that sat atop the four cabriole legs, but it was the most suitable site if they were to keep an eye on it. Tarragon had no doubt that it would be taken at some point over the weekend and had cited that the full-to-capacity hotel would be a perfect cover for their in-house Fagin. Its value of £1,200 would be another draw as it would be too much of a temptation to resist.

Pru had questioned if it was wise to use bait of such a value, but Tarragon had been insistent. He had taken the measure of the other items that had gone walk-about over the last few months, and in his opinion, this piece was perfect. Once he had been satisfied that everything was in place, he'd handed over the reins to The Curious Curator & Co and had quickly returned to the Simpering Stephanie, allowing the girls to retire for the night.

Pru lay awake, the inky blackness of their room facilitating lights, sparks and swirls to form before her eyes. The wind and rain battered the window before howling upwards towards the roof of Montgomery Hall. She hoped Tarragon and Stephanie had kept on top of general tile maintenance, or at the very least were well insured. The door rattled as another gust of wind hit the front of the building.

Bree was taking first shift to keep an eye on the figurine. She was currently holed up in the linen cupboard, directly opposite the console table, the door slightly ajar giving her sight of the prize. Pru rolled over and checked the alarm on her phone. If she was lucky, she could get an hour of shut eye in before it was her turn to take over.

Tick-tock, tick-tock.

IS THERE ANYBODY THERE...?

*B*entley lay awake in his bed listening to the sounds of Montgomery Hall as it settled itself down for the night. He was troubled by the extra creaks and groans that emanated from the vast beams, walls and windows of the building as the storm picked up pace. He relied heavily on his hearing during his nocturnal forays, as the routes he used were blacker than night itself. He checked his watch, pushing on the button to illuminate the dial.

00.15hrs.

He threw back his duvet, positioned two pillows to look like a sleeping form in case his mother took it upon herself to endow him with a rare but possible visit, and quietly dressed into a pair of black tracksuit bottoms and a black hoodie. He flicked his torch on and off. He was good to go, but just in case, he slipped two spare batteries into his pocket; the last thing he needed was more damage to his shins. His impact with an old barrel in the north passage earlier in the evening had been agony, forcing a loud expletive from his lips. The ensuing knocking on the panels from the other side had chilled him to the bone, forcing him to hold his breath and freeze on the spot. Tension had clutched at his guts, fearing his maze of secrets had been discovered all because of his potty mouth. He would have to be more careful in future.

Closing his suite door behind him, he crept along the corridor, counting off the oak panels as he went.

One, two, three, four.

His fingers tentatively pressed on the carved acorn on the fifth panel. He held his breath and listened for the click. The panel creaked open, revealing a darkness before him that was deeper than the darkness behind him. He waited, to ensure he was still on his own and hadn't alerted his parents in the next suite along before stepping inside.

The panel clicked shut, leaving the corridor as silent and as empty as it had been before Bentley's arrival.

Selma moved quickly and silently like a ghost through the secret passages of Montgomery Hall. Occasionally her cloak snagged on rusted nails or fractured wood battens, making her curse under her breath. At least twice she had become completely disorientated by too many turns and too many passages that looked the same, her internal navigation system thrown into disarray.

It had taken the best part of an hour to find what she thought was the room she needed: the suite of Cecily Montgomery. She felt along the passage, the light from her torch highlighting a multitude of spiders' webs and decades of dust. She closed her eyes and tried to conjure up the plans, as well as her own distant memories, in her mind's eye.

Two left turns, ten paces, right turn, five paces...

And she was right where she needed to be. Her fingers pulled down the hook and the panel slid sideways. She waited to ensure that Cecily hadn't been disturbed before stepping out into the darkened room...

Bentley crept along his usual route within the walls of Montgomery Hall. He had discovered the secret passages quite by accident when he was nine years old. He had been harshly berated by his mother in the Belvedere Dining Room for slinging a garden slug in Cecily's pea soup when she wasn't looking. In response, he had petulantly kicked at one of the oak wall panels with his brown Clarks sandal and had promptly disappeared behind it.

It had taken him a few seconds to realise what had happened. In the darkness he could feel gossamer threads clinging to his face and a light breeze brushing past him, but before he could allow fear to touch him, he had experienced his eureka moment. Bentley had heard his mother through the panel still wittering on, oblivious to her young son's sudden vanishing act. He had become gloriously invisible. He had wanted to giggle, but quickly pushed his fist into his mouth and bit down on his knuckles to stop the sound. It was perfect; it would be his go-to place. What amazing japes he could pull off using the hidden world of Montgomery Hall.

He would be as quiet as a mouse in a house...

That had made him want to laugh even louder, it was so funny to think he was truly *inside* the house, he was part of it, and there had been no better time to explore it than at that moment...

And that was how Bentley had moved around Montgomery Hall over the years, whenever he needed to be one of the 'unseen'. Tonight, he had a mission, one that would get him out of his current predicament and ensure he kept both kneecaps in tip-top condition.

He turned left, then right and then right again and he was there. He slid the panel sideways and stepped through...

Hilda lay awake in bed listening to Millie snoring like a warthog. She was of the opinion that she had made two terrible mistakes that evening, one in agreeing to share a room with her and the other in changing the batteries in her hearing aid.

The wind howled – Millie snuffled.

The rain lashed the window – Millie snorted.

The door rattled loudly – Millie wheezed.

And just as she was about to remove the offending piece of technology from her ears, the door to the wardrobe opposite her bed burst open and a dark, menacing figure jumped out.

Hilda's heart almost gave up the ghost at first, but spurred on by her service as a young girl in the army cadets, she grabbed her walking stick and leapt out of bed. Swishing it in the air like a fencing sword, she poked and prodded at her intruder.

'Avast with you, sir...' She lashed out again, this time making contact.

A loud 'Oof' filled the room.

'Millie, Millie, we have an interloper in our room after our sexual favours... Millie, quick, wake up and give me a hand,' Hilda squealed.

The intruder, terrified at the prospect of being trapped in a room with two sex-starved geriatric wrinklies, beat a hasty retreat back into the wardrobe, just as Millie opened her eyes and returned to the land of the living. 'Ooh sexual favours, do they come in little satin bags like they have at weddings?' she dreamily enquired.

Hilda quickly switched on the light and flung the wardrobe doors open. 'Well, rub me down with a wet copy of the *Yorkshire Gazette*, it's empty!' She pushed and pulled the coat hangers that hosted their various outfits from side to side. 'I might have a bit of a problem with my memory, but I can still recall what it's like to have a virile man in me bedroom, and there was definitely one in here...'

Hilda forlornly flopped down onto the end of her bed; disappointment written all over her face. 'You know what, Millie? That could've been the last chance for me to experience a bit of how's yer father before me brain completely packs up and forgets what it's all about, and I've just given them a bloody good poke and chased them off!'

Millie giggled. She couldn't be cross with Hilda; she simply accepted her friend's wanderings and imagination as being part of her personality, something she couldn't help or control. It was her job to make light of it. 'I'm sure you've had a few good pokes in your heyday, Hilda, but whatever you do, don't brag about it at breakfast or they'll all be wanting one!'

NOW YOU SEE HIM...

*I*t didn't take Bentley long to find what he was looking
for. Once he had got over the shock of being accosted
by a screaming banshee with a walking stick in Room 32, he had
orientated himself again and quickly found the panel he needed
to bring himself out onto the corridor that housed the second-
floor guest rooms. He rubbed his painful ribs, hoping his delicate
physique wouldn't be marred by a bruise. After that little
escapade, he had decided to veto any of his old routes that would
open out into occupied bedrooms. A full house for the weekend
was somewhat limiting his bewitching hour wanderings.

He paused and listened.

Silence.

A muffled cough from behind the door nearest to him made
his heart jolt ever so slightly. He held his breath. The ancient
springs of the four-poster bed in the Dunlevy Room squeaked
and groaned under the weight of its occupant, accompanied by
another cough and then silence. He had hoped that the four-
course dinner, followed by the copious amounts of alcohol the
guests had enjoyed before, during and after, would ensure 99 per

cent of Montgomery Hall would be deep in the land of nod by now. Another loud snore confirmed that belief.

Moving on tiptoe he made his way to the ornate walnut console table. The dim fire escape safety lighting was just enough for him to admire the prize he had spotted earlier in the evening for a few seconds, before he plucked it furtively from its resting place and carefully wrapped it in the felt pouch he had brought with him for the occasion.

This would easily fetch eight hundred quid, maybe even a grand if he pushed his mover for extra funds. Enough to pay off his debt with a little left over.

If time hadn't been of the essence, Bentley would have danced a little jig of delight on the knees that were now ensured a safe and flexible future, but he needed to be on his way with his spoils and back before dawn. He crept down the first flight of stairs and paused again to listen. Looking over the galleried landing, down the next flight into the Great Hall, he could see old Bert Lowey, Montgomery Hall's in-house security man and gatekeeper, and Fred, the waking desk clerk, huddled together under the orange glow of the reception nightlight, playing a game of cards. Bert had been with the family since before Bentley was born and had never once detected anything untoward or criminal on his nightly rounds in all that time. Bentley was pretty sure the rumours that circulated amongst the staff were true. Bert had eagerly serviced Cecily as much as he'd serviced the Hall and grounds, and had thus been promised a job for life as his reward. He checked again, wondering if he could make it down and across to the staff entrance without being seen.

Mmm... much too risky.

Instead, he opted to return the way he had come, through the passages and tunnels of Montgomery Hall. He quickly returned to the second floor, pressed on the panel that had only moments ago afforded him access to the treasure that was now hugged close to his chest, and without a sound disappeared back into the darkness.

~

Squished up in the little cubbyhole, filled to bursting with cleaning products, a teetering stack of toilet disinfectants, crisp linen sheets and plastic bags, Bree was apoplectic with excitement, albeit with a silent show of enthusiasm due to her supposedly being 'undercover' and incognito. She sighed. If someone had asked her ten years ago what she would see herself being today, she very much doubted, *'sitting on a floral duvet cover crushed in a small closet with an aqua-blue toilet freshener shoved in my right ear'*, would have been her answer.

The sight of Bentley Montgomery pinching the Lladro statue and legging it down the staircase had been a relief to her aching bum and numb legs. She hadn't immediately left the closet, which was just as well as no sooner had Bentley disappeared down the staircase he was back again, standing inches away from her hidey-hole. The door was slightly ajar, allowing Bree to watch silently.

Bentley hesitated and then made his way back the way he had come, moving further away from her along the corridor. She edged her face closer to the opening, trying to keep tabs on him. She still couldn't believe she hadn't seen him until the last minute; it was as though he had appeared from nowhere. No sooner had that thought entered her head when she realised he had just done exactly the same thing again, only this time in reverse.

One minute he was there, walking away from her, the dim fire safety lighting casting a weak orange glow around his silhouette, the next – nothing.

He'd vanished.

Pushing herself out of the closet, Bree shook some feeling

back into her left leg before quickly lolloping like Quasimodo back to their room to tell Pru of her findings.

'Pru, Pru... quick, wake up,' she breathlessly squealed. 'He's stolen it, I know who dunnit!' Her left leg took that exact moment to become devoid of all feeling. She rumpled into a heap on the floor and disappeared from view.

Pru jolted upright on the bed. 'Bloody hell, Bree, take more water with it next time...' She looked down in an attempt to give her friend some sympathy, but seeing the tangled mass of Laura Ashley bedroom fabric she'd dragged in with her, the most Pru could conjure up was a snort of laughter.

'Glad you think it's funny, Sleeping Beauty. Whilst you've been snoring away, I've solved the case – it's the son. Bentley Montgomery has stolen the ornament and he just vanished into thin air with it!'

HELLO...

*a*ndy checked his phone for the umpteenth time since dinner. He was becoming increasingly concerned that he hadn't heard from Pru. He'd been keeping tabs on the weather warnings, and as much as it was pretty dire where he was staying, it was even worse at Little Childer Thornton. The B&B at The Bull and Duck in Nether Walloping was quaint and cosy, but it was also on the flood path from the nearby river, making him wish he'd brought his trusty Hunter wellies with him. He checked his phone again, more from habit than expecting it to look any differently than it had two seconds ago.

Tap, Tap.

'Andy, it's me...' Lucy's soft voice just about reached his ears. He jumped up from his bed and opened the door for her.

'Luce, everything all right?' They hadn't long parted company in the bar after a few wind-down drinks. The day had been a long one, tiring and emotional, but it had resulted in the arrest and detention of their only suspect in the double murder. The evidence gathered had ensured he would be going nowhere except prison for a very long time.

Lucy smiled. 'It's a quicker jaunt than we originally expected.

Their force DI has just phoned; they're going to release us as from tomorrow morning.'

Andy couldn't hide his delight. He enjoyed out-of-force assist jobs, but his own towering stack of enquiries and investigations would be in danger of toppling over if he didn't get back to them soon. 'Great, I could be in my own bed by this time tomorrow night…' He made a show of banging his hand down on the hard, lumpy mattress.

'There's a debrief at 9.30am which we don't have to go to; the DI said we can head back any time after breakfast.' Lucy gave him a cheery wave as she shut Andy's door and disappeared onto the landing. Her disembodied voice drifted back to him. 'Just thought I'd let you know…'

Grinning to himself, Andy lay back on his bed, adjusted several lumps underneath his back to make it more tolerable, and reached for his mobile phone.

Pru finished the coffee that Tarragon had given her. Even though the news had been shocking, it had not surprised him in the least, and it certainly wasn't going to detract from his hospitality skills towards his guest. He wandered over to the window to watch the storm, which had been increasing in its ferocity hour by hour. It did nothing to soothe him; it just heightened his despair.

'I'm so sorry, Mr Montgomery, but there is no doubt. My colleague saw him take it, I just feel dreadful that it's a family member and a close one at that.' Pru hoped she sounded professional, but supportive. The coffee was starting to curdle with the glass of wine she'd gulped down with Bree before she had sought out Tarragon at the earliest opportunity. She checked her watch.

02:15.

'I need to speak to my wife, but we will be dealing with this in-house as a family matter, you understand?' Tarragon gave Pru a wan smile.

Pru nodded, quietly thankful that they wouldn't require any further involvement from The Curious Curator & Co. 'Absolutely, Mr Montgomery. I'll leave it with you.' She got up to leave.

Tarragon raised his glass at the portrait that hung over the fireplace, the gaze of Hugo Montgomery, his grandfather, feeding the disappointment he was feeling towards his own son. 'Enjoy the rest of the weekend, Prunella; let me have your account before you leave, and if there is anything else I can do to make your time here more pleasant, please do not hesitate to let me know.'

Pru considered herself dismissed.

Climbing the staircase back to her room, she couldn't help but feel a little sympathy for Tarragon and his predicament. She also couldn't wait to tell Andy how their first investigation had panned out. Bree was waiting for her.

'How did it go?' Bree had agreed with Pru that it would be better if just one of them broke the news to Tarragon, rather than have him feel overwhelmed with the two of them staring at him whilst he digested the fact his son, and eventual heir to the Montgomery fortune, was a thief.

'Not too bad, but I wouldn't want to be Bentley at this particular moment in time.' Pru grabbed her mobile phone and checked it again.

'I'll put the kettle on; there's two sachets of hot chocolate here. Do you fancy one?' Bree nipped into the bathroom to fill up. 'It'll help us sleep after all the excitement.'

Pru nodded absent-mindedly as she checked her watch again. 02:43. She quickly penned a text to Andy in the hope he would eventually get it. Her fingers deftly tapped over the small keys.

Can't tell you how much I need you right now. Honestly think someone is going to be really killed before the weekend is over, it's all kicking off...

'Shit...'

Bree emerged through the bathroom door. 'Shit what? What have you done now?'

Pru sighed. 'Not one bloody text has sent since we've been here, and I've just pressed send halfway through with my fat fingers and it's actually gone!' She sat staring at the blue text bubble that now had the word 'Delivered' in grey underneath. Pru grinned. 'Oh well, at least I told him how much I was missing him at the beginning of it – just hope it doesn't ping too loudly and wake him up...' She quickly added to her story.

The Curious Curator & Co. have solved their first crime; it was the son that did it! Dad's not too pleased and is going to deal with it himself, so don't be surprised if Bentley Montgomery is found deceased somewhere, lol. Missing you lots and lots, can't wait to see you, hope things good your end. Love always, Pru x

She pressed send... and sat staring at the second part of her message, which was now side by side with an exclamation mark in a red circle and the words that were becoming increasingly familiar to her ever since she had set foot inside Montgomery Hall.

Not delivered.

$\approx$

Andy's phone vibrated and pinged, rousing him from his slumber. He'd nodded off with a re-run of *Midsomer Murders* on the small wall-mounted TV, a half-drunk cup of tea on the bedside cabinet and the phone still clutched in his hand.

He rubbed his eyes and opened the text. He muttered the

words to himself as though he was lip-syncing to a song. He read it again, taking in what appeared to be a plea from Pru. He didn't need to read it for a third time.

Ignoring the hour, he jumped out of bed, quickly pulled a sweatshirt over his pyjamas, and rushed to the room next to his: Lucy's room.

She answered on his third frantic knock. Pulling a robe around her, it was her turn to rub her eyes and yawn. Taking in his tense expression; Lucy had worked with him long enough to know something was amiss. 'Andy! Whatever is the matter?'

He ran his fingers through his hair, shaking his head. 'It's Pru, she needs us…'

EVERY BREATH YOU TAKE...

*D*ragging a dead weight through the passages of Montgomery Hall was harder than expected. Every now and then a stray limb would bend back on itself and snag against the perished wooden frames. This in turn would cause a mini avalanche of plaster and daub to scatter, sending up a cloud that couldn't be seen but would permeate the nostrils. The scraping and swishing of Bentley's body against the floorboards as it travelled from passage to passage, turning left, turning right, with Selma at the helm holding him by his ankles as she navigated and dragged him through the maze, was chilling.

This hadn't been in the plan...

Selma's first thought had been to utilise the dumb waiter, but quickly dismissed it as a bad idea. She remembered only too well the creaks, groans and thunks it made on both the ascent and descent. It would have the whole of Montgomery Hall wide awake within seconds. This left her with only one option, which just so happened to be the most difficult and the most strenuous; she'd have to cart him down to the cellar herself utilising the passages and what she fondly called the 'long drops', shafts that ran from the top to the bottom of Montgomery Hall. She could climb down on the ladders, but Bentley would have to be rolled over and chucked down to the next floor. That made her wince as she considered what injuries could befall someone after being dropped from such a height.

She laughed. 'Oh, my poor boy, broken bones and a few cuts won't bother you now, will they?'

She cast her torch over Bentley's face. His tongue was swollen, lolling from the corner of his mouth; his eyes still held the startled look of someone who only moments before had been smugly celebrating a bit of graft by thieving from his own family – totally oblivious to the cloaked figure that was inching towards him in the darkness.

Selma had been forced to act quickly. To say she had been surprised by the appearance of someone else in the secret passage was an understatement; she'd nearly had a bloody heart attack. Her reaction had been swift. Bentley had gone down like a sack of spuds with a quick, powerful uppercut from Selma. She had heard his teeth clack together as he crumpled to the floor. Her cloak swirled behind her as she straddled him, hands around his throat, squeezing.

It was to be a premature kill for Bentley, far earlier than she had planned – but to her credit, it was also going to be a deliciously silent one.

She had to give him some kudos. Bentley had a bit of fight left in him, but he was no match for her. He had bucked and fought, trying to throw his assailant from him, his feet shuffling and scraping on the wooden floorboards, to no avail.

If Bentley's tongue hadn't suddenly swelled to reach gargantuan proportions that had filled his mouth, making him incapable of speech, he would have screamed for help, for someone to save him from this monster who was weighing him down, such was Selma's strength.

But he couldn't and he didn't.

Instead, he had silently mourned a life that had been wasted and a birthday he wouldn't reach, before allowing death to finally take him. With one last fatal spasm, his foot kicked out, propelling the black felt pouch he had been clutching before he fell, across the floor. It skittered sideways and came to a halt, nestled in the dark corner of the passage. Out of reach as much as Bentley was now out of time.

His lifeless body had lain sprawled amongst the dust and debris, the silhouette of Selma cast by Bentley's dropped torch spreading itself across the walls, reminiscent of the opening titles of an Alfred Hitchcock movie. Selma hadn't felt grief, she hadn't felt remorse, she had felt absolutely nothing for the tragic body before her.

'I don't do sharing, Bentley, never have, never will...' she had spat as she grabbed his foot and pulled. Whistling to herself she had hauled him around the first corner.

So that was how she had found herself in this current predicament.

She paused to catch her breath, confident that she had found the shaft she had been looking for. The wooden ladder attached to the brickwork was exactly where she had remembered it; it disappeared down into the blackness, but she didn't need light to show her the way. She had instinct and she had knowledge. Manoeuvring Bentley's body to the edge, she pushed him over. There were a few muffled thuds as various limbs hit the sides of the shaft – and then silence. She cocked her head and listened.

Nothing! Just the reed-like whistle of the wind finding nooks and crannies in the aged brick.

It was too soon for silence; there should have been a much louder thud as he hit the floor in the cellar passageway. Shining the torch into the abyss she saw why. Bentley, annoyingly inconsiderate as always, was firmly wedged halfway down.

'Well smack me on the arse with a Lipton's cheese paddle, that's a bit of a bugger...' Selma couldn't believe her bad luck. If Bentley remained there, she knew that within forty-eight hours there would be ghastly odours emanating from him, which in turn could jeopardise everything she was working towards once they permeated the Hall through the cracks, crannies and air vents. She backtracked along the passage until she came to a section where it opened out into a storage space. Grabbing a large chunk of 4 x 3 rough sawn timber, she quickly made her way back to Bentley.

Testing the first bar, she was relieved to see that age hadn't diminished the quality or the strength of each rung on the ladder; they held her weight admirably. Carefully inching her way down, she stopped just short of Bentley's body which was now folded in half with his head tucked between his legs.

'Well, that's one way to kiss your ass goodbye...' She laughed.

Utilising the timber, she pushed and prodded Bentley until eventually his body relinquished its hold. Unfortunately, it also took the opportunity to relinquish a rather loud emission of air that had been held in his lungs. It travelled across his slack vocal cords.

'Eeeuurggghhhaaah...'

Selma froze. The shaft acted as an echo chamber, bouncing Bentley's last breath from wall to wall down into the depths. She waited with her own bated breath, grateful that at least his last emission had been from his mouth and not his jacksy, as after all she now had to follow him down.

Taking each rung carefully, she descended into the darkness to join him. Annoyed that her hand had been forced to despatch Bentley sooner than she had planned, but grateful that at least this way she was now free to concentrate on Tarragon, Stephanie and, of course, the matriarch herself, Cecily Montgomery.

'One down, three to go...' Selma chanted to herself as she measured each rung with her ditty.

She lowered herself further into the depths of Montgomery Hall Hotel, oblivious to the fact that her plan and murder tally calculations were now very much out of date.

WHEN THE WIND BLOWS

'Was that you, Ethel?' Clarissa sat bolt upright in bed.

Ethel groaned and popped her head above the duvet. The pink sponge rollers tightly curled around her hair and the pale blue net holding them appeared first, quickly followed by her rheumy unfocused eyes and a sunken mouth, minus her famous dentures. Her hand shot out to grab her spectacles from the bedside cabinet. She popped them on her nose. 'What's the matter, can't you *sch*leep?'

Clarissa chose to remain silent. Out of bed now, she had her ear pressed against the bedroom wall. Eventually she spoke. 'I thought you'd guffed at first with eating all that rich food at dinner, but it's coming from the wall...'

Ethel shook the water from her dentures and savagely shoved them back into her mouth. 'I can't hear anything, and walls certainly don't fart, Clarissa. Are you sure you didn't dream it?' Ethel harrumphed, annoyed that her beauty sleep had been disturbed. 'Remember the last time we shared a room together? You were wailing all night about getting dressed for sex – I mean, really! At your age!' Being half asleep hadn't impinged on Ethel's delight in a bit of banter at Clarissa's expense.

'It was *success*... as in dressed for success, I was dreaming about having my own business. Honestly, Ethel, that train of thought says more about you than me!' Clarissa popped her slippers on, checked the bedside clock, and yawned. Another squall of hailstones hit the window of their room, followed by a loud boom which she took to be the gusting wind hitting the side of the building. She shivered. As warm as it still was in their room, the sound of the storm outside chilled her.

Clarissa was enjoying their weekend jaunt so far: the meal had been very nice, the sherry had been even nicer, Psychic Selma had been a bitter disappointment, but the touring actors, the Dingleberries, had been such fun. The only bit she hadn't been enamoured with was Montgomery Hall itself. Beautiful if may be with plenty of history, but it gave her the creeps. Everywhere you turned there were eyes peering down from dismal portraits keeping tabs on you. She pottered over to the window and looked out across the gardens. It was hard to see anything, apart from the tops of the trees fiercely bending and snapping back with each forceful blast of wind.

Ethel swung her legs out of the bed. 'Just going to powder my nose; won't be a minute.'

'Aye, fill your boots... er... actually no, Ethel, don't, not literally anyway.' Clarissa smiled to herself as she continued to watch the storm.

'Eeeeeeeeeek...'

Ethel's high-pitched scream made Clarissa jump. She quickly turned and started to make towards the bathroom. 'What is it, dear, what's happened?' She flung open the bathroom door, to see Ethel standing mesmerised, staring at poor Hilda who was happily ensconced on the toilet, nightdress hitched up, bloomers around her ankles, and holding a dog-eared copy of Agatha Christie's *4.50 from Paddington*.

'*Hilda*, you almost scared the life out of poor Ethel. What on *earth* are you doing in our bathroom?' Clarissa quickly adjusted Hilda's nightdress to hide her blushes and provide her with a bit of cover whilst Ethel, holding up the door frame and puffing like an old steam train, fanned herself with a couple of sheets of 2-ply toilet paper, hastily pulled from the roll, as though that action would miraculously calm her frazzled nerves.

Hilda grinned. 'Morning, ladies, you're most welcome to share my facilities if you wish, but can you just wait until I've finished?' She promptly went back to reading her book.

Clarissa looked at Ethel, Ethel looked at Clarissa, each wondering which one of them had forgotten to lock the bedroom door the night before.

Hilda momentarily broke away from the task at hand. 'Oh, and if you're feeling a bit frisky whilst you're waiting–' She gave them a saucy wink. '–there's a rampant man in me wardrobe!'

Selma reached the last rung on the ladder, glad to have both feet on terra firma. Poor Bentley was piled in a broken heap on the floor. She cocked her head and studied him. Clearly yoga had never been his forte, judging by the resulting lack of flexibility in both of his legs. He reminded her of a resting ventriloquist's dummy, limbs akimbo and with that vacant, chilling stare they all had. Fortunately, she didn't have too far to drag him.

She inched along the passage, and as with the other access points she felt for the lever and pulled. The panel slid open, revealing the dark, cavernous depths of the cellar. To the right was a door that led to where a vast stock of wines was housed. To the left was floor-to-ceiling shelving, which held all the dry foods, packaged bedding, towels, and on a separate shelf unit, the domestic cleaning products. Ahead was her destination.

Once again Bentley became nothing more than a human

broom, sweeping the floor with various body parts as Selma hauled him to the far corner. She opened the huge stainless-steel door to the freezer, which released a blast of freezing cold air. Selma welcomed its fleeting effect; she hadn't realised how much she had been sweating during her exhausting endeavours. She pulled and tugged, but Bentley's body juddered to a halt.

'Come on, come on – I haven't got time for this…' she snarled.

His left arm had wedged itself between the bottom of the door and the threshold. She used her foot to kick it out from under the door, and as she did so, his watch flipped from his wrist and fell to the floor, unseen by Selma.

'Welcome to your final resting place, Bentley my lad – well, at least until they find you, but I don't think that will be for a while…' She worked studiously around him.

Five minutes later, Selma stood back to admire her handwork. The muslin sheet she had wrapped him in had actually made him look like a half-side of beef, which was really rather perfect because he was now lying side by side, propped up against another lump of frozen produce also wrapped in a sheet.

Shutting the freezer door behind her, Selma mentally patted herself on the back for a job well done.

Oh, Selma – if only you knew…

INTUITION...

*L*ucy sat down on the small stool and flopped her elbows onto the mahogany table in front of her. The temptation to rest her head on her arms, just like she used to in maths class at school, was all-consuming; only this time it really was due to tiredness and not algebra overload and boredom. She checked the time on the Bull and Duck's ancient clock above the bar against her own watch.

06:23.

She stifled another yawn, which made her eyes water. Andy was already outside, loading up their car. She watched him through the leaded glass window, battling the gusts of wind that forcefully pelted the torrential rain against him as he tried to close the tailgate. It gave plenty of resistance, refusing to yield to his strength. He gave one last pull, his feet almost lifting from the ground, before it conceded and closed with a bang. He momentarily disappeared from view before the latched door to the pub opened and blew back against the arm of a worn leather armchair. Andy was almost pushed inside the small pub, bringing with him a flurry of leaves and a page from the local village newspaper that had taken refuge in the entrance porch.

He stamped his feet and shook the rain from his hands. 'Bloody hell, it's getting worse out there...' He gave Lucy an apologetic smile. She was exhausted, but although he did feel a little guilt for disturbing her sleep, the niggle he had felt after receiving Pru's text had developed into an uncanny feeling of urgency. He usually trusted his spider senses; they had rarely sent him in the wrong direction, either in his personal life, or, more importantly, in his job. He'd emailed DI Murdoch Holmes to tell him their outside Force assistance was no longer required and asked for a couple of rest days for them both. He had wandered around the pub, one arm in the air holding his phone, trying to elicit a signal. When he'd found it, he'd stood rooted to spot, fearful that even a tremor of hair would lose it. The return email had been short and sweet as Holmes wasn't one for verbose responses, but it had sanctioned his request with the expectations that he and Lucy would back-fill at short notice in the future, should this be required.

Lucy smiled back. 'No probs, but if this turns out to be nothing, then you owe me!'

'Honest, Luce, if I could get through and put my mind at rest, there wouldn't be a problem. Neither Pru nor Bree's phones are connecting, same for the actual landlines for the hotel, and I'm not yet at the point of asking any of our lot to make a visit to check...' He used his handkerchief to dry his face. 'It would be a bit embarrassing if they're all safe and sound drinking gin and the local plod come barging in, frightening all the old dears just because some antsy boyfriend got the wrong end of the stick.'

Lucy wanted to reassure him, but deep down she did think he was overreacting. 'Well, hopefully we'll find out in a couple of hours, won't we?' She didn't hold out much hope of it being a straightforward, not-without-incident journey. This weather was not going to calm down; if anything, it was getting worse. More flood warnings had been announced and plenty of amber alerts had now been changed to red. 'Andy, you are sure about this, aren't you?'

He thought for a minute. 'No, not sure at all, but it's something I've got to do. I can feel something isn't right.'

~

'Has anyone seen Kitty this morning?' Pru edged herself past Ethel and Clarissa, and took her seat at the next table with Bree. Breakfast was being held in The Orangery, which was unusually dismal and dark due to the continuing weather outside. She imagined how it would look in summer, with sun streaming through the large roof lantern, dappling the dark green ivy. She made a mental note to coerce Andy into a romantic weekend away in the warmer months. She could just imagine the two of them picnicking in the grounds, lying on a blanket under one of the huge oak trees and walks by the river. She squinted her eyes, peering through the window into the gloom, trying to make out where the track of the river should be. Since yesterday it had clearly burst its banks, spreading murky water as far as the tree-line to the woods. What had been a lazy meandering stretch of water was now something akin to a reservoir, spreading out across the grounds of Montgomery Hall. She wondered how the bridge they had crossed to get here had fared.

Pru checked out her own breakfast of scrambled egg and wholemeal toast against Bree's plate, piled high with crispy bacon, black pudding, a tepee made up of several plump sausages and a grilled tomato. 'Blimey, Bree, who on earth needs that much sausage?'

Cassidy couldn't help herself. 'Hey, Chels, they're talking about you and Beefy Bruce again!' She let rip with a most inelegant snort of laughter.

Chelsea bristled with indignation, which was actually a first for her. 'Boring! It's not very funny, either, it's not like I've not heard that one before, and anyway you've had your fair share of...'

'Girls, please!' Kitty Hardcastle, closely followed by Frank Atkins, their coach driver, regally propelled herself across the room as though she was on castors. 'Prunella, I really do think you need to rein these two in.'

Pru attempted a response through a mouthful of toast. She wished Kitty had made her dramatic entrance two seconds earlier, before she'd savoured the moment and bit into it. Kitty was the past president of the Winterbottom WI and had ruled with a rod of iron, accompanied by plenty of funny asides behind her back from some of the group when she overstepped the mark with her snobbery. Pru swallowed and dabbed at her chin with the napkin. Any other time she would have probably used the back of her hand, but in Kitty's presence, etiquette was everything.

'Point taken, Kitty, but even you have to admit they are a handful.' Pru returned to the task at hand, pushing the scrambled egg on to the remaining piece of toast as Kitty flounced off to her own table.

'No guessing what those two would have been up to last night.' Bree shovelled another rasher of bacon into her mouth as she nodded her head towards Kitty and Frank. It was common knowledge amongst the WI ladies that Frank frequently serviced more than just his fleet of coaches. 'Oops, eyes to three o'clock – someone's on a mission...'

Pru looked to where Bree had indicated to see Tarragon Montgomery striding towards their table. He was slightly dishevelled but holding his own.

'Ladies, my apologies for disturbing you at breakfast, but when you have finished could I ask that you attend my office?' Tarragon's calm request belied the worried expression on his face.

Pru nodded. 'Of course, is there something wrong?'

'My son has disappeared…'

The silence that followed evidenced his chagrin at Bentley's behaviour, but also his concern. He gave them a curt nod of his head and checked his watch. 'Twenty minutes sufficient?'

They watched him confidently stride across the marble tiles of the orangery and through the double doors. Pru knew that his bearing was an act, one that was honed to perfection for his guests and one to show his heritage.

It was a heritage that had brought nothing but tragedy and grief to his bloodline if her research was anything to go by.

A BIRD IN THE BUSH...

'Right, actors and–' Llewelyn Black took in the ratio of females to males in his troupe and quickly decided he would err on the side of caution, lest he should feel the wrath of over 50 per cent of his company. '–and, er… actors.'

It had been a long time since equality had done away with the term 'actress', and although it hadn't yet fully embedded itself in the Dingleberry Amateur Dramatics Society of Chapperton Bliss, he knew he would have a mini riot on his hands if he didn't start acquiescing in some way, and now was as good a time as any. If truth be known, he didn't hold with all this 'feminism' stuff. The days when women knew their place were, in his not so humble opinion, better for it.

Francesca Moore leant back in her chair and clicked her fingers. 'Wakey wakey, Llewelyn, we're waiting!'

Llewelyn grimaced, his face taking on the expression of someone who had just detected a slight whiff of something disgusting. 'I'm not a dog, Francesca; you don't have to click your fingers as though I need to be brought to heel!'

'That's not what I've heard, mate–' Dirk smirked, and looked at the others to ensure he had an audience. '–wasn't it you who was caught in Dibbin Woods with a pair of binoculars, taking in the views of Verity Smith and her new boyfriend cavorting *au naturel* in the bushes?'

The room descended into raucous laughter.

'How very dare you! I was bird watching, I'll have you know…' Llewelyn turned several shades of purple.

'I rest my case…' Dirk was on a roll.

Marilyn Peacock, in the process of fanning herself with her copy of the script, almost slid from her chair in shock, horrified that the man of her dreams, her secret crush, was being outed in such a public way. 'I think that's quite enough, don't you?' She tutted in disgust.

Llewelyn chose to ignore the smirks from his company and cleared his throat. 'Right, tonight is the night, murder is afoot, and our amateur sleuths will be sent on a journey of investigation and discovery.' He turned the page of the script he was holding. 'You all know your roles. Dirk, I need you to quickly go over how you are going to despatch Clara. Nothing too grisly, please. I think we have few pacemakers in the audience.'

Dirk nodded. 'Strangulation by chiffon scarf, isn't it, Clara?'

Clara laughed, making a figure of eight in the air with the prop, a rather pretty pale gold scarf she had brought from the local charity shop in Chapperton Bliss in preparation. 'I shall be outstanding, I promise. I've been practising my dying moments.' She popped her eyes, flung her head back, and let rip with a series of ooh's, ah's, and gargling noises. 'See, they'll be hooked – a performance of a lifetime.'

Julie Shute wrinkled her nose. She wasn't convinced that Clara Toomey had been the best choice as the Busybody / Victim, and she herself was still smarting from Llewelyn's very obvious snub when he'd cast her as the Waitress. She was under no illusion that refusing to serve herself on a platter for him was behind his decision. If she wasn't going to serve him one way, then he had made damn sure she'd be carrying a tray for him in another. He was the epitome of a male chauvinist pig.

'I bet that *Thi*kick *Th*elma will be the fir*th*t to gue*th* who the murderer i*th* – well that*th* if the old trout can up her game on that di*th*mal performance la*th*t night!' Francesca made her way over to the coffee pot and topped her cup up.

'Blimey, Francesca, thank God you didn't get cast as the Assassin – you'd have more than a few problems with that word!' Dirk sniggered. He enjoyed seeing people squirm, and nothing beat poor Francesca and her lisp for entertainment.

Llewelyn clapped his hands to bring everyone to order. 'Okay, don't forget you can't lie – if they interrogate you, you have to tell the truth – unless you're the murderer, of course. Right, places everyone, quick run through, and then meet back here at 6pm.'

As the Dingleberries dramatically flung themselves around the room, marking places and props, all but one were blissfully unaware that they already had an audience, albeit a solitary one...

Clara's attention had been inexplicably drawn to a panel to the left of the ornate fireplace. She could have sworn it had moved and, in doing so, she had caught a fleeting glimpse of... well, she wasn't quite sure who it was, but she'd soon find out with a closer look. Mesmerised, she padded quietly across the room and stood in front of it, her fingers plucking at the edges of the panel, trying to make it move again to no avail. She tapped it gently with her knuckles, and when that failed to produce a result she began to trace the carvings, pushing and pulling.

Behind the panel, Selma had quickly pressed her back against the wall, holding her breath. She couldn't believe her own stupidity. She should have checked that the Belvedere Dining Room was vacant before scurrying like a rat through the passages of Montgomery Hall. She had slid back the panel, expecting to pop out into an empty room, ready to set the next part of her plan into motion, but instead she had almost come face to face with some wittering old biddy from the theatre company. There were no guarantees that this nosey geriatric wouldn't blow her cover and ruin the plan. Her modus operandi for the evening would now have to change.

This inconvenient rewrite of the script would be considerably fortunate for Simpering Stephanie as she had unexpectedly been given a reprieve, but it would now be at the cost of another...

THE ITALIAN JOB

*S*mithers stood dead centre of the room, head bowed, deep in thought. Master Bentley's suite was exactly as it always was, exactly as it should be. Nothing appeared to be out of place, nothing missing, nothing there that shouldn't be. He was as perplexed as Mr Montgomery and the rest of the staff had been.

Bentley, for all his poor habits and life choices, always rang down for his breakfast between 8am and 9am. When that call had failed to materialise, Smithers had taken it upon himself to check on the young master. Discovering the two pillows but no Master Bentley had been the first clue that all was not well.

'I don't care, Tarragon, he could have stolen the Crown bloody jewels for all that matters, I just want to know where my son is!' Stephanie paced up and down the room, wringing her hands. 'He's my son; if he's in trouble, he needs me.'

Tarragon continued pulling open drawers, sifting through several Ungrateful Dead T-shirts, boxer shorts and, of all things, a lime-green man-thong. He plucked it out between finger and thumb and held it aloft. 'I sometimes wonder if we know our son at all, look at this monstrosity – I think he's a stand-in for Borat and his mankini every other Tuesday...' He gave a throaty laugh.

That hint at joviality didn't go down well with Stephanie, who promptly burst into tears.

Smithers looked on. This had been a family he had been proud to serve for more years than he cared to remember. A good, strong and noble family. Now they were reduced to a woman who had the morals of an alley cat and was a gold-digger to boot, together with a delinquent son who had more hands than an octopus had tentacles when it came to poor Ellie Shack-lady and any other young female member of staff. No one was safe when Bentley was sniffing around, and, if truth be known, he was more like his great-grandfather than anyone realised. Tarragon had turned into a wet lettuce of a man upon his marriage to Stephanie. The only good one left had been Cecily. He had the greatest respect and admiration for the matriarch of Montgomery Hall, firm but fair. Cecily had stood by Smithers in his decision to make an honest woman out of Emily all those years ago, and now she too was gone. He felt his heart would break, not just at her loss, nor his complicity in her current undignified resting place in the walk-in freezer, but for the slow destruction of the family name and its values at the hands of these monsters.

'Stephanie, dear–' Tarragon shook the small plastic bag he had found stuffed between two brightly coloured thongs. He scowled. It might be his son, but the thought of what those ridiculous pants had cosseted, and, more to the point, who had seen him prancing around in them, made his stomach lurch. '–why would Bentley have a packet of mixed herbs hidden in his underpants?'

Stephanie peered over his shoulder, sniffing loudly to show her still fragile state. She examined the dried green leafy flakes in the clear bag. 'I take it you missed the Swinging Sixties then?' She cocked her head waiting for him to reply.

'Considering I wasn't born until 1970, darling, I think that's a given.' He opened the bag and sniffed. 'Eurgh…'

Stephanie curled her lip and raised an eyebrow. 'Well, he's

certainly not making a ruddy pizza, is he?' She opened the drawer to the bedside cabinet and sighed. 'And if I'm not mistaken, these aren't blow up party balloons either!' She gingerly held a packet of Durex between fingers and thumb. 'It's cannabis, Tarragon; our son is clearly smoking cannabis whilst bumping uglies with anything that's got a bloody pulse!'

~

Pru bounced back onto her bed and lay pensively supine, staring at the ceiling.

How on earth had a simple theft-from-employer job turned into this dilemma? She was still of the opinion that Bentley, fearing he had been discovered, had done a runner. 'What's your take on it?'

Bree clicked the clasp on her blusher and popped it back into her make-up bag. She sucked her cheeks in and gave herself a last check in the mirror. 'Mmm... I'm not going for the upped-and-left theory; it doesn't sit well with everything else.' She dabbed on a spot of lip gloss and smacked her lips together.

Pru sat up and grabbed her notebook. 'In what way?'

'Okay: number one, he's the heir to the Montgomery fortune. Why leg it and jeopardise that?' Bree ticked off one finger. 'Number two, no matter what the little shit has got up to in the past, Mummy has always forgiven him. What or who says that this time was going to be any different?' She ticked a second finger. 'And number three–' She padded over to the window and looked out. '–the weather! Nobody is coming or going in this, and from what I heard after breakfast, the bridge is barely holding out. It'll be completely under water soon if this continues.'

Pru dropped her pen. Bree was right, it just didn't add up. 'Right, I think we need to organise a full search of Montgomery Hall, top to bottom. Maybe he's hiding out in one of the unused rooms, probably bombed out of his brain judging by the stuff Tarragon and Stephanie have apparently discovered in his bedroom.' She swung her legs over the bed and slipped her feet into her ballet flats.

'There's only one snag with that, though.' Bree sniffed.

'What?'

'Montgomery Hall is full. There's not a room to be had, apart from one that hasn't yet been upgraded, so it wasn't available for this weekend. Might be worth checking that, and I'm sure they've scoured their own private and staff quarters, so what does that leave us – the dreaded dungeon that all haunted houses have?' Bree huffed at her Halloween comparison.

'Nope, that was the first thing I asked. Montgomery Hall doesn't have a dungeon, it's just got a cellar, but that's been searched by Tarragon himself and nothing; all as it should be, and no sign of the Beastly Bentley either.' Pru blew upwards to push away the curl that had dropped down over one eye. She shook her head in exasperation.

Bree grinned. 'Search of the grounds it is, then… but I'm not joining in with that one. No way is my waterproof mascara guaranteed for a hurricane!'

No sooner had those words left her lips than a vibrant bolt of lightning lit up the dismal sky over the treeline, which was quickly followed by a deafening clap of thunder that made the windows rattle.

As the rain once again pelted the glass, Pru had to agree that anyone who ventured out in this would definitely have to be a sandwich short of a picnic.

SINK OR SWIM

$\mathcal{L}$ucy sat rigid in the passenger seat of Andy's car; her fingers tightly curled around the edges of the grey fabric. Each time they approached a bend, her right foot would automatically jab at an imaginary brake whilst her left foot pedalled an invisible clutch. They hit a pothole in the road which forced a spray of muddy water across the windscreen. The wipers were struggling to do their job, as no sooner had they smeared an arc in the grime and rain, it would be covered again reducing vision to virtually zero.

She tried to be nonchalant in her conversation with Andy who was currently putting his police driving skills to good use. 'Maybe we should pull over and try calling again. You never know, we might get through the closer we're getting.'

Andy grunted, not taking his eyes from the road ahead of him. She could see the tension in his jaw as he accelerated and decelerated in equal measure around the bends in the country lane.

'Look–' She didn't expect him to actually look, it was more out of habit and a way to reassure him that Montgomery Hall wasn't too far away. '–the signpost says Little Childer Thornton's only three miles away.'

'Try Pru again. If there's still no signal, try the landline for the hotel–' Andy pointed to his own phone in the centre console. '– although I don't hold out much hope for that. Look over there.' He jerked his head to the right of the hedge.

Lucy could see what the problem was. Several trees had come down, and one had fallen right between two poles, their wires looped and spiralled through the branches like a knitting pattern for beginners, with dropped stitches and loose threads. She held the phone to her ear. 'Same as before – nothing on either number.'

The realisation of a confirmed incommunicado on all media seemed to make Andy drive with just a little more urgency.

'Andy, this is not like you. You really need to rein it in; we don't know anything is wrong.' Her attempt at reassuring him seemed feeble once the words had left her mouth.

He sighed. 'And we don't know if anything is right either, Lucy. It's just a gut feeling, and it's never let me down before.'

As the trees and hedges raced past her window, becoming momentarily obscured every time the wheels of the car hit a small flood throwing up mud, water and debris onto the bonnet and side windows, Lucy continued to chew on the inside of her cheek whilst she sat in silence.

'Here we go...' Andy indicated left, the *ticker, ticker, tick* from the dashboard the only sound between them as he turned into a cutaway at the side of the road. The immense iron gates pushed back against the shrubbery on either side heralded the location of Montgomery Hall Hotel in large gold letters above the forged railheads.

Considering they were the only fools that had dared to venture out onto the roads of Childer Thornton during the storms, Lucy was amused to see that Andy had actually used his indicator. 'You'd be a traitor to the BMW badge, Sarge...' She laughed.

Andy cleared the mist from his side window so he could read

the damaged sign that was pegged to the gate nearest to him. He rubbed his chin. The fierce winds, coupled with the rain, had torn it in half, leaving just the words in bold red…

WARNING – BRIDGE ACCESS ONLY

He selected first gear and pushed on, the long and wide approach driveway to the hotel opened out before them. All around trees had been uprooted, lying like wounded giants, their branches as open arms asking for help. It made him feel sad that nature could turn on itself and cause such destruction. In the distance he could make out the dark, foreboding silhouette of Montgomery Hall, the trees that surrounded and framed it defying the storm, snapping backwards and forwards with each gust. The car buffeted from side to side as it swept along the driveway, coming to an abrupt halt once it reached the fore-warned bridge.

'Well, unless Winterbridge's finest CID squad car can miraculously morph into Chitty Chitty Bang Bang, I think we might have to swim for it, Luce.' He pointed to the mini pond that rippled before them, blocking the bridge approach by vehicle.

They sat, disappointed and almost at the point of despair. Lucy's tummy rumbled loudly. She patted it as though that would do as an apology for its impolite behaviour.

'What now?' Her shoulders dropped. She was starving, thirsty and desperately needed the loo.

Andy surveyed the bridge; the overspill of the river had pooled deeply on their side to the approach, leaving just a narrow strip at the edge that was only partially covered by shallow water. He looked at the rapidly rising levels; it was now or never. If they were quick, they could make it across on foot.

'We get out and walk – carefully!'

THE GIFTS

Smithers eased himself down into the old fireside chair in the neat little cottage housed in the grounds of Montgomery Hall. 'Tawny Wings' had been gifted to him by Cecily in the summer of 1970, just after his marriage to Emily. Emily, the sweetest and most innocent girl he had ever set eyes upon, had been Cecily's dresser. Their nuptials had taken place within a few short weeks of her seventeenth birthday.

The Butler had married the Maid.

His rheumy eyes settled on the gilt-framed photo on the mantelpiece. The beautiful bohemian cream chiffon dress was caught in a moment in time, floating behind her on warm summer thermals. The sun had dappled her blonde hair with shadows from the leaves of the large Montgomery oak that for generations had stood over the family for special occasions. He had been so honoured that Cecily had allowed them that position, a position that was only ever reserved for the Montgomerys themselves. Standing beside Emily was his younger self. His chin jutted out in pride; her arm linked through his. A man in love.

He eased himself up to hold the frame, so he could bring the day closer to his memory. He traced his finger across Emily's face. She was as beautiful now as she had been then. Age had not diminished or spoilt her charm, or his love for her. The bouquet of pink peonies and baby's breath was held awkwardly in front of her, hiding not in shame, but in secret, the life she held within her.

Yes, 'Tawny Wings' had been his gift, but at a cost...

His silence.

～

Selma sat in her room pondering her next move. She had a post-dinner spot tonight, one she hoped would be a darn sight better and more productive than last night's fiasco. Her original brief had been to set the scene for the ensuing dinner-time murder by the cast of the ridiculously named Dingleberries, but she had fought for an after-dinner performance instead and won. Once her audience had hit the drinkable spirits over three courses, it would be a darn sight easier for her to 'conjure' up the spooky spirits to entertain their sozzled minds. She had stifled a snort of laughter when she'd read the Dingleberries were appearing. Honestly, fancy calling yourself after something a cat has deposited from its bum! Clearly Llewelyn Black hadn't researched the term 'dingleberry' before giving his tribe of luvvies that moniker.

Selma could normally read a room, would know at a glance who to pick on for a good interaction, that was an actor's best asset. *Know your audience* had been her mantra for as long as she could remember, but she'd really cocked up the night before with Hilda's deceased pussy.

Pulling on her wig, she brushed on a little more lace glue and patted down the hairline onto her forehead whilst verbally chastising herself. 'A sloppy performance will never do, my dear. You really need to pull your socks up!'

Her ordered list lay on the bed next to the plans for Montgomery Hall. Although structural changes had been made over the years, her nocturnal meanderings over the last twenty-four hours had proved they clearly hadn't impinged on the passages. She was still tense over her unexpected face-to-face meeting with Bentley and his resulting earlier-than-planned demise. Her belief that Montgomery Hall's secrets would have remained hers and hers alone had been a huge mistake. She should have been more on the ball, should have expected that during her absence someone might have stumbled upon them.

'Oh well, too late now...' She laughed. Slipping a tissue between her lips, she smacked down the bright red lipstick and finished with a slick of eyeliner over her false eyelashes.

'Taa daa!' She swirled around the room, the silk kaftan billowing behind her. 'Ah, Clara Toomey, yes, yes, you my dear. I see a darkness coming your way...' Her finger pointed to thin air whilst she imagined the shrew-like woman in her sights. The image brought a cackle of very feminine laughter to her throat.

Flopping down on to the bed, she took up a pencil and began to rewrite her script.

Cue the psychic from stage left, the room is dimly lit, casting shadows on the faces of the audience (ensure position of target is known in advance)...

Selma paused and chewed the end of her pencil, deep in thought.

Why ruin the whole night? This murder had not been part of the plan, but needs must, and if she played it right, there was fun to be had with this one. It would be like giving herself a little gift, an unexpected one, but pleasant none the less.

She wouldn't ruin her own performance; she would wait until the time was right.

Ladies and Gentlemen, members of the audience, for tonight's performance the role of the Victim will be played by Clara Toomey, with the special guest appearance of (blah blah blah) as Psychic Selma...

She swished the emerald green cloak around her shoulders, dipped one leg behind the other, and took a dramatic bow.

No point in revealing her true self just yet ... because it would definitely spoil the surprise.

THE GAMES WE PLAY

itty Hardcastle swept into the dining room with poor Frank still in tow. Pru wondered if he'd actually left her side since they'd arrived, but checking out Kitty's immaculate appearance compared to his dishevelled look, she was sure he'd breached her tight rein at some point. 'Gosh, Frank, you're looking a little worse for wear; what happened?'

Frank gave Pru a sheepish look and shrugged his shoulders. He was very aware that the eyes of the Winterbottom WI ladies were upon him, boring into his soul, waiting to catch him out in a lie. 'I've been outside. It's a bit windy out there, that's all. I was just checking the inflation ratio on my–'

Before he could finish his sentence, raucous laughter from Ethel and Clarissa's table interrupted him and heralded a much-expected saucy response.

'My dearest Frank, judging by Kitty's face I don't think you've got a problem with your inflation ratio!' Ethel licked her index fingers and chalked an imaginary number 1 in the air, giving a simultaneous naughty wink to evidence her quick wit, whilst rocking backwards in her chair with a fit of the giggles. Clarissa's usually sensible façade had deserted her, leaving her to dab at the tears that were streaming down her cheeks with her napkin.

'Ooh, Ethel, you *are* awful...' Clarissa mimicked in a poor impression of Dick Emery. 'Frank, I do think you need to have a quick check in the gents, though.' She pointed to her own head to guide him as to what he should be attending to.

Frank's legendary ginger toupee had taken on a life of its own in the high winds, and was now angled over his left ear like a hairy fascinator. Embarrassed, he savagely pushed it back onto his head, but only succeeded in shoving it so far over his bald spot it slid over to his right ear and dangled precariously.

Kitty quickly jumped in to distract everyone and quell their laughter. 'Right, ladies, as I'm sure you're all aware, the weather has put paid to any outdoor activities for this afternoon, so I've organised a little game of Happy Families in the lounge after lunch. Won't that be fun?'

'Will you be joining us, Kitty – or have you got "activities" of your own to indulge in?' Ethel was on a roll. 'I hear you're pretty nifty at a quick game of chess!'

Clarissa looked puzzled. 'I'm sure Kitty doesn't know the difference between a pawn and a prawn, Ethel.'

'I know, but she does like to give Frank's bishop a bit of a thrashing...' She grinned mischievously.

Another round of laughter from the ladies filled the room as Kitty stomped off towards the lounge, Frank again following in her wake. Pru felt obliged to step in. 'Okay, girls, I think poor Kitty and Frank have had their fair share of mickey-taking, and Ethel, I'm very surprised at you. That one was a little too near the knuckle.'

Ethel's eyes twinkled as she let her cup rattle back into the saucer. 'That's just your mucky mind, my dear!'

Pru laughed. 'Touché! Okay, let's finish up in here and retire to the lounge. I think a nice afternoon in each other's company will do us good – plus they've got a lovely roaring fire in there to toast our toes in front of.'

A collection of greying heads nodded their approval. Even Chelsea and Cassidy stopped taking selfies long enough to give a thumbs up.

'What are we doing?' Hilda fiddled with her hearing aid, forcing it to emit a loud squeal, which in turn made Millie wince.

'We're retiring to the lounge, Hilda.' Millie pushed her chair back, folded her napkin, and placed it next to her plate.

Hilda was clearly unimpressed. 'Why are we required to scrounge? Can't we pay for what we want?'

Millie sighed. She loved Hilda like any good friend should, but she could be exasperating and tiring to say the least. She felt like her personal interpreter. 'Don't worry, Hilda, I've got plenty of money, you can have whatever you want.' It was so much easier to just go with the flow of what Hilda thought she had heard than try to explain to her what had really been said.

To the backdrop of excited chatter, the ladies of the Winter-bottom Women's Institute quickly vacated the Belvedere Dining Room, all thoughts of Kitty and Frank's furtive liaisons carefully put to rest – until the next time they felt like amusing themselves.

Pru and Bree remained, taking the opportunity to have a quiet moment to discuss the current events that were playing out in relation to Beastly Bentley's disappearance.

Bree twirled a section of hair around her finger. 'So that's a negative with the empty room, and Tarragon said Bentley's mobile phone was still charging on the bedside cabinet.'

'I know, and like most people his age, he would never go anywhere without it.' Pru bit down on her bottom lip, nipping at the skin, deep in thought. 'I've suggested if there's no sign of him by tomorrow morning, they should think about involving the police. They rarely do much within the first twenty-four hours anyway, unless there are serious concerns that can be backed up.'

'Which there isn't in this case. They'll probably put it down to

Bentley getting a whiff of his parents' knowledge in relation to his Fagin-like activities by pinching the family silver, and he's nipped off waiting for the heat to die down.' Bree was pretty chuffed with the way her train of thought was starting to mirror how she felt a proper private investigator would think.

Pru absent-mindedly looked out of the window, checking how the weather was faring whilst she processed what they knew so far. 'To be honest, Bree, we've done our bit. We were only asked to find out who was stealing from Montgomery Hall, and we've done that.'

Bree was inclined to agree, but she knew that Pru would be itching to carry on with the missing person part of the investigation as much as she was. 'We could always dig a little deeper; it would liven up what's left of the weekend. What do you think?'

'Mmm... you know me so well...' Pru had just started to laugh at that comment, when something outside in the grounds caught her eye. She blinked rapidly, thinking the bleak, rain-sodden sky was interfering with her vision, or that maybe it was one of those imaginary shadow people, the ones you catch from the corner of your eye. Not really there but created from make-believe, and boy had her ability to create imaginary shadows been working overtime in this beautiful, but very creepy place. It was also Halloween to boot, making it all the more likely her overactive imagination would fire on all cylinders. She cocked her head and strained her eyes against the now grimy windows. 'There! Did you see that?'

Bree joined her. 'What?'

'Over there, near the tree line...' Pru's nose was almost touching the leaded glass. 'Someone ran between the hedges, across the lawn and disappeared into the trees, I'm sure they did.'

'I can't see anything.' Bree frowned. 'Hold on, wait a minute – *yes*, there *is* someone there.' She pointed towards the path that broke from the trees and led up to join the main driveway of

Montgomery Hall. 'Blimey, Pru, if I didn't know better, I'd say I knew who that was…'

This time Pru saw the figure clearly; it wasn't a figment of her imagination. 'It's Andy!' She almost choked. 'What *on earth* is he doing here, prancing around like he's in a matinee performance of *Swan Lake*?'

Bree sat down heavily on the window seat. 'And look, there's Lucy, too.'

They watched a very wet and bedraggled Andy at the front, taking long, lolloping strides that were a mixture of running and jogging, with Lucy following behind him, desperately trying to keep up and match his pace. They raced along the driveway as though their lives depended on it, the savage gusts of wind pushing them forwards, and then, just as quickly, they disappeared from view as they approached the main doors.

'Quick–' Grabbing her bag, Pru laughingly half dragged, half pushed Bree through the doors of the Belvedere room, towards the Great Hall. '–he must be really missing me!' She came to an abrupt halt by the large mirror next to a potted aspidistra. Giving a wide grin, she checked out her teeth from all angles. 'Phew, thank goodness, there's no evidence of my lunch.' She slicked her tongue across her top lip. 'I definitely wouldn't want to snog him with a bit of half-chewed curly endive stuck between my two front teeth,' she said as she giggled.

MEMORIES

HALLOWEEN 1977

*D*aniel stood for longer than he really ought to have done. It was quite something for an eight-year-old boy to actually see and experience death.

After he had taken his bow to his appreciative audience, his small hand had touched the carved lion's head at the side of the fireplace in the Somerset Room, willing him to make his escape, but morbid fascination had drawn him back.

By now David was quite dead, his slipper-clad toes swept the wood-block flooring as he lazily drifted from side to side, the bronze cord simultaneously depriving him of life whilst giving him momentum. Daniel wanted to touch his hand, he wanted to know if he would still be warm, but the fear that David's fingers might suddenly come alive and clutch at him made him hesitate. He wondered what David's small face would be like under the white sheet now that he was dead.

Would he look any different to how he himself now looked? Would they not be identical anymore? In the blink of an eye, Daniel had become a 'one off', an individual, an only child, and the sudden realisation that his mother would have only one son to love, cherish and spend her time with, filled him with a joy he had not experienced before.

'Happy birthday, Bro–' He laughed as he threw a salute to the still swinging body of his twin. *'–until we meet again!'*

And with that, Daniel disappeared through the oak panel, his cloak billowing behind him as he skipped an excited path through the secret passages of Montgomery Hall back to his bedroom.

HONEY I'M HOME

A flurry of dry leaves from the portico that had yet to be touched by rain, raced in behind Andy and Lucy as they burst through the doors of the Montgomery Hall Hotel. It took Andy, Smithers and Boris the bellboy to close them again, such was the force of the winds that battled around the old building.

'Blimey, I'm amazed we made it!' Lucy shook her head and roughly brushed her hand through her soaking wet hair, pushing it away from her eyes. She attempted a weak smile at the well-dressed woman standing before her, hoping their dishevelled appearance wouldn't negatively influence their need for a dry and safe roof over their heads. A drip of rainwater clung to the tip of her nose, elongated, and then splashed onto the beautiful marble floor, joining the rest of the rain she'd brought in with her. She couldn't have been more embarrassed than if she herself had personally produced the large wet puddle she was now standing in.

'It's the rain...' she muttered, and then wondered why on earth she had felt the need to explain the presence of the puddle as an act of nature rather than the possible mistaken belief that she had suddenly become incontinent.

Stephanie did her best to curtail the sneer her top lip was in danger of producing. 'I'm Stephanie Montgomery, how may I help?'

Andy was under no illusion that the last thing Stephanie wished to do was offer her services, helpful or otherwise. Unusually for him, he decided to use his status as a police officer. He didn't feel uncomfortable in doing this; after all, Pru's text message had asked for help and in a manner that might have needed a police response. He pulled out his warrant card, showing the badge and his photograph. Stephanie peered at it longer than he would have liked, which in turn made him wonder if it was about time he paid a visit to HQ to get a new photo done.

'I'm Detective Sergeant Andrew Barnes of Winterbridge Constabulary, and this is Detective Constable Lucy Harris. We have received information that our assistance may be needed here.' Andy felt it more prudent to carry on with this line of introduction; he could clarify later if needed. 'We had been unable to get through to confirm all is well. It appears the landlines are down due to the storm and–'

His explanation was interrupted by a commotion coming from the far side of the Great Hall. Pru, like an excited child, had knocked over the aspidistra in her haste to check her teeth and greet Andy. She was just about to emit a squeal of epic proportions and throw her arms around him, when she spotted his *I'm working* face. She had been privy to that expression before when he had been lead detective on the Winterbottom murders. She quickly pulled back, taking the time to put right the Montgomery greenery with the help of Boris.

Andy was incredibly relieved to see Pru, but did not become distracted from the task at hand. He needed to find out what was going on without causing panic amongst the other guests, and neither did he wish to impinge on Pru and Bree's investigation without first speaking to them. He watched Stephanie's right eye twitch, a barely perceptible tic, but it was a 'tell' nevertheless.

He'd had years of practice reading body language, and often the most subtle of facial movements were a giveaway.

'Are you here about my son, Bentley?' The colour had suddenly drained from Stephanie's face.

Andy quickly seized the opportunity. 'Is there somewhere we could speak in private?'

Stephanie curtly nodded and turned on her heels towards the office. 'If you'd like to follow me...'

Lucy tailed immediately behind her; Andy held back slightly as he wanted time to give Pru a quick nod to ensure all was well. He was amazed at how reserved she was; she was actually looking at him more dreamily than needily. She gave him one of her coquettish smiles and a wink. As he shut the office door behind him, he had a sneaking suspicion that Lucy had been right; he had misread the situation and in a spectacular style that only he seemed to be capable of since he had met the Loony Librarian, he had over-reacted too.

CLARA

*C*lara Toomey welcomed the soft click her bedroom door gave as it shut out the rest of the world. It heralded at least two hours of peace and tranquillity, away from the other Dingleberries, and a little bit of time for her to perfect her performance for that night.

She stood in front of the mirror and held her hand dramatically across her forehead. 'I can see the light...' She laughed, and then just as quickly remembered that in this particular scene, she was going to be the victim of strangulation. Granted it was more in keeping with the storyline, but she did prefer a more lingering death as that always gave her the chance to showcase her fabulous acting ability. She stuck out her tongue and closed off her throat by pushing her neck forwards and her head back to make her cheeks flush red, just as a choking victim would look. She then rolled her eyes and forced them to pop.

'Bravo, Clara...' she said as she congratulated herself, and clapped her hands in glee. Tonight she would stun them all with her talents.

She clicked the switch on the kettle and popped a teabag into the cup. Her fingers rustled the packets in the welcome box, looking for the shortbread biscuits, her favourite. Once her tea was brewed, she made herself comfy in the armchair by the window and kicked off her shoes. The old Victorian radiator under the bay window rattled and gurgled as it pumped out heat. Clara sat mesmerised by the trees, bending so low they almost touched the ground. They would momentarily return to their natural position, quivering until the next fearsome gust of wind caught them, and then the show would repeat itself. From her position she could already see that some of the grand oaks had lost their hold on the land, their huge roots still gripping the mud and grass as they tilted on their sides, a mushroomed shape of torn up ground lying beside them. It was so nice to be warm and safe inside, to feel contented and happy, as she was most days.

Clara had not been the grateful recipient of a good life; most of her seventy-plus years had been difficult and, at times, down-right impossible. In her youth she had yearned for true love, which had eventually been gifted to her, albeit for a short time. Her heartbreak at the loss of Lionel Toomey had almost broken her, particularly as it had been a death that was still being talked about to this day. His demise was to be her everlasting shame.

Lionel had kissed her on the cheek and patted her head three times, much like you would a pet dog, one warm, sunny Sunday afternoon in 1963. He had donned his cap, straightened his tie, and informed her that he would be late home as the vicar wished to go over his credentials. Clara had been of the belief that Lionel was to be the new organist at St Marks and All Souls church in Chapperton Bliss.

By 10.30pm that night, Lionel had failed to return home. Clara had pottered around the kitchen, toasting crumpets and making the fifth pot of tea since Lionel had departed. She was surprised that a try-out for a regular Sunday morning spot would take so long, but hers was not the place to question. At just after midnight, the village constable came calling, waking her from her restless slumber, to inform her of Lionel's sudden and terrible passing. Lionel had apparently fallen down two flights of stone steps in the rectory, instantly breaking his neck. That she could have understood and accepted, but the reality had been so much worse.

Lionel had been getting his credential checked over just as he had claimed, but not by the Reverend Caldicott himself – rather by his frisky wife, the buxom Agnes. Alas, this had not been for his expertise in pumping air into the church organ, or indeed for any other musical talents he might have possessed. Poor Caldicott had returned home early from his Sunday evensong and administering to his parish, to find his wife and Lionel in flagrante delicto. The sight of the somewhat bizarrely dressed Lionel, splayed out on the wooden kitchen table being straddled by Agnes, had sent Caldicott into a rage of epic proportions, one that would have no doubt closed the gates of Heaven to him.

Lionel had taken it upon himself to flee the scene, leaving Agnes to face the music, and in doing so he had taken a fatal tumble down the first flight of steps before somersaulting down the second set.

The coroner's inquest was one that the whole village had attended, not least because his cause of death had been at the fault of a pair of bright red sparkly stiletto shoes he had been wearing at the time. The only consolation was that they had perfectly matched his basque and fishnet stockings.

Her final goodbye to Lionel had been one of sorrow, loss and shame, and her life had never been the same again.

Clara sighed. Never a day went by when she didn't think about her Lionel, the Lionel she had loved and adored. Not the one that dressed like Judy Garland and who favoured aged pine over a decent mattress. She laughed out loud. Maybe if the stone steps had been bright ruddy yellow, Lionel wouldn't have had the misfortune to have missed them.

She closed her eyes and wondered what Lionel would be wearing when it was her turn to join him. She certainly hoped it wasn't, as rumour had it, that you spent all eternity in the last attire you were dressed in before you popped your clogs – or, as in Lionel's case, your stilettos.

It would be a bit of a bugger to be left standing at the Pearly Gates with your husband looking better in his choice of underwear than you did!

RIDE 'EM COWBOY

*P*ru couldn't contain her excitement. 'You're the best mate anyone could wish for...' she cooed to Bree as she shoved a handful of clothes into the unicorn-coloured suit-case. Every time Bree had trundled the damned thing out, Pru had been tempted to don a pair of sunglasses. She'd lost count of the number of times she had tried to encourage Bree to consign it to the attic for all eternity, but Bree had refused point blank to part with it, not even when Pru had offered her a nice sedate lilac one as a replacement.

'Not much choice, really; there's only one room available, and no way can the Delectable Detective share it with Lucy, but me bunking in with her isn't a hardship; we'll have a good laugh.' Bree carefully folded her blouse and then exuberantly pushed it to the bottom of the plastic carrier bag she was using for random stuff she couldn't be bothered to pack in her suitcase. She didn't mind moving out to accommodate Andy, and in a small way she was quite relieved to have extra pairs of experienced hands if the Bentley saga did go tits up on them.

'What do you think of these?' Pru dangled a delicate pair of lace panties and matching plunge bra from her fingers.

170

Bree curled her top lip. 'Wow, mental telepathy or what? I was just thinking of boobs and Bentley, and you wave an over-the-shoulder boulder-holder at me.' She examined the set. 'Oh dear, there's not much material to them, won't your bum get cold!'

Pru smirked. 'Somehow I don't think my posterior will have time to get cold...'

'Eeuw, too much information, girl!'

Their banter was suddenly interrupted by a light tapping on the door. Pru vaulted the bed, almost knocking Bree into the open wardrobe with her eagerness to welcome Andy. Flinging open the door she came face to face with Hilda.

'Oh...' Her disappointment was palpable. 'Are you okay, Hilda?'

Hilda bustled her way into the girls' room, her hands waving wildly in the air, a look of bewilderment on her face. 'What are you doing in my room, and where's my Millie?'

'Oh gosh, you've got the wrong room again.' Bree carefully put her arm around Hilda's shoulders and gently manoeuvred her towards the door. 'Come on, I'll help you.'

'But I think I've got larynightdress...' Hilda was not about to be consoled.

Bree side-eyed Pru, who mirrored her look of puzzlement. '"Larynightdress", Hilda? Whatever is that?'

'My throat's sore, I can hardly swallow, and I know Millie's always got stuff to suck in her handbag.' Hilda gave a sample cough to show her discomfort.

'Ah, laryngitis; you think you've got laryngitis...' Pru stifled a chuckle. The last thing she wanted to do was offend her. 'Well, don't worry. Bree will help you find Millie, won't you, Bree?' She looked up, just in time to see Andy standing framed in the doorway with a damp rucksack slung over his shoulder. She grinned. 'Okay, off you go...' She hastily encouraged poor Hilda to quickstep out of the room, with Bree following behind.

'Ooh look, you've got a man in your room waiting to ravish

you!' Hilda poked Andy in the chest with her arthritic finger. 'Did you come out of the wardrobe as well? I don't know what it is about this place; there seem to be sex pests stashed all over the place!' She tutted loudly.

Pru gave Andy a look of sympathy behind Hilda's back. Shaking her head, she mouthed the word 'dementia' whilst twirling her finger at the side of her head. He nodded his understanding.

Bree gave Andy a wink as she passed him. 'I take it I'm no longer needed then?' If she hadn't known better, she would have sworn the Delectable Detective had blushed. 'Bit warm in here, is it, Andy?'

'Erm... well, that depends if you've been hastily stripping off to cool down...' He deftly plucked Pru's plunge bra from where it had inadvertently become hooked on the back of Bree's jumper. Now it was his turn to swing it between finger and thumb.

'It's not mine, but it looks like you've got the *booby* prize, matey...' Bree nudged him in the ribs, '... See you later, guys!' She linked her arm through Hilda's and ushered her quickly down the corridor.

Andy backheeled the door, slamming it shut behind him. 'Okay, my Loony Librarian, what's all this about desperately needing me because it's all kicking off and a possible murder?'

It was not the welcome that Pru had expected from him. She had hoped for a bit of *An Officer and a Gentleman* moment, where he would scoop her up in his arms and carry her to the bed. She squished up her nose and shrugged her shoulders. 'It was half a text; my fat fingers pressed send. Didn't you get the other bit?'

He dropped his rucksack onto the chair. 'Obviously not. I didn't quite come on a white charger, it was more like a Ford Fiesta, but honestly, Pru, I read it and–'

She quickly placed her lips on his, and grabbing his hand she pulled him closer. 'Oh for goodness' sake, just take me, my

Delectable Detective...' She gave him a sultry smile and nodded towards the bed.

Andy grinned. 'It's a single.'

'I know.'

'Not much room for manoeuvre.'

'I'm double-jointed.'

Andy didn't need any further encouragement; he tenderly took her in his arms and kissed her passionately before gently lowering her onto the bed. She reciprocated, her kisses becoming more urgent as she manoeuvred herself on top of him, taking the lead.

'Yeeow, what the hell...?' He fumbled underneath him, pulling out one of Bree's three-quarter tan leather cowboy boots. 'Please don't tell me this is some form of foreplay, Prunella Pearce...' He laughed.

Pru flung her head back, allowing her chestnut curls to bounce over her shoulders and fall down her back. 'Yee haa, ride 'em, Toto!' She held on to his leather belt with one hand and flung her arm into the air as though she was clinging to a bucking bronco.

'That was Dorothy's dog in the Wizard of Oz, my little parsnip. I think you mean Tonto.'

She gazed into those bluer than blue eyes, the ones with the intense dark halo around them, and held his gaze just that little bit longer than was necessary. 'You say Tonto, I say Toto, so let's take the whole thing off...' she trilled as she ripped at his damp shirt.

Andy closed his eyes as the excitement of being so close to Pru surged through him. He could have thought of England, he might even have considered the Australian version of foreplay by shouting 'brace yourself, Sheila', but instead a witty one-liner from the great Mae West scrambled around his brain, giving him food for thought.

'*It's not the men in your life that matters, it's the life in your men...*'

And at this particular moment in time, he was so full of life he didn't think he would ever walk properly again!

FOUR GOOD REASONS

*T*arragon sat nursing a large brandy, his fingers curled so tightly around the glass, his knuckles had turned white. He checked his watch.

5pm.

Stephanie was attempting to appear busy, a ruse to quell her uneasiness and her mother's instinct that something seriously wrong had befallen Bentley. He could hear her clattering around in their bedroom, slamming cupboards and doors. He had done his best to calm her to no avail; she had carried on weeping and wailing all afternoon. Even the appearance of the detectives hadn't consoled her, if anything it had made her ten times worse.

Tarragon's life was falling apart around him and there was nothing he could do to stop the avalanche. He mentally ticked off his current misfortunes.

1. *One very deceased grandmother, trussed up like a Christmas turkey and shoved in the hotel walk-in freezer.*

Christ knows what the local authority would make of that if they turned up on his doorstep to carry out a food hygiene inspection. He couldn't imagine trying to explain to them how you hygienically prepare a 102-year-old wrinkly with a side order of dauphinoise potatoes for the evening menu.

2. One light-fingered missing son, partaker of cannabis, wearer of lime-green mankinis, and potentially a drug-dealer to boot.

Someone he should love because he was the fruit of his loins – so he'd been led to believe – but in truth he actually abhorred. Every generation of the Montgomery clan had suffered a devastating loss at some point, so how the hell had he been so bloody unlucky for it to skip one and spare his idle, dishonest offspring, he had no idea.

3. One neurotic, demanding, money-grabbing prig of a wife, who had absolutely no redeeming features whatsoever, since she had withdrawn her bedroom services a long time ago.

He still couldn't believe how he had been won over by her athleticism and wanton experimentation in his bed all those years ago. He would have been better staying single and employing the services of a local wench, just as his forefathers had done.

4. An inheritance that offered very little ready money, but included a mausoleum of epic proportions that swallowed up every single penny that came in – except for what his wife spent on her lavish lifestyle.

They barely broke even on bookings, and after this storm probably wouldn't manage to do that. He had a sneaking suspicion that his insurance company, Beggs, Alexandra and Stiff, would find some way of not paying out on his policy for repairs.

So four misfortunes, and four very good reasons for Tarragon to consider packing his bags and beggaring off somewhere warm, leaving Stephanie holding the grandmother, so to speak. He wanted to laugh out loud at his effort at a snowclone, but in view of the current situation, thought better of it.

Stephanie suddenly came flouncing into the sitting room, making him jump.

'That detective is the boyfriend of the woman you hired, did you know that?' She stood in front of him, hands on hips as though it was a challenge.

He knew better than to reply too quickly. He made a show of examining the contents, or lack of them, in his glass. He tipped it at Stephanie. 'Fancy another one?'

She nodded curtly. 'Well?'

He took the opportunity to keep his back turned to her as he poured her drink, and then topped up his own glass. 'I didn't, but I do now. It can only be a good thing, darling. Let the professionals do their job, granted it's a little restricted at the moment...' He handed her the glass and nodded towards the window. 'This weather is not helping, our phone lines are down, and our already poor mobile signal is completely wiped out. Bentley is a big boy; I'm sure he can look after himself, wherever he is.'

Stephanie's top lip curled in distaste. She took a slug of her drink and watched Tarragon as he pensively stared out of the window. If it wasn't for the Montgomery money, she'd be the one to pack her bags and beggar off to a tropical island somewhere, leaving Tarragon to clear up the mess. She had considered this on a regular basis these last few weeks; if she could have pushed Cecily more, she might have found out where the money was stashed. Now she would never know. The image of Cecily sharing her temporary resting place with half a cow and a couple of pigs, with icicles hanging from her superior nose just like Jack Nicholson in *The Shining*, made her want to laugh.

She topped her glass with more gin and took another slug. 'I think I'll have the steak tonight; it's been a while since I've had anything tasty on my lips...'

Tarragon continued to stare out of the window, not even bothering to face her. Now it was his turn to curl his lip. 'That's not what *I've* heard, darling, especially if the rumours are true...' he muttered under his breath.

MUSICAL CHAIRS

*T*he excited chatter of the Winterbottom Ladies as they made their way into the Belvedere Dining Room for their evening meal provided a theatrical backdrop for the cast of the Dingleberries. Llewelyn Black stood by the main doors counting heads and keeping an eye on where everyone sat as his actors took their places for the evening's performance. He checked his watch. 'Anyone seen Clara?'

Julie, already ensconced on Table 6 with Dirk and Francesca, finished applying her lipstick, checked her reflection one last time, and clicked her silver compact closed. 'I gave her a knock about twenty minutes ago; she was just getting changed.'

'She's late – as usual. One day that woman will be the death of me!' Spotting a couple of old dears attempting to make themselves comfortable on Table 4, Llewelyn quickly turned heel, leaving Julie to finish her conversation with Dirk. Arms waving as though he were catching a bus, he bounced across the room. 'No, no, not there; you can't sit there...' He edged past Table 2, and in his haste fell over the multi-coloured Kurt Geiger handbag that Chelsea had dumped on the floor beside her chair. His foot caught in the trailing strap, making him execute a comedic dive that almost had him landing headfirst into Clarissa's lap. He caught himself with one hand on the edge of her table, but not before his knees had hit the floor.

'Dearie me, I didn't know we had to get down and pray before the starters!' Clarissa giggled loudly as she animatedly pointed out Llewelyn's predicament to the gathered ladies.

Embarrassed, Llewelyn quickly rose to his feet. He'd gone down with such a thump, he was sure he'd dislocated a kneecap, but like a kid who has fallen over in the playground, he didn't want to roll up his trousers and check lest his humiliation be highlighted and compounded. Instead he chose to limp his way discreetly to his intended destination, Table 4. 'I said you can't sit there; it's for cast members only!' he barked, whilst pulling out a chair to lay claim to the circular six-seater.

Brenda Mortinsen blushed profusely. Her plump fingers danced nervously on the tablecloth, looking for an outlet. They found it in the shape of a napkin, she fluttered it out and then began to refold it. 'But this is where we were told to sit, weren't we, Millie?' She looked to Millie and anyone else that was available to support her statement as she finished the napkin into the shape of a butterfly. 'And we sat on this table last night.'

Bree quickly intervened. She'd seen Llewelyn in full flow earlier in the bar, and didn't fancy having any of the WI ladies in conflict with him. He was full of his own self-importance, definitely lacking in compassion towards his fellow humans, and sadly devoid of humour. 'Thank you, Mr Black, I'll take care of this–' She placed a comforting arm around Brenda. '–but I do think there is a much nicer way to speak to others if you need their cooperation, don't you?'

Llewelyn huffed loudly, clearly offended at Bree's intervention. He stood back and waited for Brenda, Millie and Hilda to move to another table, gently ushered by Bree. As soon as they had vacated their seats, he used Brenda's folded napkin to flick away imaginary specks from the table before placing his jacket over the back of one of the chairs.

He had conquered the Winterbottom Women's Institute and had now laid claim to Table 4. His world was as it should be.

This whole exchange was observed by Selma, who sat quietly and unnoticed on Table 11. She was dining solo. She twisted the large rainbow moonstone around her finger, contemplating. She already had her next victim within her sights, but wouldn't another one, quite unrelated to the reason why she was here, be like a gift to herself? She had recognised him immediately, but Llewelyn had so obviously failed to recognise her. She gently patted her red curls with her hand and choked back a snort of laughter. Hardly surprising, really.

She thought back to all the rejections she had endured over the years. The times she had been passed over for roles she would have been perfect for, given on a whim by the casting director to someone who was either younger or more aesthetically pleasing. Selma detested the arrogance of those that held your future in their hands with their scripts and productions. Men like Llewelyn Black who had denied her the chance to shine all those years ago. Her train of thought was suddenly interrupted.

'Clara, where on earth have you been? It's almost time to start. This will never do; when we get back to Chapperton Bliss, you and I need to have a word.' Llewelyn pushed Clara in an effort to hasten her doddery steps. He tapped his watch. 'Places, please, everyone!'

Clara muttered to herself. Pulling her handbag closer to her chest, she bristled with indignation. 'I'll have more than a few choice words, Llewelyn. I don't know about Francesca Moore, I think it's "more of Francesca" every Wednesday afternoon, if you get my drift!' She sniffed loudly, jutted out her chin, and sat herself down, plonking her handbag and then her prop, the chiffon scarf, onto the table. 'I'm sure Mrs Black would like to know whose floury baps you've been fondling during half day closing at the bakery!' She pointed a finger accusingly at Llewelyn.

Francesca, who was busy channelling the 'flighty' side of her character, almost fell off her chair. The first flush of guilt burned on her cheeks. Her eyes quickly scanned the other cast members. Dirk's were the first to bore into her. She squirmed in her seat. 'I *ther*tainly don't know what you're talking about; don't be *tho thi*lly, Clara!'

Dirk clenched his teeth together. Why he had believed Francesca was out of his league was beyond him, when it was now quite clear she'd been getting down and dirty with the Lecherous Llewelyn all along. 'Now it all makes sense...' he grunted to nobody in particular.

'I said it before, and I'll say it again: one day you'll be the death of me, Clara Toomey. Now enough of this nonsense, we've got a show to put on.' Flustered, Llewelyn clapped his hands together as though he were bringing a primary school class to attention.

Selma smiled.

Oh yes, one more wouldn't hurt at all; in fact, it might even add to the fun.

TAMING THE SHREW

'Bloody hell, is that the time!?' Pru threw back the duvet, skipped over her discarded clothes, and vaulted the second single bed. In doing so, she gifted a bemused Andy with the sight of her bare bottom and a flurry of chestnut curls tumbling down her back as she disappeared into the bathroom. 'I can't believe how quick that was!'

'Actually, if you're referring to me and my performance, I thought I lasted quite well to be honest – considering I haven't seen you in like, forever.' Andy stretched out his legs and grinned, waiting for her response. When he was with Pru he wanted everything to last forever; she had not only stolen his heart, but she had stolen time too. It was endless in her company.

She popped her head around the door, toothbrush waving in one hand, toothpaste tube in the other. 'It was my nap that was quick, I fell asleep…'

'Not during, I hope!' He jumped out of bed and grabbed a T-shirt from his backpack. 'What about this?' He held up a mottled black and grey affair.

Pru shook her head. 'It's a proper dinner, three-course with coffee. Maybe something a little less casual, hey?' She disappeared back into the bathroom.

Ten minutes later they were both taking their seats at Table 7 with Bree and Lucy. The performance hadn't yet started, but Pru could see it wasn't far off. The ones she had tagged as actors at the previous evening's dinner were in position, and a few others she still wasn't too sure about.

'So what's all this about Bentley Montgomery, then? Bree's filled me in on some of it before her head hit the pillow for her afternoon siesta.' Lucy took a sip of wine.

'Nothing much, to be honest. I think he's done a disappearing act as he knew he was going to get rumbled for the thefts. Bree's sitting on the fence at the moment, only because there's nothing to indicate that he knew we were on to him – so if he didn't know or suspect, then why run?'

Andy tipped his head, deep in thought, swirling his spoon in the bowl of soup that had just been placed before him. He stared into the green depths of the liquid. 'How about we just have a nice evening? No thoughts of missing persons, no drama – apart from the obvious floorshow–' He nodded towards Llewelyn and Co. '–just a simple, normal night, hey?'

Pru grinned and gave Bree a comical wink. 'Normal! When have we ever been normal, Andy?' She stuck out her tongue and went cross-eyed. 'Isn't my quirkiness the very thing you found attractive about me?'

Lucy could see where this was going and quickly placed her hands over her ears and began the 'La La' song. There were some things she didn't want to know or hear about her sergeant.

'Erm... nope not really... think it was more to do with the fact that you can put your legs behind the back of your head without really trying – or at least that's what you told me you could do!'

Their flirty chatter continued, Andy teasing Pru relentlessly, all in good fun, Lucy alternating between laughter and embarrassment, fully aware that she would never see her boss in the same light again, and Bree? Well, she was just delighted to have all her friends together and with a night of good food, wine and a bloody good murder to look forward to, she couldn't be happier.

Tarragon and Stephanie had chosen to dine with their guests rather than in their private suite, and now occupied Table 9 together. Stephanie was making light work of a bottle of 2017 Château Haut-Brion Pessac-Léognan at a mere £390 a bottle, delivered earlier in the year from Harrods, and brought to their table this evening by Smithers. It galled Tarragon to think they were on the bones of their arses and yet she was happily chugging good money down her throat at a great rate of knots.

He leant forward, placing his hand on her arm, keeping his voice low. 'Take it easy, Steph, you're quaffing that like it's ruddy water. Those two glasses have cost as much as your last Botox job, and have your forgotten what's in the freezer? We're not celebrating, you know.'

She pulled her arm away from him and fixed him with her much talked about death stare. He wasn't sure if she was really angry or if she was actually evidencing the effects of the aforementioned Botox, and had lost the ability to move even the smallest of facial muscles in response. His blood ran cold as she reciprocated with her hand, placing it gently on his forearm, just below the cuff of his jacket. She paused so as to build the tension and then painfully dug her red talons into his skin. He winced, watching it pucker under the pressure.

Yep, she was definitely angry, now he was for it.

He made a feeble attempt to placate her, but was rudely interrupted by a commotion from the table next to them.

'It's green!' Hilda's startled voice lifted above the gentle hum of everyone else's chatter.

Every head turned towards Table 8, where Hilda, along with Millie, Brenda, Florrie, Ethel and Clarissa were seated.

'Of course it's green, Hilda! It's broccoli and stilton soup; what other colour did you expect it to be when you ordered it? Pink with lilac spots?' Clarissa's spoon clattered into her bowl. She picked up the small wholemeal bap and broke it in half before reaching for the butter.

Hilda wasn't to be placated. Flustered, she beckoned over to the waiter. 'I think we all need some Femfresh for our soup to lighten it up a bit, please?'

Ethel almost choked. 'Bloody hell, I'd rather not have women's intimate hygiene products dribbled over me florets, if it's all the same with you!' She slapped the table and let out a roar of laughter, which encouraged everyone else to join in. 'Maybe you'd like to try a blob of crème fraîche instead, Hilda?' she helpfully expounded.

Tarragon was grateful for the distraction as Stephanie's nails relaxed their hold on his skin. The laughter rose high to reach the crystal chandeliers; he could almost imagine them tinkling with the vibrations, sending out an angelic refrain. This train of thought took him to how music soothed the soul and reportedly could also soothe a savage beast.

And in all honesty, there was no greater beast than Stephanie Elizabeth Montgomery, but judging by her stony face, even a full-on bloody symphony orchestra wasn't about to support that urban myth.

SETTING THE SCENE

*C*lara sat rigid in her chair at Table 4. She still prickled with indignation at Llewelyn's attitude towards her. It rankled that she had been the one he had singled out for criticism on her tardiness, when she knew only too well that some of the other Dingleberries struggled with the passing of time more often than she did.

'Clara, you're not concentrating...' Marilyn Peacock as the Spinster hissed through the side of her mouth, which was set in an unnatural grin.

'Marilyn, if you are attempting a theatrical prompt whilst facing our audience, then you really do need to be a bit more animated with your facial expressions to detract from your dentures, my dear. They're slightly awry with a smattering of broccoli bits stuck between them.' Clara pointed her finger at her own dentures and wiggled her nail between incisor and canine to demonstrate her point.

Marilyn almost blushed, although it was hard to tell, considering the amount of theatrical blending powder she had used.

Francesca stood up from the table she had been sharing with Julie and Dirk and came to Marilyn's defence, taking a seat next to Clara to split the two ladies up. This had been the stage direction in the script anyway; she had just brought it forward by a few minutes. 'Oh come on, Clara, don't be so mean, what on earth is wrong with–'

'Ladies, will you do me the honour of allowing me to join you?' Dirk Diamond in his role as the Murderer, who was following his part of the script to the letter, interrupted them. He looked bemused, popping his eyes at Clara, Marilyn and Francesca in an attempt to bring them back into line. They were quick to follow his lead.

'Of course, do take a seat...' The Spinster patted the empty chair beside her and beckoned him to sit.

They chatted between themselves, projecting their voices as one would on the stage to ensure their audience could hear them and follow the storyline. The comings and goings of the Waiter and the Waitress brought a *Fawlty Towers* element of humour to the proceedings, and Eleanor Rimple simply excelled as the Hard of Hearing Elderly Dowager, which delighted Hilda no end.

The Winterbottom ladies licked the end of their pencils and, like a good game of Bingo in the Winterbottom parish hall every Wednesday night, they bent their heads and set to on their little books, making notes and careful observations. One or two decided to try a collaborative approach by sharing their suspicions; others sat like school children in an exam with their arms covering their notes, keen that nobody else would peep and cheat and solve the murder before them.

Chelsea and Cassidy by now had consumed one too many vodkas and were fluttering eyelashes at the dishy-looking Handsome Bachelor. Each time Chelsea winked at him, his cheeks flushed pink, forcing a smattering of perspiration to pepper his top lip. Pru half suspected that probably one or the other of the girls would end up in bed before 10pm – and not necessarily alone.

As the tension began to build in the room, the Dingleberries continued to give a fabulous performance. Already half of their audience had taken an instant dislike to Dirk Diamond, such was his portrayal of the Handsome Bachelor / the Murderer although at this point they were completely unaware of his secondary role or his intent. Sympathy was being directed towards the Spinster, who was generally confused and without direction. Llewelyn was quietly seething on Table 13 as he checked his director's notes in the script. Marilyn was confused and without direction because it was quite obvious she'd hit the bloody sherry before curtain-up and had forgotten her lines.

Without warning, the lights went off. This was followed by a crashing and clattering sound as the Hard of Hearing Elderly Dowager on Table 5 screamed, her mouth frozen in horror as she waved her hands in the air. The darkness held as muffled grunts, audible gasps and the sound of a chair falling over filled the room, before it was once again flooded with light. The sudden clamour of noise, and what the Dowager could now see were the contents of her table strewn across the floor, had almost given her a heart attack. She patted her chest in an effort to appease the vital organ that was still pounding against her rib cage.

Every head turned towards her.

'This is it, ooh how exciting.' Ethel slurped loudly from her glass of port. She hunched up her shoulders in glee and leant forward in anticipation. 'Place your bets, girls; who do you think it is that's going to meet the Grim Reaper?'

Llewelyn checked his notes again. This was all wrong, it should have been Francesca screaming, not Eleanor. He licked his middle finger and feverishly flicked through the script as though that action could remedy the situation.

Dirk Diamond stood in the middle of the room over the slumped body of Clara Toomey, the Victim, his handsome bachelor features etched with confusion. He held out his hands and shrugged his shoulders as he looked to Llewelyn for direction. He couldn't believe the stupid old biddy had taken a dive before he'd even had chance to do his bit with the scarf. Maybe Llewelyn might take notice of him now and start encouraging younger members to join the Dingleberries rather than several old trouts who couldn't hold a line, let alone a stage direction. When no assistance was forthcoming from Llewelyn, he ad-libbed.

'Oh my, the dear woman, has she fainted...?' He knelt down beside her to check her pulse. The chiffon scarf around her neck, draped and flowed across the floor like a celebration streamer.

Whilst all eyes were fixed on the tableau before them, Selma took the opportunity to slip towards the back of the room. Her hand hovered over the third acorn on the carved oak panel to the left of the fireplace.

In a flash that was worthy of any stage production, she vanished.

THE ACT

A FEW MOMENTS EARLIER...

*C*lara had been less than impressed with Marilyn and her ridiculously tipsy behaviour. If she wasn't careful, she would ruin the whole scene. She nudged Marilyn's arm to deliberately spill the contents of the small schooner glass she was holding; it plopped over the rim and splattered its burgundy stain onto the white tablecloth.

'What did you do that for?' Marilyn spat at her; a look of incredulity etched on her face.

Clara tutted. 'You're drunk, and you're going to ruin the whole performance. Put it down and behave!' She looked to Dirk and Francesca for at least some support. This time Francesca chose to ignore the sniping and Dirk was now too far in the zone to care.

The lighting in the Belvedere Dining Room suddenly dimmed, allowing the stage lighting that Phil Timkins, before taking on his role of The Doctor, had set up that afternoon with the assistance of Ralf Barnard.

Clara squinted as the follow spot lit up first herself and then moved around the room to give the audience the chance to pick out the other characters. As the dimness enveloped her table, she took the opportunity to quickly take the chiffon scarf from her handbag and arrange it around her neck. The consensus of opinion had been to add to the mystery by not revealing the potential murder weapon too soon. The audience would then have to decide if it had been brought specifically for the task of murder, or if it had been an opportune modus operandi.

She sat waiting for Dirk to do his duty.

She sensed he was behind her and mentally prepared herself for the performance of a lifetime.

Deep breath, Clara, deep breath...

The seconds ticked by. She could hear Francesca orating her lines and she was aware of Marilyn flunking her own narration, which irritated her profoundly, but what she wasn't aware of was any tightening around her neck, not even a slight pull from the chiffon scarf, the theatrical pull she and Dirk had practised more times than she cared to remember.

For goodness' sake, Dirk, do your bit!

She waited, she closed her eyes, she waited some more.

And then it started.

The room was suddenly plunged into darkness as the most excruciating pain she had ever felt in her seventy-plus years thudded into her back, right between her shoulder blades. She wanted to breathe in sharply, to suck in the air and fill her lungs, but she couldn't. Her hands splayed out in front of her as she tried to grab at the edge of the tablecloth to stop her descent. She paused momentarily as her knees hit the floor. She slowly turned her head, desperate to see who was behind her, who had been responsible for the agony she was experiencing.

'You...' The dim light from the fire exit sign eerily glowed through the darkness upon the face of her assailant.

This is not an act; please can't anyone see what's happening to me...?

The voice was in her head, too quiet for anyone to hear, too hushed for anyone to react. She held out one hand, as though to beseech someone, anyone, to help her, as the fingers on her other hand pulled at the crisp cotton material. The damask cloth slipped from the table, carrying with it the silver cutlery, a plate, two glasses and her handbag. They clattered to the floor, the noise masking her own groans as she too fell beside them. Lying on her back, she looked up to the ceiling, she felt no pain, no hurt, no drama; there was just a simple peace as the brightness once again returned to the room.

How pretty the crystal lights look, like fireflies and fairies...

She watched them break away from the chandeliers and flutter around the room, her hand slowly lifting upwards in the hope she could touch one, maybe even feel their magic, but her fingers danced into the empty air.

Ah, now there was applause. They were showing their appreciation of her performance as the spotlight focused on her and her alone.

Clap, clap, clap...

If only she could stand up, she would take a bow, maybe even several, for her performance of a lifetime...

Dirk was kneeling beside her; he was talking to her, but she couldn't quite make out his words. Her eyes were beginning to cloud over; there was a desperate need for sleep.

'Dirk, I... I...' Clara's hand trembled as she lifted her finger, pointing to the grand fireplace. '... smell the...'

And with one last laboured sigh, her head dropped to one side and she was gone; gone to a place where she would at last get to see Lionel, her beloved but long-dead husband – who would no doubt be waiting to greet her wearing his much talked about basque and a pair of size 11, sparkly red stilettos.

THE AFTERMATH

*D*irk thought it prudent to stick to the script. He was quite sure that Clara was dead, but it definitely wasn't by his own fair hand; this was certainly not his doing. His fingers hadn't even chanced to touch the chiffon scarf, let alone pull it tight around her scrawny neck. He did as Clara's last words had asked and tentatively sniffed the air. He could smell nothing out of the ordinary.

He stood staring at her for a few seconds more, quite fascinated as to how quickly death could soften the lines of old age on the face of a corpse. It must have been a heart attack, after all she was getting on a bit; add to that a few scoops of sherry along with a hike in her blood pressure when Marilyn wound her up, they were the perfect ingredients for a *wham, bam, thank you, ma'am* style of passing.

'Is there a doctor in the house?' Dirk almost cringed at that predictable line. He'd begged Llewelyn to change it, but he might as well have been talking to a brick wall. Now he'd said it, it actually sounded quite appropriate. He was amazed at how the audience sat like well-behaved children, relishing the scene being played out in front of them, totally oblivious to its reality.

Ignorant to the change in circumstances, the Doctor, played by Phil Timkins, rose from his seat. 'Yes, I'm a doctor, please keep calm everyone; remain in your seats...' He grabbed his prop, which was actually his real-life doctor's bag, and hurried over to the now lifeless form of Clara Toomey. He bent down and made a show of taking her wrist to check for a pulse. He paused, moving his fingers along the radial pulse, he waited for the familiar throb.

Nothing.

'Shit...' The word crept almost silently from the corner of his mouth. He tried again, this time on her carotid artery. 'Dirk, what the hell did you do?' Fully aware that this was now not any part of the script, he quickly broke away from his character to become the real Dr Timkins BMchB, MRCGP. 'Clear the room, Dirk, make any excuse, but just do it – *now!*'

Llewelyn was already on his feet, his face almost purple with anger. 'What the hell is going on?' he growled. 'Have you all lost your minds? Are you incapable of following a script, for Christ's sake?'

'She's dead.' Phil informed him with a blunt, hushed reverence.

'*I know she's bloody dead*, she's supposed to be! She's the damned victim – what else would she be doing, dancing a ruddy fandango!?' A blood vessel on Llewelyn's temple bulged and throbbed unnaturally.

Phil turned Clara onto her side. A pool of crimson that had been contained underneath her jacket began to spread out across the floor. 'No, I mean she's *really* dead, and if I'm not mistaken this is our murder weapon...' He pointed to the moulded Dupont handle of the Robert Welch steak knife that was fully embedded in Clara's back.

Llewelyn stood stunned, his fingers nervously fidgeting with his burgundy-spotted cravat. 'Thank God I had the fish...' was all he could mutter.

Dirk, on autopilot, quickly grabbed the tablecloth from the

floor and draped it across Clara, affording her some dignity and hiding her from the eyes of the unsuspecting. He stood before his audience with an air of theatrical aplomb. 'Ladies and gentlemen, thank you for joining us for the first half of our production, *Murder at the Montgomery Hall Hotel.* Please make your way to the lounge bar for a wee drink or two during the interval, whilst you solve our mystery.'

Those who were capable of arising from their seats on their own accord did so to offer a standing ovation for Clara's most excellent performance. As the enthusiastic clapping swelled around the room, the Dingleberries could do no more than acknowledge their appreciation. They remained in character, bowed in unison and waited for the room to empty.

The Winterbottom ladies shuffled their chairs backwards whilst collecting their pencils, notebooks, and handbags, nattering ten to the dozen.

'I didn't see that coming, did you, Clarissa?' Ethel was the first to make mention of the 50–1 outsider Clara Toomey getting smoked. 'Did they mess up, though? I couldn't see how she'd been murdered. Could you?'

Clarissa was keeping one eye on their conversation and the other on Hilda, who was currently minesweeping the tables of all the after-dinner mints. She watched as Hilda hastily brushed the green foil wrapped coins into her handbag before snapping the clasp shut in triumph. 'Mmm... no, not really, I think it might have had something to do with that scarf she was wearing.'

'To the bar, to the bar, let's have another jar...' Cassidy sang her way through the double doors, closely followed by Chelsea and the rest of the Winterbottom crew, who waddled behind her like penguins at feeding time.

Their suspicions aroused by Llewelyn's odd reaction, only Andy, Pru, Bree and Lucy remained in the room.

～

In the rooms, in the walls, in the passages winding,
  The darkness, the odour, of damp and decay,
  In the walls of the rooms, it is here I'm residing,
  Come to the wall, child, come inside and play.

Selma edged her way along the passage, led by the faint light from the torch. She gently tapped it against the palm of her hand, hoping it would elicit a stronger beam. When that failed, she resorted to using her fingers to touch the wattle and daub of the walls, feeling her way as a secondary sense. Every now and then she would spike herself with a splinter of aged wood, curse quietly and then wonder if it was divine retribution, God's way of paying her back for old Toomey the Trout's very recent, and in Selma's opinion, quite spectacular, demise. She had mulled this one over in some depth during the late afternoon: the pros, the cons and the how. It had been the sudden realisation that a murder and all the histrionics that followed would be a marvellous distraction whilst she executed the next part of her plan. The fact that she couldn't be sure Clara would soon cotton on and make mention of her sudden appearance from the Belvedere Dining Room panel, was also a deciding factor.

She had only walked this route once before; her mind's eye was now choreographing the steps she needed to take, utilising all her memories, unpicking the jumble in her brain like it was a ball of cheap 2-ply wool. She stopped and listened. Her hand counted out the panels until she found the one she had remembered from all those years ago. She gently pushed until it clicked. Stepping through the opening, her eyes fell upon the untouched and unchanged room of the man himself: Hugo Frederick Montgomery. She stood mesmerised by the portrait of Cecily and Hugo that was hung with precision over the marble mantle.

Leaning closer, she found what she had been looking for, the one thing that meant she was on the right track.

The quote that Hugo would recite as his mantra, the one she always believed was his secret code, his pointer, his clue.

She traced her finger across the brass plaque and smiled.

Trust that the treasure we look for is hidden in the ground on which we stand...
Henri Nouwen

THOSE IN THE KNOW...

$\mathcal{T}$he doors to the Belvedere Dining Room remained firmly closed, keeping out those that did not need to know, and holding in those that had no choice but to know.

Andy stepped forward, holding out his warrant card. 'Detective Sergeant Andy Barnes; could I ask that you all move away from, er–' He looked down at the sprawled body of Clara Toomey outlined under the white cloth, a small red sherry stain marking where her heart would be. '–er... the lady and take a seat. Please do not leave the room.'

The cast of the Dingleberries duly obliged, all huddling together on the larger of the recently vacated tables, apart from Llewelyn. Even in the death of one of his own, he wasn't about to relinquish his control or standing.

'I am Llewelyn Black, Director of the Dingleberry Amateur Dramatics Society and lead actor,' he perfectly stated, whilst producing a small calling card. 'Clara was one of mine, not particularly good to be honest, but she could play an excellent murder victim.' He tilted his head and stared just a little too long at poor Clara's body. 'I've got to say, this truly was her best performance to date, although she could have done with dragging it out a bit more to hold the tension.'

Incredulous, Pru dropped the sides of her mouth down, wrinkled her nose, and looked at Bree for her reaction. She couldn't believe anyone could be so devoid of sympathy or understanding about what had just happened. She wanted to join Andy and help him, but knew that this was now his and Lucy's remit, not hers. The silence in the room was desperately uncomfortable; it felt the same as the dead air she'd once experienced at Winterbridge Theatre Pavilion when the curtain went down after Act 1. That time the perpetrators were an audience that consisted almost solely of an over-eighties pensioners' club and a posse from the Sisters of the Immaculate Conception; the latter having mistakenly taken the poster outside advertising *The Second Coming of Christian Messenger* as a religious celebration rather than a rip-roaring sex comedy. Even though her current mood was supposed to be sombre, she still felt the urge to giggle at the memory of a dozen robed nuns fanning themselves in horror as they executed a starburst pattern along the aisles, desperately trying to find a way out before the curtain went up on Act 2.

She glanced at Bree. She hadn't spoken a word since it had become very obvious that this was a real murder and not some fantasy guessing game. Her skin had gone quite pallid, which worried Pru. She pushed a glass of red wine towards her. 'Here, take a few sips, it'll help.'

Bree, clearly in shock, knocked back almost half the glass before she found her voice. 'It's a dead body, Pru, a real-life dead body, and we sat here and watched it happen.'

'Oh stop moaning – it's not like we charge extra for it, you know!' Dirk sarcastically spat from the next table.

Andy bristled. 'I think that's enough, don't you?' He raised one eyebrow and indicated for Llewelyn to take a seat next to Dirk. 'Sir, if you could ensure your ensemble don't hinder or interfere with the investigation or the witnesses, that would go a long way in assisting me.'

Andy beckoned Lucy, asking her to start taking personal details from the Dingleberries. She nodded several times, her lips pursed together in concentration as she listened intently. Pru strained to hear what was being said, curious as to how Andy would deal with the initial investigation.

'Pru, I need you and Bree to go to the lounge bar and ensure all the other guests are well. You are not to divulge anything to them; do not deny or confirm, just gently back-heel any awkward questions, and try to steer them to the belief that it's all part of the act.' He pulled his mobile phone from his jacket pocket. 'I need time to get things into motion.'

She wanted to hug him, even kiss him, and if circumstances had been different, she would have done. 'I'm here if you need me, you know that.' She gave his arm a gentle squeeze. 'In all honesty, I don't think anyone, apart from us in here, suspects a thing.'

He thought for a moment, his eyes taking in the lack of signal on his phone. 'Good, but ensure nobody leaves Montgomery Hall. Speak to Tarragon and tell him; he needs to know. Ask him to keep everything as normal as possible. The last thing I need is a panic on my hands.'

Pru ushered Bree towards the door. She took a brief second to turn and watch her Delectable Detective at work, and wondered if it were at all possible to feel frightened but safe, all at the same time.

IT'S A WRAP

Smithers made his way across the Great Hall towards the main doors. He was fully aware of what had just taken place; he hadn't got to his ripe old age without becoming part of the fabric of Montgomery Hall. What he didn't know about the comings and goings you could write on a postage stamp, which was why the disappearance of Bentley hadn't flummoxed him in the slightest. If he had cared a jot about the hideous boy, he might have been concerned. As it was, he was pleased to see that Ellie Shacklady was now safe from his lecherous leerings and octopus hands.

Smithers hurried as fast as his legs would carry him; there was no time to waste. He jingled the ornate keys that hung from the large brass ring clutched in his right hand. He had already ensured that all other exits had been fully secured, and the Great Doors were his last port of call, although in truth no sane person would surely venture outside whilst the storm still raged. Then again, surely it had been no sane person that had ensured the grisly demise of Clara Toomey. He was surprised that the majority of the guests had no inkling of the scene that had played out in front of them. It was true that the mind will only accept what it is told to see.

And in this case, they had expected a murder, so a murder they saw and bizarrely enough, they had given it a standing ovation.

'Smithers…' Tarragon beckoned him from the doorway of the Belvedere Dining Room.

He rattled the Great Doors, checking their security before setting off again with his jaunty half-run, half-walk gait until he reached his master. 'Sir?'

'Is the coast clear?' A bead of sweat trickled from Tarragon's forehead. He wiped it away with the back of his hand.

'Yes sir, everyone is in the Somerset Room, the Psychic Night is going to go ahead as planned, which should keep them all occupied, and the staff have been confined to the kitchens until further notice. I have been assured of their utmost discretion.' Smithers gave Tarragon a curt bow of his head.

Andy finished writing notes in his book and took one final photograph of the scene. 'This is not ideal, but in the absence of any feasible way of contacting the outside world, this is the best we've got to go with.' He checked his phone again. Still no signal. 'Are we absolutely sure the road is impassable? Is there no other route in or out of the estate?'

Tarragon ran his hand through his hair in frustration. 'No, when Montgomery Hall was built, my great-great-grandfather Ernest ensured it was built on a man-made island with only one approach road. This is the only route for vehicles or on foot, so other than crossing by boat when we haven't got a hurricane, we're stranded. As of 6pm tonight, the bridge is completely engulfed by water and the boat has broken its moorings. God knows where it'll end up.'

'Clearly old granddaddy wasn't the sociable type then?' Dirk was offering his snide comments again. 'What was he fighting off? Hordes of villagers with pitchforks because he was trifling with their wives?'

'Dirk, that'll do; you're not helping in the slightest.' Marilyn Peacock sniffed loudly.

Ignoring Dirk and his asides, Andy concentrated on the task in hand. 'Right, this is as forensically preserved as I can get it under the circumstances.'

Everyone turned to take a last look at poor Clara who was now trussed up like a roll of carpet in a large polythene wrap that Smithers had procured from the stationary cupboard. Every inch of her was encased, along with the murder weapon still embedded in her back. A good quality packing tape was wound around her, ensuring nothing could either escape or would contaminate. Andy pulled off the latex gloves he'd found in the hotel's first-aid tin and popped them into a small brown paper bag. He folded the top, taped it down, and then initialled, timed and dated it.

Tarragon looked at the large cut away in his expensive Axminster hospitality carpet. The missing Rossini trefoils almost broke his heart. The second bundle held this section of carpet spread out on the polythene. Several large brown paper bags held the other items of potential evidence, all forensically collected and stored.

'Right, I'm led to believe you have a large walk-in freezer in the cellar.' Andy directed his comment to Tarragon. 'We really don't have much choice but to store the body there; it's the only way we can preserve her until we can get anyone out here.'

Tarragon felt sick. That one word made him feel as though the world was about to fall out of his tightly clenched backside. He tried to speak, but his throat had constricted so tightly he thought he would choke to death right there and then on the spot to join Clara Toomey in a rigid pose. 'Freezer! I... I... er..., we can't do that, there's food in there, it'll contaminate the food.' He looked to Smithers for help. 'Isn't that right?'

If Tarragon could have got down on his hands and knees to pray for salvation, he would have done so. The thought of Cecily, rigor mortis having set in and then compounded by the -22°C temperature, made his blood run cold – granted not as cold as Cecily's would currently be, but cold enough to chill his own bones.

Smithers could feel himself almost revelling in his master's discomfort, but quickly realised that he too would be implicated in the cover-up and ensuing disrespectful storage of poor Cecily. If discovered, they couldn't even proffer a decent and acceptable excuse. Somehow the financial reasoning behind deep freezing the old dear, then thawing her out a week later on the shagpile rug in her suite whilst they all wept and wailed at the discovery of her apparent 'sudden' death, seemed a little far-fetched.

This thought prompted Smithers into action. 'Leave it to me, sir. I'll just rearrange the *contents*; we can utilise the smaller side section with the separate door.' He emphasised the word 'contents' and gave a reassuring smile to Tarragon.

Andy popped his notebook in the inside pocket of his jacket. 'Thank you, and do you have a drying room?' He pointed to the large section of cut-away carpet.

'Of course, sir. I'll make the necessary arrangements...' Smithers began his jaunty trot back across the Great Hall, his mind working ten to the dozen whilst he formulated his plan for the safe storage of Mrs Clara Toomey (deceased) and the saving of Mr Tarragon Montgomery's clenching buttocks.

KNOCK, KNOCK...

*S*elma spread the plans for Montgomery Hall out across her bed. Her little foray to both Hugo and Ernest's suites had not been the success she had hoped it would be. Without ripping up the floorboards, she couldn't be certain that the missing wealth wasn't secreted in any of those rooms. As a child she'd heard talk of Ernest's strange ways, the fact that for the latter part of his life, rumoured to be over twenty-five years, he had not once left his suite. Only his financial advisors and most trusted staff had been allowed entry.

'It's got to be somewhere,' she muttered to herself. Her fingers traced the rooms on the top floor of the plans, as she mentally worked out the available passages in conjunction with the rooms she had yet to search.

She glanced at the file next to her. The tip of one of her photographs peeped out from the top. She pulled it towards her. The faded black and white print had already started to produce a sepia bloom, making it all the more poignant. Gazing at the laughing, carefree faces of the subjects, she sadly wondered where it had all gone wrong. She was so engrossed in nostalgia, she didn't hear the gentle tap on the door, nor was she aware of someone standing behind her – until it was too late.

'Don't you people ever knock?' she growled whilst trying to push the paperwork back into her briefcase. The file slipped from the bed and fell to the floor, scattering more aged photographs.

'I did knock; you just didn't hear me!' Stephanie snapped back. 'They're ready for you in the Somerset Room...' Her attention drawn to the paperwork on the floor; she momentarily dismissed Selma's presence.

Selma, on the other hand, was more than aware of Stephanie's interest in what lay scattered on the patterned carpet. She was also more than aware of what would happen next. Discreetly opening her large tapestry bag, she rummaged around inside.

A spark of recognition, a sharp intake of breath, an eerie silence...

Stephanie stood stunned, her eyes darting from the photographs to Selma and back again. It took a moment, just one small moment, but that was long enough for Selma to reach a decision and for Stephanie to connect the wisps of familiarity that had tantalisingly taunted her since she had first met Psychic Selma.

'*You!*' she gasped.

Before she had the chance to utter another word, a gauze pad was swiftly pressed across Stephanie's nose and mouth. She vainly fought; she scratched with her beautifully manicured nails, and she would have bitten down hard with her pearly white porcelain veneers if she could have freed her mouth from the hand that suffocated her. A sickly-sweet smell cloyed at her nostrils, making her stomach retch as a distant buzzing like a swarm of angry bees resonated in her ears. And then darkness enveloped her.

~

If Selma could have cursed loudly, she would have done. This was the last thing she needed. Sometimes it was exhilarating to be put on the spot, to duck and dive, change plans at a whim, but this was too close for comfort.

She looked down at the sprawled body of Stephanie Montgomery and checked her watch. She had managed to drag her through the first section of passages, and if she could get through the next set of twists and turns in the time she had remaining, she would consider her next move later tonight, after her imminent performance in the Somerset Room. She hooked her hands and forearms under Stephanie's armpits and began to haul her along, her limp body leaving a ragged trail in the dust and debris. Once or twice, one or both legs failed to make the sharp turn and became wedged between the wall and the lath and plaster frame, forcing her to stop. A heel from one of Stephanie's Christian Louboutin shoes was the first casualty, quickly followed by the whole shoe on the next turn.

The minutes were ticking by.

'Stephanie, Stephanie... you just couldn't leave it, could you? You just had to put two and two together...' Selma half sang as she pulled her into the small area that opened out near to where the dumb waiter was housed. She pushed Stephanie into a sitting position against the wall as she efficiently bound her legs and hands. Tearing a strip of masking tape, she carefully positioned it over her mouth, ensuring her nose was clear.

Stephanie groaned and stirred. The whites of her eyes eerily shone in the near darkness, picked out by Selma's torch, showing her utter terror. Selma leant forward, index finger on her lips. 'Sshh, Mrs Montgomery. Now you have a little rest and I'll be back later. You can then tell me everything you know about the family fortune...' she whispered, before turning in a flurry of cloak and dust. 'Don't do anything I wouldn't do whilst I'm gone, will you?'

A cackling laugh echoed along the passage as Selma disappeared from view, taking with her the only source of light that had fleetingly stopped the darkness from eating poor Stephanie up.

Stephanie closed her eyes, her tears forming a track through the grime on her cheeks as a sob caught in her throat.

The Montgomery Curse had returned and was alive and kicking – and rather than living the dream, she was now living the nightmare it had brought with it.

SUBSTITOOTHS

*T*he Winterbottom ladies settled themselves down on the front row, eager for the evening's performance by Psychic Selma to begin. When Tarragon Montgomery had announced the doors were open and the Somerset Room was ready to welcome them, a posse, headed by Clarissa and Ethel, had ensured their pole position in the race for the best seats. This had unfortunately left two of the Dingleberries nursing a few minor injuries.

'I haven't seen an elbow execution like that since the toilet roll shortage in Morrisons. Well done, Brenda!' Millie Thomas was beside herself with glee. The sight of Brenda's chubby elbow making contact with a set of masculine ribs belonging to Dirk Diamond as she barged herself through the small gap had inspired the others to follow suit.

An array of body parts had flown into action, scattering other Dingleberries in several different directions, paving a clear path to the front. Clarissa had been the first to flop down on the velour padded chair. She patted the one next to her.

'Here you go, Ethel.' She shoved her handbag under her seat. 'Hilda, you sit next to Ethel. Millie can sit the other side of you.'

210

MURDERS AT THE MONTGOMERY HALL HOTEL

Clarissa loved the bones of Hilda, but she was still very grateful that Millie was happy to take on the 'caring' duties for her friend, as she could often become a little wearying.

As if on cue, Hilda adjusted her hearing aid, forcing it to emit a loud screech.

Wheeeeeeeeeeeeeee.

Everyone flinched. 'Ooh, the spirits are active tonight, aren't they?' Hilda muttered. 'All this screaming and wailing will wake the dead!'

Ethel sniggered. 'It was you...'

'Me what?' Hilda carried on poking her auditory orifices.

Wheeeeeeeeeeeeeee.

'There it goes again. Can someone tell whoever's screaming to wind their neck in; there's no need to be so dramatic!' Hilda harrumphed in annoyance. 'It's giving me the heebie-jeebies...'

Ethel made the wise decision to give up explaining anything to her and rummaged in her handbag instead. Plucking out a packet of mint imperials, she rustled the bag and offered them along the line. 'That's the whole object of the evening, Hilda, it's Halloween...' she wriggled her fingers in the air, '...Whooooooo! Whooooooo!'

Hearing the laughter and joviality amongst her group, Pru breathed a sigh of relief. She took her seat at the end of the front row, next to Bree. 'What a bloody nightmare, hey?'

Bree nodded. 'How on earth are we going to keep what's happened from everyone? Surely if we've got a murderer at large, we need to let them know, or how else will they stay safe?'

Pru knew she was right; she'd had the same thoughts too. She knew Andy was going to find a way of divulging just enough to keep everyone on their guard, but without hindering the investigation once he'd sorted Clara out. She'd already spotted that the staff doors to the Belvedere Dining Room had been secured and locked, and once he'd finished up in that room, the guest entrance doors would receive the same treatment. No doubt they would all be dining in another part of the hotel in the morning.

The haunting strains of Heart's version of 'Stairway to Heaven', along with the sudden dimming of the lights, signalled the start of the floorshow. Pru noticed Ethel fervently passing her sweetie bag along the row again as the ladies settled themselves, ready to be entertained. She quietly hoped it would be a better performance than the previous night.

A sudden flash of purple light heralded Psychic Selma, draped in the now familiar emerald green cloak. She made a great show of flouncing around the make-shift stage, her hands flowing over the glowing crystal ball. To a backdrop of gasps from the audience, Selma appeared to float before their very eyes.

Clarissa curled her lip and side-whispered to Ethel. 'If she's really levitating, then I'm Doris bloody Day!'

Ethel opened her mouth to reply and spat out two half-sucked mint imperials and the top set of her dentures. The mints dropped in her lap, but her dentures clattered across the floor, coming to rest next to Psychic Selma.

Pru looked on in horror.

Jeez, what was it with dentures, Ethel and hotels? Even poor Clara Toomey had fallen foul of the loose top set syndrome in the Great Hall the previous day.

Nonplussed, Ethel had a pretty good expletive on the tip of her tongue, but the absence of her top gnashers meant she wouldn't have been able to form the first two letters: *s* and *h*. The remaining letters were fortunately no trouble at all, but what good was a decent *shit* without the *sh*? Ethel snorted loudly at that thought, which in turn made Kitty, who was sitting in the row behind, prod her in the back as a warning.

'Ladies, gentlemen, members of our little gathering–' Selma dropped her voice to an eerie hush. '–the spirits are strong, they are calling out – speak to me, speak to me,' she hauntingly incanted.

'If you shout a bit louder, Ethel's teeth might have a bit of a chatter with you!' Clarissa sniggered as she pointed to the forlorn clackers on the floor.

Selma's head snapped round to glare, first at Clarissa, and then at the teeth. She aimed a rather large foot clad in a burgundy leather Doc Marten at the forlorn dentures and gave them a hefty kick. They scuttered across the woodblock, hit Cassidy's fake Gucci handbag, and came to a stop. Cassidy bent down and picked them up, and drunkenly checked her own mouth. Once relieved to know they weren't her own cheap clip-on donkey-like veneers, she passed them down the row. Brenda handed them to Millie; she gingerly held them between her finger and thumb and passed them to Hilda – who promptly shoved them in her own mouth. When they wouldn't fit, she spat them into her hand and passed them to Ethel.

'Eeew...' Chelsea couldn't contain her disgust. 'You've just put something in your mouth that wasn't yours!' She dry-retched.

Bree was quick to react. 'Bloody hell, Chels, that's rich coming from you! Remind me what's been in your mouth every Tuesday night for the last two years that didn't belong to you, either!'

'Ladies, please!' Kitty was beside herself with embarrassment. 'I will not tolerate smutty double entendres; we have an ethos to uphold.'

Pru took that as a dig at her for not being more in control of the naughtier members of the WI as their president, but considering there was a dead body currently being housed in the cellar of Montgomery Hall, she felt Bree's rather funny aside was the least of her worries.

Selma interrupted their joviality, annoyed that their banter was ruining the atmosphere. She'd been privy to enough chatter between the ladies to have picked up a few pointers, one being their earlier discussion on the merits of healthy eating. She jabbed a finger at Chelsea. 'You, the spirits have a message for you...'

Chelsea stopped examining her acrylic nails long enough to show surprise that she had been singled out for special treatment by the spirit world.

'...I can see lettuce leaves and celery... yes, yes – they are telling me you have to go vegetarian!' Selma smirked. 'No more trips to the butchers for you, my dear.'

'Blimey, no cucumber in that lot, Chelsea; you *will* be disappointed...' Ethel guffawed loudly. '...and that's *another* smutty double entendre for your notebook, Kitty!'

If Selma could have laughed, she would have done. She was becoming rather fond of this mismatch of ladies, particularly the older dears who didn't seem to have a socially acceptable filter button between them. On the plus side, they would, she hoped, come in handy for the next part of her plan. How the death of Clara Toomey had been kept from this lot, she had no idea; she had been hoping for hysterics and at least some chaos and fear from the murder to act as a cover. Maybe topping the Victim in a stage play had not been one of her brightest ideas to create an extended smoke screen, when everyone had expected her to pop her clogs anyway.

Oh well, back to the drawing board.

AN UNEXPECTED DISCOVERY

*S*mithers yanked the heavy door to the freezer open and reverently stood for a while before entering, momentarily enjoying the blast of freezing air. He shivered. It was cold, but it was also as though someone, maybe Cecily, had walked over his grave. He blew into his hands and stamped his feet.

'Forgive me, Cecily, I'm going to have to move you again...' He wondered if she could actually hear him now she was very much deceased. He hoped there was such a thing as the afterlife, but he hadn't quite made up his mind on that score just yet. Emily had been on at him for quite some time to hurry up and make a decision on where his loyalties lay. She certainly didn't want him going 'down there' as a non-believer when she was very much assured of her place 'up there'. 'Ah, there you are.' He began his little waddle towards the covered and trussed-up body of Cecily.

Smithers stopped in his tracks.

'Well, well, well – what have we got here?' he asked nobody in particular. He bent down and peered at what looked like a side of beef wrapped in muslin, only it wasn't a side of beef at all. Smithers knew every single grocery and domestic item that came into Montgomery Hall, and this one certainly hadn't been on the stock list. Neither had it been there less than forty-eight hours earlier when Cecily had been deposited. Cecily forgotten for the moment; Smithers began to peel away the cloth. He was under no illusion as to what it could be, he just didn't know who.

He folded back the top layer to reveal the head of Bentley Montgomery.

'My dear boy, what a fitting end for someone so callous, so shallow, and so entitled...' Smithers was not going to waste one word of kindness on Bentley, not one word of sympathy, one word of respect, or one word of surprise at his current permanent predicament.

He stood mesmerised by Bentley's bulging bloodshot eyes and swollen tongue that had puffed out onto his purple lips. He cared not a jot for the boy, but his heart did flicker for Tarragon and Stephanie. He quickly covered him up, ensuring the end was tucked in, just like a good corner on a bed.

He moved several cardboard boxes containing Grimsby cod and haddock from the far wall and stacked them in front of Cecily and her great-grandson, obscuring them from immediate view. He needed time to think; he had so many questions racing around his brain, and age, as expected, had slowed down this process somewhat.

What would the benefits be to reveal Bentley's murder? He had mulled that one over already, he was as sure as eggs were eggs that it was murder, after all, as daft as Bentley was at times, there was no way he would have walked into the freezer himself to sit down and die, and if the murder mystery books Smithers had read over the years were anything to go by, he was also very sure that the lad had been strangled.

He closed the freezer door. Cecily and Bentley would stay put and that detective sergeant could deposit Clara Toomey's corpse in the side section of the freezer, away from the other two bodies. He would just have to make sure he stood his ground in front of the boxes whilst it was done to ensure the matriarch of his beloved Montgomery Hall and her clungtrumpet of a relative remained undiscovered for the time being.

He grumbled away to himself as he made his way upstairs to let Tarragon know all was in order and ready for them. '... *and that's another thing, would you credit it, these dead bodies are just like buses, you wait ages for one and then three turn up at once!*'

LIKE A SECOND SKIN

*T*he banging on the wall became feebler the weaker Stephanie became. The back of her head was hurting so badly; each time she jerked her head behind her to make contact with the wall, the thump made her eyes water and her brain to feel as though it was actually rattling around inside her skull.

She had absolutely no idea where she was. The darkness frightened her and the dust in her nostrils made her want to sneeze. She wondered if she did sneeze whether it would be big enough to blow the tape away from her mouth, thus allowing her to scream. Her legs were bound at the ankles and her hands were painfully pulled behind her back, wrists tied together, making any attempt to stand up impossible. She tried to shuffle around to see if there was a chink of light that would give her a clue as to her surroundings. She felt like a caterpillar squirming as she inched around on her side in an undulating fashion. After a few seconds, exhaustion overtook her, and she flopped her head onto the floor. Her cheek caught on something, making her squeal in pain.

A splinter, sticking up from the wooden plank beneath her,

had pierced her cheek near her ear. She waited for the stinging to abate slightly, her mind working ten to the dozen. This was a chance she couldn't afford to miss.

She angled the side of her face and rubbed the edge of the tape backwards and forward against it; each time the splinter caught, it ripped it a little further from her mouth. It was a risk, as every now and then it would rip into her skin instead, but for the first time in her adult life, she didn't care what damage would be done to her face, she didn't care about Botox, about facelifts or lip-fillers; all Stephanie cared about was getting out alive and she would sacrifice everything to do that.

After what seemed an eternity, the tape pulled away enough to release her mouth, allowing her to gulp in large mouthfuls of stale dusty air. She could feel a wetness running down her face; shrugging her shoulder up, she turned her head and wiped her cheek across her blouse, pushing a metallic tang into her mouth. She licked her lips.

Blood.

A wave of nausea bit at the middle of her stomach as a pulsating swish pounded in her ears, then a true darkness over-came her as she once again slipped into unconsciousness.

Selma had closed the final part of the act with quite an impressive bit of 'room-reading', which had earned her a round of applause. In a strange way it was quite fun being in Selma's skin, not that she would want to remain this way much longer. It was surprisingly tiring constantly being in character – one that was so alien to her true persona and one that she didn't dare deviate from, lest she should slip up. The sooner she could do what she'd come here to do and be merrily on her way and back to her 'normal' self, the better.

She checked her watch. The audience were happily enjoying a

tipple or two, waiting for the second half to start. The doors to the Somerset Room remained closed, keeping them all in. She was in no doubt that this was being orchestrated to keep everyone in the dark; the detectives were trying to keep Clara's demise a secret for as long as possible. What she needed to do now would have to wait until later, the bewitching hour. She knew there was going to be a Halloween Hunt after her performance, which would mean guests traipsing around the hotel in the dark with lanterns and fake cobwebs, screaming and scaring each other shitless, so for Selma and her plan it couldn't be more perfect.

She mentally ticked off her list.

1. *Interrogate, and then dispose of Stephanie.*
2. *Continue the search for Ernest's fortune.*
3. *Decide on Cecily and Tarragon's mode of departure.*
4. *The Reveal.*

Her plan had been quite simple, assisted greatly by her secret ally at Montgomery Hall, and whichever way she decided to play it, whichever of the two endings she chose, she would be triumphant; both would give her financial security, but only one would give her the rightful status.

She just had to decide which one.

HELPING HANDS

'*A* Halloween Hunt? Oh what fun...' Ethel couldn't contain herself. She'd been bitterly disappointed with the Murder Mystery evening, as had the other ladies of the Winterbottom WI. It had all ended so abruptly and nobody had been given the chance to solve the murder. She had been pretty impressed with the way the Victim had curled up her toes, though. 'It was very realistic, wasn't it, Clarissa?'

'What was?' Clarissa kicked her shoes off under the table and sipped her sherry.

'The murder, she was very good that woman, she went down like a sack of spuds, I almost laughed. I think it was the chappie that we caught under the table with Chelsea; he's the one that did it. What do you think?'

Clarissa really couldn't be bothered, one way or the other. It was fun to be all together, but so much of this weekend had seemed like a shambles to her untrained eye. She felt they'd been moved around from room to room, as though nobody knew what to do with them. She'd watched the Montgomery Hall staff earlier in the day set up their Halloween trail around the hotel, cobwebs hanging from chandeliers, pumpkin lanterns dotted around on each landing, all with battery operated safety candles in them, she would hasten to add. It all looked very grand and very spooky, but she could feel it in her waters: there was something not quite right.

'Ah, there you are, ladies.' Pru sat herself down next to Ethel. Taking a sip from the large gin balloon, she beckoned Bree to join them. 'Right, there's been a little hiccup this evening. I don't want anyone to panic or start spreading rumours; I'm speaking to you both as I know the other ladies look up to you.' Pru paused waiting for a response.

Ethel nodded sagely, chuffed to have been included in a line-up of respected WI members. Clarissa simply waited for Pru to continue.

'Okay, there's been a little accident, which wasn't really an accident...' She blew upwards, making the curls on her forehead quiver.

Bree glared at her in astonishment. 'Er... it's more like a bloody big accident!'

Pru could see what was going through her mind, but other than blurt out that someone had been murdered in quite such a grisly and public fashion, how else was she going to explain it without causing terror and an ensuing panic.

Pru continued. 'So at the moment, we're unsure what has happened, but I need you and the ladies to keep an eye on each other, to make sure nobody is left to go it alone. Keep in pairs at the very least, and ensure you lock your room doors properly when you retire later. I'm so sorry I can't tell you any more, but once I can, I'll fill everyone in, okay?'

Ethel and Clarissa nodded simultaneously. Pru could see that they were desperate to know more, but welcomed their understanding of her predicament by not asking.

Bree was quick to change the subject. 'Right, we've got half an hour before the Halloween Hunt begins, so who wants another round before we all start scaring the living daylights out of each other?'

Ethel tipped her sherry glass in acknowledgement, whilst Clarissa hastily drained hers and held it aloft as an acceptance of Bree's offer.

As Pru and Bree propped up the bar, waiting to be served, Bree took the opportunity to chastise Pru. 'A little *accident*? Oh my God, Pru, that's got to be the bloody understatement of the year! I think having a six-inch steak knife plunged between your shoulder blades is a bit more than a "little accident"! A "little accident" is when you don't make the loo in time and suffer the consequences!'

Pru grimaced. 'I know, I know, but what the hell else could I say, hey? Like, "We've got a deranged murderer in our midst, so let's all run around the tables screaming our heads off"? You know that's what would happen if I'd told them the truth, and not least a potential heart attack or two.'

Bree couldn't help but agree, it was all such a mess, a far cry from their little jaunt to find a tea leaf amongst the staff of Montgomery Hall. She had to admit to a little flutter of excitement to be involved first hand in the murder, although gazing down on Clara's corpse hadn't quite been the highlight of the holiday so far, and had almost facilitated the reappearance of her three-course dinner. 'We could help, like we did last time with the Winterbottom murders,' she offered.

'Mmm... not sure. We did get ourselves into a bit of a pickle with that one...' Pru gave a wry smile, remembering. 'You and me both nearly ended up six feet under at the hands of Phyllis.'

'True, but this is different, it wouldn't harm, would it? Later on during the Halloween Hunt we can have a little mooch around. I'm sure Andy could use the help.' Bree gathered three drinks from the bar between her fingers.

'We'll see…' Pru followed her back to the table.

'You sound like my mum…' Bree laughed.

'Thanks for that. Nice to know I'm almost akin to a seventy-seven-year-old geriatric that regularly wears her M&S knickers back to front…'

'What's with the *almost*, girlfriend?'

ROUND 'EM UP

*A*ndy did his usual habit of running his hand through his hair in frustration. It sprang up in several different directions, giving him the appearance of Stan Laurel. Under any other circumstances, Lucy would have made some smart-arse comment and teased him, but even she knew this wasn't the time for joviality or pick-me-up humour.

'What do you mean a Halloween Hunt?' He looked incredulously at Tarragon. 'This is a murder investigation. What bit of keeping everyone together did you not understand?'

Tarragon had the sense to look a little embarrassed. 'I thought you wanted everyone to carry on as normal so there wouldn't be any panic. This was planned, and they sort of just naturally progressed from the psychic evening to the Halloween Hunt. It won't last long, and it's all inside Montgomery Hall; surely no harm can become them.' He puffed out his cheeks and blew out loudly.

Lucy handed Andy a mug of tea and took a sip of her own. 'Do you have a tannoy system, Mr Montgomery? We could always put out a call to bring everyone together again.'

Tarragon shook his head. 'We're just lucky enough in this antiquated dump to have telephones that work.'

'Except they don't, do they?' Andy made a show of checking his mobile phone for a signal again. 'So, let's look at this with a cold eye. We've got a wide selection of guests, all of varying ages and various states of health, prancing around an immense building that's akin to a haunted mansion, scaring each other half to death, with no means of outside contact, cut off from the rest of civilisation – and to top it all, we've got one body in the freezer and a murderer on the loose!' He rubbed at his temple. 'Couldn't have asked for more if I'd touched wood and wished upon a star,' he wryly added.

'Two...' Tarragon offered and then just as quickly bit his own tongue.

'*What?*' Andy tipped his head quizzically.

'Er... *too* much going on, isn't there?' Tarragon quickly recovered himself. He couldn't believe he'd almost given the game away. It was true what they said about guilt eating away at the soul. The urge to confess would sneak up on you at the most inopportune moment.

Lucy was surprised to see Andy like this; she had never known him to use sarcastic humour aggressively. She tried to soften the moment. 'If we split up and each take sections, we can keep an eye on things, and then direct everyone to return to their rooms as and when we bump into them. That would be the safest place for them. Mr Montgomery, are there any trusted staff that you can spare?'

An ear-piercing scream suddenly broke through the air, echoing from the Great Hall. Already alert, Andy sprinted to the main doors of the Belvedere Dining Room, with Lucy closely following in his wake. He came to an abrupt halt and took in the scene.

Cassidy, attached to a plastic skeleton, was chasing Chelsea around the huge circular oak table in the great hall, squealing with laughter.

'It's going to rattle me bones...' Chelsea howled, whilst picking up pace and putting extra space between herself and the bony, outstretched fingers of the fondly named Count Scapula, who was being expertly puppeteered by Cassidy. Suddenly, and without warning, a combination of too many vodkas, and her stiletto heels failing to make purchase on the marble tiles as she hit the curve, Chelsea slipped over and skidded across the floor on her bottom, eventually coming to rest in front of Ethel and Clarissa, with her legs akimbo.

'Goodness me, now that's what I call an eager beaver!' Ethel loudly proclaimed. 'Avert thine eyes, Detective...' She giggled.

'Ethel Tytherington, you are very naughty!' Pru blushed profusely. 'You really do need to take into account where you are and think before you speak.' Having heard all the commotion from the lounge bar, she had quickly joined them to ensure all her charges were safe and well. She gave Andy an embarrassed grin. 'I think I'll let them have half an hour on the Halloween Hunt in groups, and then round them up and settle them in for the night.'

'That would be a great help, particularly the older ladies in your group, Pru. Please ensure they lock their doors securely. Lucy and I are just going to go over what we've got so far, and then we'll keep Obs during the night. Speak to Smithers if you need anything, Mr Montgomery has made him available to us.' He returned her smile, keeping their interaction professional, whilst in reality all he really wanted to do was put his arms around her and keep her safe. 'I think it's going to be a long night; fingers crossed we'll be able to make some contact with the outside world tomorrow, if and when the storm dies down.'

Pru gave him one of her most disarming, supportive smiles to give him a boost. She hated seeing him so tense and distracted from her, but understood that this would potentially be her future with him. She twiddled the thumb and forefinger of her right hand around her wedding ring finger. She lived in hope.

'I'll see you later. We'll sort this lot out and then hunker down ourselves.' Pru hoped that her statement sounded convincing to Andy's ears. She already knew that neither she nor Bree would be meekly retiring to their rooms once the ladies were settled. There was exploring to be done and, dare she hope, a little bit of investigating too.

Bree took the opportunity to haul Chelsea to her feet, and in the process restore some level of decency to her nether regions, whilst Ethel and Clarissa made their way up the main staircase to search for ghosts, ghouls, spectres and sweets. The Dingleberries crew, lacking any enthusiasm for extra fun since Clara's demise, had, on Andy's advice, already secured themselves into their respective rooms, leaving Andy and Lucy, accompanied by Tarragon, to disappear into the reception office to plan their way forward. Andy was still less than impressed that circumstances had forced him to unceremoniously bump poor Clara Toomey down fifteen stone steps to the cellar before shoving her inside the freezer to become as rigid as a fish finger in the following twelve hours.

The whoops, hollers and laughter echoing around Montgomery Hall evidenced the enjoyment that the guests were having, and belied the grim atmosphere that was hovering around those that were in the know. Several guests had already discovered the 'treasures', ranging from cauldrons filled with sweets and bloodshot jelly eyes, and the odd bottle of Witches Brew beer that was hidden behind drapes, planters and on shelves.

Everyone was occupied, apart from one.

Selma had taken the time to become an observer. Sitting in the high-backed state chair in the Great Hall, she was invisible. Just like she had always been as a child, whenever and wherever she wanted. She waited until the Great Hall was empty and slowly rose to her feet. Flicking her cloak with a flourish, she wrapped it around her and pulled up the hood.

The bewitching hour was almost upon them, and what had always been a wish was now so deliciously close to becoming a reality.

A COLD HEART

*T*he coldness was eating into her bones. Stephanie blinked rapidly trying to clear the haze from her eyes, but it only served to shoot sparks of false light. She squeezed them together tightly, and then opened them again in the vain hope that action would elicit some familiarity as to where she was. She glared into the darkness so hard her eyes actually ached, but to no avail.

She was still in the *nothingness.*

That was the only way that she could describe it. A void, an abyss, a nothing.

She knew she wasn't dead. People who are dead don't feel pain, do they? Or at least that was what she had been led to believe since her childhood.

For goodness' sake, Steffy, stop crying; it's just a graze. If you can feel it stinging then be grateful; it means you're not dead...

Her mum had just carried on watching *Coronation Street,* completely ignoring her wounds. Stephanie had stood in the doorway, tears streaming down her face, her knees savagely torn by the asphalt. She had watched the blood trickle down and merge with the edge of her white school socks. Rejected, dejected, and just that little bit harder in soul than she had been before taking a tumble in the middle of Rochester Gardens estate. That moment had been a turning point in Stephanie's young life.

And she had turned.

From a sweet, gentle-of-heart child, to one that coldly took in her surroundings and had then made herself a solemn promise. A promise that she wouldn't end up sitting on a sofa in a faded velour tracksuit, fag dangling from the corner of her mouth, television permanently on with trash daytime TV, living hand-to-mouth on benefits with hand-me-down clothes from the neighbours.

If she thought about it long enough, she could still feel the heat of her young face burning with embarrassment when Barry Berkins had pulled at the back of her dress as they were playing on The Rec, revealing a stitched-in name label that didn't say 'Stephanie Birch' at all, but had shamefully declared that her pretty pink dress had once belonged to snooty Debbie Dobbins. That had been the final nail in the proverbial coffin for Stephanie. Her desire to escape from the run-down council estate and her life of poverty had burned fiercer than her cheeks.

And she had kept that promise.

Tarragon had been her way out. What had started as a brief flirtatious meeting at the Berkley Club had led her to where she was now. Well, not exactly here, not in the *nothingness,* but to her new role as Lady of the Manor. Tarragon had been well connected in the social circuit, and with a reputation that screamed money; so much money she could almost smell it on him, along with his Drakkar Noir aftershave.

But life hadn't been the privileged, carefree and exotic dream she had wished for. Granted she wore Prada rather than Primark, but she had still been on benefits and hand-outs, only this time they had come courtesy of Cecily who ruled the family name and fortune with a rod of iron. The only difference between herself and her mother had been her ability to not only turn heads but to turn a trick or two in business as well as in the bedroom.

A muffled thump on the other side of the wall she was resting upon made her jump, bringing her back to the 'now' rather than the 'then'.

'Help me, please can you hear me, I need help!' She attempted to shout, but her throat painfully constricted so tightly her plea came out strangled and barely audible. She tried again, accompanying her frantic call with a barrage of thumps and bangs with the back of her head. This time she really did see stars.

'Please, somebody... is there anyone there?'

Silence.

'Please...' she whimpered, her legendary fight and fierceness rapidly deserting her.

Her shoulders slumped heavily as her head dropped forward, allowing her chin to rest on her chest. The tears came. Just one at first, slipping silently down her cheek, then another, and another until she could no longer stop them.

'You were right, Mum, I can feel it, I'm not dead, not dead at all – I'm very much alive...'

The seconds ticked by, the *nothingness* and the silence broken only by her keening sobs and the flash of light behind her eyes that came from the rapidly spreading migraine throbbing in her head.

'Please, help me...' She paused, listening for someone, anyone to come and save her, but all she could hear was her own mother's voice, worming its way through her dark thoughts.

I'm not here to run round after you, Steffy, do it yourself...

Remembering that curt chastisement gave her a sudden rush of determination. *Yes, yes, I will, I'll do it myself...*

Flopping down on one side, she began to slide like a snake, undulating first right, then left, briefly stopping each time her head hit something. She would pause, kick out with both feet to feel her way around, and then begin the strenuous slither again.

She knew that as long as she could move forward and away from where Selma had left her, the safer she would be. She was under no illusion that when Selma returned it wouldn't be for a friendly girly get-together.

The laughter took her completely by surprise. After all, when you are facing certain death, why on earth would you dissolve into a fit of the giggles.

But she did laugh. She laughed loud, long and with ironic humour.

'Feck me, a girly get-together! Now that's a bloody laugh, isn't it?' she screeched as she slithered along to the next bit of the *nothingness.*

ROUND AND ROUND WE GO...

*P*ru exhaled loudly. 'Jeez, have a look at this–' She stood back from the door she had just opened. '–it's like a harem.'

Taking in the ornate oyster silk ceiling drapes that hung above a huge marshmallow bed, Bree marvelled at the deliciously decadent materials and colours. She tentatively touched a corded rope that wound itself around one of the four carved posts. 'Who do you think lives in a house like this?' she drawled in a near perfect imitation of Lloyd Grossman, which made Pru chuckle.

'Bit sus, isn't it? Stephanie said there was no room at the inn, hence me and you having to juggle our rooms around, but clearly nobody is staying in this one.' Pru wandered over to a set of double doors, desperately wanting to open them, but at the same time hesitating, just in case someone, living or dead, were to be standing on the other side. She couldn't quite remember which part of Montgomery Hall they were in as they had climbed so many stairs and taken so many corridors, twisting and turning in every direction during their search. She had a feeling they had bypassed the Montgomery floor which housed the family suites, so if that was the case, they must be on a floor that wasn't used.

She tried to mentally remember the outside structure of Montgomery Hall from when they had arrived, but she couldn't recall another floor, only a battlement and a small tower to the west wing.

'I think we're in the uppermost part of the west wing, Bree, not far from that turret thingy, the creepy bit, remember?' She moved back into the centre of the room and turned slowly, trying to get her bearings.

'Shit, maybe we shouldn't be here; it's like snooping rather than helping.' Bree bit down on her bottom lip and shoved her hands into the pockets of her jacket.

Pru rolled her sleeve down over her hand and pulled open the top drawer in the large mahogany dresser. She wasn't sure why she was suddenly so concerned about fingerprints; she just knew that she'd have a hell of a job explaining why her dabs were in this room, providing evidence of her nosiness if the murder investigation was brought this far up into the hallowed walls of Montgomery Hall. It was quite a masculine piece of furniture and now, having had the time to take everything in, to absorb the atmosphere of the room, she was pretty sure it was a gentleman's retreat. The drawer glided open, revealing regimented storage squares, with each square hosting a neatly folded tie. Every tie boasted a different colour, but all bore the same crest...

EFM

'Quick, come and have a look at this.' Bree was standing mesmerised at the large oil painting hanging over the fireplace. 'Stick a ginger wig on that, and who is it?' She wiggled her fingers in a spooky fashion.

Pru searched the features. The brass plaque underneath identified the sitter as Ernest Frederick Montgomery, but other than that, she really couldn't see who Bree was seeing. 'Is it Kitty?' she hedged.

'Kitty's not ginge! It's not one of ours, but it *is* somebody who's here this weekend. Come on, you must see it!' Bree danced around the room, flinging an imaginary cloak around her. 'Bloody hell, Pru, and you're supposed to be a private detective – it's Psychic Selma!'

Now that Bree had said it, Pru could see it. 'Aw… that's a bit mean. I know she's not exactly drop-dead gorgeous, but every woman has some redeeming feature, something that's pretty about her. Likening her to a man in drag is really naughty.' She grinned and pulled her shoulders up to her ears, as though that action might forgive her for secretly thinking the same.

Bree had the decency to look a bit uncomfortable, but it didn't last long. 'I'm telling you, if Selma isn't a long-lost relative of old Ernest and Hugo, then you can beat me on the bottom with the *Woman's Weekly*!'

'I absolutely adored her, you know–' Pru tried the handle to the double doors, leaning into it. '–Victoria Wood set a high bar; she was hilar– oops…' The doors swung open, leaving Pru wide-eyed and almost on her bottom. She put her hands out to stop herself from falling, grabbing hold of the nearest thing, an old librarian's ladder. Once she had fully composed herself, she took in the vast room. It wasn't what she had first thought, a luxury en suite or a walk-in wardrobe, it was actually something more fabulous than any architect could imagine. She quickly utilised the cuff of her jumper to wipe where her hand had touched on the ladder.

The room beyond the doors held the most wondrous of treasures for a librarian. The walls were covered floor to ceiling with shelves. Every shelf was crammed with books: old books, new books, small books, big books, books with red, blue, green and gold spines. Bold print, scripted print. If Pru could have found more words to describe the vision before her, she would have done, but in fact for the first time in her life she was lost for words.

'Oh, wow, this is amazing!' Bree was the first to comment. 'Not that it sort of "does it" for me, I'm more a Zara boutique girl, with rails and rails of clothes, but I could see it being your thing, Pru.' She secretly wondered how anyone of Pru's vivaciousness and zest for life could almost have an orgasm over a bundle of dusty books... Now if anyone had mentioned a six-foot-three-inch dark, muscular and available man, she would definitely be first in the queue with her tongue hanging out.

Pru was lost to her, floating to and fro, from one wall to the other, mesmerised by the books regimentally set out before her. Bree, knowing there was no distracting her friend for at least another few minutes, decided to allow her the moment before bringing her back to the task at hand. Her own interest was suddenly diverted to a large ledger that had been left open on the green leather inlaid top of the reading desk.

Forgetting all about leaving her mark on objects, Pru's fingers danced reverently over spines, stopping momentarily at a tome that had suddenly taken her interest, her breath was shallow, a small fluttering feeling like butterflies danced in her stomach.

'Oh my goodness...' she squealed.

The edge of a rare blue cloth-bound edition of *Treasure Island* teased her; it was just marginally out of line with all the other books on the shelf, which is what had drawn her attention to it. Pru desperately wanted to remove it, caress it, look inside and sniff it. She quickly glanced around to see what Bree was up to, and happy that she was otherwise engaged, she gently hooked her fingers around the book and carefully slid it towards her.

A barely audible 'click' came from behind the book, followed by a gentle swish and another click and, like a fairground carousel, the bookcase opened out and swung from the wall, making one half revolution. In doing so it took Pru with it.

'Will you look at this? It's the history of the Montgomery clan; there's some dark and evil doings with this lot – one of the eight-year-old kids was suspected of killing his twin brother–' Bree paused to take in more of the sepia-scripted words that spidered out on the aged pages. '–and he, the naughty twin, that is, drowned in a boating accident years later.' She waited for a response from Pru. Stuff like this was right up her street.

'Pru?' Bree looked over her shoulder, only to be met with an empty room behind her and a vacant spot in front of the bookcase where Pru had been. 'Stop farting around, you daft mare! Where are you?'

An uneasy feeling rose in her gut and was just as quickly replaced by a surge of panic. This felt like the basement of Winterbottom St Michael's parish church all over again, and on that occasion Pru had ended up in hospital, badly hurt at the hands of their resident mass-murderer, Phyllis.

THE KEY

*T*he last time Pru had been chucked around with such force and ejected through an opening was when she had been unceremoniously lifted off her feet and shown the doors to The Cabin Club in Granbymoor. The bouncers had caught her dancing on one of the VIP tables, swinging her Spanx pants in the air, much to the amusement of those sitting around the six-seater circle.

The joys of her teenage years had been simultaneously fun and an era she would rather forget. Besides, she'd be hard pushed to get the ruddy things off quick enough for a wee these days. Too many extra tummy bits and a set of chubby thighs would now only accommodate the roll down method rather than the straightforward whip 'em off technique.

She sat, momentarily dazed, on a cold stone floor. The side of her head throbbed painfully. It had struck the edge of the sandstone wall on her right as the impetus of what she now assumed was a secret panel, had swung her through its opening. She scrunched her eyes and blinked, trying to focus. A dim orange light flickered and then burned behind a metal cage on the far wall. She could only assume that the revolving bookcase had triggered the electrics, and then the light, into existence. She scanned the room, taking in its nooks and crannies; packing crates and boxes were stacked in careful rows on one side and a sizeable, rough-hewn wood table sat in the middle of the small room. Pulling herself carefully to her feet, she made her way over to it.

Methodically laid out on its surface were colourful trinket boxes, more books, and in the centre, a large ornate key. She picked it up and marvelled at its intricate handle. It was old; very old. She loved how it felt against her skin; she was probably holding history right there in the palm of her hand. She glanced around to see if there was a door to accommodate it, but there were only walls to the left and ahead of her, the revolving book-case behind her, and a dark corridor to the right. She craned her neck to see where it led to, but the weak lighting barely touched the first few feet inside.

Her curiosity having got the better of her; she had completely forgotten about poor Bree, who was no doubt still on the other side of the bookcase, chattering away to herself ten to the dozen, completely unaware that her best friend had been flung into the depths of Montgomery Hall and was now no longer in her presence.

Pru smiled, thinking about her, imagining her taking at least another ten minutes to realise she was gone. She felt along the bookcase again, found the book she was looking for, and pulled the spine. Once again the now familiar 'click' was followed by a swish, another click, and she was suddenly back in the library, only this time she was prepared and held on to the edge of the shelf to stop herself from falling over.

'Bloody hell, where did you come from?' Bree stood open-mouthed and wide-eyed. 'I was just about to alert the troops!'

'I know it's a bit predictable in a haunted house sort of fash-ion, but I've accidentally found a secret room. The copy of *Trea-sure Island* is actually the mechanism that makes the bookcase revolve; it starts it up when you pull the spine towards you!' Pru was beside herself with excitement. 'The bookcase is obviously duplicate-sided; that's why it didn't look any different to you when it swivelled round taking me with it.' She stood triumphant, desperate to get out all she wanted to say in one breath, but having to acquiesce to a small hiatus. 'There's a corridor or tunnel thing on one side and a key too – we need to explore,' she jabbered, before rushing over to the reading desk. She pulled open the drawers, one after the other until she found what she was looking for.

'Here–' She handed Bree the torch. '–and we've both got lights on our phones, so we'll definitely be able to find our way.'

'Whoa, hold on a minute. We've got a murderer on the loose, and you want to go blindingly snooping behind secret panels and corridors without knowing where they lead to?' Bree was shaking her head.

Pru didn't care. 'Er... yep is the simple answer! We'll just see where it leads to, and then we can go and tell Andy and Lucy. Come on, quickly. Stand on this bit here.' She grabbed Bree by the arm, halting any opportunity she might have had to have second thoughts. She pulled the blue book...

This time they both disappeared.

SNAP

'My wife is missing...' Tarragon pinched his lips together in concern, the fingers of his right hand plucking at the metal clasps on his TAG Heuer Formula 1 watch.

Andy turned swiftly away from his conversation with Lucy. 'What do you mean she's missing?'

'There's no sign of her anywhere; she's never more than two feet behind me, believe me – and that's not because she can't be without me, it's to make sure I don't mess anything up!' The bitter irony in Tarragon's voice wasn't lost on either Lucy or Andy.

Andy's heart dropped into the pit of his stomach, the spider senses that only ever hit him when he wasn't far off the mark beginning to tingle. 'When did you last see her?'

Tarragon squinted his eyes to think. He had no idea why he did this; eye squinting didn't really have a great impact on his brain and train of thought, but he knew he'd always done it, ever since he was a little boy, usually when he was trying to think up a lie. 'At this evening's dinner, she was a little worse for wear from a very expensive bottle of wine.' He made sure to include her excesses, but happily omitted his rather tart mention of her

Botox and fillers that had almost caused her to move the one unadulterated face muscle she still possessed.

Andy checked his watch. 'So you haven't seen her since Clara's murder?'

Tarragon shook his head. He felt a little uncomfortable. He was pretty sure the detective was judging him for not keeping an eye on his own wife during a particularly turbulent few hours, but if truth be known, he secretly hoped whoever it was that had seen off the old trout from the acting troupe would get a grip of Stephanie too. The idea of having years of unadulterated bliss ahead of him would be a dream come true. No wittering, no bleating, no demanding, and his bank balance looking just a tad more healthy too. No need for an expensive divorce if good old Steph was found tits up somewhere. He quickly caught himself, convinced his dark wish had revealed itself right across his face.

Lucy frowned, taking in Tarragon's facial expressions. He seemed harmless enough, more led than leader, but she still wasn't sure about him. She'd discuss that with Andy later, but first they had to ensure everyone was safe in their rooms, a lockdown of sorts until tomorrow morning. 'Sarge, I'll do a quick sweep through with some of the staff to make sure everyone is complying. I think most have returned to their rooms. Shall I meet you back here in the Great Hall when I've finished?'

Andy nodded. 'Thanks, Lucy, and if you can grab hold of Pru and Bree on your travels too, bring them back with you, I think we need to get our heads together.' This would serve twofold; four heads and ideas were better than one, and it would mean he would know that Pru was safe too.

He beckoned to Tarragon. 'We'll start at the bottom and work our way up...'

～

Stephanie howled as the skin on her hip caught on something. She stopped slithering and waited for the pain to subside, while a warm wetness seeped underneath her. Whatever it was had obviously caused quite a deep cut, probably an old rusty nail.

'That's all I bloody need, death by tetanus...' She gave a guttural laugh. Now that would be a turn up for the books; she'd always been convinced she would die from alcohol poisoning from the best of the best in the Montgomery wine cellar, or from boredom in the Montgomery bed. She began to slither again, rounding another corner.

'C'mon, Steph, pick it up, girl, we must be near an opening or something,' she muttered out loud. She was still none the wiser as to where she was. She was sure it was still within Montgomery Hall, but it was definitely nowhere she had ever been in all the years she had lived there.

A rumbling sound suddenly cut through the silence, slightly ahead of where she was making towards. The belief that this could be her saving grace gave Stephanie the impetus to push forward. It sounded just like the old butler's dumb waiter near the kitchens as it trundled along the shaft. Her pace quickened as she ignored the pain in her side.

Almost there...

Just a few more feet...

And in the same moment that Stephanie heralded hope, the floor she had reluctantly cosseted with her body suddenly disappeared beneath her.

Falling, falling like Alice down the rabbit hole...

But she wasn't Alice, and this wasn't a rabbit hole.

Poor Stephanie's head hit one side of the long-drop shaft first, her neck angled sharply as her body twisted painfully around, her weight becoming the driving force of her descent. She dropped down several feet before juddering to a halt. Her head once again acting as a wedge between the sections of graduated brickwork as her trussed body momentarily defied gravity, pinned on one side by the ladder.

She hung in limbo twisted like a hairpin, waiting for the inevitable.

Would you tell me, please, which way I ought to go from here?

How ironic that Alice had been able to ask her way, when right now Stephanie had no need of answers, she knew exactly which way she would go…

Down.

She let a small sigh escape, her mind rushing a million questions, a million answers and a million last quotes for a dying woman.

'Oh to die savage rather than average…' she murmured.

Her body juddered once and then relinquished its hold on the walls of the shaft, the resonating snap of her neck eerily filling the void. And just like that, her eyes stopped seeing and her body stopped feeling. She was no longer grateful as her mother had suggested she should be. She was just simply dead.

In the silence that followed, the malignant *nothingness* finally embraced her.

A RIGHTFUL DYNASTY

*S*elma had quite by accident spotted the 'Terrible Twosome' wandering the nooks and crannies of Montgomery Hall. It had been bad enough watching several old biddies mooching around looking for Halloween jelly sweets they could suck with their gummy mouths, without that pair putting themselves in the mix as well.

Selma had watched Pru and Bree climb the stairs to the next floor. She was pretty confident they wouldn't get up to much trouble, the whole wing was Ernest's old suite, and she had already spent more time than was necessary searching it herself to no avail. It had been as unfruitful as Hugo's suite had been. She'd catch up with them later, see what they were up to, but first she had to deal with the Snivelling Stephanie and the next part of her search.

There was absolutely no point in having loose ends when they were not part of the original plan...

She moved quickly along the corridor and turned towards the galleried landing. Counting the panels, she found the one she was looking for, tenderly caressed the fox's head, and pushed until it clicked. The panel swung open and she stepped inside, back into a familiar world.

She took in her bearings and made her way to where she had left Stephanie. No doubt Tarragon would have missed her by now. No constant moaning and bleating in his left ear would have given him a clue that her presence was no longer visible, unless, of course, he'd thought his prayers had been answered and he'd gone conveniently deaf.

'Oh, Stephanie, dear, I'm back...' she cackled, hoping her announcement would bring chills to the prissy princess's spine. She rounded the corner and swung her torch to illuminate her next victim.

The beam fanned out and settled on a vacant spot.

'Bitch...' Selma bent down and poked at the bloodied strip of masking tape on the floor. She frantically sprayed the torch beam around in the vain hope that Stephanie couldn't have got far. An acid sickness rose in her stomach. 'Bitch, bitch, bitch...'

She felt like Quasimodo as she stumbled and swayed through the walls of Montgomery Hall, her 'underworld', with her cloak billowing behind her. Turning a corner here, another corner there, picking up pace. Every now and then her torch would illuminate the 'snake' trail that Stephanie had left behind in the dust.

'Where are you, my pretty one?' she grunted, her voice becoming lower and lower. Sweat began to trickle from her forehead, mixing with the Ben Nye stage foundation she was wearing. She wiped at it with the back of her hand, totally unaware of the result. That one reckless action had swiftly removed her heavily painted-on left eyebrow.

'Come out, come out, wherever you are...' Her rough, singsong voice echoed along the passage. She rounded the next corner, shining the torch beam to assess Stephanie's progress. The slithering trail had stopped dead at the edge of the long drop. Her heart caught in her throat as she lolloped her way over and peered down.

'Oh dearie me, what have you done, Stephanie?' The relief was palpable, but at the same time tinged with disappointment. 'You've stolen such a precious moment from me, haven't you, you simpering old slapper.'

Stephanie's unseeing eyes glared out from the darkness of the shaft, the light catching and bouncing back. Her neck, angled awkwardly backwards and to one side, evidenced her lack of life, the rest of her body trussed and inflexible was wedged between the brick sides where she had tumbled down like a human Slinky.

For the second time in her short weekend stay at Montgomery Hall, Selma found herself rodding a body down the shaft as though it were a blocked toilet, using another hastily obtained plank of wood rather than a bog brush.

Stephanie's body hit the bottom of the shaft with a dull thud, much the same as her son Bentley's had. Selma followed, carefully, inching her way down, rung by rung, on the old ladder. Stepping over the crumpled body, she took time to admire the third person she had despatched, either directly or indirectly – or the fourth if she included the enchanting Estelle in that tally. She remembered Bentley's lack of flexibility when he too had been resting in this exact spot, but judging by Stephanie's current position, she had clearly been a little more hyper-mobile than her offspring. The ties around her ankles had snapped on the descent, allowing her legs to spring up, one behind her head the other sticking out to the side like a grotesque arabesque worthy of any ballet class.

'More dying duck than dying swan, methinks!' Selma dragged Stephanie along the passage, found the lever, and pulled. The panel slid open for her, once again revealing the now familiar cellar. She hauled the body across the concrete floor, utilising Stephanie's slim ankles as her holding point. Opening the stainless-steel doors to the freezer, she momentarily stood still, enjoying the chilled air around her.

'Right, this will never do. Back to work...' she muttered to herself. Her plan was coming along nicely and had been rather enjoyable so far.

Hauling Stephanie through the door of the freezer, the back of her head smacked loudly on the threshold bar. 'Oops, sorry about that, dear; that must have really stung – well, it would have done if you were still breathing!' She laughed. She pulled Stephanie over to where she had left Bentley, and without much dignity or compassion, dumped her next to him.

'Hahaha, eeny meeny miny moe…' Selma counted out. She knew one was Bentley, one was the side of beef that had already been in there when she had deposited him, and now the third was Stephanie. A hat trick of sorts, two cadavers and a steak. That thought made her snort with laughter, wondering if peas or beans would have been a decent accompaniment. 'Er… on second thoughts, maybe I'll go vegetarian after this little mission.' Her guttural laugh echoed around the freezer, and was just as quickly absorbed by the thick HDR wall panels.

She quickly composed herself, ready to get back to the task at hand. Covering the broken Stephanie with a piece of muslin to match her son, she wrapped it around her, tucked the ends in, and stood back to admire her handywork.

'Au revoir, Mrs Montgomery, you simpering, money-grabbing, trout-pouted trollop!'

If Selma hadn't known better, she could have boasted that she had done Tarragon and the Montgomery name a service by weeding out the weakness within the family. Bentley and his mother were never decent stock, not like the old days when you were either rightly born to be part of it, or, at the very least, socially cultured and adequately connected to be accepted into it.

Stephanie Montgomery née Birch, now deceased, had been neither.

THE MONTGOMERY REAPER

*T*he door to Clarissa and Ethel's room opened just enough to allow a shaft of light to escape. It broke through the gloom of the corridor and picked out a shadowy figure as it skipped and danced along the carpet runner, the flowing floral gown rhythmically sweeping from side to side. Behind that figure was a second one. This figure was less graceful, preferring to amble slowly in a pair of fluffy mule slippers, a plastic carrier bag clutched in one hand swinging randomly with each stride, making the contents clink and chink together in time to the flip-flap slapping of the mules against aged feet.

'Hurry up, Hilda, and watch that bottle of gin. I brought it all the way from Betty's store in my suitcase. Don't you dare smash it now!' Millie hitched up her nighty and put on a spurt.

'Sshh! for goodness' sake, you two…' Clarissa was mortified. Holding the door open a little wider, she hastily beckoned Millie and Hilda to enter. 'We're supposed to be in lockdown. If those detectives see us, we'll be in trouble.'

That thought made Ethel giggle loudly. 'Ooh, lighten up, 'Rissa, I've never been arrested before. It could be fun…'

'That's a lie for a start. What about that time in Watterson's supermarket? You didn't walk out of there under your own steam, did you?' Clarissa tartly snapped.

Ethel grumbled. 'It was a mistake!'

'What? Two packets of smoked back bacon and four bottles of Mackeson Stout shoved up your paisley smock, and you call that a mistake?' Clarissa tapped the side of her nose knowingly. 'PC Davenport didn't 'arf give you some stick over that, *and* you were in the local gazette too!'

Ethel harrumphed. 'What are you incinerating? Come on, out with it.'

'I'm not *insinuating* anything, I'm just stating a fact. You got locked up for shoplifting, and now you're trying to pretend it didn't happen,' Clarissa shot back.

'It *was* lovely bacon though...' Ethel teased.

Millie pushed through the door, dragging Hilda by the arm. The carrier bag banged against the door frame, clinking the bottles again. 'Right, we've got the booze and the nibbles.' She whipped out a crushed packet of Doritos. 'So who's got the cards?'

Like schoolgirls on their first ever sleepover, Clarissa, Ethel, Millie and Hilda giggled loudly as they made themselves comfortable on the large double bed, with Clarissa shuffling and dealing out the pack of cards.

'Here you go...' Ethel handed out the drinks.

Millie took the plastic beaker and grimaced. 'You've had your teeth in this, haven't you?' She could feel a tinge of green touching her cheeks as her tummy flipped.

Ethel faked a smile to show that the said dentures were firmly ensconced on her gums. 'I washed it out first, so don't be so bloody fussy. We've got two glasses and two beakers, someone's got to have the latter unless you're going to drink it neat out of the bottle!'

'Yay, I've got a king and an ace!' Hilda shuffled the rest of her cards, threw them down on the bed and, with a flourish, ripped off her nighty. The long thermal vest underneath did little to support her deflated boobs. They dropped heavily to sit on her knees.

'What on earth are you doing?' Millie looked mortified.

'It's strip poker, isn't it?' Hilda adjusted her droopy baps, pushing each to one side so she could lean forward and grab a handful of crisps.

'Goodness me, Hilda, you've shoved them under your armpits. You look like you're playing the bagpipes...' Ethel couldn't contain her laughter. 'We're playing Twenty-One, you daft mare!'

Amid the chinking of glasses and the gentle scuff of plastic beakers, the ladies chattered ten to the dozen, excitement tinged with a little apprehension fuelling them on. They were now fully aware, courtesy of Chelsea's hasty liaison behind the aspidistra with Dirk Diamond, of the real nature of Clara Toomey's dramatic performance during dinner. As disappointed as they were that their Murder Mystery night had been cut short, they had respectfully afforded a little sadness for the woman whose true dying moments had gone unappreciated by the vast majority of the audience.

'That's the thing with reaching our lofty ages; we're closer to the Grim Reaper than the stork, so there's not much that'll faze us.' Clarissa was the first to make that observation, which was heartily agreed by the other three.

'It does bring us to the question, though – who *did* murder Clara?' Ethel was deep in thought. Their experiences with mass-murderer Phyllis Watson had made them all amateur sleuths at some point, not that that observation was particularly useful, as not one of them had correctly guessed that one of their own had been picking them off one by one in various ingenious ways.

They sat in silence contemplating that question, all four of them eager to be in the mix, but not knowing where to start.

'We could have a bit of a nose around, couldn't we? That would be exciting, and we might even find something that could help that detective boyfriend of Pru's.' Millie crammed another couple of Doritos into her mouth and followed up with a large swig of gin.

Completely ignoring the fact that they had been confined to barracks under the threat of imminent death at the hand of an unknown assailant, the ladies continued to plot and plan what they would do, how they would carry out an investigation, with the excitement of finding something that nobody else had spotted that could potentially lead to an arrest.

'Mmm... that's all very well and good, but just how far would we get pottering around the corridors of this place in our nighties before we're spotted?' That was more of a statement than a question from Clarissa.

'We could use my wardrobe...' Hilda helpfully offered.

Ethel smiled affectionately. 'And is your wardrobe a door to another realm, Hilda dear?'

Hilda thought for a moment before answering. 'It's a door to a secret passage...' She folded her arms in triumph, delighted that she had something to say that would hold her friends' interest. 'I've not been inside as I didn't have a light, but it looks like it goes on forever. I bet you we could mooch around this old place without anyone seeing us.'

'Oh, Hilda, that wasn't real. There was no intruder coming out of the wardrobe; it was just a dream.' Millie vainly tried to placate her.

'It wasn't a dream, I'm telling you. I had a better look and the back of the wardrobe is a sliding panel.' Hilda was adamant.

'Hilda, love... you've got dementia, remember?' Ethel soothed.

'If I've got bloody dementia, how am I supposed to *remember*, Eth?' Hilda's quick-witted retort made Clarissa laugh. 'It wasn't a dream, I had another look and found it.'

Clarissa, Ethel and Millie sat mesmerised as Hilda regaled them with her earlier five-minute wardrobe adventure, still unsure if this was simply one of Hilda's imaginary events, or if it was possible that she was telling the truth; after all, old manor houses were renowned for having priest holes, cubbies and passages.

'Come on, I'll show you...' Hilda quickly donned her nighty again, much to the relief of her friends. 'Have you got a torch?'

Clarissa had once been Brown Owl of the Winterbottom St Michael's Brownie pack in her younger days, and much like her counterparts at the Scout group, she was always prepared. She shuffled over to her tapestry bag and pulled out two small LED pocket torches. She retained one and gave the other to Millie.

'Right, ladies, we're on the cusp of an adventure if Hilda is right, so what are we waiting for?'

Within minutes the shadowy forms of four elderly ladies, varying in height and size, tiptoed along the corridor towards Hilda and Millie's room, eager to get started on their most exciting adventure.

They were blissfully and eagerly leaving the stork behind them to go in search of their hastily named nemesis, The Montgomery Reaper...

AHEAD OF THE GAME

*a*ndy knocked gently on Pru and Bree's door and waited. He had encouraged them both to bunk up together whilst he and Lucy carried on with the investigation. Together they had a better chance of being safe. He didn't like this situation one bit, to be incommunicado from the rest of the world, and in particular his colleagues, was as bad as it could get under the circumstances.

He checked his watch and ran his hand through his hair in frustration. He mentally kicked himself for not getting the second key from Bree before she had room-hopped to share with Lucy. He hoped against hope that they were both fast asleep and blissfully unaware of the developments with the missing Stephanie, but a niggling feeling had him believe that fore-warned would be forearmed. Knowing what the two of them were like for getting themselves ensconced in the midst of drama, the last thing he needed was for them to take it upon themselves to do a bit of snooping.

He knocked again.

'Pru, are you awake?'

Silence.

'Andy...'

He quickly turned around, his heart beating just that little bit faster, not through fear, but from being startled. 'Luce! Any news from the staff?'

Lucy shook her head. 'Nothing. Nobody remembers seeing Stephanie since dinner. Smithers was of the belief that she was doing pre-performance checks with Selma, but that's it, nothing since.'

Andy pondered on that for a few seconds. 'What about the building search, anything from that?'

For the second time in as many minutes, Lucy shook her head. 'No, every room that could be searched has been; guests' rooms have all had a knock under the guise of checking how many guests to each room. I think everyone is aware that something has happened; they're just not sure what, which is causing quite a bit of consternation and unease.'

Andy gave Pru's door one last knock. When it still failed to elicit a response, he reluctantly accepted they were both in the land of nod. 'It's a balancing act...' He sighed. 'Keep them in the dark and all stays relatively calm, but there's a risk that they're not alert to potential danger; or tell them there's been a murder and all hell breaks loose, but at least they're on their guard.'

'And then we get overrun with "sightings" and red herrings from overactive imaginations!' Lucy helpfully offered.

'Yep, Catch-22. They can be a waste of time, or we could be cutting down on potential information. Come on, back to Tarragon's office. Let's pool what we already know and make a decision from there, but first things first: we need to speak to Selma. It looks like she may have been the last to see Stephanie.'

As Andy and Lucy made their way down the main staircase to the Great Hall, they were eagerly watched by Selma herself, relishing her invisibility behind the panelled wall. Utilising one of the sliding air vents, her view was somewhat limited through the trefoil pattern, but it was enough to see – and to hear – what she needed to know to keep one step ahead of the game.

⁓

'This is sooo exciting–' Bree stood in the centre of the room, marvelling at the spookiness of it all. '–a revolving bookcase *and* a secret room; how much more brilliant can it get? This is a real-life haunted house!'

Pru laughed. 'It's not haunted, well not that I've noticed, but it is a bit spooky, I'll grant you that.' She opened one of the trinket boxes on the large table. An array of coloured beads and bangles sat knotted and jumbled together on the red velour lining. She picked up a solitary jewelled ring and turned it under the weak amber light from the wall cage. A dull sparkle reflected back at her. 'I'm not into expensive jewellery, but I don't think these would pay a month's mortgage. I think they're paste, like costume jewellery.'

Bree joined her, letting the beads hang through her fingers as she held them aloft. 'Mmm… I'm inclined to agree with you; pretty though.'

They continued to search around the room, moving the packing cases to one side and then tentatively opening one to see what treasures it held. 'Oh, that's nice…' Pru held a heavily embossed book in her hand. She opened the cover, allowing the musty-sweet aroma of aged pages to evaporate upwards as she admired the endpaper decorated with deep red pictures of wreaths, flowers and goblets. Amber staining and the brown spots of foxing randomly peppered the frontispiece, and, as she carefully turned the pages, the rest of the book, showing not only its age but the conditions in which it had been kept.

'I thought you only moaned like that when the Delectable Detective was on form–' Bree snorted. '–honestly, Pru, how can anyone get that dreamy over a book is beyond me! Is this the key?' She held the ornate metal key in her hand.

'Yes, that's it. Now, are you up for doing a bit more exploring, or are you going to be a scaredy-cat?' Pru challenged with a grin.

'Lead me to it,' Bree responded, albeit whilst chewing the bottom of her lip in nervous anticipation. 'I'm an intrepid explorer, mistress of the mystery, nothing can phase me!' She grinned and then just as quickly pulled down the sides of her mouth, deep in thought. 'Pru…'

'What?'

'Can you go in front?'

THE MAZE

'Well I never, it's like *The Lion, the Witch and the Wardrobe...*' Clarissa stood back in amazement after having just gingerly stuck her head through the panel in Hilda's wardrobe. '...I wonder where it leads to?'

Hilda sat smugly on the end of the bed, pleased as punch that she had proved her friends wrong, that she wasn't all dreams, fantasies and imagination. 'See, I told you, didn't I?' She watched Ethel and then Millie check out the void behind the cream polyester blouse that was hanging on the rail.

'Right, we need to do this methodically; no getting separated, we need to stick together. I'll lead. Ethel, you get behind me, then Hilda, and then you, Millie; you can bring up the rear.'

Millie thought about that formation for a few seconds. She jutted out her chin and hoisted her ample boobs with her folded forearms. 'Er... may I ask why I'm being the one that's left at the back? In the films it's always the one at the back that gets picked off!'

'You're the most er... robust of all of us, Millie.' Clarissa was going to say 'largest' but thought better of it.

Ethel had no such qualms. 'The fatty at the back is the least likely to get dragged off Millie; too much like hard work to pull all that wobbly lard any great distance.'

Before Millie could provide a tart reply of her own, Clarissa had arranged their line like any good Brown Owl would, leaving Millie no choice but to be last.

Clarissa stepped through the panel, closely followed by Ethel. Hilda had a firm grip on Ethel's dressing gown cord, and in turn Millie had twisted the end of Hilda's belt around her wrist. It fleetingly crossed Ethel's mind that they looked more like the elephant parade from Disney's *Jungle Book* than an elegant line of genteel ladies embarking on an adventure.

'If we alternate the use of our torches, we won't drain both batteries at once.' Clarissa was in full Brown Owl mode now.

The four ladies of the Winterbottom Women's Institute began their journey through the dusty passages in the walls of Montgomery Hall, none knowing where they would lead to or, in fact, what they were actually looking for. It was just an awfully big adventure, where consequences hadn't been considered.

At the same time as Clarissa and friends were enjoying the excitement of the unknown from an easterly direction, making towards what they thought was the centre of the Hall, Selma was also ambling, with cloak in full flow, along her familiar path from a westerly route, heading to the same location. At the same time Pru and Bree had started to head towards the heart of the Hall from the north, eagerly seeking a door that would fit the key that was clutched in Pru's hand.

They were like rats in a multi-choice maze, scuttling from different directions, but all leading to the same destination. Some unwittingly, some randomly, and only one with knowledge, which, in the eyes of any outside observer, was a recipe for potential disaster.

FLIP, FLAP, FLOP...

'It goes on forever...' Pru shone her torch along the length of what she had at first thought was an extension of the corridor, but was in fact a dilapidated passage. The heavily patterned oppressive wallpaper that had given a claustrophobic feel to either side of the walls that led from the secret room, gave way to an unfinished daub and wattle mix between dry wood slats. It had crumbled over the years, leaving a fine carpet of dust and tiny specks of rubble on the wooden floor. She could see where the wall of the passage turned a sharp corner to the right, the beam only illuminating to where her eye could see.

Bree wasn't happy. 'I think we should turn back and let Andy know. This isn't good, Pru, anyone, or anything could be hiding around the next corner.' She knew her breath was becoming short and sharp as fear gripped at her stomach.

Pru was having none of it. She was already ahead and at the corner, and before Bree could utter another word, she had disappeared from view. Bree quickened her pace, almost breaking into a little run to catch her up. 'Didn't you hear what I just said?'

'I did, but come on. It's the chance of a lifetime to mooch

around a creepy old mansion's secret passages, and maybe find a clue to our murderer – you're being chicken!'

'I'm not being chicken; I'm being sensible…' Bree pouted, and then just as quickly cringed, wondering when she *had* actually become 'sensible' – she'd never ever been sensible, so why start now? She grabbed hold of Pru's arm, as though that one action would afford her safety if the boogeyman came looming out of the darkness ahead.

Crack, thwump…

'What the bloody hell was *that?*' Bree's stomach lurched.

They both froze on the spot. Pru quickly turned the torch off, leaving them to be swallowed by the darkness. She didn't know if that was preferable to being on show to whoever was up ahead, or whether she should have blinded them with fifty lumens of light.

Slip, slap, flop, flip, flap…

Bree gripped Pru's arm even tighter, her fingernails finding the soft skin of her forearm, hoping the tactile action would bring her some much-needed gallantry. It didn't. She turned to run, but instead knocked into the wall, sending something crashing to the wooden flooring.

Bang!

An ominous silence followed as they both held their breath.

Flop, slap, flop, flip…

Pru's false courage suddenly failed her. 'Oh my God, oh my God, we're going to die…'

'It's dark…' Millie moaned from the back of the line.

'Well it's not much bloody brighter up this end either!' Ethel testily snapped.

'I'm scared…'

The WI line stopped in its tracks.

'Who said that?'

'Me.'

Clarissa huffed loudly. 'That's not much help. There's four of us. It wasn't me, so that just leaves Ethel, Hilda or Millie, so which one of us is almost wetting their knickers?'

'It's me, Hilda, and I haven't wet me knickers – I haven't got any on, I never wear 'em for bed.' She tittered.

Clarissa sounded shocked. 'Goodness me! Far too much information, dear. Did your mother never tell you you'd catch your death of cold?' She didn't wait for a reply and instead blithely carried on in her quest to see where the passage led. Up ahead her torch picked out a wall facing them. 'I think this might be the end of our journey, ladies. It's a dead end.'

'Oh that's such a shame; can we go back now?' Millie's sympathy for Clarissa's spoilt adventure was definitely not genuine. All she wanted to do was turn heel and get herself tucked up in her bed. She had suddenly begun to rue the moment Hilda had suggested this little romp. She kept checking behind her, just to reassure herself no sex fiend or murderer was following in her footsteps, desperate to get their hands on her wobbly flesh.

'No, look...' Ethel tilted her head and leant over Clarissa's shoulder. 'Turn your torch that way, no, no, that way... to the left. See it?'

The beam picked out a sharp turn to the left where the passage continued. 'Oh my days, this just gets better and better...' Although minus her knickers and starting to feel the chill, Hilda had pushed aside her fear and was starting to warm to the adventure. She quietly wished the warmth would gravitate to her lady garden, which was currently on the verge of developing an early morning frost. She jiggled her legs and did a little dance on the spot, trying to elicit some friction that might assist.

Slip, slap, flop, flip, flap...

'Hush, Hilda, keep those bloody mules quiet! Why you can't

wear ordinary slippers like the rest of us, I'll never know.' Ethel was quite perturbed.

'I'm just warming up me...'

Bang!

Hilda's explanation was cut short by the loud noise that echoed ahead of them.

'Oh Jesus, Mary and Joseph...' Millie gasped, frantically crossing herself.

'I don't think they're going to be of much help, Millie...' Ethel turned heel, eager to go back the way they had come, but was quickly gripped by Clarissa, stopping her momentum.

Clarissa slowly and cautiously edged her way forwards, accompanied by the *flip, flap, flop* of Hilda's slippers following behind her as she peered around the corner...

Selma stopped in her tracks and listened.

First a flapping and slapping sound had echoed through her domain, which had suddenly reminded her of the robust massages of obese clients at Tommy's Turkish bath house in Brigham's town centre. Not that she had regularly frequented the place; it was just the odd occasion when needs must before a takeaway from the Phát Phúc Noodle Bar next door. That odd sound had then been followed up by a loud bang.

She listened intently to the distant voices, mere whispers to her ears, but she was in no doubt that whoever it was had encroached upon her private world.

A fury rose in her chest, threatening to explode, but with nowhere to go it just made her heart pound painfully against her ribs. She balled her fists tightly, her nails digging into the palms of her hands, and although she couldn't see it, she knew that the skin on her knuckles had turned white.

The roar built in her brain.

This is my *home; this is* my *place…*

She could control it no longer, lungs fit to burst it gushed from her mouth. A savage, gruff, devilish voice that rasped into the darkness.

'Get out, get out, leave this place *now*,' she growled.

THE WATCHER

*W*hat followed was like a scene from a *Carry On* film.

Selma's rather masculine roar circumvented the heart of Montgomery Hall's secret passages. It whirled ferociously from corner to corner, first rushing from the west, then north and finally east, before tapering and completing the square by settling silently south.

That was just enough time for Pru and Bree to take it upon themselves to suddenly find their legs. Pru was the first out of the corridor, turning left in panic, closely followed by Bree. Neither had any idea where they were going or where the passage was leading them to. They only hoped they were going in the opposite direction from whence the fearsome roar had come.

At the same time, poor Millie, who until that moment had been reluctantly bringing up the rear of the little WI posse, took it upon herself to almost knock poor Hilda on her bare bottom in her haste to escape. She bypassed Ethel and shoulder-barged Clarissa at the front. A loud screech suddenly filled the passage, followed by a sharp *pheeeeep*, which only added to the terror and ensuing confusion.

If they had known that Hilda's hearing aid had decided at that moment to misbehave, perhaps the chaotic clambering over each other would not have been quite so brutal. As it was, it became every man – or woman, in this case – for themselves.

One of Hilda's mules found its target.

'Yeeeeow! Mind my shin…' Ethel bent down to rub the painful area. Unfortunately, this action caused Clarissa to fall over her bent body. She went sprawling forward, grabbing Millie's dressing gown as she crashed to the floor, taking Millie with her.

At that moment, two figures, arms flailing in the darkness, rounded the corner. Hilda let out an ear-splitting scream of terror.

'Aarrrghh! Take them, not me…' she yelled, her loyalty to her friends fading with each horror-struck moment.

The apparitions screamed back, having been confronted by a screeching banshee and a large bulky monster rising up from the floor, its several hands clawing at the blackness, whilst three heads bobbed backwards and forwards. Clarissa's torch beam rolled around the floor, giving off an eerie backdrop to the small passage.

'Pru!'

'Ethel!'

'Is that you, Bree?'

'Clarissa?'

'It's me, Millie…'

A stunned silence followed.

'I'm not sure who I am; I seem to have forgotten…' Hilda's forlorn voice broke through the electrically charged air.

The six women stood shell-shocked but relieved, their respective heartbeats slowly returning to somewhere near normal, the fearsome roar still ringing in their ears.

'What on earth are you four doing here?' Pru shone her torch at each face in turn. 'Well, I'm waiting...' Her schoolmarm voice indicated she meant business.

Millie and Hilda looked uncomfortable; Ethel really couldn't care less, but Clarissa at least had the decency to squirm a little. She reluctantly became the spokeswoman for the foursome.

'Hilda found a secret panel at the back of her wardrobe–' She pointed an accusing finger at Hilda. '– then Ethel said we should go on an adventure.'

'I did not... it was your idea, 'Rissa, not mine!' Ethel spat indignantly.

Millie stepped forward. 'I said all along that we should go back, so don't blame me.'

Pru shook her head and eyed the motley crew. It was actually worse than dealing with a kindergarten class of naughty kids in the children's section at the library. 'Ladies, please. Now is neither the time nor the place for bickering...'

'Actually, Pru, what are *you* doing here?' Clarissa smirked.

Bree looked at Pru and raised both eyebrows, the torchlight coming from below her chin giving her a spooky set of jowls. 'Er... yep, what *are* we doing here, Pru?'

As the Winterbottom ladies argued between themselves as to the merits and pitfalls of their separate adventures, Hilda's slippers, Bree's clumsiness, followed by which way was the safer and more suitable to return to their respective rooms, Selma watched and listened. She was only feet away from them, but, as always, invisible, wherever and whenever the mood took her.

And right now her mood, albeit more of a rage, told her to bide her time, to remain unnoticed. Her time would soon come.

Audentes fortuna iuvat...

If Selma had not been so intent on revenge and so focused on wealth, she might have noticed the mysterious shadowy figure keeping to the dark edges of the walls, silently following her – but, as with all psychopaths, her arrogance was so strong, it afforded her very little margin for error, or to believe she was not the only hunter in the game.

The Watcher knew otherwise.

Selma scuttled along the passage, pausing to catch her breath. The anger had been so intense it had seeped from her pores. She could feel rivulets of sweat pouring down her face from beneath her wig. The itching to her scalp was becoming quite unbearable the hotter she got. She leant against the wall, scratched just underneath the front of the ginger hairpiece, and then threw caution to the wind. Whipping it off, she used all ten fingernails to rub and scratch her head vigorously. She couldn't wait until the time came when she could do away with this character, return to her good self, and be who she was meant to be. She had excelled with her acting prowess for this little jaunt, but if all went well and according to plan, this would be her swansong, her last ever performance. She massaged her forehead and followed up with another fabulous eight-finger, two thumb, scratch.

It felt so good.

What was not so good was Selma had now slipped up. She had lost control and overstepped the mark; she was not following the plan. Actions the Watcher was now only too aware of.

ABIGAIL

*S*mithers sat forlornly in the staff kitchen, his heart heavy and his mind not on the role he was employed for. He was trying desperately to put some semblance of order to what had befallen his beloved Montgomery Hall. The last few days had been a nightmare and he wondered what he would now have to do. He despised having his hand forced.

'Penny for them…' Ellie dropped the log basket beside the fire and wiped her hands on her apron. 'You look as though you have the weight of the world on your shoulders.'

Smithers nodded. 'Aye, lass, I have that, but it's not for you to fret about. All will be resolved in due course.' He hoped that would reassure the youngster, to have his troubled woes on such innocent shoulders would have been more than he could have coped with.

'Would you like a cuppa?' She jiggled the bright pink mug towards him.

He nodded in appreciation. 'Thank you, Ellie, that would be grand. I think Mrs Smithers has left some homemade ginger biscuits in the barrel over there; maybe we could treat ourselves to one or two to cheer us up.' He gave her a gentle, fatherly smile.

Ten minutes later the barrel was half-empty, and Ellie and Smithers sat in quiet contentment in front of the roaring fire, biscuit crumbs adorning their respective uniforms. The wind still continued its onslaught on the large scullery window, battering and banging the heavy ivy boughs against the leaded glass. Every now and then rain would hit hard to provide another sound to the orchestra of weather.

Smithers rested his head against the high wood back of his rocking chair, the chair he had sat in both as man and boy over the very many years he had been at Montgomery Hall. He rubbed his hands along the armrests, feeling the indents and scratches of memories worn deeply within the wood. This chair was his now; no other member of staff ever sat in it; to do that would have been viewed as sacrilegious to the true master of the house.

He smiled knowingly to himself.

'How is Abigail doing, William?' Ellie loved to listen to the tales that he would tell of his daughter. She had left Montgomery Hall and Tawny Wings, first to attend university to study Egyptology, and then to travel the world. Ellie rested her chin in her hand and dreamily watched the flames flicker high, spark and then glow. Abigail's adventures were something she could only dream of. A gust of wind blew down the vast chimney, causing the flames to brighten and dance again; they reflected in her eyes, giving her a look of wonderment. She would love to be that capable and educated enough to just up and leave, to set for the four winds and discover new places.

Smithers watched her intently. 'Well, the last letter we had was only a few weeks ago. She was thoroughly enjoying this latest dig; there have been some quite remarkable finds, truly history in the making.' He was so proud of his Abbie; she had worked such long hours at the Farmers' Arms in the next village, taken every shift available so that she could ease the financial burden on him and Emily for her university fees. That was why Bentley had galled him so: privileged to have the best education, spoilt to have the finest car, indulged so that he had the most exotic holidays, whilst his girl struggled and Bentley had remained unappreciative. Knowing what he knew, and with his silence bought and paid for, he had no choice but to stand and watch the injustice every single day.

He would do anything for his Abbie, and as long as he had breath to take, he would ensure that one day she would have what was rightfully hers.

In that moment he knew exactly what had to be done.

THE INTERVIEW

*T*arragon sat quietly in the Great Hall, looking every inch a man broken in spirit. Being complicit in the concealment of Cecily's death, something the police were still unaware of, a dead geriatric thespian in his cellar, and a missing wife and son, had given him just cause to feel his whole life was imploding.

Andy and Lucy observed his misery. They had run out of platitudes and their usual chin-up style of encouragement. The disappearance of Stephanie Montgomery was puzzling at the very least and worrying at the most.

'Is there anything more that you can think of, Mr Montgomery?' Lucy craned her neck, waiting for a response, her notepad balanced on her knee; pen poised.

Tarragon shook his head. 'No, we sort of had words; well, she did. If you knew Stephanie like I do, you'd know that it's never wise to go head-to-head with her.' He thought about that comment for a few seconds. 'That's not a confession, by the way, I haven't done away with her, if that's what you're thinking.' He coughed to clear his throat.

'At the moment, Mr Montgomery, we have two members of

your family missing: your son and your wife. A cast member from the dramatics group that you hired for the weekend is dead and currently ensconced in your walk-in freezer, keeping company with a dozen boxed crates of steak and kidney pies. Don't you think that's a little suspicious for a long weekend? I'm sure you can see where we're coming from.' Andy waited for a response, watching every tic, flinch, eye and body movement that Tarragon made.

Tarragon rummaged around in the pocket of his jacket, brought out a monogrammed handkerchief, and nervously wiped his brow. His mind's eye conjured up the Dingleberries' old dear, almost side by side with Cecily, frozen like two pieces of Grimsby cod. His stomach lurched as a wave of nausea washed over him. 'It looks awful, I know it does, but I don't have any answers.' He hoped his voice and his face hadn't betrayed the thought he had just had.

'Could Bentley and your wife be together? Has there been any talk of marital discord, any hints that she just might take off, leave you?' Lucy felt a little uncomfortable suggesting Tarragon's marriage was on the rocks, but often that was the most obvious if there were no signs of foul play.

'Stephanie would never leave. She loves the status and the money that goes with our marriage, and I'm afraid my son is a chip off the old block. He would never give up on the luxuries he's accustomed to... and, of course, his inheritance.'

This was the inroad that Andy needed. 'Correct me if I'm wrong, Mr Montgomery, but I was under the distinct impression that yourself and Montgomery Hall are in some sort of financial crisis.'

Tarragon looked crestfallen. 'It is, we are... I am. Look, all businesses and families have difficulties; ours are no different.' He used his handkerchief to give his forehead another once over. 'There was a family fortune – maybe there still is, I don't know. It was amassed by Ernest, added to by Hugo, my grandfather, and vanished somewhere in between.' He paused, giving himself time to think. It was unusual for a Montgomery to air their dirty laundry in public, let alone to two police officers, but he could already see that this pair weren't going to extend the leash they had around his neck. 'We've searched stocks and shares, we've looked at property portfolios, land acquisitions, everything, and there is not one penny to be found. If Ernest and Hugo had tuppence to rub together, its well-hidden, so, yes, we are struggling somewhat at the moment.'

Lucy raised one eyebrow at Andy. He read her signal. 'Okay, I appreciate the family history, but let's keep looking. If there are any places in the Hall that haven't been searched, then search them now. Keep everyone in twos, and if any guests are seen out of their rooms, please ensure they are actively encouraged to return for their own safety.' He popped his notebook back into his inside jacket pocket.

They watched Tarragon, the weight of the world on his shoulders, haul himself up from the chair and make his way towards the staff quarters.

'He knows something, doesn't he?' Lucy kept her voice low.

'Definitely, and I'm going to find out what it is.'

LLEWELYN

*L*lewelyn Black paced up and down his room, a silent chagrin eating away at the very bones of his tall frame. This weekend had developed into a disaster; nothing had remained within his control, and for him control was everything.

He momentarily thought about Clara Toomey, but just as quickly dismissed any sympathy he might have felt for her. The stupid woman had ruined everything. Not content with actually dying on the job, she had thrown the whole of the Dingleberries' future into uncertainty. Already three of the cast members were talking about disbanding. He had tried to reason with them, but to no avail, and their conviction that any one of them could be the next victim of an untimely death bore heavy on them. Shutting themselves away in their rooms, Llewelyn had been left to wander the corridors of Montgomery Hall alone, his humiliation burning deep.

He pushed the heavy brocade curtain to one side and looked out of the window into the darkness. He could see very little, save for his own reflection. Large diagonal ticks of rain hit the glass, leaving their mark, and backlit by the murky moon the woodland trees swayed and snapped in the wind.

Uneasy lies the head that wears the crown... He puffed out his chest, full of his own self-importance. 'Heavy my crown may be, but it need not stop me from riding forth into action,' he muttered. He admired himself in the mirrored wardrobe as he donned his burgundy quilted smoking jacket. 'Into the breach, dear friends...' He gave a flourish with his wrist in his usual dramatic fashion.

Gliding across the room, he gently twisted the handle and opened the door, just enough for him to check out the corridor. A medley of voices, high-pitched and excitable, met his ears as several ladies from the Winterbottom coach tour bustled towards his room. The *flip, flap, flop* from a pair of tatty mules one of them was wearing set his nerves on edge, almost as much as the unsavoury polyester nightdress the tubby old trout at the back was clad in. He had visions of static sparks dancing between the hem and the carpet runner. He smiled to himself; it was probably the most friction the old prune had experienced in the last thirty years. He strained to hear what they were saying.

'Oh my goodness, that was a bit of excitement, wasn't it?' Tatty mule woman gushed.

'Who would have thought, secret passages behind wardrobes and in the walls of Montgomery Hall! If we'd had one more of us, we could have been the Famous Five!' The tubby trout at the back laughed.

Llewelyn pricked up his ears. *Secret passages, Famous Five, magic wardrobes...?*

He wouldn't mind a bit of that, it would certainly soften the current bout of boredom and ennui he was experiencing; it was Halloween after all, and what else was there to do in this soulless mausoleum?

He dropped the door handle, letting it quietly click back into place.

Hurrying to his wardrobe, he flung open the doors, pushed aside his tailored clothes and began gently tapping and pushing the wooden panels at the back. To his great dismay they were as solid as the rest of the furniture in his room.

Muttering to himself, he popped the kettle on, set up his mug and poured a sachet of hot chocolate into the bottom. The spoon clattered against the ceramic sides.

So much for adventure and excitement. He didn't think he could be more bitterly disappointed than he already was. The old biddies were clearly all airheads with overactive imaginations. He ripped open a little packet of shortbread biscuits and took a delicate bite as he once again swept the curtain to one side to bleakly stare into the beyond. The weather hadn't abated in the slightest: rain continued to pelt the windowpane, giving his reflection a distorted outline. He stood mesmerised by the fluctuating pattern on the leaded glass, his face elongating like melting wax as rivulets of water drew his reflection downwards. He was turning into the man who was slowly draining away. His melancholy weighed heavy upon him, becoming all-consuming until his awareness of his surroundings faded around him.

This was to be his downfall.

A low rumble, followed by a click, alerted him. His eyes adjusted their focus, quickly fading from his own reflection to sharpen the distance behind him. The wood panel of the wall next to his wardrobe slid back to reveal a figure emerging from the darkness beyond. He was temporarily baffled, his brain trying to figure out the reversed image that reflected back at him.

'Good grief...' was all Llewelyn could mutter before the figure was upon him, looping a ligature over his head and around his neck. He felt the soft velvet of the emerald cloak brush the side of his face, a sharp contrast to the tautness around his throat as his fingers scraped and clawed, trying to bring relief. It was futile. The skin on his neck puckered and bunched together like the drawstring on Clara Toomey's theatrical make-up bag.

He momentarily bemoaned the fact that the object of his imminent demise was an item of his own apparel, *The Winterbottom Amateur Theatre* crested tie that had been draped over the back of the chair. As a cast member he had been given the opportunity to purchase one in 1984 and it had adorned his neck on many occasions, just as it did now. It reflected back at him, fragmented by the diamond lead lights of the window. This honoured piece of fabric had subsequently been beautifully embroidered with the company monogram by the fair hand of his long-deceased mother, keen that he should have personalised items befitting his potential future success on stage. He had thanked her kindly and had worn it to special occasions over the years. It was admired by all, not in envy as Llewelyn had believed, but in laughter for the unfortunate acronym it bore.

If his assailant hadn't been in the process of choking what little breath he had remaining from his lungs, he would have sighed in resignation at his stupidity.

Somehow, dying with a tie wrapped around one's neck with gold ornate letters stitched upon navy silk spelling out the word 'TWAT' was not going to be his finest hour.

However, there was to be one consolation for Llewelyn Kitchener Black. He would, through simple coincidence, with no stage direction whatsoever, get to watch his own final performance reflected back at him, along with the image of Psychic Selma's eyes glinting with a strange kind of madness.

If he could have bowed to evidence his finale, he would have done, but instead, a long-forgotten piece of poetry from his student days drifted through his mind as tiny lights sparked and danced before his protruding eyes as he gasped his last breath.

'Dying is an art, like everything else. I do it exceptionally well.'
Sylvia Plath

NIGHT, NIGHT

*P*ru flopped backwards onto the bed, flinging her arms above her head whilst simultaneously kicking off her shoes. One dropped with a thud onto the carpet, the other flew sideways just missing Bree.

'Oi, missus, watch where you're disrobing. You'd never make a stripper – half the audience would be rendered unconscious!' Bree flicked the kettle on. 'Actually, I've changed my mind, how about this?' She deftly retrieved a bottle of Merlot from the wardrobe and held it aloft for Pru's approval. 'I think we need it after our little adventure!'

Pru grinned, which was approval enough for Bree. She grabbed two glasses and poured a large serving in each. 'So, are you going to tell Andy?'

'What? That we completely disobeyed orders and went on a ghost hunt in the middle of a murder investigation!?' She took a swig of the rich red, savouring the slight burn it gave to her throat. 'God, my heart though, I thought I was going to die of fright when that lot emerged out of the darkness.' Pru started to laugh. 'I'm actually surprised that none of the ladies keeled over; their constitutions are a lot less sturdier than ours. Tell you what, that ghostly roar was brilliant, it fooled me. The staff must have rigged up some sort of amplifier nearby.' This was the train of thought she was going along with rather than the other option – that Montgomery Hall was *really* haunted.

The possibility of losing one of their own made the hairs on her arm stand on end. She could just imagine the hysterics from Kitty if she had allowed that to happen. She was also pretty sure Kitty had never inadvertently killed a WI member during her reign before handing over the mantle of president. Fortunately, once Andy had given out his order, Kitty had been more than keen to remain in her room, with Frank displaying the same sort of enthusiasm by being almost adhered to Kitty's posterior as they crammed themselves into the lift, so as luck would have it, she would remain oblivious to the night-time antics of the WI posse.

'Did you see that Dirk guy from the Dingleberries leaping two stairs at a time to get to bed? He was like a ruddy gazelle on heat...' Bree grimaced. Dirk Diamond was definitely not her type, but he had impressed others in their group. She pulled up her pyjama bottoms and tied a bow at the front, giving the waistband a little tug to ensure they would remain in place.

'I'm not surprised. I saw Chelsea *and* Cassidy disappearing into his room for a little "nightcap"!' Pru used two fingers on both hands to indicate inverted commas around the word *nightcap*.

Bree pulled a face. 'Jeez, I don't think I could ever be that desperate!'

'What? For Dirk or for Chelsea and Cassidy?'

'Dirk, of course. Mind you, nothing surprises me these days. Take that Psychic Selma, for instance. I know beauty is in the eye of the beholder, but blimey, she certainly hit every branch of the ugly tree on the way down – with a considerable amount of force, I might add.'

Pru giggled, imagining Selma with her vibrant ginger hair

dropping through branches like a displaced squirrel, her trademark cloak billowing behind her. 'She is odd, isn't she? I feel so uncomfortable when she's around, like she's eyeing everyone up, and she keeps disappearing at the drop of a hat.'

Bree topped up her glass. 'That's probably just her mystique; here one minute, gone the next. Although I do think she would be more at home captaining a rugby team with that jawline!'

Adjusting the pillows behind her, Pru relaxed back into their softness, the wine already starting to have the desired effect. 'I was just thinking…' Her hand moved to the pocket of her knitted jacket, feeling the cool metal between her fingers, she brought out the old key from the secret room. In all the commotion with Clarissa and the ladies and her keenness to return them to their respective rooms, she had completely forgotten about it.

'The key–' She held it aloft. '–we didn't find out where it goes.'

Rolling her eyes, Bree tutted loudly. 'Honestly, don't you think we've had enough excitement for one night? I know I have.'

'Come on, just one more little jaunt?' Pru gave her friend a pleading puppy-dog look.

'Don't do that to me, I don't always melt at your command. No, no, no and no again, I'm tired. I've already got my PJs on, and it's something we should do in the morning after we've told Andy all about it.' Bree pulled back the duvet and slid into her bed.

'Okay.' Pru sounded disappointed. She lay on her back staring at the ceiling, willing herself to generate the energy to get up and change into her own pyjamas.

'Night, night,' Bree murmured, already touching the edge of somnolence.

'Night, night,' Pru murmured in reply, her fingers caressing the key.

The idea that she would wait until Bree had slipped into a deep sleep before she would tiptoe back to the secret passages of Montgomery Hall had already begun to form in her mind. There might not be lashings of ginger beer for this adventure, but the prospect of finding where the key would fit would more than make up for that little disappointment, and, after all, the Famous Five never gave up, did they? She knew Bree would be furious with her, but sometimes you just have to do what a girl's got to do. She was one half of the Curious Curator & Co, so it was about time she did a bit of investigating.

She had heard a quote once that *adventure is just bad planning* … and in her heart, she knew that this plan couldn't be *more bad* but *so good* all at the same time.

THERE WERE FIVE IN THE BED...

*S*elma paused; the exertion of the last few days was seriously starting to take its toll on her. Not only was Llewelyn Black a lot heavier than her previous 'casualties', but he was also incredibly gangly. He reminded her of a scarecrow, all floppy arms and legs, with very little substance to his middle.

She had roughly dropped him halfway along the passage, not even bothering to sit him upright. He leant heavily to one side, his tongue hanging from his open mouth was almost sweeping the dusty floorboards.

'Not so sure of yourself now, are you?' she scoffed as she rubbed some feeling back into her fingers. She studied him for a while. This kill had been so deliciously satisfying, not one that she had pre-planned, but when an opportunity arises it is always wise to take it.

'Remember me, Llewelyn? No, of course you don't...' For the second time in as many hours, she whipped off her wig. 'How about now?' She leant forward and grinned, as though posing for a photograph with him.

Llewelyn's unseeing eyes gave nothing away. His tongue

continued to unattractively loll from the corner of his mouth as Selma danced around him.

'It's me – you know, the one that wasn't good enough to appear in your production of *Blithe Spirit*.' She dropped herself down next to him, as though she was enjoying a friendly tête á tête; the only thing that was missing was a nice glass of scotch. 'I would have made the most perfect Charles Condomine, but no, you dismissed me as though I was nothing.' She used the tip of her index finger and thumb to grab hold of Llewelyn's tongue, pulling it sharply to ensure that it now definitely touched the floorboards. She swept it backwards and forwards, making a slithering track in the dust.

'You did offer me a job, though; you threw an old broom at me and told me I just might make the grade as a stagehand–' Selma made an exaggerated intake of breath. '–I did say I'd make you eat your words, but I think I've gone one better – *you're* the one that's now sweeping the boards, albeit with your vicious tongue rather than a wooden pole and a set of bristles.'

Happy that her narration had been completed, she grabbed the coil of rope and wrapped it tightly around Llewelyn's ankles. This time there would be no need for planks of wood to rod good old Llewelyn down the shaft; she'd planned this one a little better.

Finishing off with a double column rope tie she hauled the body to the edge of the shaft. Ensuring he was headfirst, she looped the end of the rope around one of the oak uprights and slowly lowered Llewelyn down. Even in death, she felt the need to give one last jolt to his thick, arrogant skull. When he was a little less than six feet from the ground, she let go.

The resounding *whump*, followed by a gut churning *crack*, was a joy to be heard.

Ten minutes later Llewelyn Kitchener Black became the third of Selma's victims to grace the cold floor of the Montgomery Hall Hotel walk-in freezer. She stood back to admire her handiwork once again. Bentley and Stephanie sitting side by side were now joined by Llewelyn. Clara Toomey had been placed in the other section, which rather spoilt Selma's tableau. Taking it upon herself, she decided to retrieve Clara and bring her to join the party.

Hauling a frozen corpse wasn't as satisfying as dragging a more malleable body, a few boxes of sausages had taken a spill when Clara's feet had hooked on a pallet, but it took only minutes to realign her before attempting to reposition her in the only available space against the wall, next to the side of beef. Clara was seemingly objecting to this course of action by toppling to one side. Selma gripped her, and in doing so caught the muslin sheet on one of her rings, pulling it away from the piece of meat.

'Bloody hell...' Selma's voice had once again dropped several octaves in surprise. She would never admit to shock, so surprise was more than adequate for this purpose.

The frosted face of Cecily Montgomery stared back at her.

She counted again, *one, two, three, four* and now *five*. Five bodies in total.

'Well, well, what have we here? Another murderer in our midst, but how fortuitous that I won't now have to seek out Grandmama and do away with her myself. Someone has clearly taken the trouble for me!' Selma mentally ticked Cecily from her list. If truth be known, she was just a tad disappointed that someone had taken a liberty and snatched that bit of enjoyment away from her, but in the long run it would save time. 'Just one more to go...' she whispered, '...but not before we've had a little chat.'

A deep resonating laughter swirled around the cellar and lifted itself up through the shaft, out into the passages of Montgomery Hall Hotel. If it had chanced to spread further, it might have changed the course of events, but it stayed itself just short of Prunella Pearce's ears.

A very dangerous game was now afoot.

FLYING SOLO

*A*s soon as Bree had settled into a steady, rhythmic breathing pattern, peppered by staccato snores and little clicks in her throat, Pru knew she was well and truly dancing with Morpheus.

She silently slipped from her bed and grabbed her trainers and a fleece jacket from the back of the dressing table chair. Tiptoeing out of the room, she let the door close with a soft click, before pausing near the linen closet in the corridor to put on her shoes and jacket. She felt guilty about leaving Bree behind, but the note she had left on the bedside cabinet explained everything, and besides Bree knew her so well she would understand the driving force behind her decision.

Curiosity might have killed the cat, but not to know the origin of the key would be even worse than death itself to someone of Pru's naturally inquisitive nature.

The twists and turns of Montgomery Hall's corridors and stairs eventually took her to Ernest Montgomery's room. She slipped in quietly, grateful that she had not inadvertently bumped into Andy or Lucy on her nocturnal wanderings. She knew she was being terribly blasé about her own safety. After all, whoever had decided to plunge a perfectly good steak knife between the shoulder blades of poor Clara Toomey still hadn't been caught. Then she really wished she hadn't gone along that train of thought; it had given her a sudden attack of the jitters, but as soon as she held the key in her hand again and felt its coldness and antiquity, any uncertainty soon dissipated.

She stood on the library bookcase footplate, found the blue book, and pulled it towards her. The click-swish-click heralded the start of her merry-go-round journey. The bookshelf completed a half revolution, and she was back in the secret room. All was as it had been during her unexpected visit earlier. She shone the torch in a sweeping arc, picking out the shadowed entrance to the corridor.

'Come on, Pru, old girl, you can do this...' she whispered to herself, but what had seemed like a good idea a few hours ago was now becoming more of a fearful reality than just a passing fancy. She hesitated; the queasy feeling that was building in the middle of her stomach made her tummy flip. 'Would Miss Marple turn round and go back? No, she jolly well wouldn't, so get a move on.'

Her self-supporting words gave her that little surge of encouragement to move one foot in front of the other, so that eventually the blackness was behind her rather than in front. She kept sweeping the torch from side to side, the heavily patterned wallpaper preparing to make way for the wattle and daub walls once more.

Pru followed the same path as before, but this time she turned left instead of right. The passageway led out into a narrow room, a wall facing her and a further two corridors either side of it. She stood, trying to get her bearings.

'Now which part of the house is this?' Backtracking in her mind's eye as to where Ernest's suite was housed, to the twists and turns she had already taken, she came to the conclusion that she must have found herself at the centre of Montgomery Hall.

'Mmm… but wasn't that where we all were before?' she muttered to herself. She tried to understand how they had all come from different directions but had ended up in the same place, scaring each other half to death. 'It's a square in the middle of a room!' Her sudden eureka moment had given her the answer. She was standing in the middle of Montgomery Hall with four passages travelling from the north, south, east and west, and they all led to the walls of whatever it was in front of her.

Excited, she began to walk around it, turning right each time, feeling her way along the smoothness of the plaster, her fingers touching the wooden joists as she bypassed each passage that serviced that part of the wall.

Why hadn't any of them noticed this before? Rough walls, wattle and daub until you get to this Tardis-type thing in the middle, and then it was perfectly finished with rather nice wood detailing.

Pru stopped suddenly, facing what she had counted as the third side to the cube. She placed the palms of her hands on the wall, feeling for anything out of the ordinary. She traced an outline, barely visible with the naked eye, but the sensitivity of her fingertips picked out each ridge. Up, along and down.

'It's a door… a concealed door!' She almost squealed with excitement, but quickly caught herself. She didn't want her voice eerily echoing along the passages. She had no idea how many entrances there were or where they originated, and the last thing she needed was to scare poor old Hilda and Millie with her dulcet tones creepily seeping out of their wardrobe.

Her fingers continued to probe, looking for the lock that would marry with the key. She felt every single inch, to no avail. She couldn't understand how you could have a door, but not have at least a handle, if not a lock on it.

She leant against the opposite wall and studied her 'door', tapping the key in the palm of her hand to aid her thought process. If it was another secret room, what could it be hiding or protecting?

'Oh gosh, maybe its gold, family jewels or money,' she muttered to herself, half-smiling at the prospect – and then another, more sinister, thought crept in. 'Or festering dead bodies and a murderer!'

Suddenly she didn't feel so brave or so adventurous anymore.

'Time to go back and find Andy, methinks…'

Popping the key back into her pocket, she swept the beam of the torch ahead of her, then behind her. A smattering of perspiration peppered the small of her back as she realised she had the choice of four passages to take, and having walked the cube several times she now couldn't remember which one she had come in from.

'Oh gawd, which one should I take?' The wobble in her voice evidenced the first flush of panic.

North, south, east or west?

'Eeny meeny miny moe…'

BEING MOTHER

*T*he feeble glow of the dying embers in the huge
fireplace of his suite made Tarragon feel even more
melancholy and alone. Sleep was eluding him, and so he had
welcomed each striking hour of the grandfather clock with
increasing fear and trepidation. He swilled the amber liquid in
his glass and slugged it back in one gulp. The photograph of
Stephanie and Bentley, held in a Louvre silver frame, quivered in
his hand.

As much as Stephanie drove him up the wall, and Bentley
filled him with despair every single day, he would miss them.
Although his bank balance wouldn't, he would, in a strange sort
of way. He still couldn't get his head around the possibility that
she had left him, and even more bizarrely that she had taken
Bentley with her.

Had it been planned? Not as far as he could see. She had taken
nothing. Her expensive designer clothes were still hanging in the
walk-in wardrobe, her millions of ridiculously high-heeled shoes
sat regimented in their individual little boxes and, the most
telling of all, her dozen rolls of sparkly tit-tape remained
untouched in their box. He knew from experience that Stephanie

would never in a million years venture anywhere without being able to hoist her droopy Elmer Fudds to an acceptable level, so she would have taken at least one roll to keep her going until such time she could garner another supply.

The thought of her hiding out somewhere and having to pop to the local shop for milk and cornflakes whilst they bounced and smacked her knees, made him smile. She had been on at him for ages to fork out on a boob job for her, but he had steadfastly refused, stating that Montgomery Hall was more in need of an uplift than she was.

Unfortunately she hadn't taken that as a compliment, and Tarragon had the misfortune to nurse a split lip for several days afterwards.

His musings were cut short by a light tapping on the door to his suite. He checked his watch. It was probably the two detectives; maybe they had found Stephanie. Woozy from the drink, he swayed as he got up from his chair.

'Come in...'

The door slowly opened, and an unexpected figure appeared, the light behind them casting a ghostly aura.

Tarragon blinked to clear his eyes, to bring them into focus. 'Selma?'

'Good evening, Mr Montgomery, I think we need to have a little chat.' Selma, without further invitation, swept across the room and sat down in the chair opposite the one that Tarragon had just vacated. Her cloak draped gracefully across the arm of the green leather Eton wingback chair. She nodded at the crystal glass that was sitting empty on the drinks table. 'I'll join you in a nice whisky too, if you'd be so kind.'

Tarragon stood stunned, unwilling to believe that a hired outsider would have the nerve to enter his private quarters, take it upon themselves to plonk their bottom down in his wife's chair and ask *him* to pour *them* a drink. He paused momentarily before finding himself doing just that. He handed Selma a glass, placed his on the table, and sat down opposite her, adjusting the cushion behind him.

Selma took a small sip and placed her glass next to his.

'What do you want?' He was curt but polite.

'A little bit of family history wouldn't go amiss, Mr Montgomery.' This time Selma didn't bother to disguise her voice.

There was a small flash of recognition from Tarragon, but he couldn't quite place it. Granted both he and Stephanie had commented on the masculine stature of their weekend entertainment artiste, but now he was really beginning to wonder which side of the duvet cover Selma had been born on – striped or floral – but in this era of being politically correct, he certainly wasn't about to mention it.

Selma indicated for him to drink up. 'Shall I be mother and pour us another one?' She pottered over to the drinks cabinet leaving Tarragon lost for words. 'And whilst we enjoy it, I'll tell you a little story, one of tragedy, greed and madness in equal measure...' She handed him the glass.

Tarragon greedily drank from it, gulping down the smoked woody liquid, barely registering the slight bitter after-tang. He sat mesmerised as he listened to Selma narrating a story that began in the late 1800s, an empire rising from the backs of poverty and hard labour. As he listened to the deep, monotone voice of his uninvited guest, his eyelids drooped heavily, and his breathing became slower. A warmth spread through his blood, even though the logs on the fire had now sparked their last.

'And so you see, one generation after another, after another – secrets, lies and hidden fortunes. What I need from you, dear cousin, is just where it all is... You can do that, can't you?' Selma leant forward and took the glass from Tarragon's now limp hand.

'Mmmleeurgh, I... I...'

'Oh come now, you can do better than that–' Selma swirled the undissolved crystals at the bottom of the glass. '–if you don't sing like a birdie, Tarragon, then you'll sadly leave me no option but for me to take you with me to find it.' She stood up, wrapping the cloak around her. 'Let's call it one last little jaunt before you join your beloved Stephanie, shall we?'

Tarragon was powerless to resist as he was lifted from his chair, his legs bending at the knees, unable to hold his own weight. He was dragged across the room, half-standing, half-slumped. One foot splayed out uncontrollably and hooked itself on the leg of the drinks table, pulling it over. It thumped softly to the floor, the only evidence that all was not well as the haunting sing-song voice of his cousin caressed his ears.

'There were two left in the bed and the little one said... it's all mine!'

HANGING ABOUT

*T*he Watcher had stood for long enough; he had heard all he needed to hear.

He quietly slid the air vent back in place, his heart chilled by the monster that had been created. If he didn't act quickly there would be further tragedy at the Hall. He needed to think carefully about his next move, how he was going to right this terrible mess without allowing the police to know the truth behind the family shame, and what his part had been in it.

He had to protect the Montgomery name at all costs...

He slipped silently along the passages, the same passages that Selma had laid claim to as her own, but in truth, he himself had been privy to since he was no more than a boy. It amused him to think that Selma was so arrogant to think that this realm belonged to her. In fact, it was the same attitude that Bentley had displayed, and look where that had got him.

He had been trusted to guard the secret the passages held, and he would do so until his dying breath.

The panel in the Belvedere Dining Room slid back, allowing him to re-enter what he called the 'real world'. He padded silently across the Great Hall and disappeared through the doors to the cellar.

What was left of the night would be given to formulating his next move.

～

Selma roughly shoved Tarragon against the wall in the north passage. He could barely hold his own weight and slowly slid down, landing in a heap on the dusty floorboards.

'Take a look around, Tarragon. This is what I've been reduced to, scuttling around the walls of this place like a cockroach–' Selma arced her torch around to show him the delights of spider-webs, woodlice and broken slats. '–not very salubrious, is it?'

Tarragon tried to lift his head; his eyes so heavy he felt they would never open again. He wanted to reply, but no words would form over his fat, swollen tongue.

'I'm not going to do away with you right here and now, I have to keep looking. Time is running out for me, and, true to form, you haven't been particularly helpful.' She dragged a rope from the corner and proceeded to tie a hangman's noose with it. 'I've had the most delicious idea for you, and I'll be able to relish it from afar... well not that far, maybe just the other side of this wall.' She gave the wall a double knock and released a chilling laugh.

She slipped the noose over Tarragon's head and adjusted it, just tight enough around his neck to keep it in place. The other end she looped over the roof beam and then attached it to the pulley in the dumb waiter shaft. 'Four floors of delight, Tarragon, a whole four floors. Once the staff start their early morning routine, bringing this down to the kitchens to start serving up the breakfasts, it'll be au revoir for Tarragon the Tepid – and it won't be quick, it'll be a nice, slow strangulation.'

Tarragon could barely register his imminent demise. His

scrambled brain was telling him to move, that he needed to push himself into action, but his limbs simply wouldn't respond.

'You'll be swinging like the churchyard bell by 8.00am.' Selma checked her watch. 'Which won't be too long now.'

And with a flurry of her velvet cloak, she vanished into the darkness, leaving Tarragon to whimper in fear.

ACCIDENTAL HERO

*A*ndy checked his notes for the umpteenth time in the last half hour, and then checked the signal on his phone. 'Nothing. How about yours, Lucy?'

Lucy yawned and spun her phone around. Pressing her thumb on the button she waited for it to spark into life. 'Zilch.'

They had both waivered any chance of sleep to continuously search Montgomery Hall throughout the night. Andy was not convinced that Stephanie had left the hall, Bentley, maybe, now they had found evidence of his drug-taking, but Stephanie was another matter. A high-maintenance woman like that doesn't just up and leave without taking anything with her. Even though they had found no evidence of foul play, he knew it was only going to be a matter of time before they did. He looked out of the window. The storm had abated slightly, but not enough to encourage him or any of the staff to start searching the grounds just yet. So many trees were down, making it too dangerous for a search of the woods. The telephone lines hung like strips of overcooked spaghetti, wrapped around the sycamore trees at the top of the driveway.

'Well, the landlines are not going to be up and running any

time soon.' He also knew this would affect the wifi and any other modes of communication devices the hotel had.

'Blimey, Sarge, was that your stomach?' Lucy couldn't help but laugh at the loud gurgle that came from the other side of the desk.

'Yup. I don't know about you, but I'm bloody starving–' Andy angled his empty mug towards her. '–I could do with a fresh cuppa. I can hear them in the kitchens; shall we go and see what we can scab from them? They might even have a bacon butty in the offering.'

Pru had lost track of how many turns she had taken. Twice she had doubled back on herself, trying to find the passage that would lead her to the secret room and Ernest's library, but each time she had found herself back where she started.

'It's like a magic maze...' She tutted loudly. She rummaged around, trying to find anything that would act as a marker. She had to start thinking methodically, and marking her starting point was the best she could think of. She found a half brick amongst a pile of broken cement, and taking that she used it to pinpoint the passage she had just come out of. If she remembered to always move to her right, she would be able to walk down each passage until she got back to the brick, or at least until she found the right one to take her back to the room. She started off along the wider of the four passages, her torch illuminating trembling cobwebs as spiders scuttled away to safety. An uneasy feeling crept along her spine; she had been wandering this passage much longer than the other ones.

'*Mmmfph... pleeeeeese... help meeeee...*'

Pru stood rooted to the spot, her heart thudding against her chest. She tilted her head and listened intently.

Nothing.

'Is there anybody there?' Her voice sounded weak and scared, but then again she *was* weak and scared. What if it was a trap and the murderer was waiting for her up ahead?

'*Help me...*'

Pru's flight or fight was triggered. If she opted for the first choice, she didn't know where she would end up and she might be running back into trouble. She didn't have anything to protect herself, but she couldn't just leave someone who was clearly distressed and needed help. She felt the key in her pocket, solid and unyielding in her grip. She could always poke someone's eye out with the end of it if she had to – she was quite aware that her mum had always nagged her with the immortal lines of *Pru, be careful, or you'll take someone's eye out with that!* Now she really could.

She ran towards the pleading voice, skidding around another corner until she came to a halt in a cloud of dust and debris.

'Tarragon!'

The whites of his eyes were picked out by the torchlight, bulbous and glazed showing his terror, a rope tied around his neck. She followed the rope upwards, over the beam and to the open hatch in the wall. She knew immediately what it was; the mechanical workings were visible over the edge and the rope was double hitched to the bar.

'The dumb waiter, don't let it start up!' Tarragon wailed.

No sooner had those words left his lips, than a clicking and whirring sound drifted up the shaft. The rope tightened as the dumb waiter began its descent, lifting Tarragon up from his sitting position until his toes were barely keeping contact with the floorboards.

Helpless, Pru began frantically looking for anything that she could use. Grabbing a large piece of wood she wedged it between the pulley and the sides of the shaft. The dumb waiter shuddered to a halt, groaning as the mechanism tried to fight against it. It didn't hold, snapping the wood like a matchstick.

'Stop, stop, stop, stop...' she screamed, her voice bouncing from the walls of the shaft. She ran to Tarragon and, using all her strength, she wrapped her arms around his knees and lifted him up, trying to make some slack between his neck and the tautness of the rope.

'Please, can anybody hear me? Please stop it from going down any further...'

JUST HANGING AROUND...

'Mmm… can't beat a bacon butty with brown sauce. Andy licked his lips and took a swig from the builder's mug of tea that Emily Smithers had given him.

'Nah, not having that, bacon butty with ketchup. Brown sauce is a heathen's way of eating one!' Lucy coughed, showering breadcrumbs down her sweatshirt.

They sat together in front of the scullery fire, glad of the warmth and very appreciative of the hospitality the kitchen staff were showing them. The ovens were working overtime cooking fresh bread and sausages sizzled on industrial size griddles, while plates clattered, and knives and forks rattled together. The normal routine totally belied the fact that the sausages had probably been bedfellows with Clara Toomey's frozen corpse, two people were missing, and he still had a killer on the loose.

'How many for room service this morning?' Emily, her round happy cheeks beamed across the large wooden table, adding to the ambience of the room.

Boris the bellboy adjusted his cap and hollered back. 'Just bringing the waiter down now. We've got three on the first floor and another six on the second floor.' He slammed his hand down on the large green button, setting the dumb waiter into motion. It whirred and rattled, announcing its descent as Boris stood whistling and tapping his fingers on the shelf.

'Bejeezus, what the hell...?' Boris pulled quickly away from the hatch as the metal pulley ropes juddered to a halt. A loud clunking sound echoed from the top of the shaft. 'That's all I need; it'll be me running up and down the stairs with coddled eggs and toast all morning if that packs up!'

Andy paused mid-mouthful and raised his hand in a staying motion. 'Shush, listen...'

The kitchen fell silent for a matter of seconds before a loud *crack* came from above, making Boris jump. The dumb waiter whirred into action again, the pulleys continuing their rotation.

'Can anyone hear that?' Andy dropped his plate and joined Boris at the hatch.

'Please, can anybody hear me? Please stop it from going down any further...'

The distant ghostly voice echoed down the shaft.

It took just a few seconds for Andy to react.

'That's Pru! Turn it off, quickly. Do it *now*,' he yelled.

Boris slammed his hand onto the red button, an alarm sounded, the stop light dimmed and then faded, and the dumb waiter fell silent.

'Pru, Pru, can you hear me? Where are you?' As hard as he tried to stay in control, Andy's voice belied his feeling of panic.

'At the top of the shaft... I need help. You need to send it back up and then lock it at the top, don't let it drop again...'

Pru's distant, wobbly voice was music to his ears. He nodded to Boris. 'Send it up, slowly.' He had to trust that Pru knew what she was doing to alleviate whatever the situation was up there.

The dumb waiter shuddered into life again at the touch of the green button. Andy watched the pulley change direction. He turned back to Boris. 'How far up does this go?'

Boris shrugged. 'Dunno, covers all three floors, the two for guests and then the private suites.' He chewed the inside of his mouth deep in thought.

'Lucy…' Andy jerked his head towards the double kitchen doors, and he was gone before Boris could get another brain cell into gear.

~

The loud *thunk* as the dumb waiter began its ascent was music to Pru's ears. She wanted to cry, desperately needing an outlet for the rush of adrenalin that was surging through her. Her legs were like jelly, wobbling as she tried to lock her knees to keep Tarragon suspended whilst they waited for the rope to slacken.

'It's okay, Tarragon, I won't let go, I've got you…' She wondered how much longer she could keep his weight. Her arms and shoulders ached terribly.

If I get out of this, I'll never, ever snoop or ignore Andy again. I promise, I really promise…

She looked up at Tarragon's face. The purple flush of his skin and the puckering around his neck from the thick rope looked horrific. Her torch was propped against the wall, where she had dropped it, throwing an eerie light upwards and allowing her to see him. Like a theatrical production, they were caught in the spotlight.

'You're going to be okay; I promise… just keep looking at me. Any minute now and you'll be down.'

Pru had never been so relieved for one of her promises to realise itself so quickly. No sooner had she reassured Tarragon than he dropped like a sack of spuds backwards. She still had hold of his legs behind his knees, which ensured he did a half back flip before banging his head on the floorboards. She stumbled forwards and fell on top of him.

'There you go, better a bump on the head than being stone

cold dead!' She knew she sounded flippant, but it was the first thing that came to mind.

She then did the most inappropriate thing she had ever done in her life.

She began to howl with uncontrollable laughter, much to the indignation of poor Tarragon, who was lying on the floor, a massive egg of a bump beginning to protrude from the back of his head as he frantically removed the noose from around his neck.

THE REVEAL

'*H*ope it's a full English, I'm starving…' Ethel closed their room door behind them. 'Are we giving Hilda and Millie a knock?' She patted her handbag, a regular habit that gave reassurance that she had her worldly possessions with her, in particular her spare set of dentures. After the fiasco at The Old Swan Hotel in Harrogate with a 'borrowed' set from lost property, she had commissioned a second lot of clackers that she carried with her all the time to avoid any future embarrassment.

'Aye.' Clarissa was not one for multiple words first thing in the morning, and their adventures the previous night had left them without their much-needed sleep. She did have to admit it had been fun, and sharing a bottle of sherry afterwards in their room, going over their little jaunt, had been the icing on the cake. The weekend hadn't been too bad after all.

'Oh look, here they are.' Ethel stopped at the top of the staircase, waiting for Millie and Hilda to catch up as they gave a jaunty skip along the corridor. Their nocturnal wanderings had, it would seem, given them all a spring in their step.

They began their descent, Hilda coming up the rear with Millie, holding on tight to the immense banister, Clarissa leading as she always did and Ethel floating from one side of the staircase to the other.

Dirk Diamond caught up with them. 'Come on, ladies, you're causing a bit of a rolling roadblock here, keep to the right – hold on tight...' He edged his way through them.

'Well, I never...' Hilda harrumphed with indignation. 'You can keep your rolling bollocks to yourself, young man!'

'Ladies... please!'

The Four Wrinkled Dears, as they had christened themselves the previous night, didn't have to turn around to know who was remonstrating with them, it was only ever Kitty who could put that much disapproval into just two words.

'Yeah, yeah... whatever!' Millie giggled; their adventure clearly having given them a shot of sass. 'Oops, here come the detectives.'

Thundering towards them, Andy and Lucy dodged Dirk Diamond on the last turn of the staircase as they rushed to make to the third floor. At the same time, Bree, who had just woken up, was rushing down the first flight, still in her pyjamas, waving a note in her hand. 'Andy, Andy... I've got a note!'

'Can't stop now, got to find Pru...' He rushed past her, Lucy following in his wake.

'But...'

As Andy reached the first landing, a flash of green rounded the corner and hurtled into him, knocking him backwards. He instinctively reached out, grabbing the first thing to hand, the emerald green cloak that was draped around Psychic Selma's shoulders. He teetered on the edge of the top stair. It was only a matter of seconds, but in that time he took in her vibrant red curls, the bronze clasp, and the look of horror on her face – that was currently sporting only one eyebrow.

Andy lost his footing and fell, taking Selma with him.

They rolled and tumbled down each stair, knocking into the wall, then the carved ornate rails of the banister, finally coming to rest sprawled out on the marble tiles of the Great Hall.

A deathly silence fell over what had been a busy area with guests eagerly making their way to breakfast. The Four Wrinkled Dears, grateful that they had vacated the staircase only moments before Andy and Selma's tumble, stood with their mouths wide open, so wide in fact that for the second time in as many days, Ethel's top set of dentures dropped down, lost their hold on her gums and rattled across the floor, coming to rest by Andy's outstretched hand.

And they weren't the only thing that his fingers were almost touching.

The vibrant red curls belonging to Psychic Selma lay in a heap next to Ethel's loose dentures, like a half-dead Texel guinea pig.

A collective gasp filled the Great Hall as Psychic Selma, still dazed, sat in the middle of the floor. Red hair now gone, the dark curls of a masculine short back and sides were revealed to all. She quickly patted her head, as though she needed confirmation that it had parted company with her.

'It's a man...' Millie squealed.

'Er... no shit, Sherlock!' Dirk Diamond observed with amusement.

'Get him, it's him... he's the murderer... it's Daniel Beaumaris!' Tarragon Montgomery, leaning over the galleried landing above, wildly waved his arms, an accusing finger pointing at Selma, the purple lividness around his neck clearly visible.

Still lying on the floor, Andy briefly looked up, relieved to see that Pru was safe and well, standing behind Tarragon. Lucy had already made a dive for Selma / Daniel, but the brief pause had given just enough time for him to scramble to his feet. The cloak flapped as he leapt across Andy, his Doc Marten boots clattering on the marbled floor. He knocked Kitty sideways and she fell heavily onto the chaise lounge, her feet kicking out, tipping the aspidistra over. It crashed to the floor, spreading soil and pottery shards everywhere.

Chaos ensued.

'Quick, someone grab him!' Dirk was happily giving out orders without actually daring to go hands on himself for fear of his dashing good looks being somewhat rearranged by a fist. 'He murdered Clara...' It was only now, with startling clarity, that Dirk realised that Clara's last words hadn't been to tell him to *smell* something odorous – she had simply been trying to tell him that her killer was *Selma*.

Daniel Beaumaris barged into Clarissa, and in the process suffered a first-class blow to the face from Ethel's handbag. 'Go ahead, make my day, punk!' she screamed as she followed up with another swing of her charity shop PVC bargain. Daniel dodged it, and terrified by the screaming banshee assaulting him, fled back up the stairs, his cloak billowing behind him. He ran along the corridor, shoulder-barged the doors to the Somerset Suite, and disappeared inside. Slamming them closed behind him, he engaged the lock.

This hadn't been in the plan...

The doors trembled and bulged with the weight of the mob on the other side. It was only a matter of time before they would give, and he would be arrested.

He ran to the fireplace and touched the familiar panel.

He was home.

ROCK THE BOAT

JULY 1989

*T*he Bella Beaumaris ploughed through the waves as Peurto
Banus became a speck in the distance.

*Daniel sat on deck, a decent Scotch in hand, with his feet up on the
cream leather seat. The sun blazed from a cloudless sky as gulls swooped
and squawked overhead. He knew that he should be content, that his life
was one of privilege – but he had once again reached a stage where
nothing satisfied him.*

His danger zone.

*He traced his fingers across the tanned skin of his chest and stared
just that little too long at his father on the bridge. A man who had never
shown him one ounce of affection, a man who preferred one son over
another, and when that special son had gone, had chosen to neglect the
one that remained.*

*Philip Beaumaris checked his Rolex watch and beckoned Daniel
over.*

*He took just a little bit longer to respond than his father would like,
as he knew that was a sure-fire way to annoy him. When he eventually
reached the bridge, Philip offered him the duties and dipped below to
join his wife in their regular afternoon siesta.*

Bringing the yacht to anchor, Daniel pulled the awning down and padded across the deck to the drinks cabinet. He poured himself another large Scotch, added the ice and topped it with a splash of ginger tonic. After that fateful day and the loss of David, his father had never been the same with him, as though he knew Daniel had somehow been involved in the tragic accident and its aftermath.

'Cheers, Daddyo...' Daniel held the glass aloft, a mocking toast to a man he hated almost as much as he had hated his own brother.

It was time for change. A time to put his acting skills to the test once again, to put Daniel Frederick Beaumaris into the costume box and develop a new character for his portfolio. This time he would go it alone, no need for the family wealth that had brought him only apathy and lack of ambition.

Whatever he now became would be of his own means.

Draining his glass, he returned it to the bar, and with his lifejacket hanging from one shoulder he launched the rib from the stern, tying it securely to the cleat, ready for his discreet getaway. He placed his Gucci Guccissima loafers by the bridge, dropped his Cartier Pasha watch onto the deck, and then crept down the steps to the engine room.

The stage was set for a most unfortunate accident, the sinking of The Bella Beaumaris – only this time he wouldn't be around to take a final bow in acknowledgement of his stunning performance. For all intents and purposes the tragic drowning of Mr Philip Beaumaris and his beautiful wife, Josephine, would only be overshadowed by their missing, presumed drowned, son...

... Daniel Frederick Beaumaris, RIP.

THE NEMESIS

*D*aniel sat with his head in his hands, the wattle and daub wall comforting against his back. He used one clenched fist to thump softly against his forehead, as though that action would destroy the memories that were haunting him. Flinging his arms around himself, he gently rocked backwards and forwards. He had failed to find the Montgomery fortune, and in accepting that failure, he had sealed his own fate.

His life had been good as James Littlewood Esq., entrepreneur and playboy, until his out-of-control gambling and crossing the wrong people had forced him back to England and to Montgomery Hall.

There would now be a price on his head.

He needed time to gather his thoughts, find a way out of this mess, and salvage something to save his own neck.

A sudden movement alerted him to the presence of someone else in the passage, someone else who had dared to enter his realm. He felt for the Strider folding knife on his belt under the cloak. Holding his breath, he waited silently in the corner.

'Come on, Danny, this needs to stop…'

The gentle voice caressed Daniel's ears, making him feel like a child again. He relaxed his grip on the knife handle. 'You?'

The Watcher moved into the light so Daniel could see him. 'Enough now, there's been too much heartbreak, too much death. Those other people... they didn't deserve that.' He shook his head in sadness as much as despair. 'We had an agreement, Danny.'

Daniel's voice broke. He ran his hand through his hair, sweat plastering each strand. Trying to think of an acceptable reply, he stared pleadingly into the eyes of the one person who knew him better than he knew himself. 'I... I... they were in the way; they were going to ruin everything.' He paused to collect his thoughts. It had been such a long time since anyone had made him feel so small. 'I needed the money...'

'And if you had got what you wanted, would the killing have stopped?'

Daniel bit his bottom lip and looked directly at his childhood nemesis.

There was a stark coldness to Daniel's eyes, no remorse, no guilt, nothing. Just a vacant darkness, the same darkness he had held since he was a boy. And in that moment, the Watcher knew.

He smiled at him. 'Well, in that case, Danny, if you need money, I shall help you once again...' He held out his hand to show his offer was genuine.

Daniel took it and pulled himself up from the floor. 'Do you know where the Montgomery fortune is?'

The Watcher nodded. 'Oh yes, it's been my life's work to guard it, Danny.' He found his bearings and began his slow walk. He patted his jacket to reassure himself that the heavy antique key was resting nicely in the pocket. Daniel followed behind him, his face smeared with stage make-up, his emerald cloak acting as a comforting protection around him.

'If you would just like to follow me, Danny, all will be well.'

An eerie silence followed the two hauntingly sad figures as they disappeared into the blackness of Montgomery Hall's secret world.

SCREWING IT UP

'$\mathcal{H}$onest to God, Pru, I don't know how many times I have to tell you! Will you *ever* listen to me?' Andy carried on searching the Somerset Room with Lucy whilst Pru stood, suitably chastised by the window.

She fiddled with the twisted bronze tie-back that held the heavy brocade curtain. 'I know, I'm sorry – I just thought I might be able to find out something to help.' She waited for a response from him. When none was forthcoming, she thought it would be a good idea to add to her narrative. 'And if I hadn't gone snooping, then Tarragon would be dead now, wouldn't he?' She hoped she would be in a little less trouble with him once he realised that.

He turned back to her. 'Pru, I love you; that's why I get cross when you deliberately ignore the advice I give you. I'm not ordering you to do anything, we have an equal relationship, but what I am doing is giving you advice based on my experience as a police officer.'

She nodded. 'I know, but I need to tell you about…'

'Not now, Pru, I've got to interview Tarragon, get the background on Daniel Beaumaris. It might give us an idea as to where he might go.' He beckoned for Lucy to follow him. 'I need you and Bree to get something to eat and then go and wait for me in the lounge bar. I can't afford to be worrying about you when I'm trying to hold this investigation together under the most trying of conditions.'

He gave her a peck on the cheek and as quick as the kiss had been, he was gone.

Pru sat down heavily on a nearby chair. She had well and truly screwed up, and to add to her embarrassment she had been admonished by her Delectable Detective. It stung, but it was also quite exciting to be with a man who could take control. It made her feel safe – but on the other hand, he had also just dismissed her and what she was about to tell him. He had absolutely no idea about the passages.

'Right, you, breakfast–' Bree stood in the doorway pointing at her. '–and I don't know why I'm still speaking to you. How could you, Pru?' Bree was properly miffed with her.

For the second time in as many minutes, Pru found herself apologising again. 'I'm so sorry, I just got carried away with all the mystique and adventure. I still need to tell Andy about the passages and the cube thing in the middle of the hall.'

Bree half smiled at her. 'I'm sure Tarragon will impart that vital piece of information when Andy interviews him. Come on, let's go and see what mystique we can find in a couple of grilled sausages and a piece of toast, and you can tell me all about the cube thingy you've found.'

Tarragon sat with a blanket around him, huddled in front of the fire in the kitchen. He gazed at the flickering flames, wishing they would bring him warmth, but the chill of the last few hours still remained stuck to his bones.

'Mr Montgomery...' Andy took the chair opposite him. 'I need to ask you a few questions.'

Tarragon nodded, a lump forming in his throat. 'Daniel Beaumaris is my cousin, he was supposed to be missing, presumed dead, drowned in 1989–' His voice broke. '–he was never a great loss. We mourned him as any decent family would, but his behaviour bordered on the psychopathic. His own mother and father, my aunt and uncle, always suspected he was involved in the death of his own twin. Can you imagine at eight years of age, that he could be capable of harm to another?'

Nothing ever surprised Andy. The cruelties of man had been indelibly etched on his soul during his first few months as a probationer constable many years ago; he still carried it to this day, and it was added to every time he investigated a crime. He listened intently as Tarragon told him of family feuds, secret passages, and missing fortunes. He was surprised that Tarragon could have lived in Montgomery Hall all his life and actually knew so little about its vast architecture and layout. 'Do you know why he has returned, and why he would want to harm you?'

'Money. He's after the legendary missing fortune, well, the supposed missing fortune. Honestly, it's just a myth; there is no fortune. If there had been, my grandmother Cecily would have...' Tarragon broke off his train of thought and went back to staring at the fire. 'Have you found my wife yet?'

Andy shook his head. 'Not yet.'

'In that case, before we go any further...' Tarragon stood up from the chair and blinked rapidly, clearing his head. 'I need to tell you about Cecily.'

THE LEGACY

'Why have you never treated me as an abomination like the others did?' Daniel skipped behind him, just like a child would.

'We all have our failings, Danny. None are so perfect that they can rise imperiously above another–' He held his torch out in front of him, lighting the way. The Watcher knew in his heart that this would be the only light that Daniel would ever see, so devoid of empathy and conscience, there would be only one place he would go when the time came. '–What we need to do now is protect the family, don't you agree?'

'Yes, yes, of course.' Daniel excitedly flapped his arms as he skipped further into the depths of Montgomery Hall.

The Watcher set his lips thinly as he continued ahead, not daring to turn to look at his charge for fear his face would reveal his intention. 'Let's play another game, shall we? You are so good at acting; I never did understand why you gave that up.' He didn't wait for Daniel to reply before adding. 'Let's be treasure hunters this time.'

'Ooh yes, I can be Captain Jack Sparrow. I've got a cloak; he had a cloak, didn't he?' Daniel childishly enthused.

The Watcher really didn't care if Captain Jack had a cloak or not, but he chose to agree to keep Daniel in his current mood. They continued on until they came to the quadrangle, an area that Daniel was familiar with, where the four passages converged.

'We're here…' The Watcher waited for him to catch up.

Daniel stood puzzled. 'Here? Where? I know every inch of these passages; this is just the walls to the elevator shaft, it's just a great big square, there's nothing here.'

'Is it really, Danny?' The Watcher serenely smiled as he pressed his hand on the wall.

A loud click filled the quadrangle of passages. Daniel stood mesmerised as he watched a portion of the wall between two wooden joists slide open to reveal a huge vaulted door.

The Watcher produced a key from his pocket with a flourish, inserted it into the lock, and pushed the door open. He flicked on a light switch and stood back. 'After you, Danny boy…'

Daniel stood framed by the doorway, the light inside casting an angelic aura around him, which belied his true self. He took in the vast array of antiques stored on bespoke shelving, paintings carefully positioned on the walls, a table in front of him held display trays of bejewelled rings that sparkled in the light, casting glints of colour that made the ceiling come alive. Dark blue velvet busts were methodically positioned to show off their treasures, necklaces that dripped diamonds and emeralds.

Daniel gasped. Initially lost for words, he then found his voice. 'The Montgomery fortune! I was right all along. I salute you, Great-Grandpapa, what a way to invest and stash it!' He grinned as he stepped unfalteringly through the doorway. His eyes narrowed and sparked with pleasure. 'Why have you kept this a secret? This place is crumbling, almost bankrupt…' He let the delicate pearls from one of the Montgomery triple-strand necklaces, roll across his fingers, the emerald and diamond clasp almost taking his breath away. 'Can you imagine what this lot is worth? You could save Montgomery Hall.'

The Watcher observed Daniel closely. He was under no illusion that the next unfortunate grisly murder would be his own if he lapsed in concentration. It had been one thing to direct a production staring a madman, which he had orchestrated from the beginning, but it would be quite another to bring down the curtain. 'It is not always about their value, it is their beauty, their rarity. No money in the world can buy that,' he uttered, more to himself than to Daniel.

Daniel laughed loudly as his attention was drawn towards one of the paintings. 'My God, do you know what you've got here?' He raised his arm and stretched out his fingers, not quite daring to touch the panel in front of him, the brush strokes on the canvas catching the light making the colours almost iridescent.

'I do.' The Watcher remained solemn.

As if not believing it himself, Daniel felt he had to orate the words to make it real. 'The Blue Lady of Hallows Beck...' he reverently whispered and then blew out his cheeks emitting an appreciative whistle. 'At sale it would fetch probably $30 million plus.'

'Very impressive, Danny, I'm glad to see you have still kept up with your interest in the arts – just a shame that interest is not for its wonderment but only for its value.' He wandered over to the far wall and readjusted the position of a Victorian gilt vase. 'Hugo was very particular about his father's treasures. This room–' He waved his arm to encompass the four walls. '– was specially commissioned. Soundproofed walls, hidden from view with humidity protection and specialist lighting – it was ahead of the times in its build. Impossible to get into or out of without knowledge – and this.' The Watcher held the key aloft, as he watched Daniel's eyes dart around the room, taking everything in, and probably mentally racking up the pound signs too. 'All of this is a legacy for the right Montgomery heir...'

Daniel, too engrossed by what he now considered to be his

fortune, failed to watch his chaperone as he made his way back towards the open door.

'...and sadly, Daniel, that is *not* you!'

The greed that had once spurred Daniel on had also blinded him to his own fate. He had become complacent, believing that only he was capable of cruel acts, that only he could carry out the will of others. Daniel had lost sight of who he was dealing with until he saw the spark of determination and coldness in the eyes of his temporary companion.

'Wait...' With that realisation came a rage tinged with fear that suddenly burned in his chest. Daniel flung himself across the room, knocking over a suit of armour that clattered against the wall.

A heavy fourteenth-century sword that was resting on a wall bracket slipped with the vibration. It held for a matter of seconds before it dropped downwards, the blade catching Daniel across the shoulder and neck. It slashed through his skin, severing sinew, muscle and veins, but his anger was so intense he felt nothing as he stumbled, hands outstretched, trying to stop what he now knew was a trap.

But his efforts were futile.

The door to the chamber slammed shut, entombing him with the treasures he had spent so long trying to discover. He brought his fists down again and again on the door, one hand now slick with the blood that poured along his arm from the gaping wound.

'Wait!! Wait!! You can't do this to me – I'm a Montgomery! Did you hear me? I'm a Montgomery!' A wracking sob, followed by a feral wail, filled the room, heard only by Daniel himself as the walls absorbed his fear. 'You're dead, I'll rip you limb from limb...'

Hearing nothing but his own heartbeat, the Watcher calmly turned the key and gently slid the outer panel into place so that it once again became a nondescript wall. He popped the key back into his pocket and patted it. Standing head bowed, as though he were by a graveside showing due reverence to the dearly departed, which Daniel would ultimately be, he allowed a sigh to echo through the passages. It was a sigh that held remorse, guilt and anger, but above all resignation.

Content that all was again well with the world of Montgomery Hall, he ambled along the north corridor whistling a jaunty tune. He was quite looking forward to a nice cup of tea and a scone. He had other matters that still needed attending to, but he would think so much better after a little rest.

Daniel, on the other hand, would never again enjoy such simple pleasures. He leant heavily on the door, his life slipping away. He hoped it would be quick. The thought of dying a slow and painful death over many days, maybe even weeks, filled him with horror. He knew his nemesis would never return, so that mode of death was becoming a very real prospect.

He slumped down to the floor, his back to the very door that could, under other circumstances, afford him his means of escape. He held his head in his hands, wondering if he changed a habit of a lifetime and begged the heavens for his own life, whether there would be anyone there to hear him. Clasping his blood-soaked hands together, he sat in quiet contemplation. His thoughts were not of remorse, or of empathy or concern for anyone else but himself. His jailer had seen in him what he was only just beginning to see in himself.

A soul that has conceived one wickedness can nurse no good thereafter...

Daniel began to laugh. Good old Sophocles, he was absolutely spot on in his analysis of the human psyche. David had definitely been his one wickedness, a wickedness that had led him onto the darkest of paths.

Daniel closed his eyes and waited, counting the waning tempo of each heartbeat.

As the hours and days progressed, the laughter would transition into the babbling of a madman as the insanity completely devoured his soul. His screams would go unheard, absorbed by the walls of Montgomery Hall, until death would finally arrive to take him.

In the rooms, in the walls, in the passages winding,
The darkness, the odour, of damp and decay,
In the walls of the rooms, it is here I am dying,
Come to the wall child, come inside and pray.

FIVE LITTLE FISHES

*T*arragon composed himself before leading Andy and Lucy down the stone steps to the cellar. The last time he had been here was to spearhead the posse that assisted in the undignified placing of Clara Toomey's body in the freezer. He shivered.

'What I'm going to show you might shock you, but we didn't really have much choice at the time.' Tarragon led the way towards the freezer. 'I need you to keep an open mind and remember what my wife can be like; you go against her at your peril.'

His hand hovered over the handle and as he pressed it, his foot kicked something out of the way. He looked down, taking time to register what it was. He picked it up and turned it in his hand. 'It's Bentley's!' He held it out to Andy. 'It's my son's watch. We bought it for him for his twenty-first birthday.'

'Did he come down here often?' Andy rummaged around in his pocket for an evidence bag. He always carried a few spares, along with his little tub of Vicks VapoRub for the very smelly dead body jobs. He indicated to Tarragon to drop the watch into the bag.

'Not really, unless he was on the mooch for some of our better wines in that section over there.' He pointed to the ante room which held the hotel's stock, along with some of Tarragon's finer, more expensive, wines that were reserved for family only.

'Right, that's something that needs looking into, but for now let's get back to the task at hand. What are you trying to tell me about Cecily?' Andy rubbed at his shoulder and winced. He must have knocked it harder than he first thought when he'd tumbled down the stairs with Daniel.

Tarragon took a deep breath, opened up the door, and walked in, Andy and Lucy following close behind. 'This…' He raised his arm and pointed his finger to where they had left Cecily two days previously. His eyebrows knitted together in a frown.

One, two, three, four… five!

He resisted the temptation for his mind to offer up a little ditty about catching a fish alive. Five muslin covered shapes when he had previously left only one. They hadn't had a delivery of meat since before the storm hit.

He felt sick.

'One of those is Cecily. We think she died of natural causes, but Stephanie wouldn't let me call the police or an ambulance – not even a doctor. She said it would ruin the weekend.' He felt drained.

'Ruin the weekend!? A bloody cold ruins a weekend, Mr Montgomery. The death of your grandmother should have destroyed it.' Lucy couldn't hold her tongue.

Andy took control. 'Which one is Cecily? What are these? Are they kitchen supplies for the cook?' He yanked at the muslin cloth on the last bundle in the row.

Llewelyn Black stared back at him, his bulbous eyes showing no sign of recognition or life. Andy couldn't help himself. 'Christ on a bike, when did *he* go missing?' It was bad enough to have a Misper on Stephanie and Bentley without an extra AWOL showing up as a stiff. He thought that was a rather ironic choice of word considering he was currently standing in a freezer. His fingers pulled at the cloth covering the next one.

Clara Toomey.

And the next one.

Stephanie.

Tarragon grunted loudly, a mixture of a strangled sob and his wife's name. Her neck still bent at an awkward angle gave her the appearance of an unused marionette.

Andy inhaled deeply. 'I take it the first one is Cecily?'

Tarragon nodded.

It was obvious to the three of them that when the last cloth was pulled back it would reveal Bentley.

They weren't disappointed.

Frantic at the position he was now in, Tarragon desperately tried to think of an explanation for the extra bodies. It ironically reminded him of the bags of gratis prawn crackers you often got with a Chinese takeout. Unexpected, but very welcome. Not that he would let the detective know that he was actually welcoming the loss of Stephanie and Bentley. Granted he was a little upset, but that would soon pass. It was a bit of a family trait to never let emotional attachments define you.

Tarragon pulled his handkerchief from his pocket with a flourish. He thought it best to provide a decent show of shock and heartbreak before he spoke, and besides, it would give him time to think. He had known Cecily and Clara Toomey were down here, but where the hell the other three bodies had come from he had no idea. He stared just that little bit longer than was really necessary at the faces of Stephanie and Bentley. One with a neck bent like an old hairpin, and the other resembling a bloated purple space hopper. It started in his chest, but quickly rose into his throat, a most unexpected snort of laughter. He quickly shoved his handkerchief over his mouth and nose, and at the last minute turned the laugh into a wail of grief. He dropped his head to hide his face as his shoulders bobbed up and down, not in sadness but in mirth.

The unfortunate side-effect of death on Stephanie's Botoxed gob had frozen her skin behind her head, making her look as though she had been through a wind tunnel. Tarragon was pleased to know that for once in her miserable, self-centred life, she would have been utterly content with the results if she had been here.

'Sadly, you're no longer here to appreciate it though, are you, dear…' Tarragon laughed, and then just as quickly side-eyed Andy, mortified that his head-thought had decided to pop out of his mouth accompanied by a chuckle. His mind worked quickly, trying to cover his faux pas. 'What I meant was I'm so sad you're no longer here for me to appreciate; you were a dear…' He looked at Andy and then to Lucy with a mournful expression.

'How many bodies were you expecting to show me, Mr Montgomery? One? Two? Three? Please do stop me when I get to the right number!' Andy took out his phone, swiped to camera, and started taking photographs. 'I need you to go with Detective Harris and wait for me in your office.'

Seeing the thin lips and the look of determination on Andy's face, Tarragon meekly obliged, following Lucy up the cellar steps and leaving Andy to continue his cataloguing of the scene. All the while suppressed laughter continued to bubble in his throat.

He reached the top step and held on to the ornate door handle, forcing Lucy to pause ahead of him, concerned that he might take a tumble if the colour of his face was anything to go by. 'Are you okay, Mr Montgomery?'

Tarragon tipped his head to one side and smirked. 'Rub-a-dub-dub, five bodies in a tub–' He giggled like a child. '–or a walk-in freezer – take your pick!'

Lucy gently took his arm, aware that he was bordering on an

emotional episode. 'Come on, let's have a nice cup of tea, shall we?'

Tarragon nodded. 'I'm a little teapot short and stout, here's my handle…'

And he laughed, and laughed, and laughed.

THE TRENDSETTERS

*E*thel bumped her suitcase down the corridor towards the elevator, closely followed by Clarissa. 'Did you check that we've got everything, nothing left in the drawers?'

Clarissa huffed. 'As long as you've got your teeth, Eth, we should be okay. You just concentrate on getting downstairs in one piece... Oh, there's Millie. Millie, dear, is Hilda with you?' She turned her attention away from Ethel.

Millie came bustling towards them, her legs taking little steps but in haste. 'Oh my goodness, she's refusing to leave. She said she's not packing until Frank confirms he can get the coach over the bridge safely. Has anyone seen Kitty to ask?'

'Did I hear my name being taken in vain, ladies?' Frank sauntered from the direction of his room. He looked behind him furtively. 'Er... Kitty... er... yes, she went down for breakfast ages ago – I think. I haven't seen her, to be honest, not since last night anyway.'

Three of the Four Wrinkled Dears stood their ground. Not believing him for one second, they peered past him, eager to see where Kitty was. They saw the door to Frank's room open;

Kitty's head pop out, and just as quickly disappear back inside again as soon as she spotted them.

'Meow, Kitty, Kitty,' Clarissa purred. 'I think you forgot to let the cat out before you went to bed last night, Frank!' She gave him a mischievous grin.

Fortunately for Frank, the arrival of Chelsea and Cassidy to the mix diverted attention away from him and his nocturnal gymnastics with Kitty Hardcastle. The girls breezed through the little group, dragging their leopard print weekend bags behind them, giggling like schoolgirls.

'Phwoar! I'll tell you what, Dirk Diamond can raise my curtain anytime!' Chelsea flicked her hair behind her and gave Cassidy a coy look. She smacked her lips together, evening out the thick blob of gloss she had just smeared across her lips. 'Here, 'ave a look… look how chapped they are.'

Cassidy stopped to get a better view. She squinted her eyes and peered at the offending pout. 'Mmm… are you sure you're slapping that gunk on the right lips? After last night I can't tell which ones were used the most.'

'Ouch, cruel or what? That just smacks of jealousy, you old cow–' Chelsea had started to turn several shades of pink. '– just because he chose me instead of you!'

Clarissa looked on in despair, shaking her head. 'Oh the uncouthness of youth…'

Ethel twirled her suitcase around and presented a pretty good Elvis lip as a sneer. 'She's almost middle-aged, and even now I've got bloody knickers older than her. She should know better.'

Millie smiled. 'What, like we did? They all look at us as though being old means we're past it. They forget; we were the innovators, we were the ones that set the trends – we staggered along the path they're now treading full of cherry brandy and Party Seven, whilst they were still on formula!'

'Aye, we were that…' Clarissa, with a twinkle in her eye, gave Ethel a wink. 'Remember the Isle of Wight festival, Eth? We were there, weren't we? Bob Dylan, The Who, Moody Blues, Richie Havens… It was a time to be alive.'

Ethel nodded. 'August 1969 – I had my first whacky tobaccy there.' She giggled, remembering the horrendous coughing fit she had endured after the first two tokes on the burning weed, before blindly stumbling around to throw up behind a haystack.

'It wasn't your *first* first, if I remember rightly, Eth.' Clarissa was feeling quite naughty. 'What was her name?'

Ethel blushed. 'She was only in my tent to braid my hair, and don't you dare ever mention that to my Albie. It was a long time ago and it's all swept under a bush now.'

'I'm sure it was, dear…' Clarissa spluttered.

'Eeew, you lot were at a rock festival?' Chelsea looked horror struck.

Millie shook her head. 'See what I mean. Chelsea, we were shocking the world before you were born – we put the *va* in vajazzle, my dear.'

'It's we put the *be* in bedazzle, Millie, unless you've been adorning bits we didn't know about in your spare time!' Ethel chuckled.

The saucy exchanges between the ladies and the ensuing laughter was evidence of a new day with a glimpse of normality, something Smithers was grateful for. He watched them cram into the elevator, taking their high spirits with them.

He discreetly slipped out from the Somerset Room and ensured the doors were locked securely behind him. It was time to tidy up loose ends and ensure everything was in order, as it should be now that a full police investigation was under way.

GREMLINS

*P*ru sat in the Great Hall watching the comings and
goings of her WI ladies as well as the Dingleberries.
All were hopeful that now the storm had abated there would be
news from the outside on the murder of Clara Toomey, and what
chance they might have of safely leaving Montgomery Hall.
Although they were all now privy to the death of Clara, the
discovery of the rest of the Frosty Five in the cellar had been kept
from them for obvious reasons. The last thing Andy needed was a
panic on his hands.

'Here you go.' Bree placed a coffee in front of Pru. 'Brenda's
having a good old moan in there, she's encouraging an uprising
amongst the ladies.' She took a bite out of her toast and rubbed
the crumbs from her chin. 'Apparently she'd rather brave the
swollen river, falling trees and damnation than stay here "another
minute longer and be ravaged to death by a madman".' Her
impression of Brenda was spot on.

'I'll just drink this and then I'll round them up. We can't go
anywhere yet. Frank hasn't come back from checking out the
bridge to see what the water levels are like, and I haven't seen

Andy, so I don't know if we can leave, even if it's safe to do so.' Pru anxiously bit down on her lip.

'I think this might answer your question...' Bree pointed to the main doors of Montgomery Hall.

Striding through them was Detective Inspector Murdoch Holmes. He carried the air of a man who was in charge. Three smartly dressed detectives followed behind him and a slightly built woman carrying a large black and silver case brought up the rear of the team. The doors slammed shut behind them as Andy and Lucy appeared from Tarragon's office.

'Sir.' Andy gave his boss the expected respectful greeting.

'DS Barnes–' Murdoch stood, taking in the vast entrance hall. '–this is Dr Lesley Ferebee, forensic pathologist.'

Andy held out his hand. 'I think we're going to have our work cut out with this one. Five bodies, two crime scenes, and a maze of passages we haven't even started to investigate.'

Dr Ferebee set her lips in a thin line and nodded as she reciprocated his handshake. 'Call me Lesley. If one of your team could lead the way, I can get started.' She was clearly a woman who expected professionalism and full cooperation.

Holmes shook his head to contradict his DS. 'It's six bodies. We've got an ongoing murder back at HQ, Andy. There's evidence that links it to your suspect, not least that he's been posing as the deceased here for the last three days wearing her clothes.' The tic in the corner of his eye set up again, evidence his stress levels were rising. 'I just hope his ruddy testicles weren't snuggled up in her underwear too! I see your friends are here – what is it about murder and mayhem that follows those two around?' He indicated to Pru and Bree, Pru having slunk down in her chair trying to become invisible. 'What about our suspect? What's the update on him?'

'I've spoken to a reliable witness; he saw Daniel Beaumaris making across the grounds towards the tree line. We've got teams out there now, and as soon as the weather is stable enough, air support will carry out a search with their thermal imaging equipment.' Andy was relieved to have back up and extra hands. After Lucy had squealed in delight at suddenly spotting a weak mobile phone signal, they had eventually been successful in calling the troops in; and combined with the abating weather and receding river levels, the investigation and search process had been rapidly put into place.

Holmes seemed momentarily appeased, before squaring up to Andy again. 'Just one thing that's been troubling me...' He paused, taking in his team around him. 'Can anyone tell me how you can go from one body to five in less than forty-eight hours? It's like a scene from *Gremlins* – have you been bloody bathing them after midnight!'

Pru wanted to laugh out loud at Holmes' attempt at humour but held back for fear of exacerbating the already tense situation. She watched Holmes follow Andy and Lucy into the office before she spoke. 'I saw Smithers talking to Andy before. There's nothing he doesn't know, and I heard him say that he's known Daniel since he was born.'

'In that case, how come he didn't recognise him when he was dressed up as Psychic Selma?' Bree mused.

'Mmm... not sure. Maybe because he was supposed to be dead, and the brain doesn't always register something if you're not expecting it. Anyway, if things get sorted I hope we can leave soon.' Pru sniffed loudly. 'I think I'm getting a cold, unless it was all that dust in the passages – *oh my goodness!*'

A PIECE OF HISTORY

'What?' Bree found it most disconcerting that every time Pru let out one of her surprised *Oh my goodnesses*; it set her nerves on edge, wondering what on earth would come next.

Pru rummaged around in her pocket and pulled out the key. 'We never did find where this fitted, did we?' She felt quite disappointed. 'I thought it might have been that cube thing in the middle of the passages, but apparently it was nothing exciting at all. No secret room, no treasure; it was just the elevator shaft. This is just a piece of Montgomery history that we found.' She tenderly touched the metal, her fingers tracing the ornate scrolls.

She would never know, but in her imagination she could dream up visions of secret trysts and furtive meetings. To her the key would always hold a little magic, a little mystique. It could open the gateway to boudoirs or treasure chests for all she knew, but for now, she would simply be its keeper.

'Pru, Bree...' Lucy, being more detective than friend at that moment, stood awkwardly in front of them.

'Luce, are you okay?' Bree's instinct was to give her a hug, but she knew better, much the same as Pru had with Andy. When they were working, it was arm's length to avoid causing conflict.

Lucy nodded. 'It's looking that at some point later today everyone can go home once we've got personal details, verified everyone, and got quick first accounts out of the way. By then the river level will have hopefully dropped even further. The bridge has some damage, but it's not impassable.' She fidgeted with the cuff of her sweater, pushing it further up her arm. 'Andy and I will, of course, be staying on until Dr Ferebee and Holmes release the scene.'

Pru could see the weariness in Lucy's eyes, although a quick glance at Bree and then another one at herself in the art deco mirror over the reception desk, made her realise that lack of sleep had turned them both into extras from the *Night of the Living Dead*. She thought that was quite appropriate, considering they'd just survived Halloween in Montgomery Hall.

'Great, I'll let the ladies know. Some are straining at the leash to leave, but we've got one or two rebels who would quite happily stay another night or two.' Pru shrugged her shoulders and held out her hands in a 'don't ask me' motion. 'Was it all down to Daniel then?'

'It would appear so. A member of staff saw him running across the grounds, so our search is focused out there at the moment, but we have teams systematically walking the passages. Holmes and Andy won't leave a stone unturned, I promise.' Lucy gave her friends a thumbs up before making her way back to the office.

Pru looked dejected. She was gutted that their investigation into Bentley was the only part they had solved. Accidentally stumbling on a couple of murders was, in her opinion, the icing on the cake for excitement, but it had taken Tarragon to point the finger at the culprit. However, she had saved his life, so that was pretty good in her books. 'So that's a wrap then?'

'Looks like it; a long weekend, five murders, more secret

passages than your Famous Five could ever wish to stumble upon, a murder mystery we didn't get to solve, a really crap psychic who turned out to be a raging axe murderer in drag, and our ladies… what did they end up calling themselves?' Bree cocked her head.

'The Four Wrinkled Dears!' Pru giggled.

'Yep, that was it, and our Four Wrinkled Dears having the time of their life mooching around in their nighties looking for some action. Seriously, you just couldn't make it up!'

'Come on, let's round them up and give them the news.' Pru was quietly relieved to be going home, back to Winterbottom, Binksy her cat, and her little library. A piece of normality – and maybe a good old-fashioned firkle and bonk with her Delectable Detective when he could spare the time. 'Oh, and he wasn't an axe murderer, he was a strangler. It would appear he had a very strange obsession with the throat.'

Bree couldn't help but snort with laughter. 'Jeez, are you sure you're not talking about Chelsea Blandish and her nocturnal activities with Dirk Diamond?'

Pru thumped her friend on the arm. 'Ooh, you are naughty – but I like you! Right, less chat, more action; we've still got work to do. Fancy a takeout and a bottle of red at mine tonight, once we get home? We can write up our theft from hotel notes for The Curious Curator & Co's records.'

Bree didn't hesitate with her reply. 'As you've just mentioned food and alcohol in the same sentence – count me in!'

GOODBYE DEAR CECILY

*S*mithers watched the black zipped body bags being discreetly taken from the rear of Montgomery Hall. There was only one that made his heart hurt. This was not the way he had imagined Cecily to leave. Under other circumstances she would have been taken with great respect, pomp and ceremony down the main staircase, across the Great Hall and through the grand entrance doors – not through the servants' entrance as though she was something to be ashamed of. A lump painfully formed in his throat as he swallowed the desire to cry.

If Bentley had lived, Smithers would have never forgiven him.

He sat down heavily in his favourite chair, threw extra logs onto the fire, and used the aged black poker to stir up the embers underneath. He sat in contemplative silence for a while watching the flames flicker and build.

Remembering how this unfortunate series of events had begun.

~

Halloween Eve 2021

The visit to her room had been Bentley's one last chance to save his neck or, more aptly, his kneecaps.

He now sat in his own room, contemplating how his approach to Cecily, his great grandmother, for more money had turned so hate-fuelled so quickly. She was a harridan of a woman at the best of times, but she had excelled herself today.

The prospect of being cut off without a penny filled him with horror and brought the realisation that he would probably struggle dreadfully to get around without both kneecaps if he didn't pay his debts before the weekend was out. Was it worth trying again? He had thought so until waiting to enter Cecily's room he had heard her chunnering away to herself about cutting everyone off, making sure that none of them got 'another penny' from her.

If Cecily followed up on her threat, he was not going to be the only family member that would be losing their meal ticket. The prospect of his mother being unable to afford her Botox sessions made him wince. If her face returned to normal, she'd have more movement in that rancid mouth of hers to continue making his life a misery with her constant griping.

*He hadn't meant to push Cecily so hard; he'd just wanted to stop her from making that phone call, the phone call that could have destroyed his life. As it was, he had just set in motion the very thing that truly **would** destroy his life – by stealing his own last breath before Halloween was over.*

Devil's Night had claimed its first victim and Bentley had been the perpetrator... an action that had not gone unnoticed from behind the walls of Montgomery Hall.

'William, dear, are you all right?' Emily bustled around her husband, placing a cup of tea on the table next to him. 'I'm needed back at the house; Mr Montgomery has insisted on refreshments for the police officers. Is there anything you need before I go?'

Emily had jolted Smithers from his daydream. He shook his head wearily. He loved how his Emily cared for him, he was always her first concern, after, of course, their daughter, Abbie. 'No, you go, dear, I'm fine. It's just been quite a traumatic few days and it's been difficult to see how Mr Montgomery's mental health has declined, but I'm sure all will be well in the end. A spell at the Springfield Sanatorium will do him the world of good.'

Smithers sighed gently, closed his eyes and at last allowed sleep to take him.

GOING HOME

*T*he unfortunate demise of Llewelyn Black had left the Dingleberries director-less, causing a flurry of uncertainty amongst them – and for some, a flurry of relief. In his absence, Caryn Davies had been the one to volunteer to take his place. Consigned to wardrobe for the last five years by Llewelyn, she was delighted to suddenly shoot up the ranks and become temporary director of the Dingleberry Amateur Dramatics Society, albeit because nobody else wanted it. She stood proud at the front of the coach.

'Right, everyone, let's quickly take our seats, I'm sure we all want to be on our way. This certainly hasn't been the weekend we thought it would be.' She counted heads. 'Er... we seem to have one extra...'

A murmur rippled along the rows as heads turned so each could check for themselves.

Caryn started counting on her fingers, how many had arrived at Montgomery Hall on Friday? She then deducted how many had been the victim of Daniel Beaumaris, and as such wouldn't be needing their return seat. 'Yep, I'm still one over.' She counted heads again, but before she could comment further, a high-pitched squeal came from the back seats where Dirk Diamond had ensconced himself.

'Oh my goodness, silly me – I seem to have got on the wrong bus.' Chelsea giggled as she staggered along the aisle in her six-inch heels. 'Honestly, they all look the same to me!'

Francesca couldn't resist. 'I*th* that the bu*theth* that all look the *th*ame or the men you've entertained thi*th* weekend, Chel*th*ea?'

For the first time that day, the Dingleberries allowed themselves a collective, much needed chuckle as they watched Chelsea totter down the steps and disappear in front of their coach. Even Marilyn who had been in the depths of mourning for her Llewelyn, faltered a smile.

'Okay, all correct, off we go…'

The tyres to the Dingleberries coach slowly caught on the tarmac, throwing a wash of water to the side as it began its journey home, leaving behind memories of Llewelyn and Clara who had both sadly and unexpectedly taken their last curtain call at the Montgomery Hall Hotel.

'Come on, Chelsea, get a move on, girl.' Bree hauled her up the coach steps by the shoulder pads on her faux snakeskin jacket. 'It's always you. Do you live and breathe trouble?'

'I was just exchanging phone numbers with Dirk, if you must know; we said we'd keep in touch. He's very good with computers, said he's going to help me do an update on mine.' Chelsea tipped her chin and gave Bree a superior sniff.

'That'll be you playing with his matrimonial software at the weekends then, Chelsea.' Ethel laughed so hard she brought on a coughing fit.

'Ladies, please!' Kitty begged.

'Blimey, here we go again – the wrath of Kitty Hardcastle. Kitty, are they the only two words you know?' Clarissa shoved her handbag on her lap, grabbed a tissue from its depths, and handed it to Ethel.

A gentle rumble of commotion ran along the coach as the Winterbottom WI ladies took to their seats. Bree was almost contemplating handbags at dawn between Hilda and Brenda over who was going to have the seat by the window.

'You promised me the window seat on the way back,' grumbled Hilda. She stood in the aisle adjusting her hearing aids.

Brenda remained firmly ensconced in the seat in question. 'You'll have to wait, I'm just trying to unpick my crotch, it's got a big hole in it…' Brenda held up her latest work in mulberry and grey 3-ply, the wool hanging from the needle.

'I wouldn't advertise that too loudly, my dear!' Clarissa chortled.

'*Crochet*, it's *crochet*, Brenda!' Mortified, Millie felt the need to correct her. Not only was she chaperone and translator for Hilda, but she was also now seemingly carrying out the same duties for Brenda.

'Right, ladies, let's get ourselves sorted. We're just waiting for Pru to hand our keys back in, and then we'll be on the road, so let's sit down and get comfortable.' Bree carried on checking heads to ensure all were now present.

The Winterbottom WI ladies would soon be home.

A DECENT PROPOSAL

*P*ru stood outside the great doors of the Montgomery Hall Hotel and looked up at the windows, searching for any sign of Andy. Just a small wave goodbye from him would lift her heart, and at this moment in time it seriously needed lifting quite a bit. The commotion coming from the open doors of the coach as her ladies rearranged seating, berated and generally teased each other was comforting. A little bit of normality amongst the chaos that had been present during their special weekend away. She turned to make her way to the coach steps where Frank was impatiently waiting.

'Pru… wait…' Andy came lolloping across the grass, skittering gravel as he hit the driveway. 'Phew, I don't think I've run that fast since I was in uniform!' He put his hands on his knees and bent forward, giving himself time to get his breath back.

'I've never seen you looking so dishevelled before, my Delectable Detective…' Pru gave him a saucy grin. 'Oh wait… maybe I have.' She cheekily poked out her tongue and laughed.

He gave her an impish grin back, his blue eyes mesmerising her. 'This isn't how it was supposed to be – I had everything planned, then it all went wrong. I had to go out of Force on a murder enquiry, but Bree said, and Lucy did too, that maybe I could... oh blimey!'

He stood in front of her, looking every inch the awkward schoolboy; he even began to scuff his shoe in the gravel. 'Pru, will you... erm...'

He suddenly dropped to one knee. Pru darted forward to grab his arm. 'Are you okay? You nearly fell over then.'

'I'm trying to propose, you bloody loon. That's what men do, they get down on one knee! I love you and want to spend the rest of my life with you. Will you marry me?' He held out his offering, relieved that he had been able to get all the words out in one go.

There was a palpable silence as Pru looked at him, stunned.

'Well?'

'Oh my goodness, of course I will!' Pru blushed and gave him her hand. 'I honestly thought you'd never ask.'

Andy placed the ring on her finger to a backdrop of rousing cheers, whoops and hollers from the Winterbottom Women's Institute ladies, who were now craning their necks out of the open windows of the coach, desperate not to miss such a romantic gesture, particularly one that involved their president.

'No privacy, I see–' Pru grinned, and then just as quickly followed up with, '–dear God, what on earth is this?' as she undulated her fingers, trying without success to elicit a sparkle from her recent romantic acquisition. The lime green and strawberry jelly sweet ring that now adorned the third finger of her left hand sat in stark contrast to her Pandora bracelet.

'Ethel gave it to me, it's from the Halloween Hunt Haribo bowl; it's only temporary, honest, Pru. I've got a proper one, just not on me. Ethel said to go for it, that life's too short to wait for the perfect moment – so I did.' Andy looked panic struck, as though Pru would suddenly devour the confectionary ring, smack her lips together and call off their ten-second engagement. 'I just didn't want you to leave without knowing that I love you, even if you are bloody impossible at times.'

Pru rose up on tiptoe and planted a kiss on his lips, not caring who would see. She wanted to shout to the world that she, Prunella Pearce, was in love and now engaged to be married to her Delectable Detective. 'It's beautiful because you gave it to me.' She quickly turned heel towards the coach, pausing to give a coy backwards glance over her shoulder. 'Although I do actually prefer the lemon and strawberry ones!'

Pru climbed up the steps and stood next to Frank, who was already behind the wheel, engine running. She gave Andy one last wave and turned her attention to the passengers. 'Ladies, all eyes this way for a minute, please. Can you all just check that you've got everything with you? We don't want to have to be turning around for missing dentures, hearing aids or–' she glared at Chelsea, '–underwear!'

No sooner had she uttered the words, she remembered she still had a little something that needed taking care of. 'Frank, I won't be a minute.' Running back down the coach steps she made her way towards Montgomery Hall and burst through the doors into the Great Hall, her eyes searching until she found the person she was looking for.

'Mr Smithers…'

His kindly eyes met hers. He was quite taken aback to be afforded such respect. 'Ah, Miss Pearce, I can hardly ask you if you have had a nice stay, can I? Such a sad, sad state of affairs, but here at Montgomery Hall we do prevail.'

'It must be awful for you, I'm so sorry. Andy… er, Detective Sergeant Barnes, told me you have been here since you were a little boy, I know you will have a deep connection with the hall, so I'd like you to have this.' She gently pressed the key into Smithers' hand. 'I found it on our wanderings in a secret room behind the library, I should have left it there, but I was just so curious.' She felt guilty, as though she had been a trespasser.

Smithers reverently turned the key in his hand. 'Thank you, Miss Pearce. I don't think it actually opens any doors now, but it is still a family treasure. I'll look after it, I promise.' He placed it in his pocket and patted it affectionately. 'Have a safe journey.'

'We will, Mr Smithers, we will…'

Smithers watched the young woman with the chestnut curls and mesmerising green eyes skip back to the coach and take her seat by the window. The doors hissed shut at Frank's command as the engine rumbled into action, taking the Winterbottom ladies home, and with them some of the secrets they had discovered at the Montgomery Hall Hotel.

EPILOGUE

ONE WEEK LATER...

*S*mithers watched the line of police vehicles turn a circle outside Montgomery Hall, taking with them the last search team, their evidence bags and equipment. He waited until the trees had devoured them before he returned inside. The dull thud of the doors echoed around the empty Great Hall, giving a finality to the moment.

He engaged the locks and dimmed the lights; the late afternoon sun dipping low had begun to cast colours through the stained-glass window above the staircase. His footsteps tapped on the marble tiles as he made his way to the Montgomery fireside chair, a glass of Tarragon's best whisky in his hand. Easing himself down into the worn leather, he plumped the cushion behind him and took a moment to appreciate the silence.

After all the excitement and drama, Montgomery Hall was quietly settling.

An overwhelming sadness crept over him. The rich colours of the wood that held the Hall together no longer cast their warmth, the tall windows reflected only fading light and the grand staircase failed to offer a welcome. The passages he had known from boy to man now only afforded him a path to a horror he himself had created and for which he now held both keys.

He looked up at the imposing portrait of Ernest Frederick Montgomery, the man himself, and tipped his glass at the stern face that looked down upon him.

'Your good health, sir...' He took a small sip.

The next portrait for his attention was the more modern pose of Hugo Frederick Montgomery. At any other time he would have been loath to toast the man who had defiled his sweet Emily all those years ago, but not now. This toast would simply be a reluctant one as he offered his gratitude for the child he loved as his own, the true heir to the Montgomery fortune. The child that would soon inherit all.

His adoration of Emily had been used to the advantage of the Montgomery family. He had eagerly agreed to marry her, heavily pregnant with Hugo's child, to conceal the patriarch's disgraceful behaviour and resulting mistake. But Abigail had been no mistake to Smithers; she had been the miraculous blessing from that bargain, along with Tawny Wings and his loyal silence.

'To you too, sir.' He took another sip. 'I have a story to tell, of mystery, lies, deceit and murder, but, of course, you already know the beginning so there will be no "Once upon a time" for you...'

Smithers could still feel the surge of power he had felt that fateful day when his hands had reached out to Hugo at the top of the cellar steps.

Just a gentle push, a little nudge – that was all it would take...

He had stood at the top, his breath caught in his throat as his fingers reached out. He had watched Hugo tip forwards, stumble and then bounce down the remaining ten of the fifteen stone steps, hitting each with a resounding *crack*. Smithers marvelled at the wonderful shapes that broken bones can make, spread out on the cold stone floor, a puppet without its strings.

What a terrible accident, they would say.

What a tragedy, they would cry.

But what a wonderful and fitting end, Smithers would whisper into the darkness.

'It was the rumours, Hugo. We all knew what you were doing. Old age hadn't tamed you or slowed you.' He could feel the anger beginning to surface. 'She was just a child, Hugo, just a child. You had no shame; she was just another Emily to you.'

And so Hugo had become his first.

He drained his glass and once again enjoyed the silence.

'It took a lot of intricate planning to orchestrate the murders of Stephanie and Bentley, you know.' He held his glass aloft and pointed his finger at his old master. 'Montgomery Hall had to be saved and Cecily's death avenged. That pathetic wastrel killed her – her own flesh and blood snapped her neck like it was a chicken bone, did you know that?' He didn't expect Hugo to reply, but he was quite enjoying his little narrative and confession. 'Granted, Clara and Llewelyn weren't part of the plan, and nor was that poor Estelle woman, but sometimes a little collateral damage can happen.'

He knew there had been very little he could have done about that, Daniel had taken those gruesome murders upon himself, and in the process had become a liability – his liability, which he had reluctantly taken care of. He had also not expected the quite delightful Prunella to immerse herself in the walls and the darkness of Montgomery Hall by galloping to the rescue of Tarragon, the last in line to stand in the way of his Abigail. He now accepted that lacking mental capacity and being sectioned was almost as good as being dead, so all was not lost.

He poured himself another drink and returned to the Montgomery chair, the ice clinking against the crystal glass. His fingers caressed the leather of the arm, knowing that both Ernest and Hugo had done exactly the same, their fingers tracing time on the worn leather.

'I myself have morals and ethics that would not allow me to personally carry out what needed to be done, but of course, as you would expect, I knew someone who would be a willing but unwitting conspirator. Someone who lacked the very principles that I possess.' He swirled the rapidly melting ice around the glass. 'And Daniel Frederick Montgomery, third in line to your fortune, couldn't agree fast enough once I found him!'

He checked his watch and counted up the days and hours. He wondered if Daniel would have met his maker by now. He hoped he had, as much as he had never liked the boy, he did not wish him a lingering and painful death. He had walked away, knowing he was the only one privy to what would be Daniel's final resting place. There would be some 'tidying up' and a removal at a later date, but he would deal with that as and when the time came.

Smithers laughed to himself.

Just how many buttons do you have to press to activate a psychopath?

Just one.

The one marked greed.

He took a large gulp of the amber liquid and relished the taste. For the last time, he raised his glass to his masters. 'Oh there is such an irony to this story, Hugo, *that* is what makes it even more delightful in the telling.' He stood to attention in front of Hugo's portrait, pride surging through him.

He was the protector, the keeper of secrets, the caretaker of Montgomery Hall – the Watcher...

'So often there is a predictable end to a murder mystery book, isn't there? The final words of *the butler did it* is such a terrible cliché, don't you agree?' He straightened his tie and buttoned his waistcoat. Pausing to raise his hands to the galleried landing, he took a bow, his performance over.

'Only this time ... I really did!'

. . .

Some are born to wealth and greatness; others are born to offer their servitude to those who are privileged to have that wealth and greatness.

Both are an honour.

THE END

ACKNOWLEDGEMENTS

I usually start with *'I never quite know where to start with acknowledgements'* and then rattle on for eternity – and to be honest, after four previous attempts, there's sadly still no sign of improvement!

I am always so very grateful for the smallest of things as much as the biggest of things in my life. I could probably write something akin to *War and Peace*, trying to thank everyone from our postman to my eighty-five-year-old hilarious auntie, who the delightful but very inappropriate WI lady, Ethel Tytherington, is based on.

To the wonderful ladies of The Women's Institute. Without you there would be no Kitty, Ethel or Clarissa, and no tales to tell. Your kindness, generosity and fabulous sense of humour became the inspiration for my characters. I loved your excitement and enthusiasm to be included, and hopefully I have created them just as you asked, like you, full of mischief and so much larger than life.

Thank you for inviting me to speak at your meetings and thank you for all you selflessly do for others.

For Loulou Brown. It was an absolute pleasure to work with you again and to get *Murders* into shape; you made the whole process so simple, straightforward and stress free and, best of all, you 'get' me, my humour and my style of writing.

This is a special thank you to Tara Lyons from Bloodhound. Tara, you are an absolute dream to work with. Not only did I gain a fabulous Editorial & Production Manager when I signed with Bloodhound, I also gained a beautiful friend. Thank you just doesn't seem enough. I wish you all the love and luck in the world with your own wonderful book in memory of your beautiful daughter, Sofia.

Written In The Stars is a charity anthology in aid of Great Ormond Street Hospital and The Butterfly AVM Charity, for Sofia, and I'd love that if you have read this far, you would consider purchasing it. All proceeds will go to the two charities. I know it would mean the world to Tara and her family.

I was honoured to be asked to participate in two charity auctions this year, one for Ukraine and one for Tiny Stars NeoNatal at Wirral University Teaching Hospital. I was amazed that so much was raised, almost £1,000 between both charities, to be named as characters in *Murders at The Montgomery Hall Hotel*. Andy Shute, who was the highest bidder for the Ukraine auction, asked that his beautiful wife Julie be included rather than himself. Julie sadly passed away with cancer at the age of fifty-four in 2015. She was, and still is, so very loved by Andy and it truly was an honour for me to create a character for her. Caryn Davies and Lesley Ferebee were the highest bidders at the Tiny Stars auction. They are amazingly loyal supporters of the neonatal charity and the excitement of the charity luncheon, hosted by the lovely Mandy Molby who does so much for local charities, added to the atmosphere and excitement of the bidding.

Grateful thanks to Shelley and Sean Prince from the delightful *Hollin House Hotel* in Bollington, Cheshire. Hubby and I, along with our doggie, enjoyed an overnight stay here as part of my research for the Montgomery Hall Hotel. Shelley's hospitality and kindness as she gave me a guided tour around *Hollin House* was so very much appreciated. Such a beautiful setting with fabulous history and atmosphere ... and their full English breakfast is to die for!

To my lovely friends, Howard Smith and Jools. I don't know

what I would have done without you. Our three-way conversation and your advice whilst I desperately tried to figure out the best place to insert a steak knife into a human body for maximum effect and a quick death, was invaluable. The laughter was really appreciated too. I promise I'll keep all the really sharp knives in the drawer when you come for dinner!

I very quickly discovered how amazing readers and book bloggers are. There are too many to mention individually, and I would hate to miss someone out, so this is a collective thank you. A bit like a group hug. As writers, where would we be without them? Our words wouldn't be heard, our stories wouldn't be told. They would lie dormant on paper or screen, meaningless. They only come to life because people read them, enjoy them and spread their love of our books.

Once again (I have to mention him as I truly am the doting elder sister), to my very handsome, debonair brother, Andy Dawson – for no other reason than him being handsome, debonair and, of course, my brother. Love you, Bro.

To my sister Claire, so far away but you will always be in my heart.

To my beautiful daughter, Emma and my gorgeous grandchildren, Olivia, Annie and Arthur. You are my sunshine, you make me smile every day, I'm so very blessed to have you in my life.

And last but definitely not least, to my handsome and very funny hubby, John. The love of my life, my bodyguard, chauffeur and human SatNav. The man who makes me laugh every single day (and frequently think of murder too). He has endured hours of torment as my muse and 'go to' for ideas for this book and my previous ones. He rolls his eyes and groans but still continues to reluctantly participate in the most bizarre acts all in the name of research – well, at least that's what I tell him it's for! Without his love and support there would be no stories to tell – and I'd still be driving around various parts of the UK, panic-struck and lost.

I hope I haven't missed anyone out, but knowing me and my scatterbrained head-thoughts, I probably have. I'm so sorry if you haven't appeared here because of my forgetfulness, but please know there's a humongous 'thank you' in my heart for you. You will always be so very much appreciated.

Gina x

A NOTE FROM THE PUBLISHER

Thank you for reading this book. If you enjoyed it please do consider leaving a review on Amazon to help others find it too.

We hate typos. All of our books have been rigorously edited and proofread, but sometimes mistakes do slip through. If you have spotted a typo, please do let us know and we can get it amended within hours.

info@bloodhoundbooks.com

Printed in Great Britain
by Amazon

18127032R00212